May Laffan

Hogan, M.P.

A Novel

May Laffan

Hogan, M.P.
A Novel

ISBN/EAN: 9783337001964

Printed in Europe, USA, Canada, Australia, Japan

Cover: Foto ©Andreas Hilbeck / pixelio.de

More available books at **www.hansebooks.com**

HOGAN, M.P.

A NOVEL

BY THE AUTHOR OF

"FLITTERS TATTERS AND THE COUNSELLOR,"
"CHRISTY CAREW," &c.

NEW EDITION

London
MACMILLAN AND CO.
1881

"Whatever may be thought of the purity of the Irish Parliament during the brief period in which it exercised an independent authority, there are certainly few things more absurd than the charges of bigotry that are frequently directed against it. . . .

"It is worthy, too, of notice that the Liberalism of the Irish Parliament was always in direct proportion to its political independence. . . .

"The purely national and secular spirit the Irish Parliament had fostered perished with its organ. Patriotism was replaced by sectarianism. . . .

"It is obvious, in the first place, that one important effect of a purely secular political feeling will be to weaken the intensity of sectarianism. Before its existence sectarianism was the measure by which all things and persons were contemplated. But when a purely political spirit is engendered, a new enthusiasm is introduced into the mind, which first divides the affections and at last replaces the passion that had formerly been supreme."—LECKY, *History of Rationalism.*

HOGAN, M.P.

CHAPTER I.

"Studies serve for delight, for ornament and for ability. Their chief use for delight is in privateness and retiring ; for ornament, is in discourse ; and for ability, is in the judgment and disposition of business."—*Bacon's Essays, Civil and Moral.*

THE schoolroom of St. Swithin's Convent presented a scene of unwonted bustle and confusion one fine, hot morning in the middle of July. Breaking-up day, or, as the Mother Superior preferred to call it, "the closing day of the scholastic year," was an event of no small importance and solemnity. The whole community, from the Superior and the members of the Council down to the fifteen-year-old novice, were intensely impressed with the sense of personal and individual responsibility.

Each had her own share of the burden. That the invited guests were all the right ones—that the *déjeûner* should be faultless, or at least equal to those given by the convents whose celebrations had preceded this one—and that the prizes should be judiciously bestowed—was the special anxiety of the Superior. The musical display, and the examinations (scientific, linguistic, and other), concerned the respective class-mistresses, who, between rehearsing and cramming, had had a busy time of it for some months beforehand. The lay sisters had scrubbed and polished with extra zeal ; and even the old gardener had been up and out at six in the morning, to rake the gravel walks and trim the sunburnt grass edges in the little lawn.

B

The schoolroom had been specially arranged for the occasion. At one end was a sort of amphitheatre of benches raised above each other. Four pianos, placed back to back, stood as close as possible to the pupils' seats. At the opposite end were chairs and cushioned benches for the visitors, placed in a semicircle. An arm-chair with a huge crimson cushion, having before it a table on which were piled the prize books, occupied the central and most conspicuous position. The whitewashed walls of the room were decorated with evergreens. The school maps had been taken down, and their places supplied by pictures executed by the pupils: chalk heads of Zingari women, scratchy and nightmare-like; dropsical infants, with prematurely intellectual countenances; landscapes of the approved pen-knife and stump school; sewed pictures, and Madonnas in Berlin wool, all in bright gilt frames. A pair of globes stood in readiness in the corner, whence they could be most easily dragged out when wanted. Everything was as clean as possible; even the statue of " our Lady," which occupied the place of honour on the oratory, had been scrubbed to its pristine whiteness, and the flower vases before it supplied with a perfectly new set of paper roses and lilies.

The " exercises," as they were called, were to commence at twelve. By eleven o'clock the schoolroom presented an extraordinary scene of commotion. Nuns in their Sunday habits and full-dress cloaks, the long trains of which, for safety's sake, they had tucked under their elbows, were bustling about in great excitement among their pupils, who, to the number of seventy, of all ages from four to twenty, and dressed in white, were coming and going, chattering, gesticulating and laughing, with the exuberance of animal spirits peculiar to their age and proper to the occasion.

At first glance the scene seemed one of utter confusion and objectless Babel; but on closer examination the crowd might be seen to be formed of sundry distinct, though often changing groups—the nucleus of each being, in every instance, a nun.

In the corner inside the door, a scene from Molière's *Avare* was being rehearsed by a set of girls. "Maître Jacques," with her fingers stuffed in her ears, was shouting her part to the teacher, who, with a book of "Elegant Extracts" from French literature open in her hand, was listening with intense anxiety, and correcting whenever her ear caught a mistake.

"Oh! Bride Sweeny, darling child, sure you won't say *naysaire* for *nécessaire*. That's I don't know how often I've told you."

"I won't, sister," replied "Maître Jacques," removing her fingers, and falling back to let "Géronte" speak her part. "You needn't be afraid."

"I'd be everlastingly disgraced if you did," continued the sister. "The first class have got off their '*Esther*' beautifully; and you know the Bishop's a splendid French scholar. Sure, you might all slip out here in the garden, and we'll go over it all once more from the first."

"Ah, no, sister; we know it by heart now, an' we'd only be dirtying our shoes; and besides, Mother Paul's coming down to go over the problems on the globes. Julia Casey's not up in hers yet."

"That I'm not," assented Julia Casey, who was muttering 'Géronte's' speech to herself: "I always confuse the latatudes an' the long-ditudes; an' I'm dead sure I'll either smash that brass thing or let it fall—that quadrint, you know,—sure I'd die, an' they all lookin' at me!"

"Oh, Sister! Sister de Sales!" wailed a pretty little girl as she broke into the circle, "I've lost one of my bronze shoes; an' what will I do? I'm to be in the first thing, and right in the front before the Bishop."

Away ran the sister to look for the missing shoe. Miss Casey went to take her finishing lesson in the use of the globes, Miss Bride Sweeny to get up her answers in French history of the Merovingian epoch. Everybody was rehearsing. Eight small children, who were to play a concerted duet, were being instructed by an old nun how to take their seats decorously on the music-stools. A harp was being strung; and just beside it a big girl, who was to

recite a Birthday Ode to His Holiness Pius the Ninth, was
impressing a difficult stanza on her memory by the aid of
thumping the window-shutter with her clenched hand at
every word. One nervous young lady, the centre of a
sympathising circle, was in tears.

The din was at its height when a side-door opened, and
a nun of tall commanding figure appeared suddenly on the
scene. A hush fell on the assembly. " Mother Prioress !"
breathed the nuns, all standing at attention. The lull
only lasted an instant, however. The noise broke forth
afresh, and with more intense vigour. Petitioners rushed
up and barred the passage.

" Oh, reverend Mother, mayn't Sister Wenceslas take
this tuck out of my dress ? Look, Mother, 'tis a show;
'tis so short."

" Ah, reverend Mother, won't you cut my piece out of
the programme ? I'm frightened to death. I'll never——"

" Mother ! Aloysia Kelly has lost one of her shoes ; and
what's to be done ? She never can stand up before the
Bishop with only one on."

But the Mother Superior heard nothing : she passed on
up to the table without a word, and taking up a little bell,
rang it vigorously. Perfect silence followed this signal.

" The Angelus, children !" commanded she, in a loud
voice, kneeling down as she spoke with her face to the
oratory. Every one followed her example.

For an instant you might have thought the room was
empty. Through the open windows the sound of the
chimes in the convent clock-tower, and the echoes of the
city bustle, poured in and mingled with the clear responses
of the girls' voices. The rustling of the leaves of the trees
in the front, and the smell of the mignonette and lavender
in the garden under the windows, came in with the warm
air. It was a glowing hot day; and the nuns in their
heavy stuff robes seemed quite overcome.

The prayer was soon over : the excitement of the occasion appeared to be rather incompatible with the duly
reverential performance of the pious exercise ; there being
clearly noticeable a general tendency to giggle and fidget

more than usual, and one tall, black-eyed girl, who was
going home for good, actually forgot to bless herself at
the close.

"To your places, children!" cried Mother Superior,
speaking while in the act of rising, and almost simultaneously with the last Amen, in order to stem the inevitable outburst at its commencement. "The Bishop has
arrived, and is in the parlour. You may speak," she
added, with the tone of one making a concession, "until
the guests all come in."

She was an experienced commander, and well versed in
the arts of ruling—the chief of which is to know when to
submit; and she divined pretty accurately that no power
of tongue or bell would stop them to-day.

The girls all swarmed up into their places on the raised
benches; and the river of talk, which had momentarily
disappeared underground, welled forth from its hiding-
place with redoubled intensity. The class-mistresses
walked about the room, picking up bits of papers, ends
of ribbon, leaves of books, and hair-pins, the jetsam and
flotsam of that stormy sea of feminine humanity. The
Prioress, meantime, had seated herself in her own chair,
on the left of the Bishop's, and was surveying the scene
with complacency. Everything was ready. The seventy
pupils, all dressed in white muslin, with white thread
gloves and blue bows—most of them fat and wholesome-
looking—formed an imposing body, filling as they did one
whole end of the room, from floor to ceiling.

"Now, Mother, everything's right, I hope," said the
"mistress of the schools," a fresh-complexioned, bright-
eyed woman, about forty years of age, advancing, as she
spoke, close to her chief.

"They've only sixty children at Saint Gengulph's" (be
it observed that the prefix "saint," is always pronounced
long and full—by no means the disrespectful abbreviation
the English and their imitators make it), "his Lordship
has just told me," whispered the Superioress. "He was
at their distribution yesterday."

St. Gengulph's was a rival establishment.

" Sixty !—now, Mother !" cried the head-mistress, exult-
ingly. " And did you get a programme ?"

Mother Superior nodded.

" Oh ! and what did they learn of music, Mother ? Was
it the overture to *Faust ?* Oh ! I do hope it wasn't ; it's
perfectly dreadful when you know the priests have heard
the same pieces the day before !"

" Better for you not to know, then, Sister," replied the
Superior, tantalisingly. The sister darted a scrutinising
look at her chief's countenance, and apparently read there
a confirmation of her hopes, for she walked off to her post
with a confident and smiling air. After a final glance
round, the Mother Superior left the room to receive the
guests in the parlours, while the pupils beguiled the timé
as they chose.

" A carriage !" announced a girl, who had taken advantage of her seat next the window to scratch a peephole in
the muffed glass, and was enjoying the somewhat limited
view to be had thereby. The excitement rose almost to
shrieking-point. " It's the Bishop !" cried one. " It's
not ; he's come already : 'tis papa !" said the black-eyed
girl, who was going home for good. With an exception
or two, the interest was only increased when the sentinel
announced the modifying intelligence that it was only a
confectioner's cart with things for the *déjeûner.*

" Carriage, indeed !" scoffed the big girl—a Miss Brangan. " Augh, then, Biddy Sweeny, ye're the judge of
carriages : not know a cake van from a carriage !"

Miss Sweeny was just launching a retort to this insolence, when the door opened, and a lay sister beckoned and
called : " Mary Rooney, your aunt, Lady Shanassy's in the
parlour,—come." Next to the Bishop, who was the
reverend Mother's first cousin, Lady Shanassy was the
star of the occasion. An awestruck murmur went round
the benches ; Miss Brangan's scornful look disappeared ;
and Bride Sweeny forgot everything, in order to stare at
Miss Rooney's progress from the topmost seat to the door.
Gleefully conscious of her importance and reflected glory

as the relative of the great lady, a little fat, red-haired girl picked her way through the crowd to the door.

"Stop, Mary darling!" called the head-mistress, "your sash is crooked;" and kneeling - down, she, with deft touches, flirted the offending ribbons into their proper position—the one hundred and forty eyes above losing not one iota of the manipulations. At last, the door being shut, their owners resumed conversation.

"Will ever I know my questions in globes?" soliloquised Miss Casey. "What's this it is now? Sister Paul says she'll ask me, 'Given the day of the month and the hour in Rome, to find where's the sun vertical.' *Rome*," repeated Miss Casey emphatically, fixing the name in her memory by hammering her knee with her fist. " Find the meridian of the sun for the——"

"*Meridian* of the sun, Julia Casey!" interrupted a neighbour. "Declination, you mean."

"It's not," snapped Miss Casey, contradictorily. Nevertheless she borrowed a book to make sure.

"I'm certain to forget the name of that old first *Maire du Palais*," moaned another girl. "An' I'm not like you, Mary Anne; I never can remember a thing I don't know till 'tis too late."

Mary Anne was the neighbour who had corrected Miss Casey: a bright-eyed girl with a quantity of black hair hanging in two plaited tails down her back. Her face was beaming with good humour, for she confidently expected several first prizes. "What matter?" laughed she. "This business doesn't count for prizes, you know. Anyhow, I think I'm safe."

"Humph!" grunted Miss Brangan, who was stupid or idle, or both, casting a sour look in the direction of the prizes. " I wish I was safe out of it; papa'll murder me for not mindin' me French. Anyhow, 'tis the last of these old botherations I'll be ever at, so I'm not caring. Julia —Julia Casey," raising her voice, "are you going to Kingstown for the vacation? I am; an' I'm going on the Pilgrimage to Lourdes in September. Yes, an' papa an' Aloysius."

Miss Brangan, the daughter of an alderman, and entitled
to five thousand pounds' fortune, troubled herself but little
about her examinations. It was not that, like Gallio, she
"cared for none of these things," but she felt that she had
enough without them. She would have liked, just as much
as Mary Anne, to be called up for half a dozen prizes, and to
play the best solo on the piano; but some sense of fitness,
just as much as indolence, told her that it was more suitable
to Mary Anne than to herself. Mary Anne's father was
poor, and the family lived over their shop; whereas Alderman Brangan lived in Mountjoy Square, and had men to look
after his shop,—or rather shops, for he had several. They
were not at all in the same set, though in the same business. "Whiskey people" are not by any means equal and
alike, though people will persist in saying so; and it was
an understood thing that Mary Anne had need of all the
accomplishments she could acquire. Miss Brangan thought
there would almost be something *infra dig.* in troubling
herself about that sort of thing. And she knew very well
also that she would incur the risk of being thought clever.
Fortune and cleverness together would constitute an anomaly; cleverness is understood to be the peculiar appanage
of dowerless spinsters, and even then is but a questionable
commodity, and one by no means in demand in the market
—that is, *per se;* indirectly it has a value of its own, for
it is considered rather as a proof of antecedent culture, and
consequent respectability, in its possessor.

The doors were thrown open now widely, and the guests
thronged in, headed by the Bishop of Secunderabad, presi-
dent on the occasion in lieu of a still higher dignitary of
the Church, who was indisposed or busy. An immense
number of priests—not less than forty—with a sprinkling
of gorgeously dressed ladies, pre-eminent among whom was
Lady Shanassy, in a robe of violet silk, slashed with velvet,
a voluminous white lace shawl, yellow bonnet and gloves
to match. The nuns entered by a door leading to their
part of the house, and took up their position behind the
visitors. The Bishop, when all had settled down in their
places, gave the signal, and the performance commenced

with the overture played by eight hands on four tolerably wooden-toned pianos. Fortunately, the instruments were a good distance off, and as the windows were open, a fair share of the noise passed out, so that conversation could go on without intermission. The Mother Superior was seated beside her distinguished relative, to whom, as he plays a small part in this story, we must devote a few words of description.

A man of about fifty-four—spiteful people would say sixty—years of age, the Bishop was under the middle height, slightly corpulent, but still trim and active of figure. His shapely hands and feet, clear hazel eyes and dazzling teeth, somewhat compensated for such defects as a general coarseness and indistinctness of feature. The lower part of his face was heavy, and gave him, until he spoke and his countenance lighted up, a sulkiness of expression quite belying his natural disposition. Indeed, a more jovial, sociable gentleman could hardly be found than his Lordship of Secunderabad, or one more in request by society. Unattached to any particular cure of souls, unless the chaplaincy of a fashionable convent be accounted such, he had plenty of time to devote to the exigencies of his numerous and widespread acquaintances. Dr. O'Rooney, as his name indicates, came of a good old Irish stock. He had been educated at Maynooth, where, as a matter of course, he had distinguished himself; and his first appointment was to a little mountain curacy on the confines of the Dublin diocese. After some ten years of country life, he was changed to a city cure. Here his social talents and agreeable manners stood him in such good stead that, on the death of the aged parish priest of St. Columbkille, Father O'Rooney was appointed amid universal acclamation to fill his place. He was not an ambitious man, and would have been well content to end his days in Columbkille Chapel House; but a Bishop was needed for Secunderabad, or a parish was needed for some curate on his promotion; and Father O'Rooney, with grief in his heart, though wearing a martyr's smile of resignation on his lips, left the pleasant pastures of St. Columbkille, the rich dinners, the

politics, municipal and imperial, the match-makings and
diversions of Dublin city, for the unknown and remote
regions of Secunderabad.

Ere he had been many years in India, a severe attack of
liver complaint forced him to return; and whether the
diseased organ proved obdurate to medical treatment, or
whether Dr. O'Rooney had made up his mind not to face·
India's malignant climate again, is unknown. Certain it is
that Secunderabad knew him no more, and the Bishop
remained in Dublin, retaining his episcopal title and privileges.

All who had known him during his tenure of the
Columbkille parish flocked round .him again; and his
services were in immense request for masses and other
ceremonies. One fashionable convent, the prioress of
which was his cousin, made him its chaplain. Then, a
Bishop's spiritual services being naturally of greater value
than those of the inferior clergy, command a higher fee.
The class of people who set store by a flourishing wedding
notice in the papers, took care to secure it by engaging
"the Right Reverend Doctor O'Rooney, Bishop of Secunderabad, assisted by, etc. etc. etc.," PPs., and CCs. In
short, this Lord Bishop unattached had very fine pickings
among that ambitious class who were not sufficiently high
placed in the social scale to venture to demand the services
of the Primate or the Cardinal, and whose love of show
would not let them be contented with the ministrations of
their own parochial clergy. He was a very useful personage, on the whole. Whenever higher ecclesiastics found it
inconvenient to preside at meetings or festivities, of whatever kind, Bishop O'Rooney was always ready and willing
to supply their place. On this occasion a much more exalted dignitary had been invited; but a sudden summons
to Rome had prevented him keeping his engagement.

The overture had just been finished, amid universal
applause, and the class-mistress was in the act of announc-
ing the second item on the programme, when the door
opened, and the portress thrust her head into the room
and beckoned the Superior. She rose and stepped hastily

into the passage, where she found a group of four ladies, one old, three young, who were waiting for an interval of silence to come in.

"My dear Mrs. Rafferty!" exclaimed the reverend Mother, embracing the oldest lady of the group, and kissing her on both cheeks in French fashion,—"and Eily and Aloysia, my darling children!" and they, too, were kissed on both cheeks.

"This is a young lady friend whom we brought with us, reverend Mother,—Miss Davoren," said the matron, who was the mother of the two other girls. A slender girl of eighteen, quietly dressed in gray silk, bowed in acknowledgment of the Superior's salutation.

"I'll take you in in one minute," said the Superior. "Eily, my child, how fat you've got! And Anastatia, my dear, you'll excuse me keeping you waiting, but there's a recitation going on just this moment, and you know it takes so little to put the children out. How is Mr. Rafferty? and why did he not come? and Stanislas?"

"Mr. Rafferty couldn't come. Augh! ye know, reverend Mother," said Mrs. Rafferty, sitting down and fanning her rubicund visage with her pocket-handkerchief, "gentlemen can't get away from business that way. Stanislas 'll come to take us home; and he said his Lordship's young nephew, Mr. Hogan, was very apt to come in with him."

"Oh dear, yes," said the Superior. "He will look in upon us; but I don't expect him till late. He's going away to-morrow morning to Switzerland, for the long vacation. I wanted him to go to Lourdes: there's a lovely pilgrimage just getting up now. Mary Brangan is going in September, you know."

"Is she, now!" exclaimed both the girls together, looking, as they spoke, not at the nun, but at their mamma, with a sort of meaning telegraphic stare. The communication seemed to suggest a great deal more than the Superior had any idea of.

"We're going down to Bray on Saturday. No; not Kingstown this summer. It's got that common, you know. I declare now, what with goin' there every Sunday, we do

be sick of it. Miss Brangan's to be there now, is she?
Well, it'll be new to her, you know. Mr. Rafferty's
thinkin' of movin' on to the Square shortly. Murtagh's
house is to be let—just a door or two from the Alderman's."

"That will be very nice for Mary to have such friends.
I thought Eily was here with her. I must introduce you
before she goes." Mother Superior saw everything, and
was delighted to accommodate her friends.

Meantime, the young lady in gray had been standing
apart, quietly examining a vase of wax flowers. She had
been forgotten for a moment or two; but while examining
with amused wonder the stiff fuchsias and petunias under
their glass shade, she had smiled at the easy success of the
Raffertys' stratagem. She knew they had been watching
their opportunity for a long time, and wondered which
was the object of their desire—the rich widower Brangan
père, or the heiress his daughter. It was time to go
now. The Mother Superior turned towards the stranger
graciously.

"You have never been at any of our exhibitions, Miss
Davoren?"

"Never. I have only been once in a convent before."

"Ah, indeed!" Something in the young lady's tone as
well as her accent, which was vastly different from that of
the others,—not Dublin, and yet not English of the very
decided sort the reverend Mother was most accustomed to
hear,—struck her as remarkable. She stood aside when
they got into the passage leading to the schoolroom, and
marshalled the young ladies before her. As she followed,
walking beside Mrs. Rafferty, she bent and whispered in
that matron's ear,—

"Who is she? Protestant?"

"Good family. Her brother's in college with my
nephew Stanislas. She's not Protestant, for she goes to
Gardiner's Street Chapel regularly."

"It's not a Protestant name, certainly. I suppose
they're half,—you know, mixed mar'ges no doubt."

Then they swept in, with great rustle and commotion,
past the Bishop and the attendant priests; the girls on

the benches feasting their eyes in admiration and envy on
the rich new dresses of the ladies.

"Julia," said Miss Brangan, "those are the Raffertys.
Look at that blue silk ; my new one that I'm to wear
going away is done just like that, panier and bouffawns.
I'm sorry I didn't have that yellow lace. I might have,
if I liked it. You've not seen it yet. I got it made
lovely. What a notion I had of going home in the old
school sack ! I'm leaving all me old dresses behind me
for the poor. What a show I'd be in plain skirts and no
tablier till me new ones was made ! Isn't that a nice-
looking girl in the gray silk, do you say? H'm. She's
a nice complexion, certainly, but I don't care for the way
her body is done, at all. Pleats are gone out entirely ;
it's——"

But here a young lady with a very tremulous soprano
began to sing one of the melodies, accompanying herself
on the harp ; and Miss Brangan's dissertation as to the
successor of "pleats" was lost for ever.

Miss Bride Sweeny—or Biddy, as her friend maliciously
chose to style her—had not yet forgotten the little unplea-
santness of the morning. She did not like to be reminded
of her plebeian patronymic in that manner. Bridget was
an ugly name to begin life with, in a world the ups and
downs of which no one can foretell. It was in vain that
she had tried to have her second name, Geneviève, accepted :
it would not go down ; and the next best thing she could
do was to adopt the compromise Bride. Sweeny *père* had
made a nice thing of it in whiskey lately ; and it was quite
on the cards that he would be a town-councillor at the very
next election, and perhaps have a house " *on* the Square "
too. Anyhow, she wasn't going to be put down by that
Mary Brangan. So after a while she leaned forward, and
said, in a whisper to which malice lent distinctness—

"Mary Branigan !"

The lady addressed flushed crimson, but pretended not
to hear. Biddy Sweeny knew her weak point, and how
to touch it.

"Mary Branigan, I say. You're the next : mind yourself now in your Silvio Pellico, and don't go smash the way you done yesterday."

"The way *you done!*" mimicked Miss Brangan, scornfully. "You'd better mind your English, Miss Sweeny." She carried the day; as indeed she generally did, for her opponent was too hot-tempered to guard herself. Miss Brangan returned to her discussion of the toilettes.

"Thanks be to goodness, Julia Casey, I'm done wid it all. This day week where will I be? On the Pier, listening to the band, or at the Flower Show. Oh, laws!"

"Don't be tantalising me!" returned her friend, who was not to "finish" till next year. "Sure, 'tis sick and tired of it I am; I'm coaxing mamma to give me a nice mixture dress, tight to me figure, for the vacation. Please goodness, I'll see something of fashions beyond silk thread hair-nets instead of invisible nets, and aprons fastened at the side instead of behind. Faugh! that's all we can have of them here."

Further discussion was stopped by the appearance of the gentlemen of whom Mrs. Rafferty had spoken : her nephew, a medical student of Trinity, and the Bishop's nephew, a barrister twenty-eight or nine years of age. The gentlemen, who walked in unceremoniously, shook hands with the Superior Mother and the Bishop, and took their places among their friends in the back seats.

"How do you do, Mrs. Rafferty? You must be nearly half through by this, are you not? No? my, my! that's a sad business; I've come too soon!" So spoke Mr. Hogan, seating himself between Miss Davoren and the lady addressed. He cast a sharp, scrutinising glance at his pretty neighbour; but her head was bent over the programme, and he could not see her very well.

"How is Mr. Rafferty?"

"Well, thank you, Mr. Hogan. You're a great stranger these times; only the Bishop told us you were comin', I'd hardly expect to see you even here."

"Can't help it, madam; I am so hard-worked, you know. I'm off to-morrow morning to the Continent. Yes; a friend of mine, Mr. Saltasche, is going over with me as far as Paris. He happens to be an excellent traveller —knows every place abroad. You've been, of course ?"

"No, never. What's this now, girls?" said Mrs. Rafferty, looking at her programme as she spoke, "That's Miss Brangan called out now to say this 'Sil—Sil '—what ? Augh, somethin' Frinch. I must listen to her anyhow. How stout she's got !"

Mr. Hogan had pains to conceal his amusement. He looked for a moment or two at the great fat girl, who, dressed in a costume of white stuff, which accentuated her stout figure most ludicrously, was reading or rather muttering something out of a book. Then he turned aside to his other neighbour. "That is an Italian recitation, or supposed to be, is it not?"

"I believe so," she answered looking up demurely; but her eyes met such a fund of quizzical enjoyment in his that she was fain to drop them again until Miss Brangan, red as a peony, had returned to her perch and the ironic gratulations of Bride Sweeny. Miss Davoren was puzzled to know who her neighbour was. Could he be the Bishop's nephew, alluded to before ? She darted a criticising look at the two gentlemen. Hogan was slight, but compact, and looked somewhat taller than his relative : he resembled him in complexion and feature. But the culture and quick intelligence so lacking in the physiognomy of the elder man were apparent in the more vigorous and clean-cut features of the barrister. He was not handsome, but there was nothing insignificant in his expression and bearing ; and under the heavy eyebrows was a pair of gray, bright eyes, observant and humorous.

He stooped a little towards her, and said courteously, "Might I ask what comes next? Grand Fantasia,—something to make us all talk : I suppose the aim or end of most drawing-room music. Then, oh my! why, they have a German recitation, 'Joan of Arc,'—aw, *Skiller's*. That's very deep ; quite beyond me. I've read it in the English."

"Indeed." Miss Davoren was perfectly grave, though she was thinking to herself how evenly the balance had been restored between her neighbour and Mrs. Rafferty.

"I've seen 'The Robbers' in French. I forget whose translation it was, though. It is quite tantalising to hear that *Lebt wohl, ihr Grotten und ihr kühlen Brunnen* ('Farewell, ye grottoes and cool streams'). I am sure the thermometer must be ninety, at least, in this room."

"More: look there!" Hogan indicated with a glance one of the occupants of the front benches.

"Poor Lady Shanassy!" Her ladyship had untied the yellow ribbons which confined her bonnet, and was lying back, gasping for breath, in her chair, yet smiling politely. Her double chin waggled about helplessly, and her round, red forehead shone with heat. It was stifling now in the room. The air that came in at the windows was hot and dusty. The mignonette seemed to have exhaled all its sweetness, and the geraniums and roses in the bouquet before the Bishop were shedding their petals on the red cloth. The priests lolled on their chairs, and talked all the time to each other, or whoever was near. It was positively too hot to pay attention.

"What's this, now? glory be to God!" ejaculated a great fat priest: "the globes, alannah! The three Muses 'tis we have."

"Beggin' your pardon, Father O'Slattery," said a curate on his right, "there was nine of them."

"So there was," assented the big priest. "You were at school since I was. Graces, I mint to say: 'tis all one as the same."

The three muses were Miss Sweeny, Miss Rooney, and Miss Casey—the last-named holding the dreaded "brass thing, the quadrint," gingerly in her white-threaded-gloved fingers, and repeating the "rule" all wrong to herself with fearful frowns. Miss Casey was first, and said her rule off glibly, but inaudibly, staring all the while at the red cloth on the table with an expression at once aggrieved and ferocious. The globe was twisted and made to squeak. Miss Casey did not drop her quadrant, but was so frightened when her turn came that she never remembered whether she had said everything wrong or not.

Hogan looked on with genuine amusement. It was the

first time that he had witnessed one of these exhibitions;
and he had little idea of the treat in store for him. Knowing
the three performers he found something intensely incongruous in their proceedings. Lady Shanassy, who in her
day had stood behind the counter of her husband's grocery,
and whose niece, Miss Rooney, might be called upon to
do the same thing, no doubt was as edified as she seemed
to be at the learning displayed. He looked all round at
the phalanx of countenances : before him, where the girls
were seated, and behind, to the guests; but the children
looked tired and hot and nervous, and the priests were
chattering and laughing and yawning. He caught the eye
of his cousin the prioress, and shook his head. She did
not know what he meant, and was too far off to speak to
him. Then he turned to his neighbour, whose name as yet
he did not know.

"Dear me!" said he, "why, this is astonishing learning!
What in the wide world? Whoever expected young ladies
like these to know such things? I must make a note of
it, and keep clear of them ever after. How in the world,
now, could I ask such a bluestocking as that" (nodding in
the direction of the bewildered Miss Casey) "to dance a
quadrille with me! I'd as soon think of engaging in conversation with Caroline Herschel or Mrs. Somerville."

"Poor things!" said Miss Davoren, who was trying hard
to keep from laughing. Something in the voice made him
look sharply at her. Was she making fun of him? She
was as demure as possible, and seemed absorbed in Miss
Rooney's manipulations of the globe.

"What does it all mean?" asked he, when the interesting exhibition was over, and the globe, protesting all the
way, was wheeled back to its corner.

"I am sure I don't know. I never was at a school in
my life," replied she. "I begin to fear my education has
been sadly neglected."

"Do you like fables,—La Fontaine and Æsop, and that
sort of thing?" This was à propos of the closing piece,
"Le Cigale et la Fourmi," recited by a tiny, fair-haired
girl of five.

" Exceedingly ; Æsop's fables were a great delight to me. He leaves so much to your imagination, you know. When I was a child I used to divert myself making up stories out of them—reading, in fact, what was to be read between the lines. You remember that charming one, 'The Dog and the Shadow'? Now, what sort of disposition had that dog? You can imagine him courageous, risking mortal combat ; or cowardly, prepared to fly directly he had accomplished his act of spoliation. Another thing, too. Did he, or did he not, attempt to secure his own piece as well as the other? and what were his sensations on seeing the dog in the water mimic his actions so exactly?"

" Ah, ah!" said Hogan, laughingly. " That is an interesting question indeed : but perhaps he abandoned his own piece as some sort of compensation to the other dog; it might have been an amicable exchange, now, concluded after a negotiation."

" Yes; one could fancy a bargain," said Miss Davoren, drily, " both parties willing and agreeable. Now they're distributing the prizes. We shall get out soon, I hope."

The Bishop, upon whose knee the little pupil who had recited the French fable was now seated, handed books to the girls, as they came up in order of merit to receive them. To the surprise of her class and herself, Miss Brangan was awarded no fewer than three firsts.

" It's a scandal!" loudly exclaimed Bride Sweeny. " Mary Anne Kellett ought to have got them. Mary Branigan, you're no better than a——"

" Stop," said a nun, catching the speaker by the elbow. " How dare you make remarks on what your superiors have decided! I'm ashamed of you, Miss ; the guests barely gone to their luncheon, and such conduct beginning."

Miss Sweeny, impulsive in everything, plunged headlong into a book-closet, and burst into tears. The other girls were racing up and down the room—some quarrelling over the books, more than one crying with disappointment, and all bursting with excitement and long pent-up feelings.

Miss Brangan, with three gaudy red and yellow bound
books tightly tucked under her arm, her red countenance
all aflame with mingled defiance and triumph, stood with
her back to the chimney-piece, stoutly repelling the taunts
and innuendoes of her companions. With the presence of
mind and clear-sightedness that characterised her, she had
realised the situation at a glance, and had taken up her
position accordingly.

Knowing well that she was not entitled to a single
reward, she had understood that on the occasion of "her
going home—for good," her teachers had felt it desirable
that she should be able to present some certificates or guar-
antees of her progress in her studies. After seven or eight
years spent in St. Swithin's, during which time the convent
exchequer had been the richer by some five hundred pounds
of Alderman Brangan's money, it was only natural that at
the end of that period the young lady should give some
evidence of either talent or culture. Besides, the Alderman was wealthy and of high position; and who was
Mary Anne, compared to Mary Brangan? Mary Anne
would be indemnified next year, " ad majorem Dei gloriam,"
as the reverend Mother, who liked Mary Anne, said to herself with a sigh, when signing her name in each prize book.

"Never mind," said Mary Anne heartily, to some condol-
ing friends. "I earned them, if she's got them; an' what
do I care? Not one button! "

The nun who had reproved Miss Sweeny was standing
near, and heard this. She cast a scrutinising look from
under her black veil at the speaker. Not a trace of envy
or discontent could she discover on the open brow of the
girl; and she nodded her head with an approving smile.
She had seen perfectly that Bride, between whom and the
heiress was a feud of old standing, had only made the
injustice a peg on which to hang a quarrel; this she, by
her prompt action, had prevented. Mary Brangan was
leaving for good; "and a good riddance, too!" thought
the sister, glancing at the truculent countenance of that
young lady. "She'll be married in less than six months,"
and a little curl of disgust passed over her lips. "But

Mary Anne," and she looked again at her, "what rest will she find for the sole of her foot in the world?" questioned the nun, whose experienced eye read in the clever, bright, refined face a presage of trouble and conflict to come. "We'll have her back here. That's the sort that always do come back."

"Mary Brangan! Where's Mary Brangan? Darling child, come out in the garden with me."

The speaker was Mother Paul, the mistress of the novices and teacher of the use of the globes and arithmetic, and Mary Brangan's favourite nun. Not, indeed, that she cared one bit more for her than for the others; but it was the fashion to have a favourite nun, to whom to apply for advice in difficulties such as peculiarly afflict schoolgirls; for example, scruples in matters of confession, difficulties of belief—mostly, indeed, quite imaginary, or resulting from a deficiency of imagination; and Miss Brangan, of course, followed the general rule.

"Now, Mary dear," began Mother Paul, a little old lady whose countenance expressed chiefly amiability and simplicity, "I've got leave to be absent from the *déjeûner* on purpose to speak to you. You know, dear child, it is a serious thing your leaving us this way for good, to enter on a scene of temptations and—and—ahem! constant struggle and watchfulness; don't you, now?"

"Yes, Mother," answered Mary; who, indeed, looked forward to life as a scene of eternal vacation, and whose imagination was revelling in visions of fashionable attire, late lying in bed in the morning, and never hearing bells ring for imperative duties.

"Come down here, child: the shade of the apple-trees is better than this glare, and you've got nothing on your head."

The pair walked down a cross path bordered with lavender bushes and great clove carnations, the flowers of which were drooping in the heat. The *parterres*, glowing with geraniums and sweet-williams, looked hot and garish, and the perfume in the close air was stifling. They passed through a little swing gate into an orchard, where the trees hung over the gravel walks and formed shady avenues. Mother Paul turned down the first path, and continued speaking, with an anxious, serious tone and look that contrasted strangely with the bearing of her companion.

"Keep faithful to grace, dear child. I know you'll go to weekly confession and communion; and you will come to your monthly meetings here on Sundays and feast-days?"

"Oh yes, Mother," answered Miss Brangan dutifully; but not without some misgivings that Sunday meetings might interfere with those promenades on Kingstown Pier to which she looked forward with such delight.

"But that's not enough, Mary dear; there's a great deal more than that necessary. Oh, it's terrible how girls are led away! Now, there's fast dancing: that's the hardest thing of——"'

"Oh, Mother!" interrupted Mary, almost with a shriek, "I'll promise you ever so faithfully: never, never!—now see if I will."

"Ah!" sighed Mother Paul, looking up to the blue sky through the lattice of fruit-laden boughs overhead, "girls have promised me that often; and actually at their very first ball—their *first* ball, Mary—have basely yielded to the temptation of the devil!"

"Laws!" said Mary, meditatively and wonderingly. Then, moved by curiosity, "Who was it, Mother? Was it the Raffertys?"

"I wouldn't tell you, dear child, for the world, that would be a sin against charity; so don't be losing your time asking me. But, Mary dear, I was wanting to speak to you most particularly about what you know you're most inclined to—love of dress, darling child; and oh! above all things, light reading."

Miss Mary assumed an air of resignation and *quasi*-penitence. She knew very well that Mother Paul was referring to that going-away dress which was at this very moment causing such heart-burnings and envy in the dressing-room, where it was ostentatiously spread out in strong contrast to the "sacks," as she disdainfully termed the school uniform frocks of the rest. As for the "light reading," that was the natural consequence of her once having brought to school, in a fit of bravado pure and simple, a yellow-backed railway novel, which had been pounced on and confiscated immediately, and the rumoured awfulness of which had thrown the school into a state of effervescence, and had invested herself with a delicious halo of wickedness and audacity that lasted nearly a week.

"Love of dress," continued the Mother, "is a snare and a delusion; and it is degrading to every one; but it is especially revolting in a child who, like you, has had the benefit of years of training and religious education."

"But, Mother," expostulated Mary Brangan with a perceptible pout, "papa wishes it; and people must dress accordingly."

"Oh! I know, I know, dear," said Mother Paul in a resigned tone; "obey your family. Of course you must appear according to your position in life; only remember the example of the Saints. St. Elizabeth wore a hair shirt under her royal robes. Never neglect to mortify your own inclinations: that's the surest road to salvation."

Mary listened devoutly to this somewhat vague direction, and began to wish the four o'clock bell would ring and call Mother Paul to her dinner. She intended fully to "mortify her inclinations," and had a vague idea that after a week or two she would get up and go to eight o'clock mass every morning. That, as she had been in the habit of so doing for years, would not be very difficult; besides, to the intrinsic meritoriousness of the practice was joined the consideration of meeting lots of girls, and of forming new and desirable acquaintances.

"You'll promise me, Mary, faithfully, never to read any book that hasn't got your confessor's approbation. Oh, Mary dear, if you only knew the——"

"I do, though, Mother Paul; and I'll never read anything at all, if you like,—there now!" vociferated Mary, who had just caught sight of a group of heads in the dressing-room window, and was seized with a sudden alarm lest any of their owners should meddle with her new dress. Biddy Sweeny would be capable of trying it on. How she burned to get away!

Mother Paul, whose veil prevented her seeing Miss Brangan's movements, stopped, and turning round, looked into her companion's face. Miss Mary was flushed a little, and her black eyes sparkled ; the faint breeze that was just stirring the boughs lifted her ripply brown hair, and swept some of it across her forehead — white and un-wrinkled yet, but hard. She was not pretty, for she had not a good feature in her face ; nor interesting, for she had a determined, bold expression ; but she had a beauty of her own at this moment—the beauty of youth and fresh-ness and vigorous strong life, eager for action and enjoy-ment, eager, and daring, and ignorant. Mother Paul read it all with one look ; and she smiled with a smile that was half a sigh, thinking how near the child was to her now, standing there in her white robe of innocence, a picture with a framing of fresh flowers and leaves ; and to-morrow busy with the gauds and pomps and vanities of this world, and far from her for ever.

"Oh! Mary dear, don't be in extremes. My child, that's what alarms me for you : you're always in extremes. And another thing,—now you'll find the time hang very heavily on your hands at home. Go on with your Italian, dear. You read your piece quite nicely to-day ; and don't forget it."

"Augh! what's the good, Mother Paul!" Mary was getting cross now ; the burden laid upon her was begin-ning to be more than she could bear. "I know as much as any one else ; where's the use of them things?"

"You never can tell, dear ; you may be going to Italy one of these days ; you never can know what may happen."

Miss Mary had an eye for an absurdity, and stifled an inclination to giggle. She thought that a poor reason, but did not say so.

"I think that's not very likely, Mother." She had already fixed on a receptacle in the lumber-room for her school-books, and beheld in her mind's eye, with intense

satisfaction, Silvio Pellico and Veneroni's grammar repos-
ing in undisturbed peace at the bottom of it.

"Now, dear child, I must go. I'll come down and bid
you good-bye at five, when the carriage comes for you.
You'll remember everything, Mary, and be a good, pious,
Catholic girl, and do St. Swithin credit, and your religion.
Now remember, Mary, it's matter of confession if you read
anything but what Father McQuaide approves."

"Oh! now, Mother, do you *think* I'd do such a thing!"
Mary was positively indignant. They were now at the
door of the schoolhouse. Mother Paul smiled as she
passed through into the monastery, and breathed a
prayer—good, pious soul—for her pupil's welfare; and
Mary, having closed the door after her with a sigh of
relief, tore up the dressing-room stairs to look after her
property.

The *déjeûner* had been going on for some time, and not
a few of the guests had departed; still talking and
laughing, eating and drinking, were being carried on
with vigour. Lady Shanassy was seated near the Bishop,
and the Mother Superior was busy catering for their
wants. The nuns acted as waitresses and hostesses at
the same time, and ran hither and thither with jellies and
ices and more solid comestibles. Plates and glasses
rattled and clashed occasionally, and great jolly peals
of laughter shook the very windows. None of the pupils
were present, save the Bishop's little friend Angela Carey,
who was seated beside him, drinking coffee out of his cup,
and being fed with all sorts of good things; there was a
separate repast provided for them in their own refectory,
and which they were all too excited and busy to eat. The
large parlour seemed cool and airy in comparison with the
schoolroom: the blinds were all drawn down, and through
the wide-opened sashes the air streamed in fragrant and
fresh from the shaded lawn without. The gaudy hues of
the ladies' dresses, and the brilliant pyramids of flowers on
the table, were toned down by the shade to a mellow
richness which the stained oak of the floor and walls
enhanced. The nuns, in their picturesque religious garb,

with pale refined faces, ministered to the wants of their guests. To Miss Davoren, at least, who was observant and impressionable, it formed a pleasant and suggestive picture. The Rafferty girls were too well used to it to think anything about the occasion extraordinary or out of the common; and sat with handkerchiefs carefully spread in their laps, and nibbled and gossiped with the priests, their neighbours. Lady Shanassy and Mrs. Rafferty professed themselves delighted with everything: "lovely" and "beautiful" were the mildest terms by which they could measure their admiration.

"'Deed, yes," said the Bishop; "Saint Gengulphus is beaten all to nothing entirely. Where's John?"

"At the other end," said the Superior. "I hope he's getting something to eat; it was so provoking I didn't know about the trains sooner. Poor Father Carey got scarcely anything. Lady Shanassy, let me give you one small bit of this cream: the lobster salad, then? They're made at home, so I can assure you they're good. And you think our music was better, my lord? Poor Mother de Sales will be so glad."

"Won't you be glad of your holidays, Mother? you must be entirely wore out," said Mrs. Rafferty, who was holding a chicken bone most genteelly in her pocket-handkerchief, and picking it deliberately.

"'Tis done now for another year. We go into Retreat to-night for ten days. Father Maloney will open it to-morrow morning, and dear knows that it will be a relief. I daresay in another hour there won't be a child of the seventy left."

"I should fancy *they* will find that a relief," observed Mr. Hogan, who had come up from his end of the room. Indeed, the laughing and romping without could be heard distinctly.

"What do you say, Angela?" asked the Bishop. "I wager you're sorry to go away, hey?"

"Berry," replied Angela, speaking thickly through a mouthful of pink jelly, and looking up confidently from under her yellow curls. "Uncle John's gone away."

"Yes; gone to catch a train, my dear. Poor man, didn't get his lunch."

"I hope you don't forget that I have to do the same thing, sir," interposed his nephew, in a low tone.

"Business, Mrs. Rafferty. Gentlemen have not the elegant leisure of you ladies. Might I ask," and he dropped his voice again, "who is the young lady in gray who sat beside me?"

"Ah, then! and you don't know? Why, I thought you knew her perfectly, you an' she seemed such friends. She's a Miss Davoren. 'Twas through Stanislas I came to know her; he an' her brother's great friends; she lives out at Green Lane."

"Oh, to be sure; I remember meeting him: Dicky— Dicky Davoren, a handsome little fellow, with Stanislas."

Then Mr. Hogan and his uncle took their leave of the assembly, and mounting a car outside the gate, sped city-wards as fast as possible.

"God be praised that job is over, anyhow!" said the Bishop, twisting himself comfortably back in his seat. "Fine lot of girls she has got there, too. I hope next year will be as good a one. What a headache all that racket has given me!"

"Me, too; though I was not so long there as you, sir."

"The drive will do us good," returned the Bishop, drawing a deep breath; "and now, my dear boy, what's this you're going to do? and when may I see you back?"

"I can't just say that, sir; it will depend on how I get along. I wasn't telling you about my friend Saltasche, was I? No. Well, you must know him; I got some work—cases for opinion—through him when that last Lead Mines Company was being wound up. You surely know Cosmo Saltasche?"

"Bless me! of course I do: the fellow who is at all those Charitable Association meetings and Hospital Boards. Yes; a regular swaddler!"

"On the contrary, a most liberal man; great friend of Monsignor Bursford's; says he met him in Rome."

"I fancy now I have seen that Saltasche at Princess

Galichini's; and no doubt it was there he met Bursford too."

"A very genial, pleasant sort of fellow, a great friend of Lord Brayhead's and Lord Ramines'; he has asked me to dinner to meet them."

"He has,—eh,—has he?" said the elder man, with a dry sort of smile. "Queer couple to hunt together as ever I heard of. One a fierce old Orange bigot, the other a blackleg—I believe he was drummed out of a London Club for misconduct. I dont care for ayther of them; you and the likes of you have nothing to do with that sort: far better keep to your own people."

Though the Bishop spoke in this slighting way, he was secretly delighted, and his nephew saw it plainly. So with a mock air of submission he said,—

"You are the best judge, sir, of course; but a public man can't pick and choose, and I might miss many a good thing by confining my acquaintance to those of my own religion."

The Bishop did not reply. A large carriage, drawn by a pair of showy bays, whose harness was almost covered with brass, with men-servants in green and gold liveries on the box, overtook their car; as it dashed past, a stout lady inside, dressed in brown, with a gorgeous hat and feathers, leaned forward and honoured the Bishop with a stare which was half recognition, half curiosity.

"Ah, then! 'my God!" cried he, astonished, "who is this that is?—I know her surely."

His nephew burst out laughing. "I should think so, indeed; it's the big fat girl, Miss Bran—something or another. Just as I was leaving the hall I saw her trapesing down the stairs, got up to kill, and looking over her shoulder at her long-tailed gown. You ought to have seen the faces of the girls looking at her. It was a regular comedy."

The Bishop laughed too. "That girl will have money —lots of it. Her father's Alderman Brangan. The Raffertys are making up to her: I can see that clearly. Faith, then, Stanislas Mulcahy might well suit her. The money's

there, for certain: more than can be said of the Rafferty
girls, for all the talk that he can give them four thousand
a-piece.   I don't believe it, for I know where he got it.
There's the Brangans' connection, too, into the bargain."

"Do you mean the gin-palace connection, sir?" answered
the barrister, with a curl of his lip.

The Bishop looked at his nephew angrily; but he had
no time to say anything in reply, for the car drew up at
that moment at the door of his own house, which was
situated in a quiet street on the north side of Dublin.

"I ordered dinner at six," said he, leading the way in.
"I hope it is not spoiled: hey, Martha?"

"Glad to see you, Master John," said the housekeeper,
an old woman who had known Hogan from the time he
was a child, ignoring her master's question to greet his
companion.   "Where were you this long time, alannah?"

"Now, Martha," spoke the Bishop peremptorily, "don't
be gosthering with that boy, but bring up our dinner.   I
have to go out at eight o'clock."

Then they walked into the sitting-room, where a round
dinner-table was laid for two.   It was a comfortable room,
and furnished with solid, heavy furniture.   A red Brussels
carpet and rug, with heavy curtains of the same colour;
half a dozen morocco-covered chairs; and one arm-chair,
well stuffed and cushioned, stood before the Bishop's
writing-table.   The sofa was brilliant with bead cushions
and antimacassars of all colours and designs.   No flowers,
statuettes, or pictures spoke for the taste or refinement of
the occupant.   The bookcase contained three shelves, two
of which were occupied by theological books, well coated
with dust, the top held a double row of modern novels,
chiefly Trollope's.   A few large photographs from Rome,
relics of his travels, hung upon the walls: St. Peter's, the
Coliseum, and Trajan's Column, looking ghastly and unreal
in thick black and white.   Over the fireplace a common
print of His Holiness, in the well-known attitude of benediction, looked down on a choice collection of cigar boxes,
pipes, and matchstands, mixed up oddly with rosaries,
prayer-books, and reliquaries.

His lordship drew a pair of Berlin wool-work slippers from under a table, and having got rid of his neat kid boots, slipped down to the cellar for a bottle of champagne, while his nephew, spying a newspaper with which he had some connection, hastily opened it to look if some verses sent in by him the day before had been printed. He found them as he expected in the poet's corner, but had not time to read the effusion before his lordship returned; and as he by no means desired his relative to know anything of the matter, he was obliged to replace the newspaper in its basket. The Bishop objected to literature. He knew the world—at least, the world of Dublin; and was well aware that the reputation of being literary does not serve a young professional man; and as John O'Rooney Hogan owed everything to his uncle, he was bound to defer to his prejudices. The barrister's father had been a tradesman in a little inland country town; and he, an only son, had been destined by his mother for the Church. For this, however, the youth had shown but scant inclination, and after absorbing the very limited stock of knowledge to be procured at the diocesan college of—— he returned home to take his place in his father's drapery shop. This was even less to his taste than the clerical career, but his efforts to free himself from the toils of the hated business were unavailing. After a year or two of discontented servitude, the fates willed it that his father should die suddenly, and he found himself, at the age of nineteen, master of his own destiny. He confided his wishes and aspirations to his mother's brother, the then P.P. of St. Columbkille. Father O'Rooney good-naturedly consented to give him a chance, and carried him up to Dublin. After a severe and continuous course of study he passed a brilliant entrance examination into Trinity College, and, without being afterwards distinguished, got through his legal and other studies with the reputation of being a sure and solid, if somewhat slow student. He eked out his resources by teaching; and on his mother's death, which happened the same year that he was called to the English Bar, found himself possessed of some twelve hundred pounds' worth

of railway stock, and not a single encumbrance, wherewith
to face the world. He was clever and good-looking, very
gentlemanlike in appearance, and had an irreproachable
accent—a most important item in our inventory of his
qualifications.

The bishop's interests in this world (his lordship would
deny that he had any) were centred in his nephew; he
looked upon him as a son, and, like many parents, thinking
in his conceit that lack of opportunity and deficient instruction alone had hindered himself from rising to the
highest pinnacle of eminence, he determined that the
young man should enjoy every benefit that adverse fate
had denied himself. His great aspiration was to see the
barrister a judge. He felt that he ought to, and might,
be on the woolsack; still, he thought he could die content
if he could once see him in the robes of even a puisne
judge. But "*ottenuto che l'avesse, si poteva esser certo che
non si sarebbe più curato degli anni, non avrebbe desiderato
altro, e sarebbe morto contento, come tutti quelli che desideran
molto una cosa assicurano di voler fare quando siano arrivati a
ottenerla.*" And we may be very certain that the Chief
Justiceship would haunt the dreams of Judge Hogan and
his uncle, Bishop O'Rooney.

The dinner appeared directly. Martha was punctual and
orderly, and the fillets of sole were perfection. Neither
of the gentlemen had much appetite, as we may imagine.

"Those Raffertys are keeping up great state and style
now," began the Bishop; "but he isn't solid. No, Assumption has told me she had always trouble enough to get the
money out of him for the girls' bills when she had 'em
there."

The Bishop deemed it well to give his nephew all the
information possible about their acquaintance. Nothing
gives a man so much the air of society as knowing everything about everybody. And it is quite easy to possess as
much information as a French *chef de police*, without being
in the least a gossip or ill-natured.

"They're moving into the Square in November, when
they come in from Bray; by the same token, I believe

they're paying fifty pounds a month for the house they have there."

"Whiskey, is he not?" asked the barrister carelessly.

"I believe tea and sugar also. He was a great friend of the late Lord Mayor. There's daughters there, too; but no money. No," said the bishop, shaking his head critically, "I don't believe there's any; but it's a fine connection,—they are hand and glove with the Muldoons, the attorneys."

"Bah!" said Mr. Hogan contemptuously, setting down his glass of champagne. "People that are the laughing-stock of Dublin for vulgarity; common publicans, too,—traders. Faugh!"

"And isn't it good enough, sir?" thundered the angry Bishop. "Now, John my boy," he continued, in a quieter tone, "don't let any one hear *you* sneer at trade. You're in a fair way enough; but a rash speech like that would be enough to tumble you over. I've not helped you to where you are without trouble and expense; and, as I judge by you now, you seem to forget yourself altogether, just because a couple of swell Protestants have asked you to dine, and you must therefore be turning up your nose at these decent, useful people. Depend upon it, John, the only way to get on—and I know the world—the only chance of consideration or respect you can have from the Protestants, is to let them see—you being a Catholic—that you have the confidence and respect of the Catholics. The Government can't do without the priests; and what use would you be without *their* back? And to make little of Catholics and Catholic society, is not the way to go about getting that,—I can tell you, sir."

"I am fully aware of that, sir," replied the young man in a deferential tone; "but I flatter myself you would wish me better than to see me tied for life to one of the Misses Rafferty or Brangan. I shall have to marry a Catholic I suppose;—have no wish to do otherwise," he added hastily; "but there are better class Catholics in Ireland and England than these."

"But the capital,—the money?" interposed the Bishop hastily.

"I don't mean to marry till I am more settled in life,— at least, sir, unless I find it indispensable. Do you know, sir, that Lord Brayhead is nearly related to the Chief Justice, and his son is to be member for Blankshire directly? He belongs to the Reform Club." And Hogan fixed his keen gray eyes on the old gentleman's face, to watch the effect of his well-calculated words.

The frown vanished from the Bishop's face, and he filled himself a sparkling glass.

"Well, well, my boy, do as you like; it may be an opening: only remember to act with prudence always, and don't be in a hurry,—wait patiently, and the world will come round to you. 'Fair and easy goes far in a day.'"

Then the Bishop and his nephew helped themselves to cigars, and were soon enveloped in a fragrant cloud of tobacco smoke. It was not long before St. George's chimed eight, and his lordship jumped up and rang the bell.

"Coffee for Mr. John, Martha. I have no time. Did you get any news of Mrs. Doolin since?"

"Augh! yis thin; she'll never pass the night, me lord. Master John, darlin', don't go now till I give ye your coffee."

"Good-bye, my boy," said his lordship, shaking the young man's hand heartily. "I won't see you for a couple of months, anyhow. Gobless you, and take care of yourself. Write from Paris, and mind you go see Father Pat Kelly at *Saint Sulpice.*"

The Bishop was gone, and Hogan waited to drink his cup of coffee. Presently Martha appeared with a tray.

"Well, Martha," said he pleasantly to the old woman, "how is the world treating you these times?"

"Augh! thin; I can't complain as times goes. 'Tis yourself is scarce and rare this while back, Master John."

"Term time and circuit, I'm busy, Martha, thank God!"

"When 'll we have the weddin', Master John?" asked she slyly, handing him a cup of fragrant coffee."

"That's what you're thinking of, Martha, is it? It is more than I am."

"Augh! now, sure you wouldn't let us go till we see you settled in the world, jewel. Nothin' would give his lordship such pleasure, or meself ayther, wid respect to you."

"I'm young enough, Martha, and so are you," answered Hogan between two sips.

"Dear, but 'tis yourself has the fine sootherin' tongue, an' always had, indeed. Himself done well to make a counsellor out ov you, Master John, honey!"

Master John finished his cup of coffee with a good-humoured smile.

"You never forget old times, Martha," said he.

"Ah no, thin! Do you remember when you blewn out the gas, an' had like to kill yourself, the night you first came up from the country, in Columbkille Chapel House? Dear! dear! but you wor' the boy thin, Master John;" and the old dame laughed and laughed until she had to put the corner of her apron to her eyes.

Master John laughed too, but not quite so heartily; and declining more coffee, set off home to prepare for his journey the next morning.

CHAPTER II.

"But not their joys alone thus coarsely flow,
Their morals, like their pleasures, are but low
For, as refinement stops, from sire to son
Unaltered, unimproved, the manners run." * * *

NOVEMBER had well set in ere Mr. Hogan returned to town,
refreshed and reinvigorated for his winter's work by a long
walking tour through France, Switzerland, and the north
of Italy. He had enjoyed the company of well-selected
and congenial travelling companions ; and his party, unlike
most travelling parties, had all returned home on as
friendly terms with each other as when they started.

His first care, of course, was to go and see his uncle, the
Bishop. Him he found looking well and jolly, after a six
weeks' stay at a famous boarding-house in Kingstown, much
patronised by the rural clergy, and where his lordship
loved to spend his vacation in the society of his old school
friends.

After the first greetings were over, and the young man
had answered the Bishop's inquiries about his foreign
friends, the conversation imperceptibly glided into the old
grooves ; and naturally the first topic that presented itself,
and the most agreeable—personal affairs—was awarded the
place of honour.

"I want you, sir," began the barrister, drawing as he
spoke an envelope out of his pocket, "to arrange a small
matter for me. I find this invitation to read a lecture on
St. Ignatius Loyola before the Catholic Young Men's
Association of St. Columbkille next Thursday. Now,
next Thursday won't suit me, and I'd like to put it off.

Saltasche is giving a dinner-party, and he wants me to meet—er——"

"Put it off, hey?" cried the Bishop, astonished; "and what on earth would Father Taggart say to that?"

The Bishop was intensely amazed at his nephew's proposal. The idea of putting off a lecture, to deliver which was such an honour, and moreover, thereby to incur the risk of offending such a valuable supporter as a parish priest, seemed incredible to him. Besides, his name would be in the papers, and perhaps a report of the lecture as well; and everybody knows what an important thing it is for a rising young barrister to get and keep his name well before the public. Hogan had always recognised the truth of that axiom, and from the beginning had steadfastly kept it in view and shaped his conduct accordingly. So much so, in fact, that he seemed to have made it an integral part of his plan of life to appear on every platform he could make his way to. Little by little he came to be known, and through the influence of the Bishop and his friends had managed to secure a fair practice: nothing very brilliant; but sufficient with his own means, and what he made by his contributions to journalistic and other literature, ·to keep him pretty comfortably. He owed a good deal to his own exertions—not that he was very hard-working, but that he was steady and regular of life ; but he owed still more to his friends, and particularly to his clerical friends. Of this we may be sure the Bishop was well aware ; and it is not to be wondered at, then, that his lordship was amazed at the notion of his nephew throwing over Father Taggart for a dinner party— and a Protestant dinner-party! There was a ring of independence and audacity in the proposition that sounded strangely unbecoming.

"Well—er—it will be only postponed. I'm getting up the lecture in first-rate style for him, I assure you ; and— er—there are to be people there whom I may find useful."

"Now, John, I have told you before, I don't like your consorting with Protestants. 'Pon me word," reiterated the Bishop, waxing warmer, "I don't like it at all. People

in general are against it. There's loads of Catholics in
Dublin wouldn't know them at all. Haven't you society
enough in your own class ? Why, there's Mrs. Rafferty.
Mother Assumption has told me she says she wouldn't
lose her time askin' Protestants to her house. It is not
approved of at all."

"Oh, that reminds me I have arrived home in time for
their housewarming. It's to-night." And the young man,
not sorry for the opportunity of changing the conversation,
took a gorgeous white and gold card out of his pocket:
"'Dancing at ten.' H'm; they're very early in the
season, are they not ?"

"Rather ; but then you see they're new people—ahem !
and by getting the start of everybody, and asking a lot of
the ball-giving ones, they secure invitations for the rest of
the season."

"They are sickeningly vulgar, to be sure," said Hogan,
calling to mind Mrs. Rafferty's appearance at the convent
entertainment in the summer.

"The father and mother *are* plain people ; yes, plain,
worthy people. The girls are very well educated—very."

"H'm ! to be sure," assented Hogan, absently. He was
thinking of the women he had met abroad : clever, well-
bred Englishwomen, bright American girls, who had been
"all over" and "all round;" the pleasant artistic and
literary talks, the clear bright air and crisp autumn landscapes. To come from all that to fog, and mud, and
commonplace, narrow-minded mediocrities. "Not know
Protestants !" How droll it sounded, after the glimpse of
broader, larger life he had just had!

"Now, my lord, I must be gone. I've a good deal
to do, you know. I'll drop round on Sunday afternoon.
Good-bye."

When he got into the street—which he did quickly, for
some sort of impatience had come upon him—he drew a
long, deep breath. Foggy and close as the air was, it
seemed strong and bracing after that of the room he had
just left. However, he was a practical, clear-headed young
man ; and he shook off the mood and train of thought sug-

gested by the talk he had had with his relative, with a
smile at his own absurdity, and started off down town on
business intent.

It was very late in the evening, almost half-past eleven,
when he reached Mrs. Rafferty's house in Mountjoy Square.
He had no difficulty in discovering the mansion, and was
not a little amused at the appearance it presented. An
awning stretched from the hall door across the pavement,
the steps were carpeted, and a couple of big policemen had
enough to do to keep back the crowd of ragamuffins who
were swarming up the rails and criticising the appearance
of the supper-table, which was ostentatiously exposed to
their consideration,—the slats of the Venetian blinds
having been purposely opened. From the drawing-rooms
above, the sound of the music and dancing might be heard
across the Square ; as the night, though clear and moonlit,
was close and muggy, there was a valid excuse for opening
the windows to their widest extent, and so securing the
desired publicity and renown simultaneously with the necessary ventilation.

Mr. Hogan acknowledged to himself as he took off his
top-coat in the hall, that if the rest of the entertainment
was on a par with the arrangements, Mrs. Rafferty was sure
of a success. For new people, they seemed to have managed very well indeed. And he surveyed the stands of
hothouse flowers and the fountain of perfume which was
playing on the centre table, making the hot air more sickly
still, with calm approval. At all events, there was plenty
of evidence that they had not spared expense ; and people
are usually pleased by that compliment to their importance.

In a tea room on the first lobby, Mr. Hogan found one
of the daughters of the house ministering to the wants of a
group of people, the foremost of whom seemed to be his
old acquaintance Miss Brangan, taller and stouter than
ever, and radiant in a voluminous blue silk. She was
accompanied by her papa, an alderman of nineteen stone
weight, between whom and herself there was a striking
resemblance ; and her brother, a young gentleman of no

small consequence, who had just left one of the diocesan
colleges. Hogan shook hands with the Alderman, and
having secured a cup of coffee, drew to one side and looked
about him. Mr. Aloysius Brangan was conversing with
Miss Rafferty in a patronising, offhand manner. Hogan
was struck by the rare richness of his brogue.

"You're very lucky to have such a fine night," he was
saying. "At Kelly's, the other night, it poured rain on
us. It's as dry as a bone, and moonlit."

"So 'tis," she answered. "We waited on purpose to
have the moon."

Mr. Aloysius Brangan stopped in the act of raising his
cup to his lips.

"Waited on purpose!" he exclaimed, in blank surprise.
"Augh, then! and how did you know you were going to
have it?"

"Looked at the almanac, of course," returned she with a
faint giggle, glancing at Hogan, who was obliged to leave
the room abruptly.

Mr. Brangan saw he had committed a blunder of some
kind; but with creditable *aplomb*, turned off the maladroit-
ness by saying, with a sort of bantering air, as of one
superior to all that sort of thing :

"You shouldn't believe everything almanacs tell you,
Miss Rafferty."

As Hogan was passing up the stairs, he was joined
by a trio of college lads with whom he had some slight
acquaintance. One of them hailed him by name. He
turned round :

"Orpen, is that you? How did you come here?"

Mr. Orpen, a pale-faced gentlemanly-looking young man,
of about twenty, glanced over his shoulder and whispered
confidentially:

"Don't know, my dear fellah. Mulcahy is a relative of
this lot, and he brought us."

Further explanation was impossible, for they found
themselves in the presence of the lady of the house, who,
dressed in gorgeous amber satin, had taken up her position
near the door to receive her guests. The rooms were full;

and as the lions of the evening, the Lord Mayor and his party, had arrived some time before, dancing was going on.

Mrs. Rafferty introduced Hogan to the Lord Mayor, who shook hands amiably with him.

"Glad to see you, sir. Doctor O'Rooney quite well?"

The minor satellites who were standing round looked respectfully at the recipient of so much honour, who indeed comported himself with astounding easiness, and entered into almost familiar conversation with the Lord Mayor and those select members of the corporation who were grouped about him on the hearthrug. His Worship wore his chain of office over his dress coat; he was a little fat man, with oblique eyes of no colour, mutton-chop whiskers, and three chins. His manner was pompous and self-conscious, as became a self-made man. It must not be supposed, however, that he owed his wealth and high position to either talent or industry. His father had been a working man; and at the age of twelve Mr. Bartholomew Malowney had entered the grocery and public-house of old Barton Rafferty as messenger. From this humble post he had risen to be barman, and after five years' experience of trade, during which time he had been distinguished chiefly by his rare capacity for keeping sober during business hours, he found a friend to be his surety with Trebblex the brewer, for the entry and stocking of a licensed house in Liffey Street. Father Dorney, the then incumbent of St. Columbkille—he was our Bishop's predecessor—lost no time in recommending this thriving young publican to the good graces of Miss Bridget Slattery, a penitent of his, who possessed five thousand pounds in her own right; and a match was speedily declared. So, as the profits on whiskey, especially in the retail trade, are enormous, it is not surprising that his Worship had the reputation of being very wealthy.

"What do you think of the news from France now?" ventured Hogan carelessly, for he knew exactly what the answer would be.

"Bad job, sir. Ah! what they want there is a king or the Impress; they want a strong hand over them, them Frinch."

" Couldn't get along with a Republic now, you think ?"

" Nothin' of the sort. Ah! that Imperor—poor man, God be merciful to him!—he was the one for them: a tight hand is what they require."

" You're right there," put in another City father, also a publican and sinner.

Hogan was listening with a polite smile of acquiescence, all the time scornfully contrasting the speakers with the *haute bourgeoisie* of the French provincial towns through which he had been travelling—well educated, clear-headed Frenchmen, amongst whom he had spent some pleasant and profitable hours—and then turned to the last speaker, who continued with an air of omniscience :

" There ar'n't any eminent men among them at all,— not one fit to come to the front. They're a poor lot compared to what they were—a poor lot, sir !" and the City father gave a sigh as of one who remembered better days.

Hogan smiled sardonically. Remembering the leading article in that morning's *Enfranchiser*, he wondered to himself what their views would be next week ; and as he often wrote for that journal, resolved to treat these worthy citizens to some novel doctrine ere long.

"What a meeting that was in Glasgow !" Hogan said this to Alderman Brangan, in the hope of bringing on the Home Rule question, and taking the opinion of the " whiskey faction " on it.

" Yes, faith !" answered he ; "an' what it manes I can't make out. What do those Glasgow Irish know or care about it ? It puzzles me intirely."

" You don't go in for it, then ?" put in the barrister quickly.

" I don't see how we're to get on," broke in the whiskey importer, Rafferty, " if the trade between the two countries is to be interrupted. And, faith, that's what it means with a large party of them. No one need tell me, for I see and hear it every day."

" Augh !" growled the chief magistrate ; " I don't know nor care what it manes. Trade never was better all over the country,—never to my knowledge, than this year."

Never, indeed! The street leading to the chief of his Worship's public-houses was almost impassable at the moment he was speaking, owing to the crowd of drunken men and women who had just been turned out in obedience to the regulations, and who were brawling and staggering along the thoroughfare, making night hideous with their din.

"But throughout the country the feeling is intensely in favour of the movement?"

"Ay," rejoined the Lord Mayor carelessly; "but it's not so in Dublin, I can tell you."

"You're a Home Ruler, Mr. Hogan, ain't you?" asked a little wizened man, a wealthy salesmaster, whose hands had completely disappeared up his coat-sleeves.

But Hogan, to his delight, was prevented answering this question by the hostess, who led him up to one of the Misses Malowney, and introduced him for the next dance. As they crossed the room, Hogan caught a glimpse of a face in the crowd which seemed familiar to him. It was that of a beautiful girl who was standing in a crowded corner. She looked at him, too, with a glance that had something of recognition in it. He puzzled himself for some minutes trying to think where it was he had seen her before. The floor was too crowded to dance with any pleasure, and he contrived to place himself and his partner at an angle where he could observe the young lady whose face caused him so much perplexity. She had fine brown hair, rippled, and with a dash of gold in it; blue eyes with dark lashes and pretty sweeping brows; an exquisite neck and shoulders. There was something distinguished in her appearance, as well as in her manner, which was excessively quiet and in no way self-conscious. High-coloured, dashing Miss Brangan, with her roving black eyes and fur-belowed silk train, seemed to attract far more attention and observation, if not admiration.

Mrs. Rafferty, roaming about, on hospitable cares intent, caught her nephew, Stanislas Mulcahy, by the arm, and whispered to him anxiously, "Stanislas, d'ye see Miss Davoren anywhere? I'm fairly dazzled, and me eyes is no good. Where is she at all? I'm afraid she hasn't danced yet."

"Over there by the door, do you see?—in white, leaning on her brother."

"I'm all right. Now, Mr. Malowney, allow me to get ye a nice partner for the next. She's a connection of Lord Rathbone. Come along o' me;" and taking that gentleman by the arm, Mrs. Rafferty advanced towards her guest with a solemn air. She was intensely impressed with the importance of the task she had undertaken. Mindful of the large sum of money the entertainment was to cost, she was consumed with anxiety lest anything should go wrong, any important guest be neglected, or any solecism, whether of behaviour or arrangements, be committed. She had taken all possible precautions ; the list of guests was very satisfactory. The Lord Mayor and his family, and nearly all the Roman Catholic members of the Corporation, were present. The Lady Mayoress had opened the ball, with the master of the house, just as she had done last Monday night at Mrs. Kelly's. More gentlemen than ladies had been invited ; so there was no likelihood of complaints on the score of partners. Nearly all the eligible men of her set were present—some well-known doctors, for years looking out for heiresses,—dancing at every ball, promenading Grafton Street on week-days, and the Pier on Sundays,—most of them in debt, and all tolerably fast living,—putting off the day of retrenchment and economy until the rich heiress should turn up to make everything square, and bring them the connection which their own idleness and self-indulgence had prevented them making. Lawyers there were also, chiefly of the briefless variety, on the same errand bent ; a few young men connected with Catholic legal functionaries, who were beyond Mrs. Rafferty's ken, and a few college boys brought by her nephew. Business men of every description formed the majority of the male division.

Then for girls there were the Misses Malowney,— Aloysia Margaretta and Augustina Eily,—"beautifully educated" and gorgeously attired, who were of course the first in importance as the daughters of the Lord Mayor; then Miss Brangan, and a host of nieces, cousins, and connections generally. On the whole, Mrs. Rafferty felt that so far she could hold her own with the best of the ball-givers of her acquaintance. As for the supper, it had been ordered from the Lord Lieutenant's own caterer at so much a head, and she had no misgivings on that score. So she sailed about the room, pairing off the right couples together, taking care that the Misses Malowney got the most eligible of all the eligible young men, and that her own daughters came next in order of precedence. She was inclined to be gracious to Miss Davoren; so she brought her a very select partner in the person of Mr. Laurence Malowney, the Lord Mayor's eldest son.

The crowd was tremendous in the ball-room; it was quite impossible to dance; and after several attempts Hogan and his partner relinquished the endeavour, and got into a corner to wait for some of the couples to retire, and give them place.

"There are far too many," said Hogan; "we never could get through that crush." He was perfectly content to look at Miss Davoren; and he had at last recollected where he had met her—at the Convent last July.

"Yes," answered Miss Malowney, with a cross look at her flounces, a part of which had been carried off by a couple who had just plunged past. "It's nonsense to be askin' so many at once. However, that's the way now. Every one must be invited, or they'll only be offended. They ought to do like the Moores—give two balls, and divide the people that way."

"This is the only ball they give in the year, you see."

"I know; and it's a great mistake too. There's no comfort in going out at all now. There, see!"

Hogan looked in the direction indicated, and laughed at the elbowing and struggles of some half-dozen couples who seemed inextricably entangled.

Miss Malowney declined to risk another turn, and they took up their position by the wall. Hogan found it impossible to talk to her; she was a heavy, stupid young

woman; besides he was engrossed in watching the frantic
struggles of the dancers. Just opposite, Miss Davoren and
her partner—a stout little man, who seemed terribly out of
breath and heated—halted for a moment. Hogan thought
he never saw any one so beautiful. She was very slender
of figure and graceful in her movements ; and when a
great stout woman, dressed in crimson and yellow, stood
for a minute beside her, it seemed to him as if a big full-
blown peony had suddenly been contrasted with a delicate
newly-opened jasmine star.

Meantime the dance went on; it was now about to stop;
and those who had been despairingly waiting for the first
batch to tire themselves out, dashed in recklessly. The
scene became truly awful; shreds of tulle and gauze floated
high above the heads of the dancers ; somebody lost her
head-dress ; and a quantity of little muslin roses battered
and dirtied beyond recognition were to be seen now and
again in the gaps among the dancers. Miss Davoren resisted the earnest entreaties of her cavalier to risk the
struggle ; at last, an unfortunate couple fell ; the music
ceased suddenly, and everybody crushed out and downstairs
to the cool room on the landing.

Hogan wanted to secure Miss Davoren for a set of the
Lancers just about to form ; and to that end he looked
around for his friend Mr. Mulcahy. Discovering him in a
distant corner he made towards him. " Want a partner,
eh ? " asked Mr. Mulcahy, divining his errand, and rising
from his seat.

"Yes ; that young lady in white, yonder."

" Standing over by the lady in green, eh ? Come along
then ;" and with an expression of unwillingness in his face
which did not escape Hogan's eye, his friend led the way
across the room.

"Mr. O'Rooney Hogan, Miss Davoren," muttered Mr.
Mulcahy, and was gone, in obedience to a signal from his
aunt. He bowed low and murmured the usual formula.

"I am engaged for this dance. Number five—the waltz ?
Yes, with pleasure ; that is not engaged."

Then Mrs. Rafferty, who had her eye on our hero, and

had no idea of allowing him to be monopolised by outsiders, came up, and led him off to one of her own daughters. She happened to be engaged; but he had the tact to secure a quadrille with her later on, which restored Mrs. Rafferty's good humour. A distant cousin of the house was next presented to him, and they made their way together to the dancing-room.

Having taken up a place at the sides, Hogan seeing Miss Brangan opposite, asked his partner who she was.

"A daughter of Alderman Brangan. She's only just out : she's very young." The lady spoke with the flattest Dublin brogue.

"Very fine girl, indeed." Hogan remembered her now, and began to laugh at the reminiscence.

"Rather too stout," rejoined his partner, who, as one of Mr. Rafferty's poor relations, acted as a sort of jackal to her patronesses. Miss Brangan was a rival young lady, and consequently not to be praised with impunity by any eligible young gentleman.

"Who is the young lady in white?" he said, indicating Miss Davoren. He knew perfectly well already, but some sudden whim took him to hear what his partner would say of her.

"She's a Miss Davoren; her father's in the Castle,— very good family. Her mother was one of Lord Rathbone's connections."

"Ah! yes, indeed. Protestant, then?" he asked, with sudden and eager curiosity.

"No; her mother was, or is, I don't know which. She's clever, and sings, I'm told, beautifully. She has a lovely *ahxent.*"

Hogan laughed outright at the tone of the encomium. "You seem to know everybody, Miss Doyle?" said he drily, turning, as he spoke, to survey the lady herself.

"Yes," she drawled carelessly. "Going out a great deal, one comes to know names and faces."

She evidently went out a great deal. Her face had the parboiled pasty colour and her eyes the dead look that late hours and excitement always give, and her hair was show-

ing signs of over-frizzing and torturing. There was no
guessing at her age; it might have been anything from
four-and-twenty to eight-and-thirty. She was pious and
gossipping, not too ill-natured, and as Hogan divined, knew
everybody and everything,—a sort of walking biographical
cyclopædia, in short.

" Who is the little man dancing with the tall girl ? "

" That's Mr. Alphonsus Kelly ; and them two young
gentlemen is his two brothers—Paul Ferdinand and James
Hubert. They're nephews of Mr. Rafferty's."

The dance was over. Hogan led his partner back to her
seat ; he was just in time to hear a whispered and eager
conversation between Miss Brangan and one of the young
ladies of the house. The next dance was a waltz, and as
such of course belonged to the list of forbidden luxuries
yclept " fast dances." Miss Brangan, as a *débutante*, was
in a sad quandary ; she bit her lips and frowned, and
nibbled her pencil in mingled rage and incertitude. It
really was no joke,—sixteen out of the twenty-four dances
on the programme were " fast." And now was she to sit
still all night during those sixteen dances because of a
promise made to a certain Mother Paul some three months
ago ? It was perfectly dreadful. The piano, and the
fiddle, and the French-horn on the balcony outside the
back drawing-room window, were playing the " Invitation
to the Waltz." And as they played, her resolutions melted
away.

" Eily ! " she whispered imploringly to Miss Rafferty,
" look, Eily ! what'll I do ? I'll be sitting all night if I don't."

" That you will," replied Miss Eily, who " fast danced "
herself. " There's very few quadrilles."

" But what 'll Mother Paul and Father M'Quaide say to
me ? "

" *I* am not going to fast dance," said the cousin whom
Hogan had just taken back to her seat ; " and Mary," she
continued, with a voice of frigid virtue, " at your very first
ball too, ye oughtn't to, now. *I* wouldn't."

" Augh there ! Mary Doyle yourself, perhaps you're
not asked," was the angry retort of Miss Rafferty, who did

not want Miss Brangan, one of the *élite* of her guests, to be prevented in any way enjoying herself. "Look, Mary, there's Rose Malowney—and this is her first ball—going off with Doctor MacSwiggan, now!"

Miss Brangan seemed inclined to judge the case more by precedent than on its own merits, so to say. For she was looking all round her eagerly to see who was going to set her an example of disobedience. Presently her eye fell on a couple who were moving in the direction of the dancing-room.

"Now, Eily!" she cried triumphantly, "there's Father M'Quaide's own niece, and the—ah—what's his name? I *will* do it."

"Very well, Mary—who will I get for you?"

"Whisper, Eily!" lowering her voice, "that young gentleman down there,—him with the lovely humbuggin' eyes, I mean."

"Oh, yes; that's young Mr. Davoren. I'll get him."

In a moment the couple were whirling round in the waltz, leaving Miss Doyle seated still on her sofa in all the consciousness of virtue, and wearing an expression of envy and scandalised prudery mingled on her face.

Hogan, who was standing with Miss Davoren close behind the group, heard and saw everything, and was almost convulsed with laughter.

"I am glad to see you are not troubled with scruples," said he, turning to her. "Isn't that awfully absurd?"

She was about to answer; but just then an opening appeared, and they swung lightly into the whirling circle. After half a dozen rounds, they dropped out.

"Isn't it nonsense to forbid waltzes and galops? What on earth is the meaning of it?" he continued, looking at her admiringly as he spoke.

"I don't know, I'm sure. They seem to me to be all alike—quadrilles and the others. And after all, how *could* a ball be managed without dancing? Certainly it would not be appreciated by these people."

"Well, and about the theatre? What do you think of the theatre being forbidden, too?"

"I don't like the theatres at all. They are stupid and absurd : I mean the plays they're giving now. That prohibition would not affect me in the least. All the same, it is no use defying people ; and I daresay the audiences have only increased. Perhaps a few ladies do stay away on account of the prohibition ; but the gentlemen, you know, do what they please. I don't believe one of them has given up fast dancing."

Mr. Hogan laughed. "You don't see many of them at ten o'clock mass in the morning—eh ?"

"Well, no ; it would be strange if I did."

"Do you mean to say, Miss Davoren," said he, with affected solemnity, "that you don't go to ten o'clock mass every morning ?"

"I do."

"May I be permitted to ask why ?"

"For the same reason as the gentlemen," she replied.

He thought a second. "And that is——?"

"I have something else to do."

Here some couples quitted the dance, and they took a couple of rounds more.

"Suppose we go down and have an ice ?" he proposed, as they quitted the room.

She assented, and they made their way down the stairs, which were crowded with sitters. The tea-room was now turned into an ice room ; huge crystal pitchers were filled with iced drinks, and blocks of ice and ferns made the air seem delightfully fresh in contrast to that of the rooms above.

They seated themselves in a window.

"Don't you think balls a mistake ?" asked he.

"There are more enjoyable sorts of entertainment, I fancy," she replied.

"We have got into the way of thinking here that there is no other mode of enjoying society. In fact, the social system seems to depend wholly on ball-giving. Horribly expensive notion it is, to be sure," he added, glancing round.

"Decidedly expensive, I should think," she assented.

"A little more conversation, and a little less fierce dancing, some good music, and a less costly entertainment altogether ; a few artistic, literary people, instead of——" a motion of his head towards Lady Shanassy. "Is that your idea, Miss Davoren ?"

"I confess that my ideal is something like that," returned she. "But it is utterly impracticable."

"Well, you see, fashion has decided in favour of these big squashes. Now, these people may give a Sunday dinner; and after Easter a smaller edition of this; then for the rest of the year they will have not as much as a tea-party."

"That is a stupid way of doing," rejoined Miss Davoren. "My cousins in Paris tell me that every evening they can go to a friend's house, uninvited, or have people with themselves, but all without one sou of expense for dress or entertainment."

"It wouldn't be practicable here. Men won't go out unless they are fed. The Mooneys' ball, last Thursday, failed for want of men ; and the reason was the supper had not been up to the mark on a previous occasion."

"Well, of course it looks unrefined," said Miss Davoren, laughing ; "but really, to dance from ten till four without ceasing is exhausting work. And at those Parisian houses I know there is a great deal of music, parlour games, and that sort of thing."

"It would be infinitely preferable to this," said he, "were it only feasible."

"It used to be supposed that ladies made society to their wishes. I mean, everything was conformable to their tastes. It is not so now, is it ?" she asked.

"My dear Miss Davoren, that was in the old time, before the era of the convent schoolgirls. I know," he interposed, "that I am speaking to a young lady of most liberal culture. You must observe for yourself how very uninformed those young ladies are in every way. They can't talk on any subject. Some one I know says it takes five years for them to get over the bread-and-butterism they bring home from school with them. When a girl

E

leaves an English finishing school she is always fit for the
duties of a drawing-room."

"There is something to be said for as well as against
our system," she said.

"Oh, of course. But if our rulers admit that there is
to be society at all, why not go in for it intelligently and
rationally?"

"By our rulers, do I understand you to mean the priests?
What have they to do with educating us girls? I assure
you girls learn at school just what their parents are able
to pay for; and above all, just what is most likely to
please—the gentlemen."

"Ah, ah!" said Hogan, noticing her sarcastic tone and
smile; "and now tell me what are the *branches*—is that
the .term?—that please the gentlemen? Antimacassars?
piano-playing?"

"I don't know much about gentlemen's tastes; but you
know, of course, it is said that in every country women
are educated up to the level of the men's requirements,
not beyond."

"And *their* requirements," retorted he, "are determined
by *their* education. Now, who educate us in this country,
and so fix the standard, eh? You see we revolve in a
vicious circle."

"Hadn't we better go upstairs again?" said Miss Davoren,
replying only by a look to the barrister's daring speech.

Hogan returned to the aldermanic group on the hearthrug, and was speedily engaged in discussion with the
dignitaries who formed it. He declined dancing as much
as possible, except when it was with the daughters of the
hostess or of the Lord Mayor; and when supper was
announced, was deputed to the honourable post of convoy-
ing Lady Shanassy down, directly after the Lady Mayoress.
After that dowager had taken in her supplies, and was
replaced on her sofa, Hogan hastened to secure Miss
Davoren, and carried her to a corner of the supper-room,
now thronged with hungry people.

The supper was in keeping with the rest of the entertainment; everything in strict accordance with the preced-

ent set by the last Castle entertainment. Soup was no longer in fashion, so there was none. Cold fish was the rage, and hot meat; so an enormous salmon was at the foot of the table, and hot roast game to be found everywhere. Pink jellies and fruit jellies were the last novelties; and champagne, that *sine quâ non* of modern entertainments, was to be heard popping on all sides.

At the top of the room there seemed to be some unusual noise and loud talking; for a while the clatter of plates and popping of champagne corks drowned it; but at last there came a general lull, and a clear English voice was heard in altercation with one of the servant-men. The master of the house, who was just entering with a fat dowager on his arm, planted her in a chair, and straightway marched up to the scene of action. A very young, fair-haired man was holding a bottle in his hand, and trying to force another from the man-servant's grasp. Mr. Rafferty asked who the youth was, but no one could tell him. His nephew Mulcahy came up, and whispered that he had seen him enter the drawing-room at 'one o'clock, unannounced. Hogan caught Mulcahy by the sleeve, and informed him that it was one of the Lord Lieutenant's aides-de-camp, named Wyldoates, an officer of the Dragoon Guards.

"I'll settle him," said the irate host; and stepping up to the half-tipsy lad, he asked, determinedly and pompously,—

"Mr. Wyldoates, kindly inform me to what cause I may assign the honour of your presence here."

Mr. Wyldoates leisurely finished his glass of champagne.

"You—aw—have the advantage over me—aw—old fellaw."

"I have," was the reply. At a look from the speaker, Mulcahy seized hold of the intruder's arm, and the servant and his uncle assisting, the aide-de-camp was speedily deposited outside the hall door, minus his hat, which he did not return to claim.

The *contretemps* lasted only a second, and the business of supper-eating was speedily resumed—plates rattled, knives and forks jingled, as if nothing had occurred.

" Tell me," asked Miss Davoren, who had turned very pale during the *fracas*, "is that a specimen of English finish?"

Hogan laughed.

"That's a mere boy; you must not be hard on him. Mr. Rafferty will have an abject apology to-morrow morning; it's just some messroom wager. Officers, you know," shrugging his shoulders; "one can't expect anything else from them!"

"They are expected to be gentlemen, at all events," retorted she; "but the Guards, you are aware, consider themselves on foreign duty in Dublin, so they don't care how they behave to us aborigines."

"Now, now, I hardly think that," replied he, unconsciously taking the part of apologist. He was holding her plate as he spoke, standing before her. "You are a patriot, I fear, Miss Davoren. Of course you are."

"I am not exactly a patriot; but I must confess to a tinge, a very little tinge, of it," she added, in a jesting tone. What would become of us all—of our energies and intellects—if we were not given to politics and patriotism? There isn't any other outlet for either, as things are."

"How 'as things are,' now?" asked he, with a look of seriousness and attention different from his previous manner.

"Do I need to tell you that?"—looking up into his face. "This country is so cut off from the other nations of Europe,—for it is a nation, in spite of geography, ethnology, and all the rest of it. Thanks to our rulers, we have no manufactures to employ our time; and then, worst of all, these wretched castes of Protestant and Catholic hinder so——"

A look on her listener's face warned the speaker to stop. She bit her lip, frightened lest she had said too much.

"Do you say that our religion, then," said he, watching her face closely, "does not allow any outlet for intellect or energy?"

"I don't say that," she replied hastily; "taking our disabilities into account, we could, I think, show as fair an average of intellectual achievement as any other creed."

" '*Taking our disabilities into account!*' Miss Davoren, were I inclined, I could turn that proposition against you nicely."

But Miss Davoren chose not to notice what he said, and turned off the matter by asking him for a glass of water.

Then they returned to the drawing-room. On the lobby stood her brother; he advanced to resume his guardianship of her; and she, turning towards Hogan, said, by way of dismissal,—

"This is my brother, Mr. Hogan."

Designedly or not, he chose to take it as an introduction, and held out his hand to the lad, saying pleasantly that he was glad to make his acquaintance.

The college boy was a little flattered, for he knew Hogan by repute; and they entered into conversation cordially. Miss Davoren was carried off by one of her partners.

" You have to go out of town to-night ?" asked Hogan of her brother.

" I have to go out to Green Lanes. We live there ; but my sister is to stay in Fitzgerald Place."

" Do you live in college ?" asked Hogan.

" No; wish I did. It's such a bore to have to go in and out such a distance every day."

The tone made Hogan laugh. He guessed pretty accurately it was not the trouble of coming in from Green Lanes daily that bored the young gentleman.

" Do you belong to the football club, Mr. Davoren ? "

" I do."

" Do you know Mahoney Quain ? "

" Yes ; "—this with a laugh. " That's a nice boy. I'm going to the opera with him to-morrow night. He's got a song for the top gallery that'll make a sensation."

" I'm going also," said Hogan, " and I must look out for that. What's the opera ? "

" I don't know : I ain't fond of music. Do you know who that begger was that kicked up the shindy below-stairs ?—an aide-de-camp, I heard."

" It was an aide-de-camp and an officer of the Guards, I believe."

"Infernal cad," was young Davoren's comment. "He thinks he's paying the place a compliment."

"So he was," interpolated another collegian, Mr. Orpen. "I never saw such a shop in my existence, Dicky. Look at that girl over there. Did you ever see a little dog with his tail curled up so stiff on his back that his leg had sort of gone up with it, and he walked lame? Now she's got her hair drawn up so tight and stiff, her eyebrows are gone up with it. Look. I bet you my life she couldn't wink, to save her soul. Are they all whiskey people, Dicky?" continued the critic. "You don't hear these old buffers talking of anything else."

"They're not giving you whiskey to drink, Orpen."

"No; I'll allow the champagne is genuine. Supper's A1, certainly."

"Very well, Orpen. You know that's what you came for," returned young Davoren.

"I think, young gentlemen, that we're expected to dance for our suppers; so come along into the room," said Hogan, leading the way back. And the trio were speedily absorbed into a quadrille just forming.

Hogan by no means intended to distinguish any particular young lady by his attentions. He knew that a very little flirtation goes a long way with the chattering dowagers and chaperons, whose occupation in a ball-room is to watch and chronicle all such occurrences; and he did not want his name brought into any of their debates. At the same time he was considerably smitten by the beauty of Nellie Davoren; in fact, she had made on him a very deep impression. Guarded as he tried to be, his eyes, in spite of himself, followed her in the dance, and his partner's conversation fell unheeded, save for monosyllabic replies, on his ears. He had danced twice with her already, and had taken her down to supper, and before that to the refreshment-room. He wondered if he might not risk another waltz. A good half-dozen or more dances still remained; and he prudently resolved to divide them between the Rafferty girls and the Malowneys. Then nobody could be witty at his expense.

So he first inscribed their names on his card, and then walked over to her, and cut out Mr. Orpen, who, bent on the same mission, arrived simultaneously. She was almost about to refuse him, saying she did not wish to remain longer; but he managed to induce her, and they moved arm in arm to the dancing-room. She waltzed well, and Hogan felt himself fully repaid for the five sacrifices he considered himself to have made.

After-supper waltzes are peculiarly delightful : there is a swing in the music, and a lightness and exhilaration in the dancers, that make the interval between that event and the breaking-up the most enjoyable part of the whole entertainment. Hogan did not waltz very badly. He was indeed a little stiff, and looked rather too much at the ceiling; but he was light, and kept good time; and Miss Davoren was one of those dancers who carry themselves instead of making their partners feel their whole burden. They spun round utterly unconscious of everything but the delight of their own harmonious motion. The musicians played the "Wiener Tänzen" in capital time. A large detachment was downstairs at supper; so the floor was not too crowded, and Nellie and Hogan enjoyed a thoroughly good waltz. They drew up breathless at last.

"That's the most delightful waltz I ever had in my life," said he, in a tone meant to be significant, and which was certainly sincere. "What a pity it must be the last !" And he looked down straight into her eyes.

She smiled, but turned away her head.

"Miss Davoren, please tell me are you to be at Mrs. Muldoon's on Friday night ?"

" No."

"No ? Then neither shall I."

" Oh, how absurd ! Were you really going now ?" and she looked up laughingly into his face.

He took a card out of his pocket, and showed it to her.

"I shan't go, because you are not to be there. Will you go and hear Father O'Hea at Gardiner Street on Sunday ?"

" Possibly Dicky may take me."

There was not much encouragement in the tone, but the

young man determined he would be there too ; and on relinquishing her, he whispered to her brother to return after depositing his sister in Fitzgerald Place, and he would give him a lift on his way home.

It was not long before the youth returned ; and, Orpen, joining them, they donned overcoats and mufflers, and sallied forth cigars in mouths.

Mr. Orpen was indignant and disgusted, or pretended to be both.

"I didn't know a creature in the place," he grumbled, " give you my word. What the deuce did the people mean by askin' us to such a shop ? Dav., did you notice the Lord Mayor—old whiskey barrels—with his chain of office round his neck ? Law !" continued the young gentle-man, after an explosion of laughter, "why hadn't the aldermen got on their gowns ?"

"I didn't mind him so much," returned Mr. Davoren; "it was her ladyship took my eye. I was dancing with some girl who called on me to admire her 'joolery' (jewellery)."

"I wonder will the aide-de-camp get in a row for his lark to-night ?" said Hogan.

"By Jove, I expect so. Of course those people will write a complaint to the Castle about him : only too glad of the chance. Beggars !"

"Not at all," put in Hogan quickly. "Rafferty knows more than that. He kicked him out ; and that's quite punishment enough, I fancy."

"What a capital lark it was !" grinned Mr. Orpen, approvingly. "That Wyldoates is game for anything. What a joke he'll have over it to-morrow !"

"I hope he's game for a new hat. I saw his under the hall table just now," said Dicky, who did not look on the insolent aggression in the same light that his friend did— namely, as a pleasant novelty in the way of practical jokes.

"Where have you to go ?" asked Hogan of Orpen, seeing a car approach.

"Close to Charlemont Demesne," replied he.

"I'll drop you. Get up, Mr. Davoren ;" and all three drove off.

CHAPTER III

"The head of a petty corporation, who opposes the designs of a prince who would tyrannically force his subjects to save their best clothes for Sundays; the young pedant who finds one undiscovered property in the polype, or describes an unheeded process in the skeleton of a mole, and whose mind, like his microscope, perceives nature only in detail; the rhymer, who makes smooth verses and paints to our imagination, when he should only speak to our hearts; all equally fancy themselves walking forward to immortality, and desire the crowd behind them to look on."—*Goldsmith.*

MISS DAVOREN'S cousin, Dorothy O'Hegarty, sat in a sunny bay-windowed parlour of Fitzgerald Place, waiting breakfast for her young relative. The wintry November sun shone in, lighting up the silver on the breakfast table, and brightening the grim visage of Desmond O'Hegarty, staring with hard gray eyes from his gilt frame over the sideboard. Everything in the room was bright and burnished; the carpet, an old well-worn Brussels, was brushed to perfection; the breakfast-cloth was spotless; you might see yourself mirrored in the heavy old plate that decked the table and sideboard, and the fireplace was nothing short of a picture. Seated with her slippers on the edge of the fender, reading with gold spectacles on nose the fashionable intelligence in her favourite Tory paper, Miss Dorothy herself deserves a passing word of description. Tall and thin, not to say angular, with round, hard, gray eyes and bushy eyebrows, she had a good nose, in profile, —it was rather sharp at the point,—strong white teeth, and a weak chin. Like most of her country-people, the upper portion of her face was the best: from the upper lip down, few Irish faces are well moulded. There is a peculiar look, as if of a squeeze, about the chin that is easily distinguished. She had a broad forehead and thick gray hair,—on the whole a rather handsome and uncommon physiognomy, but stamped with hardness, and unmistakably cynical.

Miss O'Hegarty had quite finished the list of names at Lord Brayhead's dinner, when the door opened and Nellie entered, fresh as a rose, and without a trace of headache or lassitude—blessed privilege of *débutantes*—after her night's dancing. Her hair was not dressed,—that is, it was not plaited up in the hideous unnatural-sized braids of the day; merely rolled up in a coil at the back, and drawn tightly off her brows, it showed the beautiful Greek outline of the head; and a hundred tiny transparent ringlets clustered at the nape of her neck, and swayed with every breath upon her temples. A clear fair forehead, and eyes as limpid and soft as a May morning,—truly, as yet, Nellie was a day beauty. The bright shell-pink that the gaslights of the night before had not been able to set forth now glowed upon her cheeks, which then had seemed too pale.

As the door opened Miss O'Hegarty dropped the paper and spectacles into her lap.

"Now, child, good morning. Are you rested? No one would imagine you had been dancing all night. Perhaps you were not;—you were a wallflower, hey?" and she laughed ironically.

"Not altogether, Cousin Dorothy," said Nellie, laughing as she rubbed her hands at the fire.

"Well, well," said Dorothy, pouring out tea, "come and take your breakfast, and tell us all about it. Whom had you there?"

"We had a delightful ball; really, cousin, I enjoyed it so much. And there was the Lord Mayor and Lady Mayoress, and Alderman Brangan, and——"

"Why, you had everybody of note," interrupted Miss O'Hegarty sarcastically; "come now, tell your conquests: one of the Malowneys, I hope? They're rich, you know."

Nellie permitted herself a little curl of her upper lip. "Really, I only danced a few times with the Malowneys."

"A few times!—that wasn't bad, altogether," commented the old lady.

"There was also Mr. Mulcahy, one of Dicky's friends, and a Mr. O'Rooney Hogan."

"O'Rooney Hogan!—who's that?"

"I don't know, Cousin; he's a barrister, and very gentlemanlike indeed. Somebody said he was a nephew of Bishop O'Rooney."

"Oh! one of your own people, then. I think I've seen his name in the papers."

"He's quite a rising young man, and I heard somebody say won't be long until he gets into Parliament."

"Ha, indeed. To be sure, that's what all those creatures go for nowadays." Miss Dorothy was looking over the column of births and deaths for any familiar names. Not finding any, she resumed.

"Who was the belle? or how many of them were there?"

"There was a great tall black-haired girl,—a Miss Dorney, from Galway; but I did not like her dress."

"Galway! Dorney? Tush! that's not a Galway name," said Miss O'Hegarty scornfully. If there was one thing more than another that she prided herself on, it was her knowledge of the generic names and habitats of the Irish country gentry. Given a name, she could place and classify it with as unerring sagacity as an Owen or a Lyell would an antediluvian claw or tooth.

"You have no beauties among your set, Nellie," continued the old lady, just in the tone she might use in discussing the habits and peculiarities of a Central African tribe. "Anyhow, not among the Dublin lot. They're all overfed and underbred;" and she chuckled at the neat antithesis. "All as like as bullets cast in the same mould. I don't know what does it. Letitia O'Rourke now, poor thing, she was ladylike and refined—had a real air of civilisation about her; but her daughters, how or why I never could make out, were coarse-looking, clumsy, unfinished, and all of them with such accents! It's those convent schools."

"It must be the mixture, for they're really all mixed,"

said Nellie; "and then you know there are far more
Catholics of the common class than the other."

"I know it. That's just it. They're all new tradespeople, and of course they swamp the upper element
altogether. It must be so in their schools, even more so
than in society—their own society, I mean; and that
accounts for the commonness of all the young R.C.s now.
I declare I've often been puzzled to know how it is the
rising generation are so inferior to their parents. It's all
this frightful irruption of trade. Shoddy, my dear; it's
shoddy."

"Well, but I am sure the nuns are all nice and ladylike;
they do their best, and really you can't——"

"'You can't make a silk purse out of a sow's ear.' No,
I suppose not, poor things; but after all, Nellie, the nuns
are the very same themselves. Don't tell me. Dooly, my
butcher, had his daughter enter a convent the other day,
and his sister is in one. Ah! to be sure."

"Very well, Cousin Dolly,—if they're able to pay for it,
why not?—their money is as good as anybody else's; and no
matter who they were, I never met a nun that was not nice."

"No, it isn't, it's made by cheating; and as for Dooly,
he is charging me a shilling a pound this minute, while
he's paying the farmers not the one-third of that price for
their beasts; he's in a ring to make a hundred per cent,
like those vile coal people; and traders who go on like
that, of course may make their children into nuns and
priests, and all that's grand, and give balls to three hundred
if they like. All I say is, don't ask me to have anything
to do with them, for I abhor them. Pah!"

"Ah! now, Cousin Dorothy, what can you mean? And
there were no butchers nor coal people there last night.
They were nice enough, and very good-natured."

"No, you hadn't butchers; but you had salesmasters,
and that's not much better; and if you hadn't coal people,
you had whiskey people—wholesale or retail, or both."

"Come now, Cousin Dorothy, will you tell me if you
object to meeting Lady Plutus Grains and Mrs. Trebblex,
—and pray what are they?"

"They are ladies of family and fortune,—aristocrats who have married men of fortune : that's all, Miss."

"Well, Mrs. Malowney's only fault is, then, that she is——"

"Mrs. Malowney,—you don't know what you are talking about, child." Miss Dorothy cut Nellie short with an air of superiority. "How was she dressed by-the-by ?"

Miss Davoren proceeded to describe the dress at length; and her relative laughed heartily.

"The daughters, of course, were to match," chuckled she, "were they not ?"

"No; they were dressed in rather good taste, but very richly."

"Well, you know, Tims does that for them. They may buy Paris dresses; but figure and style, thank goodness, that is not in the market yet."

"I must go home now, Cousin. Do you want anything? Mamma has been by herself since early yesterday."

"Well, you had better take care not to excite her by telling her too much of all your fine doings. I met Surgeon Graham last week, and you know he is particular about her being kept quiet."

"I'll take care, Cousin Dorothy."

"And see here, Nellie,"—here Miss Dorothy hesitated an instant,—"Nellie! I have an afternoon tea on Monday, and if you like to come over for it, do; but mind, there · will be nobody but a pack of old women and some few young ones, or rather would-be young ones—no men, Nellie: and if there were, none for you—remember that, child. I set my face altogether against mixed marriages ; no good can come of them. Marry in your own set, or don't marry at all, *I* say ; but, if you *will* marry, gild your pill,—some rich wholesale dealer, or great stack of a tea-man that can keep you a carriage and pair. I always think of the maxim, 'Repentance is easiest in a coach and four.' Heigh-ho !"

And Miss O'Hegarty, who was perfectly serious, sighed a little absently, and leaving the breakfast table, mounted her feet again on the fender preparatory to finishing her paper.

Nellie assented gladly, for she never before had been invited by her cousin to any of these festivities, and she was curious to meet the guests, some of whom had been friends of her mother's before she had married and given up society. Nellie's mother had been ward and niece of Desmond O'Hegarty, Miss Dorothy's father ; and she had lived with him until she fell in love with, and married, Mr. Davoren. A long estrangement ensued on this step; but gradually the old friendship had been renewed, and had lasted since the birth of her first child, Nellie.

CHAPTER IV.

" And experience showeth, there are few men so true to themselves and so settled, but that sometimes upon heat, sometimes upon bravery, sometimes upon kindness, sometimes upon trouble of mind and weakness, they open themselves ; specially if they be put to it with a counter dissimulation according to the proverb of Spain, ' Di mentira y sacaras verdad,' Tell a lie and find a truth."—Bacon.

MR. COSMO SALTASCHE possessed a first floor office in a fine building in Dame Street, not very far from College Green. It comprised three apartments : two large rooms and a smaller one at the back, which was fitted up, although but seldom used, as a bedroom by the owner. One of the other two was devoted to his clerks ; his own office was a splendid, lofty room, dingy enough as to paint and paper, but furnished with fine desks and plenty of softly cushioned morocco chairs. A long leather-covered table stood in the middle of the room ; share lists, prospectuses, and blue books, with reports in various languages, filled this. Maps of estates and railways hung on the walls. Two fine windows commanded a view of Dame Street and College Green, with their motley crowds. Standing in one of these, leisurely stroking his chin and looking out towards Westmoreland Street, was the owner.

Mr. Saltasche, the grandson of a French *émigré*, was now somewhat over forty years of age ; short, but not of the shortness that would entitle him to be spoken of as "a little man." His face was handsome ; he had large brown eyes full of intelligence, an aquiline nose, and determined mouth and chin. His foreign pedigree asserted itself in the clear olive of his skin, and silky fineness of his hair.

If you were told of it, and looked for it, a certain resemblance was discernible between him and the first Napoleon; and it was doubtless with the object of helping out this resemblance, on which he prided himself enormously, that Mr. Saltasche shaved so scrupulously every vestige of hair off his face, and always wore the whitest of vests and wide turned-down collars. A capital actor and mimic, and a finished linguist, although not a classical scholar, he was considered to be a most accomplished gentleman. A long residence on the Continent had given him a knowledge of men and women that was of immense use to him; and his easy, suave manners, joined to the advantages of wealth, obtained for him an intimate footing in the highest circles in Dublin. "All things to all men" seemed to be his device, for he was as intimate and congenial with Viscount Ramines, the turfite, as with Lord Brayhead, the champion of the Church party, and patron of every proselytising institution in the kingdom.

Mr. Saltasche's religious creed was evidently a liberal one, for he had been known to attend a morning meeting for the Christianising or evangelisation of Rome, and the evening of the same day had been seen to stroll arm-in-arm with gentle, amiable Monsignor Bursford, formerly private secretary to His Holiness, and now parish priest of Green Lanes, through the grounds of his own home, Vevey House, or along the shaded highroads. To Monsignor Bursford, who since his conversion had spent his life in Italy, a chat with his versatile neighbour over old times in Naples or Florence was a delightful treat. Saltasche knew every byway of Europe. Every picture, every statue was familiar to him. He could tell you everything you needed to know —from the best hotel to the best shop where to buy a bonnet.

Such a man must have enemies; and in the body at large of Dublin society Saltasche had not a few. Most of the number were jealous of his success and prosperity. Some distrusted his silky ways; many were envious of his intimacy with the great folks, and puzzled their heads to know what could be the "open sesame" by which this insignificant nobody of a stockbroker penetrated the enchanted circle. Lord Ramines was known to be involved—so the explanation of his intimacy was of course not far to seek. But Lord Brayhead was a psalm-singing fanatic; and this fellow, who, it was notorious, believed in nothing, human or divine, must have bewitched him. He was not a marrying man, and was in consequence by no means favourably regarded by women with flocks of marriageable daughters. There was an expression in Saltasche's face, when he was off his guard (which was very seldom), that reminded one somewhat of a tiger; showing unmistakably that under the gloss of training and worldly usage was a powerful, unprincipled, and passionate mind,—that of a man capable of risking all on the turn of a card, and toppling down with one sweep the edifice that had cost years of patient scheming and plotting to rear. There was something of the Buonaparte nature in him, and in audacity and self-confidence at least, he was perhaps equal in his own way to that greatest of adventurers. His fault was a love of pleasure and self-indulgence; and on more than one occasion his lapses had nearly been his ruin. Any other man would have been swamped, but Saltasche's resources and impudence were overwhelming, and floated him over everything.

Lounging in the window was in no way congenial to him; and after some five minutes spent in looking up and down the street, he stamped his foot impatiently, and returned to his desk. He lifted a sheet of paper which was lying loosely on the blotting-book, and read a pencilled memorandum: "'Mr. Brangan and the gas companies at half-past two: and I must be on 'Change at three.' What can this fool mean?" The office clock pointed to five minutes past two, and Mr. Saltasche returned to his post of observation. In a minute or two a pleased expression came over his face. A brougham with a coronet on the panels, drawn by a pair of job horses, crossed the front of the bank; and in a few moments a tall angular-looking old man entered the office.

"I am a little late, Mr. Saltasche," he said, in an explanatory rather than apologetic tone, laying his hat on a chair as he spoke.

"Pray don't speak of it," returned the stockbroker, pulling round an easy chair and seating himself with his back to the light. After a few commonplace remarks, his visitor, who seemed fidgety and uneasy, plunged headlong into his subject.

"I have been wanting to see you on a very particular business. You know the railway to Leadmines?" The stockbroker bowed assent. "Well, I wanted that railroad to be run a good two miles closer to my estate. See,"— and as he spoke he unrolled a chart which he took from his pocket,—"the boundaries are here ; and on this side is a valuable quarry of splendid granite, worth—oh! a fortune, Mr. Saltasche. I offered the railway company as much granite as they wanted at a merely nominal price, on condition of course, you understand, that they complied with my wishes in the laying of the road. I offered, also, to assist them with my interest—very great, as you are aware —in getting their Bill through Parliament. But, no : they refused, influenced by those of whom it were useless to speak now. Hem!"

"I understand you, my lord, perfectly." Saltasche fixed his eyes on the chart, waiting for more.

"It is now my purpose to start a railway from Dublin to a point beyond Leadmines. The farmers, my tenants, will benefit enormously by it; and those magnificent granite and slate quarries will be at last practicable. Er—the forming of a company is one of the branches which I shall confide to you ; but the getting the bill through Parliament will be, I apprehend, troublesome. We may expect opposition."

"Doubtless. That once disposed of, the rest would be quite easy."

"Well, it is necessary to look ahead in these matters. This bill will be read for the first time next session. My friends have secured a day for it ; but I fear, unless some precautions are taken, it will fail. I certainly could not spare a single one of my supporters in the House. And to-day I am told that an old friend of mine who represented Lord Kilboggan's family seat for years in Parliament is in very bad health. In fact—ah—he writes to me that his physician has recommended total abstinence from all public duty ; he has gone to the south of France, and I may feel justified in saying that his resignation is imminent." And fixing his gold spectacles on his nose, Lord Brayhead stared with a woe-begone expression at the broker.

"And Lord Kilboggan's nominee for the seat may be——"

"With Lord Kilboggan I have nothing to say or to do in common, I thank the Lord. I trust I remember him in my prayers ; but, Mr. Saltasche, he is a godless man, who would not scruple to injure me in any way he could ; and if he were aware that I had any interest in the election for Peatstown he would oppose me."

Saltasche, who was dying to laugh at the idea of his lordship praying for the ungodly Kilboggan, instantly answered :

"Nothing would be easier than to find a candidate for any vacant seat your lordship may think of. But then, as things are, it must be some Home Ruler ; and—ah—hum —somebody agreeable to the priests. In fact, my lord, it is with them that you would have to treat. Moreover, as to money, you must be prepared to guarantee part, or all your man's expenses."

"I do not object to Home Rule, Mr. Saltasche. The Government has forfeited its title to our——"

"Certainly, my lord," interrupted Saltasche skilfully. He dreaded a discourse on the iniquities' of disestablishment. "But your bill is to be read. Mr. Wyldoates had obtained permission, I think ; and——"

"It was to have been brought in early in the next session," groaned his lordship.

"That would be after Christmas. It must only be postponed," said the broker, speaking rapidly and with his sharp eyes fixed on his client's face.

"As to a candidate selected or approved by the priests, do you think, Mr. Saltasche," asked the noble Churchman, his countenance presenting a diverting mixture of perplexity and disgust, "that the state of the country is such that we cannot avoid by some means that very annoying dilemma?"

"Candidly, my lord, I do not. Moreover, if a re-election be necessary, you cannot pick and choose. Of course your name must be kept out of the affair completely."

"That is why I came to you, Mr. Saltasche," said his lordship helplessly, "to talk it over. I cannot appear. I am a Conservative and a Churchman."

"It would be awkward, certainly," assented his friend, who thoroughly enjoyed the intrigue, and appreciated the position of the spiteful old wretch consenting to forego his principles, religious and political, in order to have his revenge against the railway magnates who had thwarted his schemes for money-making.

"You will make inquiries as to a probable candidate, the cost, et cetera, and come and dine with me, and we can talk it over. I can rely, of course, on your discretion?" said the nobleman, rising from his chair, and beginning to shuffle to the door.

"You may, my lord," returned the stockbroker, with a triumphant smile, rising to show his distinguished client downstairs.

A moment after the brougham and the job horses had rolled away, Mr. Saltasche was on an outside car, driving down the quays as fast as possible. At the corner of a street near the Four Courts he saw O'Rooney Hogan nodding to him. He returned the salutation mechanically as he passed; but, as if a sudden thought struck him, turned his head and looked back keenly after the young man's retreating figure.

"Where the deuce did he tell me he lived?" thought he.

CHAPTER V.

" So gib mir auch die Zeiten wieder
  Da ich noch selbst im Werden war,
  Da sich ein Quell gedrängter Lieder
  Ununterbrochen neu gebar ;
  Da Nebel mir die Welt verhüllten,
  Die Knospe Wunder noch versprach,
  Da ich die Tausend Blumen brach,
  Die alle Thäler reichlich füllten. .
  Ich hattè nichts, und doch genug,
  Den Drang nach Wahrheit und die Lust am Trug.
  Gib ungebändigt jene Triebe,
  Das tiefe, schmerzenvolle Glück,
  Des Hasses Kraft, die Macht der Liebe,
  Gib meine Jugend mir zurück."

Faust.

ABOUT five miles out of Dublin is a place called Green
Lanes, a tolerably select suburban village, consisting of one
main street lying close to the railway station, and which
comprised the usual shops and groggeries, the post-office,
and lending library. Branching off this main street were
dirty, frowzy lanes, peopled by slatternly women and
children, where pigs rooted at their own sweet wills, and
hens, as demoralised and down-at-heel of appearance as
their owners, sunned themselves and excavated their clay
baths under the road walls. Leading down to the village,
and from it in various directions, were wide highroads,
well planted and bordered by eight-foot stone walls, muddy
and dreary now to look at, on a late November afternoon.
Great elms and knotty ashes stretched their bare limbs
across in wintry greeting to each other ; and here and there

the long gray stretch of demesne wall was broken by an
entrance gate overgrown with ivy, or a narrow grated door
which gave the passer-by a glimpse of the sea view from
which the jealous proprietor had so carefully excluded him.
Scarce a house was visible, most of the mansion residences
being hidden away as far from the thoroughfare as the
extent of their grounds would permit, or cunningly placed
at such an angle as to be veiled from the eyes of such
curious persons as might chance to look in the gate-ways.
Tall shrubberies of Scotch firs and laurels made evergreen
tufts pleasant to the sight amid the wintry desolation now
reigning around.

At a corner of one of these roads, where another avenue
—also leading, but by a more circuitous route, to the
village—joins it, stood in an enclosed space a queer old
gabled house, with a yard in front flanked by high white
walls with crenelated parapets. A huge wooden gate, the
pillars of which were surmounted by griffins sadly the
worse for time and weather, gave admission to a large
gravelled square. The front of the house was quite overgrown with creepers, which stretched their long bare arms
round the latticed windows, and held even the topmost
chimneys fast in their dry and thorny embrace. At this
winter season they were hardly an ornament. Sparrows
had built in the jessamine; and their abandoned nests,
matted and unsightly tufts of straw and leaves, hung to
the gables. Large tubs, painted green, held aloes, and
stood in a stiff row across the gravelled square. A tiled
walk led up from the gate; and a wicker paling, also
overgrown with rose trees and creepers, divided the garden
and out-offices from the front. Old-fashioned pointed
windows, with queer little lattice panes, and tall stacks of
chimney-pots, one-half of which were abandoned to the
jackdaws, gave the white house a queer old-world look.

It was about three in the afternoon; a November sun
was sending pale yellow rays through the elm branches,
and lighting up the window-panes of the room where Nellie
sat at work. Dressed in a plain black gown, the girl
looked even better than in her ball-room bravery. The

ivory contour of her neck appeared to advantage circled round with the dull black, and the tints of her hair and eyes seemed more brillant for the dark relief. Her mother lay sleeping close by, and as the sunlight was rapidly drawing round to a point where it must fall upon the invalid's face, Nellie gently pulled down the blind, and then, having remembered a task downstairs, laid aside her sewing and glided noiselessly out of the room.

Catching sight of her brother in the garden from a lobby window as she passed, she went out to speak to him. The garden looked a wilderness. A few late chrysanthemums still lingered by the walls, and a pale bleached monthly rose showed its straggling petals from the hedge. The beds had been lately cleared of the refuse of the summer flowers. Blue lobelias, their tiny blossoms sadly faded, and white and red foliage plants were heaped here and there. The clay had a black and newly-turned look; the ivy on the walls looked a more vivid green in contrast. Down at the end was the kitchen garden and tool-house; and here Dicky, seated on a watercan, among broken pots, compost heaps, and piles of dead leaves, was busy driving nails into a wheelbarrow which he had just broken. He was tall, as we said before, and had long handsome features, pretty fair hair, and eyes like his sister's, only lacking her steadiness of look. He was a pretty, interesting lad, clever beyond all doubt, but idle and wild. His escapades were condoned by many people on account of his pleasing, winning manner; and it certainly was difficult to refuse him anything he asked. He had recently taken a good place at the entrance examination of Trinity College, and he found plenty of congenial spirits in that abode of learning to help him in mischief.

He looked up when he saw his sister coming down the path, and after selecting a conveniently-sized pebble to throw at the house-cat, Tib, who was following her with stealthy footsteps, and between whom and himself there existed the bitterest of feuds, resumed his hammering with deafening assiduity.

Nellie, who knew with whom she had to deal, waited

patiently, wrapping up her hands in her apron. At last, the nail being driven home, and perhaps a little beyond it, the carpenter looked up.

"Dicky," began she, "you have never been at your books at all to-day."

"Pooh! how do you know that? I was at Fitzgerald Place this morning," he added, in order to change the subject.

"Oh, indeed! How is Dorothy?"

"Blooming. Gave us no tip, though, the old—the old ——," and failing to find a proper epithet wherewith to stigmatise Miss O'Hegarty's conduct, he hurled the hammer across the garden.

"You had money the other day."

"I lost it all to Orpen. I say, Nell, what do you think? Orpen told me he took one of the waiters for old Rafferty the other night. 'Pon my word, he came up to me and said, 'I'm blest if I know the servants from the gentlemen here!' and said he was awfully near asking the man who announced us to get him a partner. Ho, ho! They looked a great deal more at home in their evening dress, though. By Jove, he said that was the way he could distinguish them."

"Which speech exactly proves that Mr. Orpen is a vulgar-minded snob."

"Snob!" echoed the collegian scornfully. "He's no such thing. His father is a country gentleman, and they're most highly connected."

"I can't see what difference that makes," returned his sister drily.

"Listen, Nell," said Mr. Dicky, jumping up all of a sudden from his can, "just—ah—lend a fellow a couple of shillings, will you?"

"What for, now, Dicky?"

"Well, Mahoney Quain has a—a tea-party in his rooms to-night, and Orpen and Griffiths are to be at it, and they're going to help me with my mathematics; so I only just want a couple of shillings in my pocket, you know—just to have them in my pocket," he repeated, and he looked coaxingly at her and held out one hand. "The governor's going into the theatre to-night, and he and I'll come home together," he added, with a pleading look.

"What did you do with the money you had last week?"

"What money? Ah! sure I never have any at all."

"Indeed you have, Dicky, and I can't lend you this; it is too bad;" and Miss Davoren put on a severe air.

Dicky caught sight of Tib, and the pebble was discharged against his fat ribs with a force that sent the luckless animal flying in the direction of the house as fast as his legs would carry him.

"Don't then, Miss," retorted he viciously; "don't, that's all, and see if I'll take you to Gardiner Street on Sunday —that's all either," and plumping back on the water-can, he began to sort out another nail to drive in the wheelbarrow.

"Listen, Dicky. I'm not refusing to lend you the money, but when *do* you mean to take to your books?"

"Ah! what do you know about it, child?" returned he, in a somewhat softened tone. "I'm not three months in yet; and look at all the hard work I did with those beastly mathematics there, to pass. Every man takes a rest after he enters, like that;" and he looked up out of the corner of his eye to see how this told.

She remained silent; she had not heard him at all, for she was thinking of something else as she watched the gradually darkening sky.

"I saw your partner, Nell, to-day;"—Dicky struck into a fresh subject—"that Mr.—oh, Mr. O'Rooney Hogan. Decentish sort of fellow that, now. He inquired for you."

"Did he?" said Miss Nellie quietly, turning to go into the house.

"Oh, Nell! I say, Nellsie jewel, you're forgetting the half-crown."

"Oh dear! oh dear!" said she, putting her hand in her pocket, and giving it to him. "Now, Dicky, don't be late, I beg of you."

"I'll take you on Sunday," vouchsafed the youngster,

now restored to good humour; "and oh! I say, Dorothy
says she's heard, next week or the week after there's to be
a command night at the Royal, and we're both to go with
her."

Nellie gave no sign of having heard, beyond an inclination of her head as she sped back to the house, and
the boy returned to his hammering with renewed vigour.

When she reached her mother's room, she raised the
blind again, and seated herself in her own chair by the
window, looking out at the sunset, fast fading now. A
gray mass of cloud, edged with a dull crimson, and through
a rift lower down by the horizon a tiny fiery speck fast
sinking out of sight. The spires of the city, lying between
her and the west, were clear and hard against the light;
and over towards the north a mist was gathering fast.
Folding her hands in her lap, Nellie began to trace over
again in her mind the events of the night; and many a
smile rose to her lips at the incongruous figures that presented themselves to her memory. Hogan's image certainly
was prominent; and from the time of his being introduced
to her to their last dance together, she followed every word
and look as far as her memory aided her. How strange
that she should meet him again there!—and she wandered
back from the pale wintry landscape before her eyes,
to that glowing, burning day in July when they sat
together in St. Swithin's schoolroom, amid the din and
crash of pianos. There it was all a white hot glare,—
white walls, white dresses, and noise. She remembered
well the headache it gave her. Her remembrance of her
pleasant neighbour was scarcely so distinct—the Bishop's
nephew, and a barrister, and related to the Superior,
Mother Assumption:—so much the Raffertys, who seemed
to hold him in great esteem, had told her. He had not
seemed to respond to their pressing attentions the other
night, Miss Nellie reflected, with the least possible tinge of
mischief suffusing her consciousness. Would Dicky go to
Gardiner Street on Sunday? and would Mr. Hogan be
there? Surely by Sunday he would have forgotten everything about it. Then she began to wonder if she could

recognise him ; and she called up one by one the features
of his face,—dark eyes, a long straight nose——Nellie
painted an ideal portrait so flattering, that had its original
presented himself before her, she would have found but
few points of resemblance in her creation. She remained
in the window-seat for a long time, weaving all manner of
fancies, as strange and unstable as the flitting shapes of the
clouds. The room was so quiet, so warm,—not a sound,
save the fall of the wood-ashes in the fireplace, disturbed
her reverie. The last pale rays of the sun fell on her
mother's portrait above the chimneypiece—a pallid chalk
head, with wide low brows and almond-shaped wistful
eyes—wistful and sad, though she was only twenty when
it had been taken. Some faces bear the shadow of coming
troubles even at their brightest and freshest. A little
glass on the table held violets,—a few pinched things that
had peeped up by mistake in a sheltered corner, and had
been summarily cut short in their unseasonable career by
Dicky. Their sweet faint odour reached Nellie in her
window-seat. A redbreast perched suddenly on a branch
beneath, and, fixing his bright little eyes on the window
from which he was used to receive crumbs, struck into a
loud shrill song. It sounded so near, Nellie almost started
and forgot dreamland. The cloud-castles were shattered,
the bright lights faded in the west, and a cold green tone
took the place of the crimson bar. The whole sky assumed
that Indian-ink colour we see only in the late autumn ;
and when she turned her eyes round into the room again,
she was astonished to find that it was nearly dark. She
felt almost guilty as she picked up the neglected sewing
which had fallen on the floor.

CHAPTER VI.

" On ne sait rien d'une nation, tant qu'on n'a pas scruté les ressorts secrets de sa vie morale et analysé les forces organiques dont un examen superficiel ne montre que les résultats."

George Bousquet, " La Religion en Japon."

HOGAN was on his way homewards from the Four Courts one afternoon. Deep in meditation, he was bethinking himself, as he steered his way through the mud, that he must, without delay, repair to the Bishop, to render up an account of his doings since their last meeting. It would not do by any means to take an independent tone with the old gentleman; and after all, the young man thought that he deserved so much attention. Then, if he should cavil or find fault, it was so easy to convince him; and he smiled as he thought of the simple artifices by which he had so often hoodwinked his venerable relative. Affairs were going on very well with him now. Briefs were plentiful, and the attorneys seemed to have taken him quite into their good graces. Before going on circuit he thought of giving a large dinner-party to some influential Dublin priests, and to some of his uncle's colleagues. One of the most approved means of "working the clerical dodge" is to give big dinners to their reverences; and this nephew of a Bishop was by no means ignorant of how much a champagne dinner at the Gresham or Shelbourne might do for him—especially now in the beginning of Term.

While ruminating in his mind a list of names to submit to his lordship's approval, he was almost knocked down by his new friend Mr. Saltasche, who was crossing the footpath of Bachelor's Walk to get to his car.

"Hillo, Mr. Hogan! is that you?—the very man I wanted to see. I had forgotten your address. Will you come down to my office with me? I want you to look over some papers, and give me your opinion of them."

"With pleasure, indeed," replied the barrister, smiling.

Both gentlemen mounted the car. Saltasche, who seemed in the best of humours, turned, as if moved by a sudden thought, to Hogan:

"Can you dine with me at the Shelbourne to-day? Have you anything better on hand?"

"Nothing doing to-day, Mr. Saltasche. Very willingly."

"I very often dine there or at Jude's—very often: it is so handy, instead of going out to the country, you know."

"You sleep in town, then?"

"Yes; I've got a little bedroom fitted up in my offices. I don't use it very often, though."

The car drew up at the door of the broker's office. He led the way up the broad, well-lighted staircase, and having pushed open the swing-door of his room, stepped in first, and held it for the barrister to enter. On turning round, he uttered an exclamation of surprise. In his own arm-chair, which had been pulled out of its place and turned towards the fire, sat a man puffing a cigarette.

"Hillo, Captain Poignarde! is that you?"

The intruder jumped up and shook himself together. Throwing the cigarette into the fire, he advanced to meet the broker.

He was by no means prepossessing, Hogan thought, who was looking askew at him as he stood under the gaslight. Of middle height, with whiskers and hair of the same faded blonde, his face bore all the marks of dissipation and vice: a furtive, watery eye, and tremulous lips, told the tale of excess. His speech proved him to be an Englishman, as unmistakably as his bearing and dress proclaimed him a military man.

"Good evening, Mr. Saltasche. Sorry to disturb you at this late hour. I—er,—just wanted to tell you——" here he became aware of Hogan's presence behind the broker's

figure, and dropped his voice discreetly—"just wanted to
tell you that I'd be obliged by your selling out—say a
hundred and fifty, or more, pounds' worth of stock to-
morrow."

The broker raised his eyebrows slightly.

"Of course, Captain Poignarde, if you require it. I
hope Colonel Anstruther is well."

"He's quite well, thank you," replied Poignarde, who
showed some confusion in his tone, and seemed fidgety to
get away.

"Well, what time to-morrow will you be likely to call?"

"Er—about twelve, Mr. Saltasche, I think. Hope it
won't trouble you."

"Dear no—not at all."

So the military man blundered out of the room, glad
to escape without further parley.

The broker turned his head and looked after him with a
sort of amused smile.

"Do you see that fellow?" said he to Hogan; "he's
going the pace; he married an heiress—ran away with her,
I believe some one told me. She, if she'd waited a while,
would have been worth her quarter of a million. Fact, sir.
As it was, she was cut off with four or five thousand; she
was only of age the other day, and this animal is squander-
ing every penny. I have heard she is exquisitely beautiful, too,—I haven't seen her."

"What could she see in him?" asked Hogan.

"God knows! I never heard the whole story. Some
schoolgirl fancy," returned Saltasche, who was busy at a
huge iron safe behind his desk.

"Look over those, Mr. Hogan, if you please," he said,
flinging, as he spoke, some parchments on the table,
"while I go to look what these fellows are after;" and he
turned and went by a side door into the clerks' room to
overlook the accounts of the day. An easy, pleasant
master, this daily advent was no terror to his subordinates.
In about twenty minutes he returned, to find Hogan, standing with his back to the fire, holding one of the papers in
his hand.

"Those I find all right and square, Mr. Saltasche,—no hitch whatever ; but this—h'm—you have seen the deeds referred to. I daresay it's all secure too."

"These belong to a Mrs. Bursford, a sister-in-law of the convert Monsignor Bursford—you know him, I dare say ? —belong to her and her daughter ; and she has sold her land in Wicklow to invest the proceeds in my care. Those are title-deeds lodged as security."

Hogan folded up the papers and handed them to the broker.

"All right, sir—so far as I can judge from the deeds."

"So I thought myself," returned Saltasche ; "but you see the Miss Diana Bursford mentioned there is Mrs. Bursford's daughter ; and about the reality of her fortune there seem to be doubts."

"It seems to be a rather common complaint in regard to that article, nowadays," laughed the barrister.

"By Jove, yes; it's something tremendous the lying that goes on in this good city about money. This young lady started in life with the reputation of ten thousand pounds fortune. I do not think for a moment that her own family had anything to do with the absurd exaggeration, but there are always indiscreet friends——"

"Indiscreet friends who will run the figure up or pull it down with equal unveraciousness."

"Just so," nodded the broker ; "and of late they have turned to the pulling-down process. However, Hanaper and Diesele, the family lawyers, have sent me these ; and further it's no affair of mine. Lord Brayhead is one of the trustees for Miss Bursford's money ; and they—the ladies —are old friends of mine. Have you ever met them ?"

"No."

"Well," said Saltasche, pulling out his watch, "time we were moving, sir, I declare. Come along round to Jude's, — I sent them word about our dinner ;" and pulling on his top-coat, he passed his arm familiarly under that of Hogan, and they turned their steps in the direction of the hotel.

The night had fallen now, and a chill north wind swept

the fast emptying streets; carriages rolled by, on their way homewards towards the squares and private streets; cabs and cars poured in endless stream to the railway stations; workmen passed rapidly in knots and couples, shaping their course towards their haunts by the river; the brilliantly lighted shop-windows began to become few and far between, and the city was rapidly putting on her more sombre and quiet attire for the night.

Jude's was well lighted up. Red lamps shone on each side of the door, and a brace of smart waiters stood in attendance in the entry. Mr. Saltasche was evidently known to them; and without a moment's delay both gentlemen were shown into a well-lighted room, through which a large fire diffused a pleasant warmth, agreeable enough to new-comers from the cold world without.

Dinner was served without delay. Saltasche showed his usual discrimination in his choice of dishes.

"Capital ox-tail soup," said he; "no use going in for *bisque* or *purée* here. Soup is not an institution of this country, you know, like our Burren Banks oysters. So we must put up with what we can get."

"This is good enough for anybody, I should say," returned Hogan; "I don't believe, excepting people who go in for style, that they ever eat it here at all."

"No; the Irish middle class, I venture to say, beat the English in point of incompetency as cooks, and upon my word that's saying a good deal. They're not so wasteful, because they're so much poorer; but they're a deal more uncomfortable."

Hogan assented tacitly. He was indeed thinking of the beefsteaks and chops his landlady served him in his lodgings near the Canal. Frightful beefsteaks, tough as leather, and chops fried and swimming in their own coarse fat. And her tea and coffee: if anything could be worse than the tea, was it not the coffee—muddy, flavourless, and usually tepid?

"The best cooks, to my mind, are the Italians,—better tempered than Frenchmen, more patient, and less nonsense about them. French cooks are perfect devils to have in a house. The Lord Lieutenant brought over his own cook, a Neapolitan. I am told the dinners are something superb. By-the-bye, I hear his brown mare, the one entered for the Spring Meeting, has hurt her shoulder."

"I don't know," returned the barrister carelessly; "I never was a horsy man, and anyhow the Castle doings are my aversion."

"God knows, I'm glad to hear you say so," returned the broker. "It is something infernal the way they are discussed in Dublin,—it is such a little place, you see. You can't turn round without every one knowing it. The most intensely snobbish place I ever was in."

"Yes," returned Hogan, "I go with you there. You see there are so many reasons for that. It could not fail to be what it is: I only wonder, all things considered, that it isn't worse."

"Worse!—that would be hardly possible, I should fancy."

"Bless us! yes, the root of it lies far back. You have to go back a century or more into the history of the country to see how deeply rooted is the class distinction between the two rival creeds. I assure you even Protestant tradesmen think they have the pull over any R. C. And that is a thing that always gathers force as it gets older. So long as the Protestants were the recognised superiors of the others, they were not nearly so stuck-up and exclusive. There was far more friendly intercourse; and, in fact, there was not the wicked partisan feeling on either sides that we have seen since the disestablishment,—perhaps since Emancipation."

"Ah," returned Saltasche, "however it came about, bad feeling was stirred up on both sides by Emancipation; the reason, I take it," he added, "that it never subsided was, your clergy learned their own strength. O'Connell taught them the trick, among others; and like all men raised at once from a very low position to a very high one—that is, politically speaking, in the way of controlling elections and so on—they have abused their power."

"Abused their power!" echoed the barrister thought-

G

fully. " Hum,—I don't know that the Government can charge them with that. They certainly have an enormous personal influence over the people ; but in political matters, why, look at this Fenian business : in all Ireland, it is a fact there was but one Fenian priest. Their lives were actually threatened,—you know that."

" I think," said Saltasche, " and I base my opinion chiefly on my experience of the Church in Spain and Italy, that the reason of the clerical opposition to that movement was the dread of the republican free-thinking spirit imported into it, far more than loyalty to England."

" Fenianism was low too," said Hogan thoughtfully, " essentially low : it had not a single supporter of the social position of those who were concerned with the Young Irelanders ; and I may tell you that priests are intensely aristocratic."

" Well, there now, isn't that what I say ? " put in Saltasche, replenishing, as he spoke, the glass of his companion ; " precisely my position. They abominate Radicalism and Republicanism."

" Well now, in America we don't find them acting in conformity with that principle. They are not struggling to overthrow the institutions there——"

" Hah ! are they not indeed ? I have studied that question closely, I assure you. You have very little idea of the condition of affairs in the States. Before we are many years older, my good sir, they will be trying conclusions over there in a very practical fashion."

" I have never studied American questions of any kind," returned the barrister ; " it is not at all an interesting country to me. I think, however, it is a general mistake to make so little account of America."

" I have very little Irish blood in me," said Saltasche, who was playing with some filberts on his plate ; " but I do believe that for anybody who is fond of studying character, individual and national, a more interesting field is not to be found in the whole world than Ireland. Dublin society is really a perfect study."

" Ay, a drop of ditchwater under a microscope ; everybody pushing upwards on the social ladder, kicking down those behind. However, the Protestants have pretty well laid down the line to our people now, 'So far and no farther,' ever since the passing of the Church Act."

"Now is that really your opinion?" asked Saltasche. "Do you think that the social intercourse between the two parties has been checked by that measure?"

"God bless me,—yes. All through the country the feeling is most bitter. Why, I know many instances of people refusing to keep a Catholic servant in their house."

"Disgusting rubbish!" and the broker curled his lip.

"You are pretty liberal in your sentiments, Mr. Saltasche, like myself," said Hogan, fixing, as he raised his glass of wine to his lips, a peculiar look on his friend.

"I am very liberal," replied Saltasche, returning the look by one equally significant. "I don't believe any man possessed of judgment, or knowledge of the world, could for a moment sympathise with the conduct of the English in this country—their conduct at this very instant. I only wonder your people bear it so patiently as they do."

"You mean, of course, their attitude socially and religiously?"

"It is one and the same. The monstrous insolence of the English is at the bottom of all the troubles here. Talk of Infallibility and the Pope's assumptions,—God bless me! what is it compared to the Anglo-Hibernian Protestantism? A trifle light as air. Their religion is themselves; and everywhere John Bull goes with his egotism and his Bible,—on the Continent, in India, Africa,—the story is identical; hatred and rebellion spring up at once. A friend of mine, a bank manager in this country, told me the rector of the parish once came to his house. When going away, he said to him, with a sort of a snigger, 'You won't take this as a visit—eh, eh, Mr.—ah—Nokes?' 'I shan't,' he replied; 'but next time you presume to come to my house, I shall take it as a visit, and I'll kick you out of the door.' He did well."

"India is a good example," said Hogan, after laughing at the anecdote. "Look at that mutiny, caused altogether

by the heartless, wanton insolence of English officers. It
does not come out so much at home. You must see them
out of their own country to appreciate their delightful qualities,—though, indeed, they do treat servants
horribly."

"Treat servants badly?" said Saltasche. "Have you
noticed that? Why, nowhere on earth are they better
fed and paid."

"I mean their way of treating them as inferiors. Did
you ever hear an officer swearing at his man, especially at
his own servant? There is something most repulsive in it
to me, that because a man takes your money to perform
certain duties in return for it, you are entitled to treat him
like a dog—like a creature devoid of all feeling or self-
respect!"

"They are the best servants in the world," said Saltasche, "the English; the most perfectly trained and comfortable, and—treacherous."

"Treacherous! By Jove! I should think they are
that; but since the days of Abraham I fancy there has
always been that class hostility. Look at the servants of
the Tichborne family. The English have some knack of
always making themselves hated by their subordinates."

"I don't believe, now," said Saltasche musingly, "Irish
servants could do that. They're not given to those deep
schemes at all, so far as I know them."

"Well," said Hogan, slowly shaking his head, "I've had
some little experience of them in the Four Courts, and, if
they don't concoct those infernal schemes their fellows do
across the water, it's merely because their heads won't hold
them."

Saltasche laughed heartily. "That was a shocking
murder down the country, eh?" said he.

"Yes, most extraordinary. The usual thing—eviction.
It's a mistake to suppose that the Land Act, however con-
ceived, will put an end to that sort of business. They
mistake the cause altogether."

"How? It is not revenge—wild justice."

"Not at all. The Irish agrarian murders are prompted

by the same motive as those French rural crimes we read
of so frequently,—intense love of the land itself; and the
landlord or his agent is not hated one bit more than anybody else that stands in their way—not a whit. It is all
nonsense to say that they hate the landlord as a foreigner,
a usurper. Mrs.——, and that unfortunate Mr.——, were
not English, and see how they were shot. Bless me!
they shoot their own relatives, if they stand in their way,
quite as readily as any Sassenach of them all.

"They do—not a doubt of it," said Saltasche thoughtfully. "Yet the English papers will insist on laying every
murder on the everlasting ' disaffection.' It has nothing
to do with ninety-nine hundredths of them."

" Nothing whatever. Believe me, they are more afraid
of each other, more disaffected and more treacherous to
their own next-door neighbours, than they are to England.
Look at the farmers ; they daren't whitewash their house,
lest a neighbour should imagine they had money, and inform the agent, and then the rent would be raised. If
they kill one of their own geese or ducks, they eat it with
closed doors and windows, for fear it should be thought
they were well off. They lodge money in the banks at
three or maybe two per cent interest, and the very same
men—will you believe it?—borrow money at *six* per cent
from the *same* bank to pay their rent. Just imagine
it."

" Well, I can believe, though it looks absurd, that there
is a solid reason at the bottom of it. If the landlord gets
a bill at three months or six months in payment of his
rent, he fancies the tenant is poor."

" That is so," continued Hogan. "Now there must be
something rotten in the state of things when it is the interest of the people to keep themselves poor, and to look
poor. There is a heavy drawback imposed on their prosperity and industry. It reminds me of the stories of the
French peasants before the Revolution. And it is such a
demoralising state of affairs. Habits such as are engendered under this *régime* are most destructive. Think of
the children who are born and brought up under such

influences.   The entire tenant-at-will system is abominable."

"I don't in the least see how it is to be remedied.
There would seem to be no medium between a confessedly
mischievous system and wild schemes framed and proposed
by Jack-o'-lantern politicians, having for object the simple
spoliation of the proprietors.   I can't see any way out
of it."

"I can't either," replied the barrister.   "It is flying in
the face of human nature to expect the landlords to work
the reform.   And what can you expect of the people?
what can they do for themselves?   Take into account
their wretchedness and degradation, and their ignorance,
they really are not one whit more civilised than the
peasants whom Arthur Young describes in France a century ago.   How, then, can you expect them to have more
just or equitable ideas?   They are in a state of black
ignorance, and it is a frightful and disgraceful thing that
there should be a penalty on industry and enterprise."

"How strange it is that the English are so devoid of
this love of the land!   An English farmer thinks only of
the ground as he thinks of a machine, which, properly
manipulated, will bring him in money.   What on earth is
the fascination it has over these Irish?"

"It has never been explained," said Hogan.   "The
French peasant is the same.   Perhaps it is some queer
lingering love of the conquered race for its own land.   The
native Gauls and the native Irish have some points of
similarity historically.   It may have had its origin in that.
Besides, the people here have no way of living save by
land."

"Extraordinary people!" mused Saltasche; "how in the
world are they ever to be improved?"

"Sweetness and Light," said Hogan with a smile, pulling
up his chair closer to the fire.

"And there the priests bar the way.   It is incomprehensible how the people follow them so blindly in refusing
the national education system."

"Tut, tut!—not so fast.   The whole cause of the dislike, or rather distrust, lies in the conduct of the Protestant party. They always wanted to force Scripture, in some shape or sort, down the throats of the children, and insisted on their right to do it. Bah! the priests were quite right to resist such aggression. And let the parsons promise what they like, from the very first time they ever established a school in Ireland, proselytism was their business. There is not a brat as high as your knee but knows that, and hates them accordingly. Besides, the people have always had the idea, and that too with solid reason, that this proselytism was not for the sake of merely winning over their souls to the rival Church, but also, mark you, as a means of obtaining their allegiance, and thereby strengthening and securing the proselytisers' own position as conquerors in a subjugated country. So at all times here a pervert, or, as the *Saturday Review* says, a 'vert,' was looked upon in the double light of a deserter and an apostate."

"Is that so now?" asked Saltasche.

"It is literally as true at the present moment as it was a century ago. Even here in Dublin, as well as in the country, any Roman Catholic 'going over' is held to have sold himself body and soul for temporal advancement."

The Church Establishment was a monstrous injustice anyhow," said Saltasche, with a great air of concession. He said this to please his friend. "High time it was done away with. A scandalous absurdity."

"Yes;" replied Hogan, raising his eyebrows slightly, "but after all it weighed but lightly on the people—as compared, of course, with former times. I almost think it would have been more expedient to have postponed disestablishment for a time, or at least to have disestablished the Scotch branch first. The priests were, I believe, the chief instigators of that movement; and since its accomplishment, strange to say, seem tolerably indifferent; one might almost fancy they regretted being deprived of their pet grievance."

"Hah! I'll tell you why. They wanted to get the money. They fully expected to get their share."

"Do you imagine they looked for concurrent endowment?"

"Hardly," replied the broker. "They know better than to take a State provision; but they thought to get it, and think they will get it still, for a Catholic University."

Hogan shook his head. "No, no," said he; "Trinity is absorbing such Catholic youngsters as want college education and degrees. I think the Stephen Green University merely draws medical students. After all, they have a very good excuse for patronising Trinity. Few people can afford to lose time and money taking out a degree that has no market value—a mere certificate. Look at me, for example. What should I be doing with a Catholic University degree? Moreover, who are their professors?—mere nobodies, or men trained in and belonging to the Queen's Universities or Trinity."

"It's a pity, Mr. Hogan," said Saltasche, "that you are not in St. Stephen's; if you were to talk that way, you'd soon make your mark."

"All in good time," laughed the barrister, emptying his glass. "I hope to be one day."

"I think," said Saltasche, "that one important feature in the case is the social distinction of Trinity. That has an attraction for Catholics of a certain grade. There is a marked desire on the part of many of the professional set to know and mix with the other persuasion. Is not that so?"

"Decidedly so. And an equally marked desire on the part of their *ecclesiastical* rulers that they shall do nothing of the kind. Anyhow," added Hogan, "if the Catholics want to get into Protestant society, they don't go the right way about it. Men, of course, know each other; but it's the *women* who bar the way. R. C. women are terribly behind the age. Did you hear the last story of Lady St. Aldegonde? She wrote to her friends, the Hawardens of Westmeath, to come up in time for the dinner on the 14th. '*We shall have only our own friends,*' said she; '*none of these dreadful Dublin lawyers' wives.*'"

"Ay," said Saltasche with a laugh, that's a good one; but," he added seriously, "what a curious affair this new marriage law is. Now tell me, if Catholics and Protestants can't marry in Dublin, why can they in London? It's the boast of your Church that her doctrine, etc., is the same and infallible everywhere. Yet this law is unknown in America, Scotland, England; and in Paris too, for a mixed marriage came off there last week."

"I confess I don't understand it," replied Hogan. "Mixed marriages are seldom happy, they say."

The broker laughed sardonically.

"That's hardly a reason," said he drily. "But I confess it looks odd to see people take a trip to London to get married, and come home coolly in spite of the awful denunciations, and live like other people, in the teeth of the priest's assurance that they are not married at all."

Hogan laughed and shook his head.

"It just proves thoroughly what the Infallibility means," continued Saltasche. "I don't wonder at the old Torys' talk of *autos da fe* and the Inquisition. 'Pon my word, I'm liberal enough, but some things do make me uneasy."

"Stuff," said Hogan; "that's all gone by and forgotten long ago—impossible and nonsensical."

"How do they arrange," asked Saltasche, "in the case of poor people who can't afford to go to London, or to buy a dispensation?" And he looked askance at Hogan.

"I know of some cases—they get married by the Registrar, and never mind the religious ceremony at all. I think it a bad plan."

"It is, begad. But in your Church they have always kept up the old tradition—one law for the rich and another for the poor."

"Bah! tell me where it isn't the same—it's human nature. Wealth has everywhere its prerogatives and privileges." The barrister laughed a little sardonically.

"Come and look in at the theatre; it's only ten minutes past nine," said the host, pulling out his watch as he spoke.

Now, Hogan had work before him at home—work, indeed, that would keep him out of his bed until quite the small hours of the morning; and he did not intend to waste any time in theatres. So he told his host plainly

that he could not bestow further time upon him, he had
two cases to get up.

Then a car was called, and Mr. Saltasche was dropped
in Hawkins Street by Hogan, who vainly endeavoured to
prevent that liberal gentleman from paying the man.
Saltasche only laughed when the barrister tried to stay
his hand, and chucking the jarvey half a crown instead of
his legal shilling, disappeared under the arches of the
theatre, while Hogan drove home alone to his work.

CHAPTER VII.

" Why should this desert silent be ?
For it is unpeopled ? No ;
Tongues I'll hang on every tree,
That shall civil sayings show :
Some, how brief the life of man
Runs his erring pilgrimage,
That the stretching of a span
Buckles in his sum of age ;
Some of violated bonds
'Twixt the souls of friend and friend."

As you Like it.

ONE Monday morning, Miss Nellie Davoren might have been observed taking peculiar and unusual care with her toilette. She braided her brown hair in the very last style, a modification of Miss Malowney's, just as Miss Malowney's was an exaggeration of "Her Excellency's." She pulled two silk dresses out of her wardrobe—a blue and a gray—and spent some time deliberating which to put on. The gray finally obtained most favour in her sight, and she decided to wear it. At twelve o'clock Nellie was ready ; and her brother, who had been shouting impatient summonses and threats up the stairs for half an hour previous, seized and hurried her off, vowing he would be late for lecture, and promising all sorts and kinds of misconduct in revenge if such turned out to be the case.

"Oh, there now, Dicky," said Miss Nellie, at last, "do not go on at that rate : you will be in long before one o'clock."

"How do you know, miss ? and what's it to you ? The idea of your talking !" returned the saucy boy, in his most scornful tone.

" Since you entered college, you have become unbearable. Do you imagine that knowing Latin and Greek gives you a right to be so impertinent? You think you're a man; but, indeed, that's not the way men behave. Look at Mr. Orpen and Mr. Hogan, how polite they are."

"Yah! because you're not their sister," retorted Dicky.

"No matter, sir; gentlemen are always polite. There now, the clock is only just ringing, and with all your hurry we are five minutes too soon."

"So much the better. Cool down and look pleasant over it."

Just then they came upon a tawdrily dressed nurse carrying a baby, and followed by a number of little children. They belonged to an acquaintance of the Davorens, and Nellie stopped to inquire for their mother from the nurse.

Dicky, who was a little in advance, turned half round with such an angry face that she hastily quickened her step to overtake him. He stood quite still until she came up, and then said, in an angry and serious tone,

"Did I possibly see you speak to that girl of the Wildings?"

"Yes; I asked for her mistress."

"Don't you ever dare to speak to her again: never notice her on any account. You hear me, Nellie?"

"I do. Why not speak to her? What can you mean?"

"I mean this, then, since you must have meanings and reasons,—she's not a person fit for you to speak to. I know what she is very well." So he did; for the "person" in question was a companion and associate of several of his college friends.

Nellie made him no rejoinder. She felt shocked and mortified, and getting into the train seated herself silently in a corner alone, for Dicky had got into the smoking compartment with a neighbour of theirs, a Mr. Saltasche. Neither she nor her father was acquainted with him, but Dicky was on friendly terms with him. Arrived at the terminus, Dicky reappeared, and sulkily informing her that he would not return to dinner, and that Dorothy must send Peter, the man-servant, home with her, hailed a cab, and putting her into it, departed speedily on his own road.

Nellie looked out of the window after his retreating form, striding along beside his companion. She had noted of late—not without much misgiving—the change in the boy's manner. A dictatorial impertinence had taken the place of his former good-humour, and sulky reticence made all question as to his employment of his time and out-door pursuits bootless and unsatisfactory. Cousin Dorothy supplied him liberally with pocket-money, which, with his own allowance, disappeared mysteriously; he was always wanting more, and always grumbling that he had never money like other fellows. A beautiful boy, he had been his mother's darling; and from the day of his birth he had been spoiled. His sister and mother, and in accord-ance with their example the servants, had always given way to him. Whoever suffered inconvenience, or came short of any comfort, it was not to be Master Dicky: and the lad took it all as his birthright. He was a fine boy naturally, and was good-natured and generous of spirit. But he had never been denied anything, and he had never learned to deny himself anything. It seemed perfectly natural, and a matter of course, that his sister should give him her allowance of pocket-money. He had the grace, to be sure, to ask her politely for it, and even to call it lending; and sometimes, when he chanced to be in a parti-cularly good temper, vague visions of paying it back would cross his brain. But he did not feel at all bound to do so. What was she but a girl? and what did women want money for? Indeed Mr. Dicky, like a great many of his kind, held the pleasant theory that women had no business to have money except for men to take it from them. If the young gentleman thought about the matter at all, his thoughts probably took that shape.

Nellie soon arrived in Fitzgerald Place. Peter opened the door, and bade her walk into the dining-room.

"Bless us, Nell! is that you?" said Miss O'Hegarty, who was busy arranging a wintry-looking bouquet in a china basket. "You look quite nice, my dear,—a great

deal too nice for my pack of old women. They'll fall on
you tooth and nail, just for the spite of it. Come here,
and see if you can arrange these. I want them for the
drawing-room by-and-by. Don't splash your dress now!
I want to go to the drawing-room to see if Peter has put
things to rights. Peter, Peter!" she called; and Nellie
was left to arrange the chrysanthemums and veronicas in
the basket.

Miss O'Hegarty's Mondays were the event of her week.
She did not go into society; at least, since her father's
death she had given up entertainments, but she had by no
means given up her circle, and had hit on the popular
and cheap device of weekly afternoon teas to assemble her
coterie. She had a large number of relatives and connections; and as since the Church Act was passed a great
many county families had thronged up to live in Dublin,
her Monday afternoons were as punctually attended as the
Drawing-room itself. Gentlemen seldom came. Now and
again some old country acquaintance would drop in with
his wife or daughters, and, appalled at the gathering of
women, drop out again just as quickly as politeness would
allow. Married ladies and spinsters of her own standing,
and young ladies who had reached the age when the
appetite for scandal may be indulged without any of the
jeune personne squeamishness, composed the majority of her
habitués. It was not without some misgiving that she gave
Nellie Davoren an invitation to one of these festivities.

Nellie very soon finished arranging the flowers, and
hastened upstairs to aid her cousin and Peter in the drawing-room. This was a large room, with a fine bay window.
The furniture was for the most part old, and some of it
had come from Castle O'Hegarty. Queer old girandoles,
with mirrors that reflected you upside-down, or broader
than you were long, as a spoon does, hung here and there
among the pictures on the walls. Dorothy had not adopted
the modern custom of hanging her walls with china until
they resembled a kitchen dresser; but had she liked she
could have made a fine display of old Worcester and
Wedgewood ware—a goodly stock of both being stowed in

a great glass-fronted chiffonier. She liked solidity and massiveness in her surroundings: the chairs and sofas were enormous of frame; but for all that there were plenty of pretty things scattered about—little lounging chairs, velvet covered, and with gilt legs and backs; a pretty little table held Miss O'Hegarty's work materials; and here and there were artistic mementoes of her foreign travels in the shape of pretty statuettes and ornaments of various kinds.

Peter was carrying in flower-pots out of the little greenhouse on the leads, and under Miss O'Hegarty's directions distributing them through the room. On a sofa-table stood the tea equipage, and the top of the grand piano was utilised to hold spare cups and plates of cakes.

"You will do the honours, Nellie. And, Peter, mind what you're about to-day, and if you must spill coffee and tea the way you did last week, don't do it upon the only lady of title in the room."

Some inarticulate growlings, as Peter descended the stair in quest of another pot of myrtle, was the only notice vouchsafed to this recommendation.

"He's getting old," continued Miss O'Hegarty, turning to Nellie,—"getting old, my dear, and past his work."

A frightful crash on the staircase followed this asseveration, and seemed to have occurred precisely to bear out the mistress's opinion,—the fact being that Peter had overheard her remark, and took the means of smashing the flower-pot as a double-barrelled expedient of revenging himself and venting his temper.

The lady divined the state of affairs, and with a discretion the fruit, no doubt, of long experience, judged better to take no notice. So she pretended not to have heard anything, and left the old gentleman to gather up the mess at his leisure.

"He's done it on purpose, me dear." Whenever Miss O'Hegarty was vexed her native Kerry brogue asserted itself in all its purity. "Just wants to aggravate me: but he shan't. He's been at it all morning. Old devil!" she added wrathfully; "who on earth would put up with him but meself?"

Peter, a shrivelled little old man, with apple and red cheeks and sly blue eyes, was one of those ancient retainers whose impudence and good-for-nothingness people feel themselves bound to endure simply because they have been in the habit of doing so for a greater or less number of years. The race is fast becoming extinct, with no great loss to the community at large. Between Peter and his mistress there was a perpetual feud going on. They were always at cross-purposes about something or another; and Dicky Davoren declared that a considerable portion of the time of both was spent devising schemes to vex each other.

"Everything's done, I do believe," said the lady of the house, giving a final glance around. "Come up to my room, Nellie, while I dress myself."

They passed up the stairs without seeming to see the irate Peter busy with brush and pan, and reached a large airy bedroom over the drawing-room floor.

Nellie sat down, and Miss O'Hegarty proceeded to divest herself of a dark morning dress, and having arranged her ringlets, put on a heavy black silk dress, with lace to match her rich head-dress.

"I hope I'll do, Cousin Dorothy," said Nellie, looking dubiously at her simple costume.

"Pooh! do, child? indeed you will. I never have a mortal but a pack of women about me—horrid lot! I hope you won't repent coming among them. See if I left the hand-glass over there."

"They are not all old, are they, cousin?" asked Nellie, handing her the article in question.

"Old: humph! If they heard you say so! There will be Mrs. Bursford. Now, she knew your mother long ago; but she's older—oh yes, much older; and her daughter, Miss Diana, is a belle. She's over thirty. Her cousins, the Bragintons, say she's thirty-five. But that's cousins' talk all the world over. You'll see them here; and an amiable collection they are. They're nieces of Lord and Lady Brayhead, and are on a visit to them,—nieces on her side, you know. And the eldest, Miss

Blanche, is going to be married ; at least so she's given out. We'll see what her aunt, Mrs. Bursford, says of it. Nellie, see if you can find the eye of that hook."

" Now, child," said Miss O'Hegarty, turning round, " let's have a look at you. Smooth your hair ; and there's hot water ; and let me see—yes ; I've got a bit of a lace collar and cuffs, which will look better than that."

While Nellie did as she was told, the elder lady rummaged in drawers and boxes, and at last brought forth a collar and wristbands of fine Brussels point, and a queer oblong gold brooch, with double rows of pearls, blackened with age, set in it.

" I 'll give you this brooch, Nellie," she said, pinning it in the girl's collar as she spoke ; " it was given to me long ago by a man whom, I daresay, your mother recollects— Laurence Lentaigne. He's dead ages ago," she added quickly, seeing a look of curiosity in the young face so close to hers.

They went downstairs now, and had scarcely reached the drawing-room when the company began to arrive. It was already a quarter-past three.

" Mrs. Fitzharmon Dillon, Mrs. Hepenstall, Mrs. Biggs," roared Peter in his broadest Limerick brogue. Another of Peter's tricks when in bad humour was to speak in the coarsest country fashion he could manage. His mistress darted a—

" How are you, me dear Mrs. Biggs ? The children all well ? My *dear* Mrs. Hepenstall ! Back from London ? We'll have tea in one instant, Nellie, love. Oh ! Miss Davoren, my cousin : Mrs. Hepenstall, Mrs. Biggs."

Nellie made a circular reverence, and hastened downstairs to see that Peter was bringing a really boiling urn. She found, as she had anticipated, that he was doing nothing of the kind ; so, as he was called away by a succession of knocks at the door, she took advantage of his absence to enlist the cook's services in the interest of the tea-drinking, and have a properly munitioned tray carried up.

When she returned to the drawing-room she found the

H

" kettledrum" in full swing. She was presented to all the
ladies, who received her graciously enough; and she sat
down by Mrs. Hepenstall, a young married woman with a
good-natured handsome face.

"Dinner at the Chief Secretary's last night." A very
dressy woman was talking in an abrupt, disjointed way.
"Their Excellencies not there—couldn't come. No. What
d'you think we heard? Corrie Vickars, the *aide-de-camp*,
got it from London by telegraph—brother in War Office.
Lord Newmarket—h'm—Lady Oaks! It's been expected
at the clubs this while back."

"Nellie dear, go and make our tea," interrupted Miss
O'Hegarty, nodding in the direction of the sofa-table.

"Lord Oaks went after by the next——"

"No, Blanche," interrupted another lady; "Lord Oaks
missed the *next* train, so he could not overtake them that
night,—he had to wait till next morning."

The Misses Braginton had commenced this anecdote
together, but gradually the younger and weaker had
dropped out of the running, and now seized the opportunity of her elder sister pausing for breath to cut in again
for the finish.

"They say," went on Blanche—Miss Braginton—"that
he missed it *purposely*."

Miss O'Hegarty took off her spectacles and wiped them.
Mrs. Fitzharmon Dillon, who knew nothing whatever of
either party, but who wanted it to appear that she was
conversant with the aristocratic doings on the other side
of the Channel, threw out the following little random shot:—

"Lady Oaks was—ahem—very fast, you know."

"That's evident," snapped Miss Braginton; "but Corrie
Vickars says the betting in London is even that Lord
Oaks will take her back again."

"Especially as Newmarket is so poor, you know:" the
other Miss Braginton brought this out with an insinuating
giggle.

A tall old lady, with a prominent hooked nose and cold
blue eyes, who was seated on a sofa opposite, turned and
looked reprovingly at her.

"Really, Blanche, you do go rather beyond your text. Mr. Vickars, I am certain, has not heard that; oh! come now."

"There are three children," continued Miss Braginton, speaking rapidly, in order to divert the stream of public attention from the channel opened by the snubbing remark of the lady on the sofa.

"Dear! dear me!" said Miss O'Hegarty, "But it's in the blood: look at her mother. You remember the Marquis of Cheltenham scandal? That was her mother, my dear."

Miss O'Hegarty did not know one of these titled people, whose names she now bandied so freely. Neither did she know anybody who did know them. Nevertheless, she could talk of them quite cleverly—even familiarly; and she was as thoroughly versed in all the bearings of her subject as a Court Chamberlain.

"I got my German governess at last," put in Mrs. Hepenstall, impatient of the ill-natured Bragintons; "and brought her home with me from London."

"Ah! did you now? Where did you get her?"

"The Brighams recommended her to me strongly."

"Ah! there now, Mrs. Hepenstall," cut in some one else, "and what is there new in style this time in London? It's ludicrous the way we're behind here."

"Yes; positively we are two years behind Paris!" This from a pretty little lady, who had just come in.

"Paris! Bless us," said the hostess, "we don't think of Paris. London is good enough for us. And I declare only for *Punch* and *Fun*, we'd never know even what clothes they were wearing over there."

"*Punch* does always give the fashionable hats, and the hair too, very correctly," said Mrs. Dillon, who was a county lady; "but *Fun* and *Judy* are not good style."

"No; nothing like *Punch*," went on Mrs. Hepenstall, speaking a little louder, and settling herself back on her chair. "I left sooner than we'd intended. Couldn't trust my chest in London these months." And she coughed in a most interesting manner.

"Tell us, what did you notice in the way of dressing
hair?" This from Miss Braginton, to whom nature had
been rather grudging in this respect, provoked a quickly
stifled smile from the other ladies.

"Well, there were several styles, but the favourite and
best seemed to be that of the Princess of ——. We
saw her last Saturday. The hair all carried up at the
back, quite high under the bonnet, plain and smooth in
front, and generally quite off the face."

"Now," said Miss O'Hegarty, putting on her spectacles,
and deliberately surveying her visitor through them, "how
about bonnets?"

"Oh! really most unsatisfactory. One good thing, you
can wear hats almost anywhere. The bonnets are getting
smaller, and prices larger—in inverse ratio—now. This
is one of Rebons's last from Paris: what do you think of
it?" and Mrs. Hepenstall inclined her head forwards.
After a general inspection and admiration of the lady's very
becoming head-piece, Mrs. Fitzharmon Dillon changed the
subject.

"When did anybody hear of the George Lamberts?"

"Oh!" cried the two Bragintons simultaneously, "she's
off to Nice. He is going on so badly. She says it's for
her health she's going. Don't believe it. You know they
went from this to Leamington. Dee Tee, my dear; and
treats her—oh! frightfully; she never has a penny in her
pocket. Never—for any purpose."

"Poor creature! She has a small settlement, has she
not?" asked Mrs. Hepenstall, in a compassionating tone.

"I don't believe it. I assure you it's quite her own
doings—quite." And the amiable Miss Braginton raised
her voice insistingly. "George Lambert's father, and the
family generally, are quite furious about her: say she
neglected him, running after all sorts of excitement. We
all know when the Buffs were here she never missed a
thing that was going. She quite neglected the man, and
he has taken to drink in consequence."

"It's rather hard on her to say that, now—don't you
think so, Blanche?" put in the frisky matron, who owned

a scampish husband too. A vicious toss of the head was the only notice vouchsafed by Miss Braginton.

"You were a great friend of hers, I thought, Blanche?"

This question came from a tall blonde woman, dressed, as blondes will dress, with a quantity of pale blue about her head and throat; her round cold blue eyes, with lashes and eyebrows of the same whitey yellow as her hair, were turned full on the corner honoured by Miss Braginton's presence.

But she got no answer; for that lady, whose versatility equalled her ill-nature, had gone down to the tea-table to see who the little girl was who was busy pouring out tea alone, and engaged speedily in conversation with her.

"Mrs. De Lancier, won't you have a cup? Do—just one! Nellie!" called the hostess, taking the cup from the lady in the low chair.

She was a Frenchified, stylish-looking little dame, with a head of dyed hair.

"Were you at the Castle on Tuesday evening?"

"Oh yes; I can't say I enjoyed myself, though. I was paired off with that dreadful old Tubbs, the Q.C. Stupid creature! I do hate Buzfuzes. I never spoke to him all dinner-time. Really, only we are obliged to go there, I'd prefer staying away. They do manage things so badly."

"I have heard," began Miss O'Hegarty in a very grave tone, "that they have given great offence there latterly, being so careless about their arrangements. I'm sure in Lord ——'s time—(he went in, you know, for being popular, and all that sort of thing, lugging up all description of rubbish to the Castle, and being that polite and affable to them)—people were greatly annoyed by his going on that way. Just as if everybody was alike and equal in Ireland! At one of the private dinners, sending Solfa, that musician man, you know, down with Miss Sheedy of Castle Sheedy! And it wasn't that he did not know, either. There never was a dinner in his time that there wasn't a rumpus after it on account of the precedence. All just to make himself popular."

"They have no business," began Mrs. Bursford, "turning

the Castle into a scramble of that kind. It's most insulting to the Conservative aristocracy here."

"I assure you," rejoined the hostess, "the drawing-rooms are the very same, if not worse. The Chamberlains must be perfect nonentities; they allow tradespeople of all sorts in; no distinction is observed at all. Really, in London you are safe not to meet that sort of mud. But here, I am told, when the people themselves don't go— these traders and shopkeepers, I mean—they send their daughters, chaperoned by some city celebrity, nobody inquires about them at all, and so the place becomes the insufferable 'omnium gatherum' it is."

A general murmur of indignant assent filled the room, now pretty well stocked with Dorothy's *habitués*. Nellie was busy at the tea-table, but not so busy that she could not catch the substance of what was being said. She was more amused than edified at the airs of the ladies. There was something unreal and artificial about them, polished and refined of manner and appearance as they all were. And knowing as she did the relationship between the Bursfords and Bragintons, she could not help noting and being shocked at their ill-concealed hostility to each other.

"Ah!" said Mrs. Bursford, "in London it really is different. By-the-by, Mrs. Hepenstall, did you see anything of Lady Dacres in London?"

"Er—no. In London it is so hard to see people. They were at their place in Leicestershire. It is really so difficult to see people in London!" Mrs. Hepenstall clearly did not like the question.

"Ah! yes; I should think so," put in Mrs. Dillon. "What an income one requires to live there! Now, when Mr. Dillon was in Parliament"——

"When Mr. Dillon was in Parliament" seemed to be the signal for a general rally of the listeners' forces in opposition to the reminiscences connected with that halcyon time. Miss Braginton threw herself into the fray.

"But it certainly is cheaper to live there than here," cried she with a sudden burst.

"The necessaries of life may be a little cheaper," said

Miss O'Hegarty dogmatically; "but house-rent alone is quite an income. My friend Lady Brooker: her house in—ah, what was the name of it? some terrace in Hyde Park—was over six hundred a year."

The little yellow-haired lady looked up from her tea and the Carlsbad wafer she was nibbling.

"My dear Miss O'Hegarty, we are not all Lady Brookers. There are cheaper parts of London than Hyde Park. It is only the nobility or very rich people who live in the Kensington or Hyde Park quarters.

"Mercy, yes, Mrs. De Lancier! I know you can get houses cheaper in London than you can in any part of Dublin; but in places you couldn't live in. You would be out of society, quite."

"You lived in Belsize Park, now, Mrs. De Lancier."

This was from the second Braginton; but the hostess adroitly shelved the question of topography by turning to Nellie and ordering her to play for the assemblage.

Miss Davoren began a brilliant drawing-room piece, and conversation went on with renewed vigour.

"In London there are twice as many sets and ranks of society as in Dublin." Miss Braginton was determined to keep to the subject.

"But, excuse me, dear Miss Braginton, we make distinctions here that they do not in London. Rich tradesfolk cannot get into society here, as there, on the mere strength of their money. We value position and family far more on this side of the water. Doctors hold a better position here—how it came to be so I cannot tell—than in England."

"And then professionals are the aristocracy of Dublin," said Miss Bursford. "On the whole, I think they are in a better set here too."

"I don't think so," said the little Mrs. De Lancier, with something of a huffy air. "*We* went into an excellent set in England, and we met professionals in every house." And she went away with quite a savage look at the Bragintons.

"I hope Mrs. De Lancier isn't put out, now," said Miss O'Hegarty, a little anxiously, looking at Mrs. Bursford as she spoke.

"Her father was an eminent doctor in England," hastily replied Miss Braginton; "and the mother married a second time—Lieutenant-General Anstruther."

"Oh, ho! If I'd thought that, I'd never have said a word. What a stylish person she is—and so young! Well, since she's English, I'm not altogether sorry she got a knock. I never could endure English people."

"Can't you, now, Miss O'Hegarty?" rejoined Miss Braginton. "So many of our relations are pure English. I assure you we are quite fond of them."

Miss O'Hegarty had one invaluable talent. No matter how grave a conversational *contretemps* might be, whether she had caused it or not, her imperturbability was unequalled. In truth, she seemed rather to court them than otherwise, and dearly loved to administer a good snub or "taking down" when a fair chance offered. On this occasion she looked coolly at the speaker, and noting the glitter of her beady black eyes and the somewhat defiant pose of her head, answered in the same tone—

"I am glad to hear you say so. You have a reason, to be sure, for feeling well disposed towards them; but, for myself, my prejudices are of too old standing."

Nellie, now freed from her duties, covered up her teapots in huge cosies, and coming up to the circle gathered near the fire, seated herself in the velvet chair left vacant by the little Englishwoman.

"I never cared for English people either," said Diana Bursford; "and I am sure on the Continent they are so hated. You see them there to perfection."

"I have known them upset a whole hotel in the middle of the night to look for a bag or umbrella. There wasn't a row at the Kater Saisons last year but what they made." Miss O'Hegarty laid her knitting on her lap. "Don't you recollect, Emma," she continued, turning to Mrs. Bursford, "at Ghent, when poor Maria Gordon was lying so ill at the hotel there,—dying, positively,—and at eleven o'clock one night there arrived an English family? They were told there was a lady upstairs very dangerously ill; and the first inquiry was, of course, as to its being infectious.

No; the landlord assured them it wasn't infectious; but would they please not to make a noise? Upstairs they stormed, calling and shouting and tumbling boxes about. They woke me at the far end of the corridor, and up I jumped and gave them such a talking to. They quieted down when I got the landlady to threaten to turn them out of the house: even that would not keep them quiet. Next morning, at five o'clock, we heard a voice roaring down the corridor—'My bawth. I want a large bawth of cold wataw. I could not exist without a cold bawth evewy morning.' John Gordon ran past the wretch, and called into Maria's room, 'My dear, I hope you're not disturbed. It's only one of these Cook's tourists trying to get up a row on his own account.' We heard no more of the bath, I assure you."

"Well, I don't dislike them, indeed," said Mrs. Hepenstall; "but it is quite true that they are very rude to foreigners at the hotels. I sat next a nice Prussian family at the *table d'hôte* at Gratz; and the lady told me she would sit beside an English family for twenty years, and never address them, for they either do insult, or have the reputation of insulting, every stranger who addresses them."

"Yes," said Mrs. Bursford; "and after all it may be some English cheesemongers who are giving themselves all these airs, and they are never done talking of themselves and their belongings. First what *I* eat, what *I* do, *my* stick, *my* dog."

"I have noticed that," said Mrs. Dillon. "I went over to Paris to bring home Katharine from school, and a lady picked up with me on the boat. All the way up to Paris she talked of nothing but herself, her family, and affairs; and at the end she gave me her card, and asked me to call upon her. 'Wednesday was her at-home day: wouldn't I come?' I just said, 'Thanks exceedingly; but—ah—you forgot I have not even told you my name.'"

Miss Braginton and her sister took their leave now, and the remainder of the visitors drew up their chairs in order to fill up the gap.

The hostess looked around her. "I really think, Miss

Diana, you might give us a song, it is such a time since I
have heard you.   Come along now, do!"

She led Miss Bursford over to the piano.   As that lady
was untying her strings, she whispered to Dorothy, "Who
is that pretty, quiet little thing sitting over there?"

"A cousin of mine, my dear."

"Very pretty indeed—very," returned Diana, glancing
approvingly at Nellie.   "How old might she be, now?"

"Oh, nineteen or so: scarcely nineteen."

"Is that all?   Really, now, I'd have said she was twenty-
two or twenty-three."

"Humph!" returned Dorothy drily, "I fancy she looks
her own age exactly; just like everybody else."

Then she returned to her guests at the fireplace, leaving
Miss Bursford to sing that patriotic ballad, "The Wearing
of the Green."

"Just like her!" thought Dorothy, rather amused, as
she resumed her seat.   "She'd make everybody out to look
older than they really are; I suppose in the hope to get
credit for the same herself.   Augh!"

"Dear me!" cried Mrs. Dillon: "'The Wearing of the
Green.'   Why, we are becoming Fenians altogether!"

"It's quite the rage just now," said Mrs. Bursford.
"Everybody has got it."

"Tell me now, Mrs. Bursford," began Miss O'Hegarty,
leaning forward and speaking in a low confidential tone,
"what's this I hear about Miss Blanche and the O'Gorman
Mulcahy?   She was saying Hanaper and Diesele——eh?"

Miss Braginton was a young lady who, owing to a variety
of reasons, had been rather long on hand; longer a good
deal than her cousin the blonde, Diana Bursford; and between the two there had always been rivalry and jealousy.
Blanche Braginton had played a trick or two in days gone
by on Diana, which would never be forgiven her, the chief
of which was in this wise.

"Diana's fortune was only three thousand pounds, and
this sum had been magnified into five by judicious puffing,
after the usual custom in Ireland—a veritable land of
promise, as far as figures go.   There had been seven or

eight years ago an Honourable Captain Vesey, who had
paid marked attention to Miss Bursford, and who, it was
thought, but for some mischief-maker, would have married
her. Who this mischief-maker was had never been openly
declared; but the mother of the young lady, after seeing
Vesey and Blanche for some time *tête-à-tête* in an ice-room
at a Chief Secretary's ball, made up her mind as to the
delinquent. Nothing could be proved. Vesey was an
embarrassed man, and went to Abyssinia. All his friends
declared there never had been anything in it; Diana's
complexion quite went off, and she and her mother left for
Italy. It was no use attempting open hostilities—the cousins
were in the same set; but all the same the offence was never
forgotten; and Mrs. Bursford found many opportunities of
revenge.

One peculiarity of the amiable Miss Braginton was that
she always fancied herself to be the recipient of matrimonial
overtures from one or more eligible parties. According to
the lady herself, settlements were eternally in process of
being drawn up; but at the last moment the papa or
sister interposed, and "the thing was off."

On all these histories Aunt Bursford cast scornful incredulity. Nothing was more amusing to their respective
friends than to hear Miss Blanche's accounts, and then to
witness the methodical way in which her aunt would sit
down and flatly contradict and ridicule every one of her
statements. Certainly, for the few months the Brayheads
patronised Dublin, Blanche's "engagements," thanks to her
aunt Bursford, were the stock diversion of her set.

Mrs. Bursford's eyes kindled, and she shook herself together in her chair. "The O'Gorman Mulcahy! Trash
and nonsense! Miss O'Hegarty, how can you imagine for
an instant there is anything in it? A man with grand-
children, and mortgaged to the chin. I have no patience
with the Bragintons——"

"Mamma," interposed Mrs. Bursford's daughter, who
had finished her song and had returned to her chair; "we
don't know,—there may be something in it."

"Now, Diana, don't be absurd; were we not at Hanaper

and Diesele's this very morning? and do you suppose for
an instant they would know anything of this and not tell
us? O'Gorman Mulcahy indeed!—as if he had not enough
encumbrances without taking home a penniless old woman!
Blanche is nothing else." Mrs. Bursford emphasised this
statement with a glance at Mrs. Dillon, who she guessed
would carry the intelligence to the Mulcahy family, as she
was on visiting terms with them.

"How late you are, dear Mrs. O'Hara!" and the hostess
welcomed a lady accompanied by two blooming girls—
Galway beauties, in town for the season. "Nellie dear,
take these young ladies down there, and see if you have a
cup of tea for them."

"You are up for a good while this time, I hope, Mrs.
O'Hara," said handsome Mrs. Hepenstall. "You must excuse me : we dine at the Chief Justice's to-night." Some
of the others followed ; and the Bursfords and the last
arrivals were almost the only ones left. Peter lighted the
chandelier, and drawing the curtains, shut out the cheerless
gray evening. The room looked all the brighter and
better, and the fine red cheeks of the O'Hara girls glowed
in the clear light of the wax candles.

"What kept you so late, Mrs. O'Hara? and where were
you this long time?"

"Shopping, my dear Miss O'Hegarty, for the Cattle
Show ; buying no end of things."

"Getting everything into campaigning order, hey,
Peggy?" cried Miss O'Hegarty, with a meaning nod.
"Look out for the Brazilian : he is to be there. How uncommonly well they look, to be sure!" she added, turning
to the mother.

"Well, I'm sure it's something to hear of a catch like
that," said Mrs. Bursford ; "it's not every day Dublin can
boast of such *partis.*"

"Quite true," assented the Galway matron, with a sigh ;
"and Dublin is that overdone with girls now, I'm sure if
they would only make up their minds to it, they would do
far better in the country. *I* never saw Dublin till I was
married."

"I never saw it either," said Mrs. Bursford. "And tell me, Mrs. O'Hara, is this South American really substantial, now? For myself, I prefer something on the spot—it is much more satisfactory, you know."

"I agree with you there," said the hostess; "but indeed times are changed; young ladies can't be picking and choosing now, as they did when I was a girl." And the veteran gave a twitch to her cap-strings.

"Indeed they are, Miss O'Hegarty," assented her compeers.

"She must have picked and chosen with a vengeance," murmured the second O'Hara girl, a saucy, black-eyed thing, not quite eighteen.

"Well, I declare!" said Mrs. Bursford, "there are no *partis* now. This new arrival, they say, has a——" (dropping her voice discreetly) "well, a tale—fact—not safe at all. Mrs. Soames had a letter from her son, warning her not to allow the Soames' girls to have anything to say to him. He wouldn't say why. Men never do tell on each other, you know."

"Dear, dear!" said Miss O'Hegarty; "there's not a good match in the market, I do declare. There's that Saltasche man, to be sure; I'm sure the conceit of him is wonderful."

"Oh, he's not to be caught!" cried Mrs. O'Hara; "that fellow won't marry, take my word for it. His game is playing up to high society. He can't marry there; and if he marries in his own set, he will have to give up his aristocratic tastes. But he'll never be caught."

"I daresay not. I can fancy his sort from what I've heard of him; and most likely the wretch is married to his cook on the sly."

"I fancied," said Mrs. O'Hara, "that last year he was paying great attention to one of those Fitzharmons of Coolmagrah—cousins of your friend Mrs. Dillon."

"Oh yes, mamma," said Miss Bursford. "Don't you recollect our seeing them all together at Ostend? They had lost a boat, or missed a train, and there they were sitting on top of their trunks."

"Don't I remember it ? There were a whole crowd of people ; and the Fitzharmons had drawn up their trunks, and were perched on top of them, eating biscuits and talking of the 'Cawstle' at the pitch of their voices. They had Mr. Saltasche with them—most devoted, to all appearance. The boasting and bragging of those Fitzharmons, it was really sickening ! "

"Now, really," said Mrs. O'Hara, not without a touch of dry humour in her voice, "I thought it was only the English who went on like that abroad, Mrs. Bursford."

"Indeed, then I assure you," rejoined Miss O'Hegarty, "wherever you hear loud boasting and bragging on the Continent, be sure our countrymen are not far off."

"Even so, now, maintained Mrs. Bursford, "they never are in the upsetting, dogmatic style of the English : besides, Miss O'Hegarty, the Irish you mean are those would-be English that are always talking of their Norman blood, and would not be Irish *in* Ireland for any consideration. I know them. When they go to England they change their tone, then it's *Ipsis Hibernis Hiberniores*, more Irish than the Irish, with them."

"They want to be Irish aristocracy over there, you may be sure ; and so well they may, for it's the only feather in their cap, once they're across the water." And Miss O'Hegarty gave her head an emphatic shake. "And this Mr. Saltasche was doing the civil to the Fitzharmons, you say, Mrs. Bursford ? "

"Well, I don't see," said Diana Bursford, "why Mr. Saltasche should be attentive to those Coolmagrah people, since he has the *entrée* of the houses of people of rank—as we know he has."

"Ah ! my dear," said Dorothy, "they have business relations together ; that's the reason of the intimacy—if intimacy there be—between him and Lord Brayhead."

"Intimacy ! Miss O'Hegarty. Why, he is a great personal friend of the family. We are to meet him at Brayhead House this day fortnight, and their Excellencies are to be there." And Miss Diana Bursford looked all round her with an air of superiority.

"Ah !—a dinner. Anybody in the evening?" asked Miss O'Hegarty.

"No," hastily interpolated Mrs. Dillon—who, though ostensibly engaged in confidential conversation with an old lady on the sofa, lost not a syllable of what was being said, and seized the opportunity to show off to her country neighbour, Mrs. O'Hara, that she was in such a good set— "nobody in the evening. We're—er—(this was drawled out with an air of affected indifference)—"thinking of going." She would have died sooner than have missed the dinner, and was only asked by the Brayheads because of a coming election in their county.

"We met Lord Brayhead to-day, he was talking in the office with Mr. Saltasche and that young barrister, his friend Mr.—ah—ah—O'Rooney—Hogan," said Diana Bursford.

A teacup crashed into its saucer at the other end of the room, where the young girls were together.

"It is not broken, Cousin Dorothy," said Nellie, with a perceptible tremor in her voice.

Impelled by some sudden and irresistible impulse, the girl rose from her place and advanced to the group at the fire. ' She passed round the back of Miss O'Hegarty's chair under pretext of ringing the bell.

"O'Rooney Hogan," repeated her cousin, trying to remember where she had heard the name before. "R. C., I imagine ?"

"Yes," said Miss Bursford; "his uncle is a Bishop, I believe."

"Bishop—hey ? R. C. Bishops don't count for much. They're useful relatives, though," returned the old lady, flashing a keen look over her spectacles at Diana.

Mrs. Bursford took out her watch. "Positively six, my dear Diana. Good-bye, Miss O'Hegarty." In a minute or two the room was emptied of the visitors. Miss O'Hegarty took off her spectacles and wiped them, then rose from her chair and yawned.

"Well, Nellie, how did you like them? Tired, eh?" Nellie was pale, and she was looking thoughtfully into the fire. "Do you like your own people best?"

Nellie only smiled in answer: her thoughts were busy with the tall Diana Bursford and Mr. Saltasche. To think of Mr. Hogan knowing these two people!

"Miss Bursford is handsome; and so stylish!" she said.

"Hum—she was better looking. Those blondes fade so. She's a long time on hand now, and would take any one, I do believe. She is quite tired of trapesing about. Bless me!—Harrogate, Brighton, Scarborough,—what hasn't Emily Bursford tried for that girl? Poor Di!" And the elderly lady smiled half maliciously. "It's very hard for girls to get married in our set," continued she, after a pause. "You can see what they are for yourself. Only for her cousins, Di. Bursford would have been married long before. One man to every hundred girls—I do believe that's the proportion—and all the women devouring each other for the sake of him. It's a frightful state of things. Look at those Bragintons: actually their own blood relations are not safe from them. There's no such thing as friendship; even relations are not friends now-a-days; one has only acquaintances. The struggle for existence has become too keen for it. Really," said she, stooping down to caress a huge black cat which had just taken his place on the rug, "only it's not my nature, I'd turn against society just as Toby does: he's a misanthrope now, is Toby. Sweet old monster! I wonder did Peter give him any dinner?"

"Toby doesn't care for any one," returned Nellie absently.

"He's a misanthrope, my dear," said his owner, "he disappears from my afternoon teas, and never comes back till the last of the visitors is gone."

Nellie now announced her intention of going home. Dorothy's talk jarred upon her nerves, and made her feel fidgety; and she wanted to be alone to think over what she had heard. So she set off, escorted by Peter, and in about an hour's time reached Church House. She crept up noiselessly to her mother, whom she found awake and uncomplaining. Mrs. Davoren was anxious to hear all the details of Dorothy's entertainment. So Nellie related everything. The invalid heard her—listlessly enough. When she mentioned the Bursfords' names, her face kindled a little, and her eyes dilated with a fixed bright look. She raised her head a little.

"The Bursfords? Yes. Ah! Emily hasn't married her girl yet. Let me see, Diana is older than Jervis. Yes. She must be thirty-two or thirty-three at least. Was it seventeen or—or—— ?" But the light faded from the invalid's eyes, the delicate flush paled on her thin cheeks, the memory had lapsed again, and she turned her face away with a petulant and drowsy expression. After a moment or two her eyes fell on Nellie's brooch.

"Where did you get that, dear ?" she asked, with a sudden return of interest.

"Oh, mamma," cried Nellie eagerly, "Dorothy gave it to me: and, mamma, she said you knew who gave it to her: Laurence Lentaigne. And she unpinned the little brooch, and put it in her mother's hand."

A bright flush passed quickly over Mrs. Davoren's face, and as quickly faded again. She laid down the little oblong bit of gold with the rows of blackened pearls on its edges.

"Laurie Lentaigne!" she repeated. "I hope it won't prove an unlucky gift, Nellie. Laurence Lentaigne was the name of the man who broke Dorothy's heart nearly thirty years ago."

CHAPTER VIII.

TWELVE o'clock, or, as it is more often termed, "last" Mass, was greatly crowded on the occasion of Father O'Hea preaching the closing Advent sermon. The reverend father was one of the best preachers in Dublin—in Ireland, perhaps. He was one of the favoured few who are born with the real oratorical talent; and like most natural geniuses, let those theorists who pretend the divine spark is due to fortuitous circumstances say what they will, had found at an early age his special vocation. Culture and practice had enhanced the precious gift to the utmost; and Father O'Hea was perhaps at this period without a rival in any part of the world—as regarded his power of attracting hearers.

In a prominent seat near the High Altar was the Lady Mayoress, accompanied by her daughters and her husband's secretary. The Raffertys, gorgeous as usual, were not far removed; and the sanctuary was crowded with the *élite* of Father O'Hea's admirers and supporters. In a central seat were Dicky Davoren and Nellie, and with them Mr. Mulcahy, now one of Miss Davoren's devoted squires. The Brangans, the Muldoons, the Gogarties,—everywhere he turned his eyes Hogan saw some one whom he knew. Right opposite him was the Bishop; and from him our young friend, who had come in late, received a reproving glance.

High Mass was sung; and when the benediction had been pronounced, and the silks and velvets had fluttered and rustled into their seats again, expectant eyes were turned on the vestry door. The organ finished a loud symphony, prayer-books were clasped noisily ; and when at last the little door swung open, and the tall figure of the great orator, clad in the picturesque robes of his order, strode forth, a hush of breathless admiration filled the great building. After a moment of prayer before the High Altar rails the priest ascended the pulpit, and, having read the text, commenced his sermon. It was, as usual, a masterpiece. The person and bearing of the speaker lent an additional force to every powerful sentence. His was indeed a remarkable countenance. Burning black eyes looked out from beneath arched, deep-cut brows ; eyes that looked all the blacker for the clear pale olive of the cheeks and forehead ; a large well-shaped and flexible mouth ; and hands so apt and skilled of movement that they seemed to speak in unison with the lips.

The greatest charm, however, the most effective weapon in all his well-burnished armoury, was his Irish brogue,— broad, rich, and resonant, lending itself to every mood ; now rising loud in a passionate storm of denunciation, now sinking low as a whisper, yet distinct and clear as a silver bell. No tongue nor dialect, voice nor accent, has the power of an Irish brogue in persuasion or exhortation. At first, the variety of tones, the grotesque cadences and inflections, strike strangely upon an unaccustomed ear ; but by degrees the earnest manner and language, the consummate skill with which the subject is presented, appeal' to and draw away the attention, the novelty becomes dulled or forgotten, the sympathies are awakened and excited, and the all-embracing enthusiastic sweep of eloquence leads the mind captive.

Hogan, from beside a huge pillar against which he was leaning, looked admiringly at the speaker. Not a gesture escaped his appreciating eye. It was not without a touch of envy that he noted Father O'Hea's triumph. How thin and cold his own outpourings were as compared with this ! He consoled himself by the reflection that the religious *genre* of oratory had its special advantages. The fervid burning adjurations of the priest to his flock would be out of place were the audience to consist of the dozen of thick-headed jurymen; and above all, reflected the barrister, there was nobody to pull him up in his gallop, no sharp-eyed counsel on the other side to interpose carpings and contradictions. And Hogan leaned back and surveyed the crowd of richly dressed people all intent on every word,— the women now pale, now red, and many of them with tear-filled eyes. He ran his eye quickly along the benches in search of one particular face: up and down each end, beginning with the gas bracket at the top, down to the end at the wall, where hung a gaudy Station picture.

At last Dicky's roving eyes met his with a glance of recognition; and beside him, in full relief against the dark fur cloak of a lady next her, appeared the clear, cameo-like profile of Nellie Davoren. Her eyes were fixed intently on the preacher. Hogan rapidly noted her dress, in order not to lose sight of her in the crowd going out; and then, mindful of the Bishop's watchful gray eyes, resumed his pose of edified attentiveness. Father O'Hea's brilliant peroration fell on heedless ears in Hogan's case; if his eyes were riveted on his face, his ears were listening to other strains, and instead of the burning words of the preacher, the clear, low voice of Nellie Davoren in imaginative tones filled his whole being.

The sermon over, the entire congregation poured out of the benches and thronged the passages.

The Bishop of Secunderabad, who wanted to join his friend Mrs. Rafferty, executed a dexterous flank movement and came up with that lady's party before they had reached the main door. The Lady Mayoress, who in her turn was being pursued by Mrs. Rafferty, halted for a moment in the porch to greet her friends. Once outside the sanctuary, all tongues were loosened. Hogan and the Davorens joined the party; the Misses Malowney and Rafferty and their various satellites poured down the steps, laughing and chattering.

"Your ladyship is coming over to lunch with us? It's only just a step. Oh, me lord!—ah, now, Mr. Hogan, prevail on Dr. O'Rooney to come and take a glass of wine." So spoke Mrs. Rafferty, on hospitality intent.

The Bishop was easy enough to persuade, and stepped into the civic coach which was in readiness, accompanied by Mrs. Rafferty and Mrs. Malowney. Hogan followed on foot with the young people, who all chose to walk; and the Raffertys' great green-and-gold liveried carriage drove off empty.

"Will you go down to the Pier to-day, Eily?" cried Miss Brangan, who rushed across the street to join her friends. She spoke *to* Miss Eily Rafferty, but *at* Mr. Dicky Davoren, the "young gentleman with the lovely humbuggin' eyes."

"No, Mary, we can't to-day; you know we must be at home for the people calling after the ball."

"Oh, sure, I forgot. How do you do, Mr. Davoren?"

Dicky had advanced, in gallant acknowledgment of the young lady's glances, to renew their acquaintance.

"How did you like the sermon to-day? Was it not splendid? I saw you were quite moved, Miss Brangan." The collegian had had his eyes about him, and had noted the young lady's total indifference to everything but the bonnets and "young gentlemen of her vicinity."

"Yes, indeed," she answered, with charming candour; "wasn't he lovely? Such an angel as that Father O'Hea— Oh! I thought I'd ha' died."

"Oh dear! you oughtn't to let your susceptibilities run away with you like that. 'Pon my word, I was alarmed for you, Miss Brangan. Look: by Jove, there goes Father O'Hea himself."

An outside car passed at that moment, carrying the preacher across town to his monastery. He smiled and bowed to the pedestrians.

"He's coming to dinner with us to-day," said one of the Raffertys, in a boasting tone. "Oh gracious! I mustn't forget to practise the accompaniments to the melodies. I disgraced meself intirely last time I played the 'Minstrel Boy' for him."

"Here we are. Come in, Miss Brangan: where's your papa?" Mr. Rafferty led the way in, and the whole troop poured in and up to the drawing-room. Here they

found those who had preceded them. Bishop O'Rooney
and Mrs. Malowney were seated on a big sofa near the
fire ; a great many of the guests had also arrived, and conversation became general.

"I hope your ladyship wasn't fatigued after Tuesday
night?" asked the lady of the house.

"'Deed, no, then ; I enjoyed meself so much. I'm
never so wearied intirely as when I've got to go to them
dinners at the Castle. Not but what their Excellencies is
kindness itself, an' everything lovely. Ye had an iligant
ball, then, Mrs. Rafferty."

"I'm really glad your ladyship liked it. I think everybody enjoyed it. It was the greatest pity but your lordship
could honour us," added Mrs. Rafferty jestingly, looking at
the Bishop.

"My dancing days are over, ma'am," returned Dr.
O'Rooney, entering into the humour of her joke, with a
mock sigh of regret, stretching one neat foot a little in
advance. "We leave the young people to do that for us
now. We must look on, just,"—and his lordship glanced
at the chattering groups behind him. He honoured Miss
Davoren with a keen scrutiny from under his brows, while
offering a pinch of snuff to Mr. Rafferty.

"Might I ask you who is the young lady in gray with
the fur jacket?" he asked of his neighbour, dropping his
voice discreetly.

"A Miss Davoren. She was here the other night."

"Davoren?" repeated the Bishop, vainly trying to connect the name with some half-forgotten reminiscence.

"Her father is in the Castle."

Then the party were marshalled down to lunch, and the
Bishop led off the mistress of the house, noting, as he did
so, that his nephew was giving his arm to the young lady
in gray with the fur jacket, instead of improving his opportunity with the Misses Malowney, Rafferty, or any other
of the eligible and advantageous connections in the room.

"Did your ladyship observe the bride at mass?" asked
some one of Mrs. Malowney, in the intervals of champagne
popping.

"Beautifully dressed, was she not?" interposed a daughter of the house.

"I·don' know, thin," said her ladyship deliberately. "I don' fancy that violent coloured bonnet becomes her at all."

"Violet! mamma," shrieked Anastatia Eily, from the opposite side of the table.

"Vi'let, then," repeated her ladyship, dutifully, but with a trace of asperity. "It's all wan as the same."

Hogan's eyes sought Nellie's for a moment; and in spite of her efforts to the contrary, a faint flash of amazement escaped hers. Dicky and Mr. Mulcahy jogged each other's elbows and grinned convulsively; but whether it was due to stupidity or politeness, scarce a trace of consciousness was betrayed by the rest of the company.

"Malowney's gone over to London last night," said the Lady Mayoress, in reply to a question of the Bishop's. "Gone on wan of thim depitations."

"Oh yes, to be sure—the depitation. I was wanted to go," said Rafferty, pompously.

"'Tis well you were out of it," said his wife; "last night was so stormy and wild."

"'Twas so: God keep us all," piously assented her ladyship. She then finished her *galantine*, and announced her intention of starting, as she had promised to visit a convent out of town.

Hogan, meantime, was dividing his attentions pretty equally between the Raffertys and Nellie Davoren.

"You danced immensely, Miss Malowney; but I really think, Miss Rafferty, *you* went ahead altogether. Poor Mr. Dooley!" Mr. Dooley was a brother of the gentleman who was to marry Miss Malowney.

"Oh! Aloysia Mary! oh, oh!" and the other young ladies giggled sympathetically.

"How many waltzes, now? just tell us, Miss——" But here Hogan became aware, from the quick glance that ran round the bevy of girls, and the warning elevation of her eyebrows by the young lady addressed, that he was trespassing on dangerous ground; and he stopped suddenly.

Miss Malowney laughed, and glanced up to the Bishop's
end of the table; but his lordship was busy with Mr.
Rafferty, and heard, or seemed to hear, nothing.

"What matter?" said Dicky Davoren; "we're not his
penitents; and Mr. Hogan won't let him tell the 'Car'nal'
on us."

"'Tis no sin to dance fast," declared Miss Brangan, emphatically, "when you don't think it a sin; an' I don't."

"Yes; that's the only way to do," affirmed a Miss
Malowney; "an' then you don't need to confess it.
Father O'Flanagan himself told us he couldn't give us
absolution for dancing fast, but if we did not consider it
a sin we needn't confess it."

"Capital dodge!" said Dicky approvingly. "Mul., my
boy, that's a wrinkle for us. I'll make short work of
'scraping my kettle' next time,"—and the collegians
chuckled together.

"Ah!" laughed Hogan; "I must make a note of it too."

Just then the Bishop rose; and Hogan, in duty bound,
got up also to accompany him.

"Tell me, ladies, are any of you to be at the concert for
the soldiers' widows and orphans next week?" As he
spoke, his eyes sought Nellie's with a look of questioning
and almost entreaty.

"We won't be there, I don't think," said the eldest of
the Raffertys: "isn't it a Protestant concert?"

"What's a Protestant concert?" asked Bishop O'Rooney,
on his way to the door, looking questioningly at his
nephew.

"I don't know on earth," replied Hogan, speaking to
the young lady. "I only saw it advertised. But I fancy
it is."

"If the Lord Mayor goes we'll be there,—not otherwise," said Rafferty.

The Bishop and his nephew now left the party. When
they got into the street the Bishop proposed a trip to
Kingstown for a turn on the Pier before going to the
Convent of St. Swithin, where he had to give Benediction,
and to whose prioress Hogan owed a visit.

"Just two," said his lordship, consulting his watch. "Let's walk fast and catch the two o'clock; then we shall just have time for a constitutional, and I'll be back by four for Benediction."

They arrived at Kingstown in about half an hour; and taking his nephew's arm, the Bishop started for a smart walk to the Lighthouse. It was a clear gray day—mild, as it sometimes is before Christmas; not a breath of wind curled the water, which lay steel-coloured under the murky sky. Scarce any ships were at anchor; half a dozen dun-coloured fishing-smacks hung windbound out under the cliffs of Howth. The man-of-war lay like "a painted ship upon a painted ocean," and the mailboat getting her fires made down for the evening trip seemed the only thing that gave sign of life. The steam tugs were out in the bay, cruising for customers, Sunday as it was. It was yet too early for the regular promenaders to appear; except nurse-maids and children, and a few of the resident dowagers, who always come down early, to secure good seats, the pier was all but deserted.

They walked on in silence for ten minutes—striding along with the business-like air of men who are taking a walk for the good of their limbs.

Hogan was the first to speak.

"How do you like the Raffertys, sir?"

"Very well indeed," replied the Bishop in a cordial tone,—"very well; fine house, good style altogether; they seem inclined to be very civil people. The young ladies are better than Assumption gave me to expect."

"Hah! reverend Mother knows them, then?"

"Of course she does," returned the Bishop. "She had them all there at school—at least, barring the last two years, when they were sent off to England somewhere. She was very angry at that."

"The papa and mamma wanted them to get the accent, I suppose?" said Hogan. "They didn't succeed, if my ears are good for anything: ha! ha!"

"No," said his lordship, with a dry little laugh, "it isn't everybody can improve his opportunities in this life." And he sighed as if the weight of some of his own shortcomings oppressed him. "Assumption thought one of them likely to enter. That second girl—at least, she was when she had her—she told me she had strong hopes of her. 'Twould have been such a good connection for the convent —and she's a fine musician, I'm told; but that going over to England has changed her entirely."

"Evidently," said Hogan, laughing heartily.

"That little Miss Davoren, now, who's she?" asked the Bishop, in an inquisitorial tone.

"A nice, ladylike little girl," returned the barrister in his most careless voice, looking away across the harbour as he spoke.

"Some of them told me she never was at school at all," went on the Bishop, in a doubting tone, as if that fact were incompatible with the account just given of the young lady by his nephew.

"She sings, and paints beautifully, all the same," returned the young man, with the slightest touch of impatience. "At least," he added, offhandedly, "I'm told so by Mulcahy, who seems quite gone about her."

To this the Bishop made no reply.

Afternoon service was going on as they passed the man-of-war; and the strains of a hymn, sung by some hundreds of men, reached their ears across the water. The Bishop had a musical ear, and but for the bad example of seeming to favour heretical ceremonies, would have stopped and listened for a minute to the fine harmony of the Old Hundredth; but he passed on without paying any attention. Climbing the steps to the top of the wall at the end of the pier, they stood and looked out seawards. Howth, save a faint, shadowy profile, was invisible, wrapped in a pale veil of sea mist. Killiney stood out bare and bleak, all its rocks looking red and cold. No green foliage or sunlight relieved the lines of white and yellow terraces along the bay. Everything seemed leaden, and the sullen rise and fall of the water on the rampart behind them struck with a monotonous iteration on their ears; a damp, chill breeze came across the bay from the north-east.

Hogan buttoned up his coat, and stood a moment viewing the wintry sea before them.

"Time we faced about, my lord," said he, taking out his watch.

"Tell me," said the Bishop, when they had descended to the promenade again, "how goes it with your friend Saltasche? What's he up to since?"

"Nothing particular since, sir. He's getting up a company, with a capital of a hundred thousand, to work Lord Brayhead's slate and granite quarries, somewhere about Leadmines, wherever that is. He wants me to be a director."

"Hey! but the qualifications, sir?"

"Oh, well! a thousand or so is qualification, you see. And I have a precious amount of work to do for them, and may as well take payment in shares as not. That will help to make it up."

"What are the shares issued at?"

"Not settled yet, sir. There's some idea of a railway to be built in that direction. I expect the Bill will be passed next session. It's to run parallel with that one."

"Humbug! Where's the traffic to come from? That region is almost a desert: I know it well, God knows; I spent ten or twelve years of my life in it." And the Bishop heaved a regretful sigh.

"Whatever the slate company may do, the railway won't obtain, I fear; at least, not in London," said Hogan dubiously.

"No, you might bet upon that. Those English are so jealous of Irish undertakings, they never will subscribe a *sou*."

"Ahem! You know, sir, they have it always to throw at us that we don't manage our railways so as to pay any decent sort of dividend."

"We ain't up to their dodges? No, I suppose not," retorted the inconsequent Bishop, who was incorrigible on some points.

Hogan let this pass. At any other time he would have diverted himself by holding a passage at arms with the old gentleman; but, having drunk two glasses of Mr.

Rafferty's excellent dry champagne, he felt the least bit
drowsy and good-humoured, and so contented himself with
an indolent movement of the chin that might have stood
for assent or dissent.   They walked on now in silence for
a good stretch of the dry sandy reach.   Everything looked
dull and cheerless, and Hogan wished himself back at his
work by the fireside in Canal Terrace.   This was not to
be, however; for the Lady Prioress of St. Swithin's had
to be visited after the Benediction, and after that came a
dinner party at the Muldoons', where there was to be, as
usual, a collection of priests, and from which Mr. Hogan
would not dare to absent himself.

"If we remain here much longer, my lord," said Hogan,
"we shall be encountering our friends; and then, how
about the next express?"

"Come along," said his lordship.   "Last Sunday I was
a full quarter late; an' Assumption hates them to be kept
waiting."

They hastened on, and took their seats in a first-class
compartment.   Scarcely had they done so when a stout
short man rushed in after them.   "Me dear Bishop, how
do ye do?   Hogan, I'm delighted to see you.   Taking a
turn on the pier?"   Without waiting for a word, he went
on, "Meself was down calling on the O'Gorman Mulcahy;
he's at the Marine, in bad health, poor fellow!"   Just then
the speaker turned his jolly red face towards the platform,
and, catching sight of some one, plunged half out of the
window, roaring at the full pitch of his voice, "How are
ye, Judge?   Come in here, Judge!   Room for ye here,
Judge!   'Tis Judge Costelloe," he explained in an aside to
Hogan and the Bishop, drawing in his head as he did so.   This
momentary delay was fatal.   Another attorney who had
also stuck his head out of window to hail the great man
was successful, and landed his prize on the seat beside him.
Hogan was not sorry for Mr. Muldoon's disappointment.
The fellow would have kicked up a frightful row all the
way; and Judge Costelloe, a most retiring, quiet man,
would have been seriously annoyed.   Besides, Hogan preferred to make the personal acquaintance of the Judge

through a more aristocratic medium than Mr. Corney Muldoon.

"The Lord Mayor is in London," observed Hogan.

"Ay," said the attorney, "and a deputation with him. Nice little bill there'll be for that journey; and all for a humbug. Look at Lord Ramines: look! look!"

Hogan, who was now sitting at the window opposite Muldoon, cleverly caught the eye of the gentleman referred to, an aristocratic and very dissipated-looking man, and was honoured with a nod of recognition as he hurriedly jumped in.

"Do you know him, Mr. Hogan?" asked the attorney, in quite a respectful tone.

The express train darted off with a jolt and scream that hindered Mr. Hogan's answer from being heard very intelligibly; and Muldoon engaged the Bishop in conversation until they reached Westland Row.

"They'll go down with a run, my lord, you may take my word for it," the attorney was saying, as the express slackened speed at the platform.

"You'd advise me to sell at once," asked the Bishop in an eager whisper, "hey, Muldoon?"

"Sold me own yesterday afternoon. Stonelock says there's a fair demand yet."

"Hah," said the Bishop, nodding his head as he took the attorney's arm to get out.

At five minutes past four the Bishop and his nephew drove up to the wide green gate of St. Swithin's. The green gate had a sliding panel set in it; and after they had rung at one of the small doors by which it was flanked, the face of a nun appeared at this, and smiling pleasant recognition to the visitors, speedily unlocked and held open the door for them to pass in.

"Day, day, Veronica: how's your toothache?" said the Bishop. Sister Mary Veronica, a jolly-looking lay sister, plumped down on her knees and kissed the Bishop's ring before answering. She was the lay sister whose duty it was to wait on him at breakfast, and open the hall door and the gate; consequently they were well acquainted with each other.

"Mr. Hogan, I'm very glad to see you. Reverend Mother will be so delighted!" And she laughed and chuckled as if she had uttered the best joke in the world. Then she turned and led the way across the front to the hall door.

How quiet and still and gray it all was! Hogan asked himself, could it be the same house that he had seen last summer? The big stone convent looked bleak and cold; the yellow blinds were all pulled down, no gas lighted yet, and only the red flickering of the fires showed at some of the ground-floor windows. A narrow grass plot, bordered by a walk which was planted with stiff evergreens and rows of chestnuts, was before the house. A double row of poplars, now bare and wintry-looking, in summer screened the wall which ran all round and kept out "the world" and all inquisitive eyes. Behind were the gardens, and another small patch, gravelled, but planted with trees, and furnished with swings and poles, which served as a recreation-ground for the children.

They reached the hall door, which was half glass and neatly curtained with white muslin. Veronica opened it, and ran off to announce their arrival and ring the bell for Benediction. His lordship plunged down a dark passage leading to the vestry; and Hogan, taking a tiny ivory-bound prayer-book out of his pocket, went by another route to the convent chapel.

A bell began to clang noisily. The scuffling and whispering of the boarders could be heard as they hastened to assemble in order of procession. Dark-robed figures flitted past in the dim twilight—the rattle of the huge rosaries alone betraying their presence. A little nun ran by, swinging a big thurible newly kindled from one of the parlour fires, and leaving a long stream of aromatic odour behind her. They had reached a big door set in a white sharp-pointed arch. Sister Veronica appeared with her office-book in her hand, and opened it; and Hogan entered. Beside the door, in the inside, stood a white-winged figure holding back with one hand a red velvet curtain which hung before the door, and in the other presenting a vase of holy water. Hogan dipped in a finger, and then, without turning an eye to the right or the left, took his place in the topmost of the three benches reserved for strangers.

The chapel, a small structure of Gothic style, and exactly proportioned, was exceedingly pretty; and the stained windows admitted a soft, rich light which set out its beauties admirably. The walls were painted cream-colour. The gilded frames of the pictures, and the deep crimsons of the carpet, and the richly-worked *priedieu* chairs, gave it a warm and comfortable look. The altar, of Carrara marble, beautifully carved and inlaid, was decked with superb bronze candelabra, the gift of a wealthy convert. These were filled with wax candles, which the sacristan sister was busily lighting; vases of wax flowers filled the spaces between the candles, and the jewelled monstrance lay ready on the snowy altar-cloth. The Bishop's faldstool stood at one side; and an embroidered cushion marked the place of the officiant at the foot of the altar. The organ began the instant the vestry door opened, and the fresh voices of the nuns and children rose together in the hymn. A few old ladies who were boarding in the house were the only lay persons in the chapel—the children being sequestered in a gallery above the enclosure railed off for the nuns.

The little chapel was warm and close; and Hogan laid down his head on his hands and yawned to his heart's content. He could with difficulty keep his eyes open; and the thick white incense that rose from the thurible was almost stifling. The ceremony did not last long, however. The Bishop, though dignified in his movements, was anything but slow; and in something less than twelve minutes Hogan found himself in the reverend Mother Prioress's own private parlour. Here there was a magnificent fire blazing; and Sister Veronica fussily lighted the gaselier, and with vast clatter produced from a cupboard wine-glasses, decanters, and cake. The bishop made his appearance ere long from an opposite door, and installed himself in a cozy easy-chair by the fireside.

"My word, Veronica," said he, rubbing his hands, "that is a fire you have!"

"And what an exquisite fireplace you keep, sister," said Hogan, admiring the brilliancy of the cut-steel fittings; "not a speck of dirt, even in the corners."

"Dirty corners is velial sins," cackled Veronica, running to open the door for the reverend Mother, whose familiar footstep she heard outside.

"Hah! are they? I wish people 'in the world' thought so," returned Hogan, thinking of the contrast presented by his own fireplace.

The Mother Superior now entered. The cold weather agreed with her, and gave her a fine healthy colour. She was a tall woman, as we said before, and her trailing Sunday robes gave her an immense look of dignity. She had a merry, cheerful face, with keen gray eyes—the O'Rooney eyes exactly; bushy brows, and large white teeth gleaming in a wide mouth, which seemed always smiling, but which could wear a determined look at times.

"My lord!" and down she too plumped on her knees: a most aggravating practice. "John, my dear child: ah now! and where were you this long time?" and the Prioress shook him by both hands affectionately. "Dear bless us—what a settled-looking man you're growing!"

"Hard work! ma'am. You look very well; blooming, indeed."

"Hum—thank God, I am. I haven't time to be ill. A great school we have now. I got eight new pupils to-day,—all from the country. Three Miss Sheas, from Peatstown. It's a great affair. They're taking every extra."

"Every extra—ho, ho!" said the Bishop approvingly: well knowing what a sum the innumerable list of accomplishments would total up.

"When are you going to take my advice, and make them all learn Latin and mathematics?" asked Hogan; "what will they do with wax flowers and the use of the globes down in Peatstown?"

"Latin, John!" returned her reverence with a little

scream; "augh now, Jig Polthogue would be more in their line a great deal."

"Indeed! why teach them Italian, then, ma'am?" returned he pertinently.

"Give them just what their parents want, I suppose," said the Bishop curtly; "what business further is it of ours?"

"Their parents don't know anything about it: how should they? And you, ma'am, ought to supply the best market value, and the most modern improvements you can hear of, in return for their money. You'll be sorry for not doing it, some of these days. See if you are not."

"Such trash as you talk, John!" interrupted the Bishop. "What do they want with all this education? What the better would one of them be for Latin, indeed? Let them say their prayers: plenty good enough for them."

"If that's so," retorted Hogan, a little crossly, "why does Mother Assumption pretend to teach them anything but their prayers? It would certainly be cheaper for them."

"Now, John dear, you're talking of what you don't know; 'pon my word you are," began the Prioress gravely. "Father O'Hea himself told me our language classes were better than those of any other convent school in Dublin. And as for music, why, we are renowned for music. My dear boy, you don't know what other schools are. And Protestant schools, too. I assure you a great many of the best class Protestant schools are not nearly as good as we are."

"Pardon me, ma'am," said the barrister, laughing heartily, "you are entirely behind the times. How is it that the best-class Catholics are sending their daughters to these new Ladies' Colleges and High Schools, to learn Latin, Greek, and mathematics, and sciences of all sorts? Why don't *you* go in for South Kensington examinations and Trinity College classes? Why have the convents fallen from their old ideal? They used to be the homes of learning and culture. Your curriculum, ma'am, is little

K

better than a swindle, and it will be a bad job for you when your supporters find that out."

"I declare to goodness," cried the Bishop, "this fellow has gone mad. Latin and Greek and mathematics for a pack of girls, indeed! What would the world come to then, I'd like to know?"

"Ah," said the Prioress, good-naturedly, "he doesn't mean it. I got a new postulant last week," she continued: "one of our own children come back to us."

"Who!" asked Hogan.

"Mary Anne Kellett. She could not exist till she was let back to us, the darling child."

"Is that Kellett's daughter of Rathboy Farm?" asked Hogan of the Bishop; "if so, she ought to have money."

"Yes,—the same. I'm glad she came, poor thing. She never could be happy with them at home: a rough lot!"

"If her father and mother are rough, why should she be less rough? How comes that, Mother Assumption?"

"Because," returned the Abbess, "she got a nice education, and was refined and improved; and she chose to enter instead of remaining at home."

"Bah! ma'am; she had no business to be refined and improved beyond her station in life. You are doing the most horrid mischief throughout the country. There's not a useful hard-working girl left, with your refining and improving them,—improving them off the face of the earth."

"There's always women enough," said the Bishop crossly: "and too many, for that matter. At the same time, I'll allow you carry off the best of them into the convents here. Anyhow, it's God's will, else they wouldn't think of it."

"Of course it is," assented the Prioress.

Between the Prioress and the Bishop there was this difference:—He considered that Catholic girls had a mission in life as well as being nuns. He held it right and suitable, in a religious as well as a social point of view, that they should marry—a certain number of them at least; although, of course, as a Churchman, he considered marriage to be an

evil—a necessary evil—a concession made to the exigencies
of poor fallen human nature. But the Prioress considered
it to be an entirely unnecessary one, to be avoided as much
as possible—a wholly inferior and condemnable state as
compared with the religious life : in fact, the mere name of
it was unfit to be breathed without a proper little shudder
of revulsion—a little fluttering of the dove-like wings of im-
maculate and over-conscious purity. Mother Assumption,
to do her justice, did indeed sometimes think of the institution of matrimony as being in some remote way connected
with the perpetuation of her flourishing boarding - school.
Like many another enormity, it tended, no doubt, to the
furtherance of that scheme best expressed by the legend
inscribed over her gates, "*Ad majorem Dei gloriam!*" and
so was to be tolerated and almost condoned.

"How are you getting on, John?" asked she. "It was
very thoughtful of you to send me the paper with that
report of your speech in it. *I* never see a paper, you
know, unless some one sends one with something in it of
interest to the community." Mother Assumption loved a
newspaper—in secret.

Those modern luxuries are not generally allowed in convents. However, as they were not known at the periods
when Saints Dominic, Bernard, Francis, Teresa, and other
founders of communities, flourished and drew up their
respective rules and codes of observances, they escaped
being placed on the index of forbidden indulgences. And
consequently, if somewhat irregular, it is not an absolutely
sinful relaxation for a nun to read one.

"I must send you a *Graphic*, ma'am," returned the barrister. "Indeed, I ought to have done so before."

"Ah! yes, now, for the Christmas holidays. The children
will be so glad of the pictures."

Her reverence did not add that she would be so glad of
the stories which usually go with the said pictures. But
her cousin was aware of her proclivities, and good-naturedly
promised a stock of the usual Christmas effusions.

"Now, you promised to select a list of books for the
library for me, John. There's not a day but what I have

girls here asking me, may they read this book or that book? and how am I to know what to recommend them? And of course, except the mistress of the schools, and she has no time, there's nobody in the house knows anything about books but myself."

"I'm sure, reverend Mother, I sent you a bundle not long ago. It seems to me you read them up like winking."

"Read them, John! I am astonished at you! I only skim through them, just to see if they'll do for the children."

"Of course, Mother Assumption," answered the barrister, in the gravest of tones, nevertheless with a noticeable compression of his lips. "Well now, let us see," proceeding to jot down in his pocket-book. "Let's see: you have the first, second, and third of 'Middlemarch.' How do you like that for the children?"

Mother Assumption paused.

"It's a lovely book—oh, most lovely! But somehow the religious part doesn't come out clear enough; an' still, I don't know—there's many a worse and a more foolish book."

"Well, yes," agreed Hogan drily; "I should say so. All the same, ma'am, I suppose I must send you the fourth volume?"

"Oh yes, John, if you please;" and the Abbess looked as if she would be pleased very much. "See, here's a list I've been given; you might send those round at your convenience."

"What's 'Middlemarch,' eh?" asked the Bishop of Secunderabad, who was sipping his glass and warming his feet at the fire. "Eh! who's it by?"

"George Eliot, sir," replied Hogan.

"Hah!" said the Bishop, as if the name were quite familiar to him. "I don't know any of his works."

"Is it true the Prime Minister of England is going to be 'received'?" asked the Prioress, changing the subject adroitly.

Hogan looked at her in utter amazement, almost doubting his ears; but the Bishop, who knew what was expected of them, replied quite seriously,—

"I heard, on very good authority, that he and all his family, barring the wife, were converted by Monsignor Capel; but it's kept quiet just at present. It wouldn't do, you know, to make it public, on account of Parliament being just going to sit."

"Glory be to God!" ejaculated her reverence piously. "Now, would the most part of the House of Commons follow his example, if that turns out true?"

"Well," said Hogan, quite gravely, "they are very much attached to him: but I doubt if their affection goes quite so far as that. My lord, is it not time we were off?"

"Now don't go yet," entreated the Prioress; "it's three months since I saw you. Ye never told me one word of the grand ball."

"Ah!" replied her nephew, laughing, "you know as much about it this minute as I do, Mother Assumption."

"No such thing, indeed!" returned she, repudiating the allegation with scorn. "There were a few here, to be sure, that were at it." She knew every dress that had been seen there perfectly. "But how did you get on?"

"First-rate, ma'am; grand affair."

"Augh," growled the Bishop, "don't lose your time, Assumption, talking to him about low business people like the Lord Mayor of Dublin and that Rafferty lot. Mr. Hogan is got above them entirely, so he is. Nothin' less than me Lord Ramines and me Lord Brayhead, the swaddler, will content him these times."

Mother Assumption knew the origin and history of this little innuendo nearly three weeks back. The Bishop was chaplain to her convent; and every morning, while he ate breakfast in her parlour after eight o'clock mass, she came down to hear all the news and exchange information with his lordship. Veronica was first, she having the pleasant task of waiting on him; and by the time his lordship had finished his cutlet and had poured out his second cup of tea, Reverend Mother had eaten her meagre breakfast in the refectory, and came to relieve Veronica and send her to the lay sisters' table.

She turned her big gray eyes with an expression of mock

horror on her cousin. "Augh now, John dear — ah now!"

The gentleman thus abjured, seeing precisely the state of affairs, was ready to burst with laughter; but he wisely concealed his merriment, and shrugging his shoulders, made answer in a lackadaisical, helpless sort of tone.

"I can't help it, Mother Assumption. What would you have? I suppose the next thing to please his lordship and you will be that I am to refuse every brief I chance to be sent from a Protestant attorney's office. People like me can't pick and choose, my dear lady."

"Take a glass of sherry, sir," said his lordship, who had been helping himself not from the decanter of sherry, but from a queer-looking little roundabout glass jar, bearing on a silver chain and label fastened to its neck the inscription "whiskey."

"No, no. I must be off. I have to dress for dinner. Good-bye, reverend Mother! I won't forget 'Middlemarch' and the list at Kelly's." And Hogan, delighted to make his escape, rang the bell for the jocund Veronica and went his way.

"Dear, dear!" said the Bishop, mounting his neat feet on the fender, "how well he's getting on these times. I'm terribly afraid though, Assumption, those swell Protestants may be leading him into—ah, hum—God knows what."

"Surely your lordship has no fear of him losing his faith?" returned the reverend Mother, with a look of genuine anxiety on her face.

"Not that—not that alone; but he's making remarks and turning up his nose and fault-finding with these friends of yours, the Raffertys. Ye see that's always the way. If girls go into Protestant society, oh, nobody's so nice and genteel and refined as Protestant young gentlemen; and then here's John, the same: the refinements and the niceness of the Protestant young ladies!" And the Bishop pursed up his lips and shook his head in a melancholy foreboding way.

"Well, I'm sure he has no reason to fault-find with the Rafferty girls. They'd every extra and everything here, and then off in England for the accent. What can he be thinking of, at all?" The Prioress spoke in an aggrieved, half-lachrymose tone. "Did he see Mary Brangan, now? She's a splendid girl, and so beautifully dressed!"

But the Bishop raised his eyebrows, and by a gesture of his face testified to the Prioress that even Miss Brangan had failed to impress his obdurate nephew. Then, after a pause, with the easy happy-go-lucky philosophy belonging to his disposition, he added, in a more cheerful tone,—

"God will provide. We must accept our lots, and just pray on. Anyhow," he added, "John had always a great taste for getting on in life."

"Indeed, then, 'twon't be for want of prayers. Sure that lamp is always on St. Gabriel's oratory for him—him and old Mrs. Doolin together," added the Prioress, who, though a good woman of business, certainly was scrupulous and conscientious. "He attends the *saw*crament regularly, doesn't he?" she added in an anxious tone.

"Oh yes," replied the Bishop; "though I believe it is *say*craments he calls them nowadays."

Who would believe the enormous difference that lies in the pronunciation of the first syllable of that word? By săcrament is understood the Protestant communion; while săcrament expresses the great fundamental dogma of the Catholic Church. Volumes would not suffice to recount the religious, social, and nationalistic differences summed up in the mere accentuation of that one syllable.

Mother Prioress seemed to be impressed by this intelligence, as well she might. The bell rang now for Divine Office; and she took her leave, while the Bishop also departed to dine with a country family in Mountjoy Square.

CHAPTER IX.

"Ein garstig Lied! Pfui! ein politisch Lied!
Ein leidig Lied! Dankt Gott mit jedem Morgen
Dass ihr nicht braucht fürs röm'sche Reich zu sorgen.
Ich halt' es wenigstens für reichlichen Gewinn
Dass ich nicht Kaiser oder Kanzler bin.
Doch muss auch uns ein Oberhaupt nicht fehlen,
Wir wollen einen Papst erwählen."—*Faust*.

LORD BRAYHEAD possessed a town house, which he inhabited for a few months in the early spring of each year,—
for the Dublin season, in fact, which is over when that of
London commences, or nearly so. St. Patrick's Ball, given
on the night of that "immovable" Feast, closes the Castle
festivities. The Viceroy and his family usually take wing
for London, and the big "whiskey men" and a few—a very
few—of the set remain to keep the ball rolling in Dublin.
The Roman Catholics are all "fasting" and "abstaining,"
and longing for Easter to remove their disabilities.

For these few months Lord Brayhead entertained hospi-
tably enough. His circle was tolerably wide—embracing
the Castle set (the private circle, of course, understood)—
the Viceroy, his family and acquaintance generally. Then
there was the usual *filling*: the Castle officials, the commander of the forces, the Lord Mayor, the provost of
Trinity, bishops, chaplains, surgeons, and physicians in
ordinary and extraordinary, legal dignitaries,—all these
were to be met at Brayhead House. There were not many
of them; and the "deadly lively" (as Wyldoates, the larky
aide-de-camp, styled them) entertainments were pretty
generally the same; except that the dishes varied with the

seasons, while the guests were the same always—at least, while the Government remained unchanged. If the Whigs or Tories went out, of course there was a novelty in the way of Viceroy, Lord Chancellor, and so on.

The first levee and drawing-room of the season had been held. Dublin was full of country people, and the hotels and lodgings were all crowded. Court milliners advertised for additional hands, and the shops were thronged all day by fresh-cheeked purchasers. Stout bucolic gentlemen, addicted to plaid trouserings, and to the distinctively provincial habit of staring about them in the streets, tried to kill time in Grafton Street, and wandered from one club to the other. The Courts were all sitting, too, and everybody seemed on the alert. Country witnesses lounged about the quays — shopkeepers and farmers dragged from their avocations in the busiest season, in accordance with the abominable centralised legal system of this country.

Hogan was passing hurriedly one afternoon from the Court of Probate to that of Common Pleas, in obedience to the summons of an attorney, when he felt his arm grasped by some one. Turning round, he found Mr. Saltasche, on whose arm was leaning a tall, elderly man, whose little sunk steel-blue eyes were bent scrutinisingly on him.

"How do you do, Mr. Hogan?" said Saltasche. "Allow me to present you to Lord Brayhead. We heard you speaking just now. I congratulate you on your success."

Hogan bowed low. He was puzzled by Saltasche's manner. Then Lord Brayhead, seeing a couple of people beckoning at a doorway, observed, after a remark or two,—

"Do not allow us to detain you, Mr. Hogan. Mr. Saltasche can finish my errand for me."

"*Fiat justitia!* my lord," said Hogan; "I need not offer any excuse,"—and hastened away; not, however, until Saltasche had engaged him to call on him the same afternoon at his office. Then the nobleman and his companion remained alone.

"What do you think of him, my lord?" asked Saltasche, placing himself so as to look straight into his companion's face.

"H'm : he is much better than I had anticipated ; much better—gentlemanlike, rather, and of good address. You say he is a Romanist. I should hardly have thought that. I am—er—pleasantly surprised."

"Oh yes: nephew to some bishop, I believe. Oh ! quite one of that party. Owes everything to them, and is bound to them altogether."

"Dear, dear ! " almost groaned his lordship, standing still ; and looked around him with an air of bewilderment. "It might, perhaps, be better to drop the idea."

"You cannot do without *some one*, my lord," said the broker emphatically, " in the place of Mr. Wyldoates ; and if not well managed, this seat may be lost utterly to you. Besides, we shall hold this man." And the broker looked significantly at his companion.

"True, true. How much would it cost ? Have you endeavoured to ascertain."

"How much ? Well, there is a parish priest there, I'm told ; nothing less, between him and the Convent, than a cool hundred will suffice ; maybe more will be required : and that's only one item. To be sure, there are loads of other things, too. And you see it is not so long off dissolution ; which must be considered in the case of Mr. Hogan. A man may like to spend his money when he has seven years before him to enjoy his purchase ; but with a general election to come on in a year or two, it's a risky thing."

"The Liberals are in possession altogether, it seems to me," said Lord Brayhead. "I don't believe we have a chance against them. The country never was so Whig before : look at the majority they hold. They think themselves that nothing can upset them. Ruinous state of affairs."

"Quite so, indeed," assented the broker, who was not attending to a word. "I think, now, seven or eight hundred pounds should do the business. If there's no opposition ? The Conservatives will hardly think it worth wasting powder on. And if he goes in on Home Rule and the Education question, with his connections in the clerical line, I can't see any danger of the priests supporting anybody else. I think, too, if properly represented to them, the Reform Club would come down with something."

"Of course, Mr. Saltasche, my name never appears; and you will undertake to bring Mr. Hogan round to our mutual views cautiously. I shall see you both to-night."

Saltasche opened the door of the brougham, which was in waiting at the entrance of the Law Courts, for his client, and watched him drive off with an amused smile on his lips. "What an old fox!" thought he. "He'll pay every penny, unless our friend here be more fool than I take him for," ruminated he. "Poor old Wyldoates must really be dying; begad, it will be a lift to young Hogan. Who the deuce is this?" And Mr. Saltasche bent his sharp eyes on a couple of people advancing in his direction. "Poignarde, and the—yes,—the wife, no doubt."

The military man whom we met before in Mr. Saltasche's office now approached. Beside him walked a young woman, not tall, and very slight of figure, dressed in a close-fitting black costume, with a thick veil over her face, through which a clear ivory skin shone more lustrous by the contrast, and which in no way marred the brilliancy of a pair of almond-shaped, hazel eyes. She was walking along in silence, and with a listless air and step—Captain Poignarde seeming engrossed in his cigar. Saltasche caught his eye; and the pair halted simultaneously.

"Captain Poignarde, how do you do?"

"Adelaide: Mr. Saltasche—my wife."

Mrs. Poignarde bent her lithe figure in the least perceptible acknowledgment, and raising her white eyelids a quarter of an inch, met the appreciating glance of the well-dressed man of the world, who was bowing before her, with cool equanimity. Saltasche had been told she was lovely and young; but he, having a standard of his own, paid but little attention to reports. While acknowledging the churlish introduction of her husband, he ran his critical eye over her; veiled, and plainly dressed as she was, he saw enough to cause him the greatest astonishment.

"Nineteen or twenty," thought he, "and clean bred.

What a set her head has!" and his practised eye in one moment took in every detail and line of her form.

"Ah, Captain," said he, reproachfully, "you never came back that day we settled, you remember. Mrs. Poignarde, your husband is a sad man of business."

Not a word she spoke in reply, only flashed a glance from him to the gallant youth beside her, who, holding with one lemon-coloured gloved hand his cigar, with the other tugged his whiskers, vainly endeavouring to grasp the purport of what had been said. His wife evidently relished the situation.

"A man of business!" she said at last. "Business!— the idea of Eric and business. What was it?" And she laughed, with a ring of malicious amusement in her voice.

He turned round a sulky countenance upon her. Saltasche, watching every stir, noted the scornful curl of the short upper lip.

"A trifle," answered Saltasche airily; "nothing worth remembering or talking about. Any time will do," he added, looking significantly at Poignarde, who returned the glance by a meaning nod.

"Mrs. Poignarde, your friend Mrs. Grey, the chaplain's wife, has been a neighbour of mine, at Green Lanes, for some time back. Has she told you that a concert is proposed for the Soldiers' Widows' and Orphans' Home situated near us?"

"I recollect. Yes," said she, indifferently; "she did speak of something of that kind."

"It is to be exclusively amateur; and you sing, don't you?" He was watching her closely as he spoke.

"Sing?—no." And she looked at him with wide-opened eyes.

"Are you sure? I'm certain I was told of your singing so well. Captain Poignarde, I must appeal to you;" and Saltasche turned to the husband.

"Don't know, 'm sure," drawled he. "She plays."

"You must hear more about it. I know you can help them; and the committee are absolutely lost for a really good performer. Oh, I won't allow you to refuse. I'll send and tell you all about it."

She threw back her head, and looked at him with an inimitable air of half bewilderment, half haughtiness. Saltasche coolly returned this with a look of the most expressive, intense admiration. A car was passing, and he signalled the driver by a wave of his hand.

"May I set you down anywhere, Poignarde ? Mrs. Poignarde, will you allow me ?"

"We're going home Park way," nodded the husband.

Mrs. Poignarde vouchsafed not the slightest attention ; and with a distant salute from her, they separated.

Saltasche, as he drove towards the Bridge, turned and watched the two retreating figures — the man slouching along by the curbstone, puffing at his cigar, and vacantly turning his head from right to left at everything that passed ; she erect and well set up, walking with a firm step, and never heeding, apparently, a single person or thing on either side. Not a word evidently was exchanged between the couple ; for the woman, or girl rather, walked along as if unconscious of her companion's presence. Nor was it until the car had turned a corner, and was quite out of sight, that she looked at her companion, and broke the silence between them.

"Eric—I say, Eric—was that the stockbroker Anstruther sent you to ?"

"Yes : an awfully rich fellow; no end of a swell. I say, if you're asked to play for them, what do you intend to do ?"

"Do ?—I don't know. I am not asked yet."

"You'd better decide, then, and at once," grumbled he, in a bullying tone.

"Listen, Eric," she said indifferently. "I don't intend to be controlled by you in my few amusements. I don't interfere with you ; so let me alone."

"I'd like to see you, that's all—damn you."

And so this happy couple strolled home.

The hours sped on till evening. Lord Brayhead got through a heavy day's work of committee meetings, boards

of governors, and such like. He visited an English railway
magnate at the "Bilton," and from him got the name of a
firm of engineers and railway contractors. Altogether, he
felt, as his carriage rolled eastward through Merrion Square,
on its way to Brayhead House, that he was considerably
nearer the object of his ambition.

It was now dark; the gray wintry day had closed
rapidly, and a biting frosty air made all the lights sparkle
with unusual brilliancy. Brayhead House, a huge red-
brick corner house, standing, like some of the fine Paris
houses, *entre cour et jardin*, with a splendid granite *porte-
cochère* and massive iron grates and railings, showed an
unusual excitement. The double, doors were open, and a
crimson carpet ran down the wide steps. The servants
were rushing about, all in their dress liveries of claret and
gold. The hall was heated with great stoves placed
beneath the staircase. White marble , statues gleamed
among stands of hothouse plants ; and camellias, like trees,
their stems hidden in masses of maiden-hair fern, stood
everywhere masking the walls.

A second hall was divided by a velvet curtain, held
back at either side by a beautiful marble figure. The
staircase was carved oak ; and off the drawing-room lobby
was a conservatory, filled with spring flowers ; great pots
of pale narcissus, Russian violets, and hyacinths of every
hue. The sweet fresh scent penetrated to the drawing-
rooms, where the maids were busy giving the final touch to
everything.

His lordship stalked gravely up the staircase until he
reached his dressing-room. Here he rang the bell ; and,
after giving some orders to the servant who answered the
summons, went to his wife's room.

Lady Brayhead was in the hands of her maid, a grim
Abigail, who left the room in obedience to a look from his
lordship. Standing with his back to the fire, he waited
for a minute without speaking.

"That invitation you despatched last night, Sophronia ?"

"Yes, Lord Brayhead," responded she meekly, crossing
her thin chilly fingers in her lap.

"Did the answer come from Mr. Hogan this morning, or this afternoon?"

"Mr. Hogan sent an acceptance by the midday post."

"Good. Sophronia! I desire you will be attentive to him; I have particular reasons for it."

"Is it true, my lord, that this young man is—a Romanist?"

To this question his lordship replied with a stiff inclination of his chin; and as he moved away slowly from the fire, added, as though prompted by an after-thought:

"I desire you will convey my wishes to your nieces in this matter also."

"Certainly, since it is your wish." And the countess wrapped herself in her swansdown *peignoir*.

She was a little old woman of sixty, with a perpetual red nose, and pinched-up, wintry little face. In the hottest day of midsummer it was her peculiarity to look cold. She was rather Low Church in her religious views; Conservative, of course, like her lord; and like him, too, abominating Roman Catholics. Ritualists she held in a horror second only to that she entertained for the Scarlet Lady herself. She was a soured woman. Of her two sons, her favourite, the second, had not lived to grow up, and the eldest, Lord Greystones, had never agreed with his father, and lived always abroad. There was a rumour, too, of his having made a low match with a barmaid, or some one even more disreputable still; and his name was never mentioned at all.

The Brayheads were not held of much account in London. The Earl was a stupid man, pig-headed and narrow-minded. He liked dabbling in business, and to be the great man of a Board of Directors or a Committee of Managers. It gave him a little importance in his own eyes. People said, too, that the guineas were an attraction. A good sort of vestryman, in short. He had never taken any part in politics, or come to the front in any useful way; and they were not rich enough to hold a prominent position in London society by virtue of their entertainments or disbursements alone. They might, had Lord Greystones been so minded, have been accounted of some use and importance through him. The heir to an earldom and sixteen thousand a year confers a vast weight of responsibility and value on his family generally. They are noticed, flattered, and made much of for his sake ; and if he fails, on the other hand, to come up to the public estimate and expectations, his family are pretty sure to be made bear the weight of the disappointment. It had been so with the Brayheads. However, London and Dublin are quite different ; and a very second-rate personage in London may become a corner-stone of the social edifice in the Irish capital.

Dinner was appointed at eight, and their Excellencies were expected. Lady Brayhead was connected with the Lady Lieutenant's family ; and at ten minutes to eight the hostess and her nieces, the Misses Braginton, took up their position in the drawing-room. After a while the company began to pour in—the Lord Chancellor and his lady, a brace of judges and their wives, the physician in ordinary, a couple of dowagers, a few country gentlemen, the provost, and a dean celebrated in the world of letters, but asked solely on account of his family name. Lord Brayhead, though he had written a book of unexampled stupidity, considered literature as the last of the professions. Miss Bursford and her mother arrived at the same moment with Mr. Saltasche and Hogan. The Bragintons instantly seized on Saltasche. "*Nil desperandum*" was the family motto ; and Miss Blanche had already planned her assault on this fortress.

Conversation went on pretty smoothly. The fact of their Excellencies being expected gave a fillip to the spirits of the guests. Her ladyship, in peach velvet and silver, with little bunches of wispy, blonde curls on each side of her face, twittered little insipidities to a grave judicial dignitary standing beside her. The physician in ordinary was talking to a deaf dowager through a trumpet, and cudgelling his brains for some news for her. The Lord Chancellor, who had met the Chief Justice of Appeal the day before at the Castle dinner, and who was to meet him the next day at the Chief Secretary's, was exchanging some commonplaces about a street accident with his brother dignitary. An agrarian outrage was the prevailing topic; and one of the bucolic contingent, a Mr. Fitzharmon Dillon, was holding forth loudly on the generally seditious aspect of rural affairs to Saltasche, who hardly had made up his mind which was the most intolerable— the fascinating *minauderies* of Miss Braginton, or the pompous twaddle of the J.P. Mr. Fitzharmon Dillon was one of that class of Irish gentry who would have it to be believed that they are suffering all the woes of exile by being condemned to live in their native country. They take care always to speak of it as "this country," in the tone Burton or Stanley might use in describing Zanzibar or Unyanyembe.

"The idea, my dear sir; that in a country calling itself civilised, in the—ah—nineteenth century, I am obliged to keep two policemen in my own house! Daren't stir without their protection." And he paused and looked round for admiration and interest. A county gentleman buried in his estate for eight months out of the twelve is obliged to make the best of his little opportunities. It is not everybody that is honoured with a threatening letter, and people have little idea of the importance conferred by being the recipient of one of these missives. It is, positively, the next thing to being fired at, and raises a man enormously in his own and public estimation. Mr. Fitzharmon Dillon had frequent interviews with the editor of *The Daily Alarmist*, who was forcing the Coercion Bill on the notice of the Government.

Saltasche was not unacquainted with the variety, and listened with an expression of compassionate deference.

"Dreadful position, indeed; dreadful, dreadful!" and he had to smile in return as he spoke in reply to Miss Blanche's *œillade*.

"Last year, after nightfall, every shutter had to be closed immediately. A mere glimmer of light, and we might have lost our lives."

"Why didn't you go away to London, Mr. Dillon?"

L

asked Diana Bursford, who was sitting close by, speculating wearily as to her probable partner at the dinner-table, and inwardly praying that the Bragintons, contrary to their customary good-natured practice, would have forgotten to put her down to a married man, or some useless "detrimental."

Poor Miss Bursford! her opportunities were not to be wasted now. Who would think that under the cold, well-bred, smiling manner there lay such a torrent of disgust, contempt, and fierce self-upbraidings? She looked round and round the room, noted with a sneer that ancient man-hunter, Blanche Braginton, playing off all the well-worn tricks in her repertory on the tough hide of Cosmo Saltasche; then noted the sofa, where a couple of women, well-dressed and dull, were keeping up a feeble trickle of small talk with some dining-out professional; Lord Bray-head, wooden as usual, on the hearthrug, and the place of honour vacant as yet for the Lord Lieutenant.

She wished the vice-regal party would arrive and decide events. Miss Bursford lived now but from day to day; and every season, as she well knew, instead of advancing her nearer to her prize, landed her farther from it. Every day was of value now. She had started in life as a beauty, and, like many girls, oblivious of the exigencies brought about by economic social change, had counted too much upon her beauty, and had flown too high. Then there came the Vesey crash; and what a long grudge she owed the Bragintons for that ill deed! After that she had abated her price by degrees; and now, to her mother's terror, had decided to take anybody who might offer him-self. She had been hawked about from London to Dublin, from Dublin to Scarborough, to Bath, Leamington, Dieppe, Florence, and Rome. If Mrs. Bursford heard of a *parti* on the summit of Mont Blanc, they would have toiled up after him, or have sat down at the bottom and waited his descent to attack him. There had been no end to their efforts; and yet here was Diana, Miss Bursford still, seated on a *causeuse* and speculating on the dark-complexioned, intelli-gent-looking young man who had come in with Mr. Saltasche, while she, at the same time, affected to join in

the talk of the group around her as anxiously and hope-
fully as if it was her first season.

"Why did I not go to London?" replied Mr. Dillon.
"Ah, well! that's all very well, but"—and Mr. Dillon put
on an air of resignation and self-abnegation—"there is not
the least use in trying to escape your fate that way. If I
am a marked man, I may"—and he raised his voice and
looked round the room—"just as well stop where I am.
Besides, it would be abandoning the field to them; it
would be—er—cowardice!"

Hogan fixed his keen eyes on the speaker. "You had
reason, then, for apprehension?" he said, with a cross-
examining sort of air.

"Reason, sir! reason!" spluttered Mr. Dillon. "Everybody knows what reason any man of property has for
apprehension in these days. But what can we expect, sir,
with a Government that panders, sir—panders to the mere
mob in this way? Communism——"

"Miss Bursford, have you heard the Italian Opera is
coming next week? Town will be very full." Saltasche
broke violently into this new topic.

"We are to have a very good company, I am told," said
Hogan.

"By-the-bye," said Lord Brayhead, "speaking of the
opera, His Excellency has been obliged to give directions
concerning the 'Huguenots.' An appointment was made
for the manager this afternoon at the Castle."

"Ah! that may be the cause of the delay of their
Excellencies," chirped Lady Brayhead, glancing at a time-
piece: "quite twenty minutes late."

"The 'Huguenots' is quite calculated to rouse party,
h'm—spirit." This from Saltasche, uttered in the gravest
tone. "Now, that Rataplan chorus, and the scene where
they clap their hands—Kentish fire, you know—that *must*
be excised completely. No one could answer for the consequences, otherwise."

Hogan, who had seen the opera alluded to several times,
was trying to make out what particularly inflammatory
material lurked in the scene alluded to.

"Very wrong, very wrong," said the host. "I quite disapprove of this conciliatory policy; it is nothing but cowardice. Why should we make such ignoble concessions?"

"Do you not think it would be better," asked a quiet, gentlemanly man of the last speaker, "to yield in trifles like this than to provoke conflict? Keep the fire and tow apart as much as possible."

Hogan, wondering and amused, and by no means certain that they were in earnest, turned and shot an inquisitive glance at Saltasche.

That mentor returned it with a knowing nod; and, under pretext of taking his young friend to admire a lately-executed bust of the earl at the other end of the room, said in a low voice,—

"I see you're diverted. Did ever mortal man hear such foolery? His Excellency, I suppose, is holding a Privy Council to decide whether the Rataplan chorus is to be excised or not. He'll send alarming despatches to Downing Street over it, to show them what he is doing. Pooh! he must give a little value for his money, you know, or seem to do so." Then, louder, "Capital likeness, is it not?"

"Oh! speaking expression. Quite so: life-like."

"More than ever the original was," muttered the incorrigible Saltasche. "There he comes now: hear the outriders?"

In fact, the noise of the horses could be heard below; and the Lord Lieutenant entered directly, and, after a few minutes' delay, the party filed off in proper order of precedence.

Hogan fell to Diana Bursford, and Saltasche paired off with the evergreen Blanche. They found themselves close to each other in the dining-room, at the farthest end from the representatives of Royalty; who in their turn were seated beside the usual dignitaries invited to meet them, and bored each other as a matter of course. Mr. Saltasche devoted himself to his dinner; and on Hogan, devoid as yet of that *aplomb* and *savoir faire* which enables a man to secure his own exclusive interests in a well-bred manner, fell the burthen of talking to the ladies. Blanche was ambitious: she saw clearly that there was no use wasting powder on the gentleman beside her until the needs of his inner man had been satisfied; so she talked to Miss Bursford and at Hogan, who was not a little puzzled at her *œillades* and affectations. She was not altogether bad-looking, and certainly possessed the manner and appearance of a well-bred woman accustomed to society. Her black eyes, however, had a beady, hard look: as to the complexion, even violet powder and a faint suspicion of rouge could not replace the bloom that had fled with youth. Her best points were her teeth and hands; and the first-named she managed to show with every word she uttered, while in using the last, which were loaded with rings, she rivalled the great Father O'Hea himself. She and her sister were the daughters of a needy and disreputable baronet; they had a small income—just sufficient to maintain them—which came to them from their mother: and they always accompanied Lady Brayhead in her yearly visits to Ireland. Like their noble relations, they were too insignificant to make any real figure in London; and though they would strenuously have denied it, they thoroughly enjoyed their sojourn in Dublin. They loved domineering over the willing serfs whom they encountered in their aunt's set, and bullied and condescended to their hearts' delight. The dresses of last season did duty very well in Dublin; as also did their second-hand gossip and scandal-mongering.

Mr. Saltasche looked up at last from his soup, and, peeping between the branches of a table vine mounted in a silver pot on the table between them,—

"Oh, Miss Bursford, I must not forget to speak to you of the concert we're getting up. You will have to help."

Diana Bursford sang extremely well—that is, in a finished, though unpleasing way—and her amiable cousin grudged her this accomplishment heartily.

"Is this the Soldiers' Home affair, Mr. Saltasche?" cried she, hastily forestalling Miss Bursford's reply. "Now really, do you think it will pay to have amateurs? I fancied you, so sensible as *you* are"—this with a killing look—"would have gone in for professionals at once. It saves so much trouble and worry; now, does it not?"

"Yes, to the amateurs it does indeed," said Diana coldly.

Saltasche looked at her for an instant; but the immovable smiling face gave no sign, except that the brows were the least bit harder looking. She looked away up the table, through the blaze of wax-lights and gorgeous bloom of flowers, past the double line of faces, some serious, some gay, to where his Excellency sat, eating nothing, and barely civil to the withered old lady beside him.

"I really think, in a charitable thing such as this is, that all the performers should be amateurs," ventured Hogan. "It takes such a large sum of money from the profits to pay professionals."

"I have got Major Sands," continued Saltasche, "of the Hussars, to play accompaniments, and the Greys say that they have quite a chorus made up. We want a good pianist for a solo or two, and a good soprano."

"Diana, why don't *you* volunteer?" asked Miss Braginton in her most acid tone, casting a spiteful look at her relative.

"That's exactly what I want, Miss Braginton," said Saltasche; "won't you join your entreaties to mine? You can't refuse us, Miss Bursford: I have heard you sing—often, you know."

Miss Braginton was outnumbered, and she went on eating her quail in silence.

Diana turned and looked full in Hogan's face. "You sing, I am sure, Mr. Hogan; you have a singing voice: I am certain you do,"—and the cold blue eyes looked straight into his. She had put on her most pleasing manner, and her tone was deferential and soft, flattering in the extreme to the young man, who was raw and unpractised as yet in the ways of such women of the world.

Hogan felt a pleased glow steal over him. Flattery's

silver tongue was new to him ; and it was with a sense of
swelling delight and pride that he recognised and accepted
his tribute. His neighbour evidently considered him
worth her attention and civility; and he returned
gratefully and cordially the glance of the practised
coquette.

"I don't sing, I assure you," said he. "I never sang
for anybody—anybody, at least, worth talking about."

"There's a confession, now ! We shall make something
of him, believe me," murmured Saltasche.

Then they passed to other topics ; and at last the signal
was given by Lady Brayhead, and the ladies sailed off to
the drawing-room.

Diana seated herself on a chair near the door. The
room was hot, and her complexion after dinner was not
trustworthy. Her cousin, who came in last, looked about,
and swooped down on her. These ladies were always
most scrupulously polite to each other, though the hatred
between them was something that could never be measured.

"Diana, love, your dress is charming ; and that blue and
salmon is perfect—suits you *so* well, dear."

Miss Bursford cast her eyes over her interlocutor's
attire, but finding nothing noteworthy, contented herself
with giving a twitch to a flounce. She knew something
was coming.

"Who was that young man that took you down to
dinner ? Did you catch his name ? Nice-looking, eh ?"
And Miss Braginton's black eyes were fixed on her
greedily.

"H'm—I didn't notice, I'm sure," replied Diana carelessly, to outward appearance at least. In reality her
guard was up. "His name, if you want it particulárly,
is O'Rooney Hogan ; he's some *protégé* of Mr. Saltasche's.
Tell me, Blanche,—is the O'Gorman Mulcahy here ?"
And Diana, who well knew he was not, pretended to look
round for that personage.

But Blanche was off. She pretended to see a signal
from Lady Brayhead's end of the room, and took her
departure speedily.

Some one began to play on a grand piano. The servants carried in tea into the back drawing-room, and the women all abandoned themselves to the state of semi-torpor in which the interval between their departure from the dining-room and the arrival of the men in the drawing-room is usually spent. At last they entered. Miss Blanche seized on Saltasche; her sister secured a military widower.

Saltasche was the least bit sulky. He had been snubbed by his Excellency; and in this wise. He had told a capital anecdote, brand new from the Paris Jockey Club; and it had fallen flat, for the simple reason that his Excellency did not know the story-teller, and had chosen to consider it a sort of a liberty for a man with whom he was not acquainted to attempt to amuse him. It was so easy for his Excellency to administer the snub; and it was done in a very common way. He had listened, or had seemed to listen, attentively until the point of the story came, and then, instead of laughing amiably and condescendingly, had thrown back his aristocratic chin in a manner that expressed in a way there was no mistaking his conviction that he had certainly heard that story before, and only needed an effort of memory to recall it. Of course, everybody had politely waited for his Excellency to laugh first, save one *aide-de-camp*, who exploded prematurely, and then chose to consider that Saltasche had placed him in a false position, and was ill-tempered and aggressive towards him in consequence.

Hogan came in last, and dropped himself, in obedience to a glance from Miss Bursford, into a chair beside her.

The rooms were looking their best now; the guests seemed more at ease; and their tongues, loosened by good cheer, kept up an endless murmur, broken now and again by ripples of well-bred laughter. The wax-lights cast a mellowed, soft light on the faces—none of them too fresh, for the Bragintons stoutly resisted the introduction of girls —of the women, and toned down the rich hues of their dresses. The Lord Lieutenant, bored to death, was talking of horses with one of his friends on the hearthrug. `Mr.

Vickars and Mr. Wyldoates, the gentlemen in attendance, stood near the door; the second named, whenever he met Hogan's eye, turning away his head. A small party—the musical clique, who always attract one another—migrated to the piano; and a gentleman, who was said to have owed his appointment in the household to his vocal powers, sat down and sang an Italian buffo song with fine spirit and execution.

"Do you know him?" asked Diana of Hogan. She was a little curious to find out the gentleman's set, and had resort to the customary device—not by any means in the "best form," as the slang goes—of putting through him a categorical list of names of people of note.

She was foiled in this; for the barrister, reading her purpose, and being very slightly acquainted with the gentleman alluded to, made answer in the affirmative. In reality, he only knew him professionally.

"What a pretty woman his wife is! Delightful musician; I heard her play the other evening."

"I am not fond of music at all—have no ear," he replied. "Moreover, I hold that pretty women have sufficiently fulfilled their duty to society in looking nice. They have no business with accomplishments."

"You think, then, that only plain women should be allowed to cultivate their minds?"

"Certainly; to me it seems a fearful extravagance for a pretty woman. They have no business being clever. When the true philosopher's millennium arrives, it will be unlawful for any woman possessed of more than a certain number (to be agreed on) of good points, to sing, play, draw, or indulge in any of the current accomplishments of the day."

"Oh dear! And a good-looking blue-stocking, or a belle who dabbles in the 'ologies?"

"I would make such infractions an indictable offence; and I would visit aggravated cases, such as the dead languages or mathematics, with the extreme penalty of the law."

"Are you serious? I think not," she said, turning and

looking directly at him. The slightly sardonic expression
of his eyes and mouth disappeared as he replied.

"I am not serious; and I am too. We are not at all
logical or consistent in our method. It is tacitly acknowledged that women who are devoid of mere personal charms
are expected to make up for the deficiency by acquired
attractions; but if accomplishments, or indeed solid
learning (for they seem to take that up now), be a marketable acquisition, why should not all women possess that
additional charm?"

"*If*," said Miss Bursford with an emphasis: "that is by
no means agreed; and for myself I quite disapprove of
ladies intruding into men's sphere. I don't in the least
see how this higher education of women is to help them."
Diana said this with real feeling, for she had tried botany
and conchology one summer, but not finding those branches
of science any special aid, she had concluded to put off the
"*blue stage*" a little longer.

"I don't see it either," returned he thoughtfully; "it
is not that women in general are in need of higher education; the mistake does not lie so much in the quality or
quantity of instruction meted out to women, as in the
mode of administering it. It is quite a mistake to suppose
that women in general are inferior in point of education
to men."

Miss Bursford set down her coffee-cup and looked at him.

"I really mean what I say," he went on. "It is notorious, and admitted on all sides, that in the lowest classes,
both in the rural districts and in the towns, the women
are infinitely beyond the men in intellect."

"Yes, yes; I have heard that. I quite recollect it.
Lord Brayhead says the chief work of the missionaries,
and that sort of people who go amongst the lower orders,
is accomplished by women, and they are so much easier to
work among and instruct than the men."

"Quite so. And even ascending a step or two in the
social scale,—getting up amongst the traders, shopkeepers,
farmers,—the women at the present moment are enormously, destructively in advance."

"I really have heard that the women of the Roman Catholic classes in this country are very well educated—play, sing, draw, dance, and all that sort of thing; the nuns, you know, are so nice."

"They can do more than that," said Hogan, smiling at a droll reminiscence which came to his mind—that of young Brangan's blunder in the tea-room at the Raffertys' ball. "But that's not the question. I disapprove of the entire separation of the girls and boys; it seems to me so irrational. They are to live together afterwards, and be companions for life; and how are they to get along? The boys are always herded together when young, and are not subjected to any refining influences. I remember at the college of St. Ignatius there was not even a woman-servant in the house. A little fellow was dying there, and he had to be carried out to lodgings, otherwise his mother could not have been near him—according to the rule she would not be allowed into the infirmary. Then later on we find them living in their clubs, or substitutes for clubs; anywhere, in fact, out of their own houses, and away from the restraints of the female society to which they are so unaccustomed, and which, I am sorry to say, is distasteful to them in most instances."

"It really looks like it," she replied; "and in London it is as bad as it can be. My friends there say the labour of collecting men for their entertainments is absolutely dreadful. Men won't go into society nowadays; you may get them to dinner-parties, but as to balls, and that sort of thing, it is impossible. I can't imagine why."

Miss Bursford was called upon to sing now, so Hogan found his way over to Mr. Saltasche, who was flirting, out of pure good-nature, as men do sometimes, with Miss Braginton. The lady continued her conversation in a *sotto voce* tone, while her cousin was singing one of the eternal Claribel or Gabriel effusions.

Mr. Saltasche made a little *moue*, as if to impress on her the necessity of keeping silence; but the young lady returned, with a pretty infantile shake of her head,—

"Don't ask me; pray don't. I have heard it *so often*—

over and over again, I do assure you.   The effort would
be quite beyond me."

The two gentlemen smiled in reply.   Both of them read
clearly the ill-nature that lurked in her words, and both
saw in it still more clearly its prompting motive—the desire
to please them, and cunningly depreciate a possible rival;
and so they smiled amiably in encouragement and appreciation of the manœuvre.   Each appropriated the implied
flattery to himself: Saltasche by virtue of his large fortune, high standing, and admitted desirability; and the
younger man with a keen sense of his new importance and
dignity.   The evening was indeed a triumph for him.   To
be admitted to such a house was in itself an inestimable
honour.   But to be invited, to be held worthy to meet the
Viceroy himself, it was almost overwhelming.   And then
Miss Bursford's manner was certainly cordial and affable
in the extreme.   He looked across the room to where she
was sitting at the piano, her cousin, Colonel Bursford,
turning over the leaves of her music.   The light shone
full on her face and figure.   "Gone off rather, I should
say," thought he, "and decidedly too thin; but what a
style and air she has!"

This was true.   Diana was looking her best.   An artful
touch of rice-powder veiled the sallowness of her temples
and toned down the sharp outline of her rather high cheek-
bones.   She was richly dressed; and her hair, plentiful,
whether her own or not, was becomingly and softly arranged.
Her small hands were white; and the wrists, rather too
anatomical for beauty, were judiciously concealed by handsome bracelets.   She sang well, but with a hard and un-
sympathetic, if highly-cultured voice.

The viceregal party left as early as it was possible for
them to get away; and after a short interval the rest of
the guests followed suit.   Saltasche, who was engaged on
a committee which had been formed to get up a concert
for a charitable institution—one of the many which he
patronised, and which in turn patronised him—remained
to the last.

"How very well Lord—— is looking!   Never saw him

better—never!" He said this to Lord Brayhead, who was staring absently into the fire. People who entertain the Castle set feel usually a sort of proprietary interest in them; so it was with the air of one deeply concerned in the matter that the host made answer.

"I am glad to hear you say so; very glad. Yes, I think he looks very well,—much better, indeed. Quite so."

"Aunt, did you observe her Excy's dress? Oh, so sweet: lemon and strawberry——" This was from the second Braginton.

"And ice-cream," muttered Mr. Saltasche, who was wanting to get off to his cigar.

"And quite new, too," said Mrs. Bursford acidly; "a rarity that——"

"No then, for I heard her say to Lady Guinevère Fraise-feuilles last week that she had been at the great Gore House Ball, and that it was so unlucky Lady de Montfort had a dress exactly the same. Both came from Paris." So spoke Miss Blanche, the well-informed.

"Well," interposed Mr. Saltasche, who did not know to what lengths this gossip might be extended by the voluble lady, "I have engaged Mr. Hogan; and now I must have these young ladies' assistance. Oh now! Mr. Papillon has also promised me; really, ladies, I am even going to sing myself. I am—in the chorus."

It was finally settled that the younger of the Bragintons was to sing in the chorus; and Hogan, who was firmly persuaded that it was out of the question he could sing at a Protestant concert, allowed Saltasche to arrange that he was to call at the Bursfords' house in Merrion Square to see the music proposed, which was in Miss Diana's keeping. As they went down the stairs, Lord Brayhead held back Saltasche an instant, and murmured in his ear, "I received a telegram this evening. Mr. Wyldoates has gone up to Paris to be under the care of doctors there. No hope of him at all. They speak of gangrene——".

Mr. Saltasche gave utterance to a sort of whistle. "I'd better tell this man, then, and see what he is inclined to do."

"I leave it in your hands entirely, Mr. Saltasche," said Lord Brayhead, turning back to the drawing-room.

And they sallied forth. The night was clear and cold, and the stars were brilliant overhead. The street was perfectly quiet and deserted; not a creature to be seen. Saltasche struck a match on his boot-heel, and lighting a cigar, took Hógan's arm and set out at a brisk pace.

"You mentioned something once, Mr. Hogan, of your intention of trying for a seat in Parliament some of these days."

"A seat! Hey? Yes!"

"A seat"—puff—"in Parliament; because if you were seriously inclined for it, I might"—puff—"put you up to a good thing."

Hogan stood stock-still with amazement, and looked at his companion; but the darkness left nothing discernible of Saltasche's face but his bright cunning eyes, which shone from between his half-closed eyelids almost as brilliantly as the burning tip of the cheroot.

"It is possible before the month is out," said Saltasche slowly and indistinctly, speaking with his cigar between his teeth, "that a seat will be vacant."

"Ha! You mean that man who was obliged to go abroad some time ago, and is at Hyères now for his health?"

"He is not at Hyères now, and his recovery is impossible. So anybody that wants can take the ball on the hop. Hum."

"Peatstown," said Hogan. "I know it. I have been there at quarter sessions; precious nest of Nationalists. Nothing but an Ultra will get in there."

"*Ultra?*" repeated Saltasche, taking the cigar out of his mouth; "Ultramontane, do you mean?"

"Tut; not at all. Very opposite. Ultra Repealer; Ultra Home Ruler. Poor Wyldoates got in through the priests. I recollect it well."

"Humph!" said Saltasche; "that was before the Ballot. They will get a taste of that novelty now. By Jove, the wind will be taken out of all our sails by that, once these country bumpkins come to understand it."

Saltasche stopped under a lamp, and looked at his watch.

"Lord Brayhead is wanting to run a railway out to Lead Mines. I'll send you from Hanaper and Die Sele's some title-deeds to look over. He owns most of the ground to be broken through : but at the same time one must be sure, and have everything in order."

Hogan murmured his acknowledgments.

"And at the same time, Mr. Hogan—I speak as a friend —now don't you think you had better consider about Peatstown ? No time to be lost. It would cost, I daresay, a thousand pounds."

"Any prospect of a contest ? In that case the Liberals might help to keep the Opposition out of it. Nay ? And then you see, sir, it would involve the sacrifice of my professional engagements, in great part. Really it is a risk to a man who has his living to earn ; only a barrister in a well-rooted practice can afford the luxury of Parliament. Moreover, Dissolution is only a year and a half or so distant."

"Nonsense, my dear fellow ; the Liberals have an overwhelming majority. They literally have booked the Government of this country for an age to come. God bless me—what can shake them with such a majority ? Besides, as a member of Parliament you will have opportunities to compensate for the loss of your time. There are committees : you are the very man for such things ; commissions and directorships innumerable. Then, the position, the social advantages !"

Position ! Social advantages !! The wily man of the world had well calculated the force of his words, and their effect on his friend. Hogan was thoroughly dazzled by the glittering prospect dangled so skilfully over his head, and was astounded at the wonderful chance thrown in his way. He had indeed entertained visions, very airy and unsubstantial visions, of risking his fate at the approaching Dissolution.

A Dissolution is the best chance for men of his stamp ; the chances being that in the general hurly-burly and scramble some small constituency may be overlooked, and either the previous member returned unopposed, or some outsider get in easily by blazoning the particular clap-trap of the hour as his motto. Hogan was on the watch for some such cheap investment for his money. So, indeed, was the Bishop; who, if the outlay were necessary, had determined to give his nephew a helping hand financially.

"I must consider about it," he said hurriedly. "Mr. Saltasche, I am greatly obliged to you for your kindness. I'll let you know in a few days."

"See," continued Saltasche, "you know Peatstown is Lord Kilboggan's place; and his family have always influenced the elections there—always controlled them, begad. They're not resident, of course. They live abroad, on account of the son's health. Well, the nephew, an elder brother of that A. D. C. Wyldoates, and a finished scamp too, is somewhere round. He is heir, you know, and it is not unlikely he'd try for it. These people," with a backward gesture of his head signifying the Brayhead family, "don't agree with the Kilboggans; never did. So what I'm coming to is: you should steal a march on them—go down and proclaim your intentions, take your soundings, in short."

"Can't do that till the man's dead, hey? It wouldn't be decent."

"Try and make up your mind by Saturday,—this is Wednesday; and come in and tell me your final decision: take care not to ventilate the thing. Good-night, then." And Mr. Saltasche mounted a car and drove to the railway.

Hogan strode on across town, ruminating the affair. He did not know what to think of it. It might, after all, be the best chance that ever would present itself to him; and, indeed, how could he hope for a better? Young as he was, he had seen fortunes lost and reputations impaired in the struggle of elections. Everything seemed to combine to favour him. The Kilboggans were in bad odour. Lord Brayhead was to assist. That was certainly an unaccountable combination. He felt sure Saltasche would not be so gracious for nothing; no doubt he would require some indemnification. But, after all, what was he indebted to him for, more than a friendly hint? And it was to be considered, too, that Dissolution was not more than a year off: if he were not to be re-elected, there would be all the money gone for nothing—a thousand at least. The honour would be dear at that price. And there was also the possibility of failure in the first instance to be considered. If the parish priest were powerful enough to return Mr. Wyldoates, he might be able to "cast" him. In those remote country parishes the priests are omnipotent. There was the Ballot, to be sure. But the Ballot Act was not long in force at the time of which we write; and Hogan, who knew the unscrupulous people whose interests were in direct opposition to and jeopardised by it, had little hope in its potentiality to aid him.

"Night brings counsel," thought he wearily, as he turned into bed; "and the first thing to do in the morning must be to see the Bishop."

M

CHAPTER X.

" To thee, King John, my holy errand is.
I, Pandulph, of fair Milan Cardinal,
And from Pope Innocent the legate here,
Do, in his name, religiously demand
Why thou against the Church, our holy mother,
So wilfully dost spurn ?"—

King John.

HOGAN'drove up to the gates of St. Swithin's shortly after
nine o'clock the morning following Lord Brayhead's dinner.
Finding the side-door ajar, as it was the hour for the arrival
of the day-pupils, he bade his carman wait, and slipping in
amongst a crowd of children, who were assembled waiting
for the ringing of the school-bell, speedily found himself at
the green baize door of the Mother Superior's parlour. He
knocked ; and on hearing his uncle's tones in reply, entered.

"God bless me, John ! what has brought you here ?"
was the astonished salutation of his lordship, who was
seated at his breakfast, and who almost jumped up, so surprised was he.

"Don't disturb yourself, my lord," said Hogan, pulling
over a chair. " I took the liberty of coming here, as I
could not see you to-night. Pray go on with your breakfast ; I'll tell my story as you finish."

The Bishop chipped his egg—a new-laid one, the produce
of the conventual poultry-yard. His breakfast was charming. The bread was home-baked ; the butter, in pretty
little round pats, and the cream in the silver jug, came
from a cool dairy situated in a corner of the nuns' own
garden ; the cloth was the whitest, the china the prettiest
that could anywhere be seen ; and the little silver teapot

and sugar-pot, which shone bright enough to dazzle one's eyes, had been bequeathed to the sisterhood by an old lady who, having survived all her relations and friends, had died in their convent.

"Well, sir," began Hogan, "you will be astonished at my news. The member for Peatstown is dying, and—ah —I have been recommended to stand for the seat."

"Peatstown! Good Lord! that's Jim Corkran's parish, that was with me at Maynooth. Whew!" And the Bishop almost whistled, so great was his astonishment.

"Mr. Wyldoates is in a hopeless state," continued his nephew; "the vacancy may be declared any minute, and a contest is not anticipated."

"A contest, at least if a Conservative opposed you, would be no hurt; for the Reform Club or the Liberal Association would guarantee your expenses, or part of them, to keep the seat to the Government, wouldn't they now?"

, "Well, sir, you see Dissolution is only a year or so off, and I think the Tories are reserving their strength for a tussle then. You see, one man more or less is nothing while the Whigs have such a majority. And they have too firm a hold on the country not to get in again after the general election. I have no fear at all of not being re-elected if I got in."

"What will it cost?" asked the Bishop abruptly. "Father Corkran won't let you off short of a couple of hundred. God bless us! the time of the last election, I remember he sent to that rich Manchester man (I forget his name) that was opposing Wyldoates, and told him the roof of the parish chapel was out of repair. The fellow sent him a cheque for eighty pounds. Corkran wasn't satisfied, but sent him back a letter to say he had a second chapel wanting a roof to it. He did; and got a fifty-pound note for it. And the cream of the joke was the Manchester man was left out in the cold after all," and his lordship laughed heartily.

"I might do it for eight hundred. And I really think I'll chance it, sir. You see this Home Rule platform is sure to rally the people."

"The people!" repeated the Bishop, folding his napkin and pulling away his chair from the breakfast-table; "it will go very much according to whether their priests are for Home Rule or not. There's the Education question; if you want to stand with them, put that first. You will not have their support unless you stand firm on that point."

"Home Rule will bring me in the votes," said Hogan in a dogged tone. "I see nobody anxious for the Education question but the priests. How does it affect the Peatstown people, compared with Home Rule? Kilboggan is an extorting, oppressing absentee. All those fellows are looking to Home Rule to settle the Land Question. They are indeed, sir."

"God help them!" was the sententious reply.

"Would the Cardinal recommend me to the clergy and the chief Catholics of the place? He has never pronounced yet in favour of Home Rule." Hogan, as he asked this question, leaned on his elbow, and resting his chin in the palm of his hand, bent his gray eyes searchingly on the Bishop's face.

"I don't believe the Cardinal has ever given it his consideration one way or the other," said the Bishop, in a slow emphatic tone. "*I* don't approve of it; and my acquaintance, so far as it goes, with the opinions among the clergy, leads me to infer that it would not be acceptable at all to the Hierarchy. However, it is neither sedition nor treason; neither, though it has begun," he added pointedly, "among the Protestants, and independently of the Church, is it irreligious. Some few priests go in for it heart and soul; more say they don't understand it; and, in fact, it is not decided yet what course is to be pursued with regard to it; nor, what's more, will it be decided yet awhile. You had better consult your own judgment in that matter. But I warn you, show a proper regard for the Education question. The clergy are set upon that."

"They'll never get it. The people are against it altogether. Look here, sir: when you can reverse the whole state of society, when you can put the Protestants at the

bottom and the Catholics on the top ; make the Protestants the low poor people, the struggling traders, and the
mushroom rich, and have the Catholics the aristocrats, the
refined, high-born, exclusive sect that the others are now,
then you may have a Catholic university, and *then* the
Protestants will be disobeying their rulers and their con-
sciences, and sending their sons to it that they may be
improved and refined by coming in contact with us. If
you had a chartered university this minute, the wealthy
Catholics would send their sons to Trinity all the same ;
and small blame to them."

"Tut, tut ; you talk nonsense. Why should not we
have a Catholic University, as well as the Belgians and the
French, and——?"

"Have it the nest of free-thinkers and atheists that
theirs are." Hogan took out his watch. "No, no ; you
misunderstand the whole question, my lord—entirely misunderstand it. A quarter past ten, sir. Well, you don't
say against my project ?"

"I'll say nothing at all. I'd like to make inquiries first.
There's no great hurry, is there ?"

"Well, no, not exactly," returned Hogan, who saw
clearly that his lordship meant to give his consent ; "I'll
call up to you some evening soon."

Then he remounted his car, and hastened to an appointment at an attorney's office before Court.

*　　　*　　　*　　　*

"Diana, is that young man to be here this afternoon ?"

These words were spoken by Mrs. Bursford to her
daughter, perhaps at the same moment that the young
man referred to was engaged in the conversation with his
uncle detailed above.

"Possibly, mamma," returned Miss Bursford, who was
stooping over a large music waggon beside her piano. Miss
Bursford was certainly not a morning beauty, like our
friend Nellie Davoren : the clear bright sunlight showed
many a flaw that the wax-lights of the night before had
not discovered ; a beauty when unadorned she certainly
was not ; and her woollen morning dress of plain design

betrayed the deficiencies of figure that a *modiste's* cunning hand had veiled or supplied in her toilette of the night before.

"We must defer our visit until to-morrow, then. I must say that I do not care for Romanist acquaintances. He looks to be well-bred and gentlemanly, I allow; but you never know what the family may turn out to be. There was Elinor Hely insisting on marrying that odious O'Ryan, the surgeon of the ——th; and what a mother and sisters-in-law she found herself set up with!"

"I think you know very well, mamma," returned the young lady, with more than a shade of sharpness in her voice, "that Mr. O'Rooney Hogan has no relatives." And she continued sorting the music into parcels, laying the separate pieces neatly on top of each other, and picking out two or three which she placed on the piano for practising.

Mrs. Bursford sighed as she rose from her writing-table; she was too well conversant with her daughter's disposition to oppose her in the matter, and too well aware, also, of the hopelessness of this new venture to think it worth risking either opposition or encouragement. She had given up all hopes that her daughter could be married by any effort of hers. She did her best; for she certainly devoted nearly two-thirds of her income exclusively to the furtherance of that great object. She carried her everywhere; she got introductions by the score; she had plenty of relatives, connections, and acquaintances. Still, Miss Bursford did not take: she was ladylike, well educated of course, and possessed a thorough finished society manner,—a bearing that procured her a due amount of deference and attention everywhere she went. Still, the general feeling in a room, when she had taken her departure, was one of relief; her cold blue eyes and distant manner with her own sex were rather repelling. She was always irreproachably dressed, and had a way, whether she meant it or not, of making any woman who was not up to the mark in point of toilette conscious of her deficiency. With men she made the mistake of adopting a totally · different manner. She was deferential, flattering, and listening to the silliest chaff with engrossed attentiveness, as if to the utterances of a cabinet minister. But she wanted softness; her blandishments were too artificial and too well-worn; the iron hand showed itself too unmistakably beneath the velvet glove. The girl was, in truth, sick of her life; fourteen years was a long apprenticeship, and she wearied for the day when she might lay aside, literally as well as metaphorically, the war paint and feathers; when she might be natural and unaffected, and, above all, independent of the mother bird, whose control, prolonged far beyond the natural limits, was now become distasteful and wearisome to her.

Sons escape the maternal rule, to them always light, as soon as they become men; sometimes as soon as they go to school. In many cases, from the very cradle up they are obeyed rather than commanded. But it is not so with the women-children; they leave school to enter upon a still harder regimen, and one that never relaxes until the door of wifehood opens for them—if they are so fortunate as to escape by that risky aperture; if not, as in Diana Bursford's case, they must only bow their necks to the yoke, and hope that time may soften its asperities and make it wear easier. It does sometimes; but, as often as not, a collar too tight-fitting and galling creates a painful raw instead of a callosity.

Nor had Diana's training and mode of life been the best suited to fit her to bear the inequalities of her lot with that patience and philosophy which, under some conditions, rise to the level of dignity. One-third of every day of her life, perhaps, was devoted to the cares of her toilet, and to practising her music. This last she disliked naturally, and had not a particle of native aptitude for it. But music, vocal or other, is an indispensable part of the equipment of a young lady, and so Diana had been forced to learn; and, by dint of much expenditure of time and money, succeeded' in singing and playing in a fashionable and mechanical manner. It was no pleasure to hear either performance; but then, it was patent to everybody that she had been well taught—*i.e.* by expensive teachers. When an audience cannot pronounce any other compliment, they are seldom chary of their acknowledgments on this particular point.

Miss Bursford and her mother had paid their tribute to society; and society, in return, graciously accorded its sense, not of gratitude—to express it more accurately, let us say, tendered a receipt for value received. There were times, it is true, when Diana was fairly tired out; and, despairing, threatened to take refuge at last in one of the new sisterhoods: and then Mrs. Bursford would rage and storm. She had, as we have said, abandoned all hopes that a husband could be caught in the ordinary way for her daughter; but she still cherished a belief in fate, or providence, or chance. She designated the mysterious hidden potentiality by all three names, varying them according to the frame of mind she happened to be in. On Sundays, or when she chanced to be in a religious mood, it was generally providence; when she coupled Diana in an especial manner with the contingency referred to, it was fate she invoked; while the good luck of other women's daughters was always ascribed to mere chance. When things seemed most hopeless, she would cast over in her mind all the odd pieces of luck that had fallen to the lot of women much older than Diana: Miss Dillon, without a penny, who was forty, and who had been proposed for [1] by her parish priest—in trust—for a grazier, of enormous wealth, who had seen her walking along the road; and Miss Hare, without a penny also, and more than forty, who married a general worth five thousand a year; then again, only the other day, old Miss Stoney getting a judge (Miss Stoney's age was notorious). So she would rake up precedents, her hopes rising in corresponding ratio with the ages and drawbacks of the personages she adduced, till Diana would fling out of the room almost in hysterics.

Miss Bursford seated herself at the piano, and began to pick out slowly and deliberately, bar by bar, and line by line, the last fashion in waltzes. When ten or twelve years

[1] The expression "proposed for," like many idioms apparently unaccountable, exactly defines the action. A proposal of marriage is seldom made *to* the lady, but *to* her guardian *for* her.

younger, she might have taken a novel and abandoned
herself to the luxury of castle-building, leaving the ways
and means to develop themselves; but it was not so now.
Romance had long ago taken wing; and feeling, not to say
love, she had never known since she was twenty-five; for
Captain Vesey had certainly carried poor Miss Bursford's
heart to Abyssinia, and left it there, for he married an
Indian widow on his way home. She took everything in
the most practical, business-like way; and having selected
a fort to be stormed, drew her lines around it, dug trenches,
and turned every available gun on the weakest points with
the skill and dexterity to be learnt only in the heavy
campaigning business to which her existence had been
devoted.

When her allotted time of practising was over, she went
to her room to make her toilette for the afternoon, and
seated herself before her mirror. The Venetian blind
pulled carefully down, and her long fair hair well in process
of the complicated brushings, spongings, and rubbings necessary to coax it into brightness and silkiness, she began
to consider her position, and calculate her chances. Brushing her hair seemed to set her thinking powers in action;
it was like a considering cap, and every vexed question
was kept methodically for this hour of the day. She was
not one of those people who, to use an Americanism, "borrow trouble" by forecasting complications or situations ere
they actually exist. She took things as they came, in a
matter-of-fact, practical way; and, turning the full force of
a somewhat narrow intellect directly upon them, just as
she did with a difficult passage in a piece of music, exerted
herself to her utmost until she succeeded, or found she had
miscalculated her forces.

She had estimated Hogan pretty accurately; and Saltasche had given her mother a rough outline of his career,
past and present, which had led that veteran to conclude,
although she disliked him on personal as well as on religious and social grounds, that this barrister was worth
looking up. He had nothing at present; but an Irish
M.P., even in the embryo stage, is always a judge or

colonial dignitary in perspective; and as to his religion, in
Ireland it was a drawback certainly, but in London it
might be rather an advantage.   People of undoubted rank
and position in England seemed to think most highly of
her uncle Monsignor Bursford; while in Dublin he could
only be spoken of with bated breath, as of some disgraceful
appendage, and always as a *convert;* her mother felt it
quite a duty to have it known that her brother-in-law had
not been *born* a Roman Catholic.

Diana reflected also that Mr. Hogan was a beginner and
a climber in society—that he knew nobody.   Lord Brayhead had taken him up, she felt certain, for some purpose
of his own, in connection, doubtless, with some of his selfish
absurd schemes.   The private opinions of his female relatives regarding that great gentleman were not too flattering.
As for Mr. Saltasche, he was utterly unaccountable; and
being a man of reputed wealth, and moving in the best
society, equally irresponsible.   She had the greatest confidence in his discernment, however, and felt fully disposed
to act on his information and suggestions.   As to intro-
ducing his friend to her own set generally, she had her
doubts as to the prudence of that.   There were too many
girls younger and more attractive than herself, who would
do their best to secure even such an uncertain prize as this
promising young barrister.   The more Diana thought it
over, the more firmly convinced she was of the necessity of
keeping him out of the way of people as much as possible.
"*Experientia docet;*" and Diana's wisdom was of that solid
kind that has been bought and paid for.

When fully dressed she pulled up the blind and looked
out, and up and down the street.   Not that she expected
to see anybody or anything; but it was a habit of hers.
Then she turned a large cheval glass round to the light,
and surveyed herself critically from head to foot.   Her
dress was a mixture of dark violet cashmere, and pale blue
silk; the lighter shade gave a golden reflection to her hair,
and a soft ruffle of cambric and lace concealed the thin-
ness, while adding to the whiteness of her neck; velvet
wristbands performed the same friendly office for her hands

and wrists. She had scarcely finished her inspection when a loud knock resounded through the house.

A sneer curled Miss Bursford's lips as the thought flashed through her mind that Hogan was so hurried to confirm his introduction to people of respectability. And she went down to the drawing-room with a leisurely step, intending to maintain her advantage by a chillingly condescending tone.

To her surprise, instead of Mr. O'Rooney Hogan, there was Mr. Saltasche's rotund figure reclining in the easiest chair by the fire. Saltasche had been a school friend of Diana's eldest brother, and was on intimate terms with the family. He managed Mrs. Bursford's business for her in general, and had charge of the investments of her money.

"Well, Miss Di., good morning; is your mother in? I can't stay a moment. By-the-by," and he got up and leaned against the mantelpiece, "Miss Diana, Mr. Hogan —er—" (Diana glanced up at him with a look full of interest)—"is pretty safe to get in for Peatstown. Try and —ah—engage him for the concert if you can. He will call this afternoon after court; about five, maybe. Tell him I am away to London to-night; will be back on Saturday morning. Can I do anything for you there?"

"No," she replied; "it would be too much to trouble you with commissions. You are too kind." She was rapidly thinking over his words, and trying to account for his evident desire to interest her in his *protégé*.

Mrs. Bursford came in now.

"Mr. Saltasche, I am very glad to see you. How do you do? Pray sit down."

"I am going over to the 'little village' to-night. I just leave you these in your own hands before starting. Just sign me this receipt for the Leadmines stock—and you, Miss Diana;" and he handed her a large roll of papers.

Mrs. Bursford took the envelope to her secretary, and, after examining its contents, locked it up. She and Miss Diana signed the prepared receipt, which he then transferred to his pocket-book.

"How very well their 'Excies' looked last night!" Mr. Saltasche observed for about the twelfth time that day.

"Very well indeed," responded the ladies simultaneously.

"He has bought a couple of Lord Newmarket's hunters at Newby's. Splendid animals! Gave three hundred guineas for one of them. Sent them down to the Curragh this morning," continued Mr. Saltasche, with the same tone of proprietorial interest. "I am told, though, that one of them has rather—ah—an inclination to sandcrack," he added, as gloomily as if the price of the animal had come out of his own pocket.

"Dear me!" said the ladies; who did not in the least know what the sandcrack was, but who felt interested and sympathetic immediately in anything ever so remotely concerning their dear Excellencies.

"You will go on Saturday to the theatre?" continued he; "it's a Command night. I shall be there if I can get back in time. Must go now. We'll meet again. Don't forget my message, Miss Diana. Good-bye. Can't I do anything for you in London? No, no: I have had lunch. Quite sure. Adieu! adieu!"

And so Mr. Saltasche took himself off, bowing and smiling to the last moment; and leaving the two ladies quite refreshed and roused up by his visit. It was just as if a wholesome out-of-door breeze had suddenly invaded a close-heated room.

Diana felt invigorated and braced up for action; as she sat down to lunch she said to her mother, "Do you think, mamma, we could get those visits paid in the Square, and be back here by half-past four?"

Mrs. Bursford paused for a second. She knew perfectly well, from her daughter's tone and the mention of the particular hour, that Saltasche had given her some hint before she came down to the drawing-room. What was the good of demurring? So she shrugged her shoulders in a helpless sort of way, and replied resignedly, "We may as well, I suppose."

CHAPTER XL

"All you sage Counsellors hence !
And to the English Court assemble now,
From every region, apes of idleness."

King Henry IV.

DICKY DAVOREN was passing through the entrance gate on his way to the ten o'clock train one Friday morning, when the postman unceremoniously stuffed a couple of letters into his hands, and, glad to be saved the trouble of going up to the hall-door, made off as fast as possible. Dicky duly qualified this impertinent proceeding; and then, casting his eye over the superscriptions, rushed back to the room where his sister was sitting, and, tossing the letters into her lap, cried impatiently,—

"Open the O'Hegarty's first, Nell, and be quick. I've only five minutes."

Nellie broke the huge violet seal, and read as follows:—

"MY DEAR NELLIE,

"I should perhaps have written earlier to let you know that I want Dicky to secure front places for us at the 'Royal' for to-morrow night. Three—please remember. Come early, and dress here. It is a Command night. Tell Dicky, with my love, that I shall require him to see us · home, as Peter pleads rheumatism to escape the 'extortion' of attending us. I hope your mother is better. My love to all of you. In haste,

"Your affectionate cousin,
"D. H."

"Well now!" exclaimed he; "and so I'm to be made

do Peter's work! My word, it's a trifle too cool of Miss Dorothy. That dirty, good-for-nothing creature kept to do nothing."

" Well, well," said his sister, soothingly, " perhaps Peter will relent, and——"

" Yah! old rascal ; relent, indeed! Give him a piece of my mind, I will. Dorothy Hegarty's getting childish. I'm to go take these seats too."

"There's nothing out of the way in that, is there? Here is the money for you. Go now, Dicky, or you will lose your train."

The young gentleman snatched the coin, and flew out of the house, running fast in order to make up for time lost. Not so fast, however, that he could not bestow a friendly wink on the nursemaid to whom he had forbidden his sister to speak, and whom he encountered in the avenue with her young charges.

He arrived at the station just as the train drew up; and in obedience to a signal made him from the window of a smoking carriage, clambered in beside his friend Orpen, who happened to be going up to town by the same train.

" Look here, Davoren," said this young gentleman ; and putting his hand in the pocket of his Ulster coat, he produced a newspaper. Folding down a sheet, he pointed out to Dicky's inquisitive eyes an advertisment from a firm of bookmakers, setting forth, adorned with the usual notes of admiration and testimonials from grateful clients, the golden harvest to be reaped from their infallible system.

" A bam., is it not?" asked Dicky, incredulously.

Mr. Orpen winked his left eye, and having folded up the newspaper, put it back in his pocket without saying a word. Then he leaned back, and proceeded to enjoy the flavour of a dirty little briar-wood pipe, which he had laid aside for an instant, with the most perfect composure and elegant indifference.

Dicky Davoren was not blessed with the virtue of long-suffering; and after a moment's stoical acquiescence in the superior attitude of his friend, gave him an impatient push.

"You're not such an ass? Come now, Orpen."

Still no answer. So Dicky, burning with eagerness, was forced to assume a look of indifference in sheer self-defence. Then Mr. Orpen condescended to enlighten him ; and taking the questions in order of precedence, answered the first oracularly,—" 'Tis, and it isn't," and then winked again.

Mr. Davoren, who by this time had got a small meerschaum lighted, and with alarming contortion of feature was endeavouring to hold it in his mouth and smoke it simultaneously, without the aid of a supporting hand, allowed his friend's utterance to pass unnoticed.

"And as for being an ass," continued he of the briarroot, "all right : I am," and he nodded with an air of cheerful acquiescence.

Dicky felt absolutely humbled and abashed ; conscious that irony of this magnitude was a weapon entirely beyond his powers, he gave in at once. Taking the meerschaum, whose uncoloured bowl betrayed its newness in a very lowering way, he laid it tenderly on the cushion beside him, and having expectorated out of window, advanced his face close to the impassive briar-root, and in an emphatic tone asked,—

"Orpen, how much are you on?"

Mr. Orpen deliberately reversed his pipe on the edge of the open window, and having knocked the last vestige of tobacco-ash out, put it in his pocket and answered sententiously—

"Every brown I can raise."

Dicky's countenance glowed, and his blue eyes opened to their very widest extent. Then he dug his hands into his pockets and began a whistle.

"I know a chap," resumed Mr. Orpen, "that won a hundred and fifty on a mere little garrison steeple-chase."

"Shillings?" interrupted Dicky, so greedy that he could not wait to hear all his friend had to say.

His companion glanced at him in a withering manner, and enunciated the single word "Sovereigns."

The train drew up at the City Terminus now, and

the two youths descended, and taking each other's arms, plunged through a number of dirty byways across town to the college.

They dashed into the lecture-room almost breathlessly, and spent the time, as far as Dicky was concerned, in happy unconsciousness of the reverend lecturer's every utterance. Dicky was deeply meditating the distinctions and differences between backing a horse and taking the odds, and calculating the amounts of imaginary investments and the intricacies of making a " safe book."

The moment they were free, away they rushed to the rooms of a gentleman commoner named Gagan. Him they found at breakfast, with a chum named Mahoney Quain, a splendid-looking young animal, over six feet in height, and renowned as one of the best athletes and wildest lads in Trinity.

"What's the row ?" growled the host, turning a pair of very bloodshot eyes on the incomers. Mr. Gagan had been making a night of it ; and the soda water with which his skip had liberally plied him had not quite rehabilitated him yet.

" Morrow, Mahoney," said Dicky. "Got out your watch ?"

This allusion was called forth by the unusual sight of a gold chain in the button-hole of the gentleman addressed.

"Yes," returned Mr. Mahoney with a grin ; " the money's gone back to the bank : here's the receipt !" and he dangled his watch in his fingers as he spoke.

"The Post Office Savings Bank is a humbug compared to a real good ticker. Mine's not half the value of yours, Mahoney. It was left me by an old godmother, for being a good boy and attending Sunday-school regularly." Orpen intoned this part of his speech with a sort of nasal drone that made the rest laugh. " It doesn't keep time ; but the governor can't take a hint, and declines to exchange it."

"That's not what we came for," interrupted Dicky. "Orpen, show thát advertisement. Look, Gagan."

Mr. Quain stooped his great back over the table, and, in company with his friends, perused the enticing bill of fare set forth in the columns of one of the most largely circulated and influential papers in Dublin.

"Ten pounds realise four hundred. Augh!" grunted he derisively, "the lowest thing they notice is five pounds."

"Five hundred it might as well be!" cried Dicky scornfully.

"What do you think of a joint stock concern?" asked Mr. Orpen. "Quain, you're in cash; Davoren, couldn't you manage twenty-five shillings—hey? Make your game, genelmen; ball's a-rolling. *Rooge ah nore*, genelmen! genelmen!!" And Mr. Orpen, whose forte lay in mimicry, gave a good imitation of a well-known roulette man of the day.

"I shan't," said Mr. Gagan; "I'm cleaned out. You did it, Billy Orpen; so put down for me, else I won't."

"Have you your Ulster coat?" suggested Mr. Quain, who was credited with a perfect genius for raising money.

"No, I haven't my Ulster coat," returned Mr. Gagan savagely; "it's pawned two days ago."

A silence fell on the quartette. It seemed as if their scheme was to fall through; but Orpen, inspired by a sudden thought, cried,—

"Day after to-morrow we give in our fees, don't we? Suppose you—ah—just postpone paying yours for a week, Gagan. I have done that: it works beautifully. They never mind a few days' delay; and something's always sure to turn up in a week."

Mr. Gagan looked a little frightened; he had not tried this expedient yet; embezzling the fees was looked upon in college as a rather go-ahead practice.

"And what if your new financial dodge turns out to be a bilk?" asked Mahoney Quain, stretching himself lazily against the opposite wall of the little grimy room.

Orpen shook his head. "Perfectly safe, my boy; take thirty, forty, whatever is given against their selection or your own, I bet you we'll win."

"Have you won anything by it?" asked the host, slowly raising his head from the back of his chair.

"No, I have not tried it yet; but a cousin of mine has

N

—a very decent fellow, Jack Warden,—I dined at his house
yesterday, and he tells me he netted a cool hundred and
fifty on a ten-pun' note; he recommended me to try this
firm in preference to his. He—let me see—I think he
took seventeen or eighteen to one against Molasses; then
their commission and charges reduced it. He is making
money at it, I assure you."

"When is the event, and what is it?" asked Mr. Gagan
a little impatiently.

"Churton races; and they settle the Monday after.
The money must be forwarded by Tuesday at latest."

"I'll close on the fees," declared Gagan energetically,
sitting up straight in the chair.

"I'm on too," said Mahoney Quain. "And I," declared
Dicky Davoren, last of all, but not a whit less determinedly.

"Is it money down now?" asked the gigantic Mahoney,
proceeding to finger over a handful of silver.

"Monday afternoon will do. Meet me at the football
gathering. Now don't forget," adjured Orpen; on whom
seemed to fall of its own accord, and by tacit consent, the
office of secretary and treasurer.

Mr. Gagan lay down on his bed in an adjoining room;
Dicky threw his books into a corner, and selected the most
enticing of a collection of novels; Mahoney Quain, who
was not addicted to literature in any shape, lighted a clay
pipe; and Orpen disappeared with his newspaper, doubtless in quest of another Joint Stock Company of subscribers. Before Dicky had finished the second page of
his romance he remembered his commission, and reflecting
that it would never do to forfeit the good graces of either
Miss Dorothy or his sister at this particular juncture—for
he was depending chiefly on their support to enable him to
raise the twenty-five shillings, that nest-egg which was to
be the nucleus of an inexhaustible Eldorado—dashed off at
once to secure the places.

In the box office of the Theatre Royal he brushed against
no less a person than Hogan, who, at the instance of Mr.
Saltasche, was also taking places in the front row.

"Who are you squiring?" asked Hogan, carelessly, on hearing him demand three tickets.

"My sister, and—a—my cousin. Front row, and as near the centre as you have them," said Dicky to the booking-clerk.

"This gentleman has got the centre seat; there are a couple on either side of his, if you could just settle between you," returned the official.

"Of course," said Hogan; "here, twenty-one, two, three, for you; give me this one." The exchange was made to the satisfaction of both, and they turned and walked out together.

"How is your sister?" asked Hogan. "I have not seen you now for a good while: come in and have an oyster." They were just at Burton Bindon's door: Dicky assenting, both entered, and were speedily engaged with a dish of bivalves, washed down with tankards of stout.

"Master Davoren, why have you never come to see me?"

"I will, indeed," returned Dicky. "I wrote down your address."

"I shall be giving a supper some night next week, or so. Where is this you are? 'Church——' what was it?"

"Church House, Green Lanes," replied the boy promptly.

"Oh, you're beside Mr. Saltasche there. Do you know him?"

"I do; he lives close to us. Awful swell place; no end of glass, and all that sort of thing. Nice, jolly old chap, too."

"Old chap!" thought Hogan; "a man I take to be only twelve or thirteen years older than myself: how these young ones run on!" and he looked at the stripling beside him. "Seventeen, I suppose," he continued, noting the clear, smooth, almost girlish face, and weedy, though promising build of the lad.

"How old are you, Mr. Davoren? Twenty?"

Immensely flattered, Dicky looked up with a pleased expression.

"Not quite," he replied. "Not eighteen yet."

" Dear me ! indeed!" Hogan threw all the wonder possible into this tone. " My dear fellow, excuse me, I must follow that gentleman going out there." Hogan ran over to the bar, paid for both, and disappeared after an attorney of his acquaintance.

Dicky sauntered out leisurely, and returned to college, ostensibly to an afternoon lecture, but in reality to lay his plans with a view to possessing himself of the needful sum of money. If he were to borrow from Orpen, that youth, who somehow always managed to have cash in his pockets, would insist on being paid out of the profits—Mr. Dicky, of course, with his usual confidence, looked upon the venture as already realised—and Orpen was such a Jew he would extort goodness knows how much percentage ; then, too, the money would be in his hands, and he could in fact lay an embargo upon it. Somehow the post of chancellor of the exchequer always devolved upon Orpen ; some eclectic affinity between him and money, thought Dicky, shaking his blonde head. He must look for it elsewhere.

The result of all his meditations seemed to be indicated by his dropping into his cousin's house in Fitzgerald Place at seven o'clock punctually, dressed with the most scrupulous care, and with a flower in his button-hole for which he had paid sixpence to the florist who lived in Green Lanes, and which, had he bought it in the Nassau Street shops, would have cost perhaps three times the money.

" The darling villain !" screamed Miss O'Hegarty, on finding him in the drawing-room when she came down ; "he's actually punctual to the minute ! And how nice he looks ! Really, Nellie," she cried to that young lady as she followed her in, " we may be quite proud of him to-night."

Nellie was not a little puzzled. She had expected, from the young gentleman's conduct of the morning, that he would have presented himself with a sulky countenance at the very last minute, and that he would have forgotten the tickets, or have gone to procure them so late in the

day that they would have been obliged to put up with a
back row.   Not so : he produced an envelope, and handed
it to his cousin, remarking,—

"Centre front, ma'am.   Twenty-one, two, and three; and
I've ordered a cab."

"The dear, thoughtful child !" cried Miss Dorothy in a
perfect ecstasy ; "and so poor Peter needn't go out with
his rheumatism."

Nellie was stroking her hair before a pier-glass, and
detected the trace of a grimace on the collegian's face; but
she wisely abstained from making a remark, feeling grateful to whatever accident had caused his unwonted good-
humour.

"Where did you get that lovely bud, Dicky?" she
asked.

"Bought it—ah—just now," returned he, glancing
modestly down at the camellia, as if overcome with a sense
of his own graciousness and amiability.

"We need not be there too soon, as we've taken our
places.   Sit down a bit, Dicky, till I get you a glass of
wine ; and tell us what you've been doing."   And Miss
O'Hegarty seated herself in her arm-chair and rang the
bell.

Peter presented himself with a countenance of super-
human crossness at the door.

"Peter ! a glass of wine for Master Richard ; and you
needn't go for a cab.   Master Richard has saved you the
trouble ; he has been so thoughtful as to order one as he
came along."

Peter cast a glance of utter scorn and incredulity, on
hearing this assertion, at both his mistress and Master
Richard.   This last-named repaid it with a broad grin of
triumph and defiance.

"I haven't been doing anything, ma'am.   College as
usual; and went and looked at the football match."

"Were you not playing, dear?"

"No, ma'am.   Hem,—my subscription is out (five
shillings), and it's got to be renewed."   Nellie, hearing this,
turned and looked at him in utter bewilderment, clearly

remembering him to have got the very five shillings from
his father only one week before.

"Oh, you must have it. I'll see that you have it, Dick;
now take your glass of wine ; you must have hurried over
your dinner."

Mr. Dick mentally placed the five shillings to the credit
of an account he was opening with his bank, which was
situated in the top small drawer of his bureau at home,
and drank his glass of sherry with infinite relish.   Then
feeling impatient to make his final move in the game, he
declared it time to be off, and marshalled his charges carefully into the cab.

When they arrived at the theatre, and were about to
pass down the tiers of seats to the front, Dicky seized
Nellie by the arm, and held her back, saying, " Let Cousin
Dorothy go first."

Miss O'Hegarty passed in accordingly, and took number
twenty-one, as he intended ; then he placed himself between the two ladies, leaving Nellie in the seat marked
twenty-three.   "Now," thought the young Machiavelli,
"if Hogan has the gumption to sit next her, she'll be in
good humour too."

They were rather early ; but Miss O'Hegarty liked to
be in before everybody else ; and in the theatre, or in
church, she almost considered it a part of the performance
to see the people come in.   Nellie leaned back in her stall
and looked round ; the gas was not fully turned on, and the
half-light had a pretty effect.   The orchestra were tuning
their instruments.

"That's a part of the performance I never could understand their having to go through in public," said Miss
O'Hegarty with a grimace.   "Just hear those fiddles
scrooping : it ought to be done somewhere at the back.
Ugh!"

Then a crowd poured in, and she began to recognise her
acquaintances on all sides.   Right opposite to them sat the
Raffertys, dressed in all the hues of the rainbow, and the
Brangans, and a tribe of their friends.   Presently people
began to crowd in behind.   Miss O'Hegarty looked round,

and found Mrs. O'Hara and her daughters attended by a couple of officers. She turned Dicky out of his front seat, and made room for Mrs. O'Hara. The young ladies did not seem inclined to be divided from their squires. The gas was now turned on full, and the orchestra having finished the objectionable preliminaries, commenced a lively waltz. Gaudily dressed people streamed in; red cloaks, white cloaks, blue cloaks, great bouquets of hot-house flowers, and gold and silver sprinkled fans, flirting and fluttering on all sides. The talking and rustling of silks rose above the music. All of a sudden a sort of commotion; then a lull. The waltz stopped suddenly, a bar of "God save the Queen" was played; their Excellencies were come, and without more ado the curtain drew up. Her Excellency looked pale and cold, and the red noses of her two old ladies-in-waiting beamed conspicuously over their ermine tippets. Mr. Wyldoates, and the other A.D.C.'s-in-waiting, settled themselves resignedly in a corner from which nothing could be heard or seen. The Malowneys were in their box too: Mrs. Malowney conspicuous by her absence; a chaperone, with a stack of roses on her head and huge knots of red ribbons, accompanied the young ladies in her stead. The Lord Mayor, of course, was present; his sons were in the pit, near the door, so as to slip out to the bar as often as necessary; and a rising young architect, and a young doctor, who showed themselves capable of appreciating the money and connection which Mr. Hogan had despised, made themselves agreeable to the ladies of the family.

One of the new modern society plays was being performed by a London company, in the usual style. The noblemen of the piece certainly did not look "to the manner born," but were very well dressed. The actresses were tolerable; a lady who had a minor part played it pretty badly, but her splendid diamond earrings and red-heeled boots seemed to compensate for her deficiencies. The first part was played by a clever actress, who might have passed for a lady in ordinary society. She was the only one of the female characters who seemed conversant with the most ordinary rules of etiquette. An "h" was dropped here and there by the diamond-earringed lady; but the youngest nobleman of the piece kindly adjusted the balance by inserting an extra one at intervals.

The first act was over, when, hearing a stir behind them, Nellie, whose attention was by no means absorbed by the piece, turned her head and met the glance of Hogan, who, followed by Saltasche, was moving quietly down to his seat. He smiled and bowed, and passed on to the farther of the two seats. Saltasche followed, and took that next her, giving, as he did so, an approving glance in her direction. Bland and smiling as ever, with a dark red camellia in his button-hole, he settled himself back in his chair to look round him; becoming aware of the presence of the physician-extraordinary beside Hogan, he touched him lightly.

"Change with me, my dear fellow; I want to speak to your neighbour."

It was done in a moment, and Hogan was Miss Davoren's next-door neighbour. She looked away across to the stage, trying hard to look unconcerned; but a bright lovely flush came up unbidden, and her eyes for an instant sparkled brighter.

Hogan caught sight of Nellie's neighbour, Mrs. O'Hara, and remembered having seen her at Lord Brayhead's dinner. He could not imagine whom Nellie was with. Presently Miss O'Hegarty handed an opera-glass to Nellie, desiring her to look at some person in the distance; and Mrs. O'Hara made some slight remark to her about the scene just going on. It was settled, then, who her companions were; and he was more puzzled than ever. She seemed to him still more exquisitely lovely to-night; her white cashmere cloak was open, showing her full white throat; a cluster of lilies of the valley, looking the very embodiment of innocence and cold white purity, nestled in the abundant coils of her brown hair; the graceful, but as yet scarcely formed contour of her shoulders and bust, showed clearly under the thin drapery, indicating a form that would mature into still more perfect womanly beauty.

Some way behind sat Miss Bursford, with the pretty, but made-up, little Mrs. De Lancier ; and across, beside and half hidden by a pillar, wearing a *burnous* of deep crimson, above which her face looked like a *relievo* of snowy Carrara marble, leaning her head listlessly on her hand, was Captain Poignarde's wife. Saltasche caught sight, as he was sweeping the circle round with his lorgnette, first of Poignarde's vapid countenance, grinning approval of the actress of the diamonds : and, impelled by curiosity, looked to the right and left of him, to see if his *piquante* helpmate might chance to be there. She was looking, as it happened, straight in his direction, and he caught the very glance of her splendid liquid brown eyes right in his. The pure oval of her face was well relieved against the braids of brown hair hanging low on her neck. White and scarlet camellia buds were set, in defiance of the mode of the day, right behind her left ear—just where the Spanish beauties put them ; the white over the scarlet, so that the one set off the ivory-white skin it caressed, and the other glowed in the setting of her luxuriant hair. Not a jewel did she wear, save a gold and diamond star, fixed in a black velvet ribbon on her neck ; and her wrists, slender, round, and supple, bore not a single bracelet. Saltasche's artistic eye revelled in the picture she made ; but not venturing to seem bold, he relinquished the glass to Hogan, and turned his eyes again on the stage. After awhile, at an emotional scene of the piece, seeing that Mrs. Poignarde, like every one else, was wrapt in attention to the performance, he took the glass, and hurriedly adjusting it, fixed it full on her. Just the graceful pose of head he had noted that day down on the Quay ; the square low brow, set in wavy brown ripples of hair ; the white lithe neck, on which her head drooped and turned as gracefully and languidly as one of Nellie's lilies ; the short curved upper lip and sweet half-opened mouth, showing little uneven pearls of teeth.

"What countrywoman can it be ?" wondered he. "The mouth and chin are too perfect and too pronounced for her to be Irish. The accent, too, I remember, was a little foreign. Could she be American ? I must find her out."

The pathetic, or rather, hysterical, love scene, was over now, and the drop-scene fell. With the exquisite artistic taste of modern audiences, it had to be raised again, to allow the spectators to feast their eyes on Lady ——'s dishevelled fainting fit.

Hogan leaned upon his elbow, and said to Nellie, "Are you not hard-hearted? I have been watching you for a symptom of a tear, Miss Davoren. Such insensibility is quite distressing."

"Have you been greatly moved yourself?"

" Er—that is not expected, you know ; you don't expect soft-heartedness from the sterner sex."

"I have noticed," said she, "that at sermons men cry more than women."

"Well, indeed," returned he, "if you could read the hearts of all present now, you would find the men more moved by that pathetic scene than you ladies seem to be."

"You don't need to take the trouble of looking so far as their hearts. Take them on the evidence of their eyes, just." And Miss Davoren smiled a little maliciously.

"Miss Davoren," said he with mock gravity, "do you insinuate that their emotion arises from soft-headedness rather than——?"

"I am sure I insinuated no such thing. Pray look! what strange being is that?" And she turned towards the stage, where the conventional stage-Irishman was going through the approved Hibernian *répertoire*.

"A foreigner of distinction!" and Hogan affected to raise his glass. "I have read of such an animal in the books of English tourists."

"Is it not too bad that such a monstrosity should be presented as a national type? The Home Rulers ought to put that down."

"We don't know that," said he drily; "only for this sort of thing, how could the distinction be kept up? And then it flatters the English so. They always like to remind themselves of their great superiority over us ; and this " (nodding at the Paddy) "is a sort of pleasing reflection for them,—like *Punch's* Scotchmen, you know."

Nellie looked up into his eyes hastily, to see how far he was in earnest; and meeting a droll twinkle there, though to all other appearance he was perfectly solemn, she laughed outright behind her fan. " Well, the Scotch are not made fun of, as we are," said she.

" Indeed they are!—and though it is the fashion here to sneer at them as being unpatriotic, calling their country North Britain and all that, they are a deal more really national than we."

" I have heard that they deny their country, whenever they can."

" That's not so at all ; rather, it's only a few. The Irish in America—the second generation, I mean—would like to pass themselves off for Knicker-Bockers if they could. I have been told so. Not that I think that matters; I wish they'd all do it," continued Hogan. " They keep pretty well to their flourishing—good gracious! From Captain Macmorris down to the present day they are at it: what in the world is the sense of it ? "

" '*My nation ! what ish my nation ?*' Is that it ? What a little gem that passage is!" laughed Miss Davoren. " Look at that man," continued she ; ." did you here him say *h*opportunity ? Is it not absurd?"

" Yes," replied Hogan ; " I fear the people who come here to learn the correct pronunciation of the Queen's English will carry away some rather erroneous impressions."

" What do you say ? People come here—to the theatre —for that purpose ?"

" Yes, certainly, Miss Davoren ; I know people who do."

" Do look at that actor," cried Dorothy,—" he with the handkerchief: that's an imitation of Charles Matthews, in ' Cool as a Cucumber.' "

" I have seen Charles Matthews : we went to see him the last time I was in London ; he was very far before that man." This was from Mrs. O'Hara.

" What a pity it is that ladies and gentlemen don't take to the profession !" said Nellie Davoren.

"Ladies and gentlemen!" exclaimed Miss O'Hegarty; "what are you saying, Nellie?"

"But, Cousin Dorothy, was not —— educated at Rugby? and Miss ——?"

"Don't let me hear you talking so, child:" and Miss Dorothy turned away with a frown. An interval for refreshment occurred now, and the gentlemen availed themselves of it extensively. In this respect the Dublin audiences are yet far behind the Londoners; but, no doubt, time and assiduous copying of the British peculiarities will soon bring them abreast of their models. The pit was emptied in a few minutes. Boys just started in life, clerks and little shop-keepers, thronged into the bars; and every beverage, from the modest glass of beer to champagne and brandy and soda water, was called for. Saltasche and Hogan went out with the crowd. Hogan drank a glass of lemonade and sherry. Saltasche set down his glass untouched, and rushed to meet Poignarde, of whom he caught sight at the door. "Come and take a glass of brandy and water." The Captain accepted with pleasure; and when he had finished, leaving his companion, a young officer, followed Saltasche back to where Mrs. Poignarde was sitting alone.

"Adelaide, you met Mr. Saltasche before."

She looked up, and bowed and smiled. He seated himself beside her.

"You don't seem to care for this play, Mrs. Poignarde?"

"Well, no; I confess I do not."

"After the London theatres it must seem very poor and shabby to you."

"Well, I did not draw any comparison between them."

"Have you been in Paris?"

"Never."

"Ah! that's a pleasure to come. You like travelling, of course?"

All this was uttered by Mr. Saltasche in his most courteous, suave tone, with the air of deferential interest which in spite of oneself attracts at last.

She glanced at him a little suspiciously, as if doubtful of

his meaning, and said distantly, "My experience of travel-ling has been limited to the regimental changes between London and Shorncliffe and Aldershot; we were in Cork, too, for a few months."

"A nice rainy place!"

"No so bad as Dublin, though;" and she shivered a little. "I was born in South America, and have a dim remembrance of warmth and bright colours and perpetual sun. It may be only a sort of instinct, but I do hate this damp cold."

He looked at her sympathetically.

"Well, we make up for it," he said, "with our gaieties. These three months to come form our season. You go to many balls?"

"Ah! I know so few of your people here. I don't make acquaintances. I wonder where Eric has gone," she added suddenly, noticing that her husband had left his seat for the second time. "Ah! here comes Mr. Grey." Saltasche bowed, recognising in him the son of a clergyman of his acquaintance; and seeing Poignarde's sullen countenance in the background, his eyes looking rather lowering from the effects of a second potation, he judged it well to with-draw and return to his own seat. So after a word of adieu, distantly and coldly pronounced by Mrs. Poignarde, he left her.

"Do you know Saltasche, Mrs. Poignarde?" asked young Grey.

"Well, hardly."

"I know him right well: he is a very rich fellow—has a beautiful house in our parish; very charitable, and that sort of thing."

"Is he?"

"He's worth fifty thousand pounds; and an incorrigible bachelor."

"Really!" She turned languidly, and cast a look across the theatre at Saltasche and his companion, who were sitting opposite. Saltasche was not the more interesting of the two. Hogan was taller and younger, and his bright thin face and keen eyes seemed to take in everything.

Saltasche leaned back on one elbow, and out of his half-closed eyes looked far more at the audience than at the play; every now and again he directed his eyes on herself. She saw this too, and was amused at it.

When the first piece was over, she observed that his companion went out, with the ladies who were sitting next him; he remained, as she did, for the after-piece. When it was finished they all rose to go; and in the throng on the staircase Saltasche pressed his way until close beside her. She was leaning on young Grey's arm, her husband following behind: and in a bevy of beautiful women assembled from all parts of Ireland, Saltasche in his own mind decreed her the palm. Standing in the full blaze of the chandeliers, amid all the glare of colours around, the slight lithe figure and small glossy head so proudly carried, attracted more admiration than the celebrated Galway belle, Miss —— herself. She seemed so utterly unconscious: not Lady St. —— herself, attended by her court, could have shown more self-possession and haughty indifference. They passed down slowly; and it was not until after a long wait below that a cab was found. Saltasche stood close at the door and handed her in. He succeeded in his aim, which was to hear the address given to the cabman.

"3 Park Villas, Inchicore," growled Poignarde.

Saltasche took out his pocket-book, and turned to the lamp to scribble it down. As he did so, he struck something with his foot on the step of the colonnade. Stooping, he found a broken fan of ivory and scarlet feathers, and on the handle a monogram, "A. C.," in curiously entwined raised letters. A smile of triumph lit up his face as he examined his prize; he rubbed the dust off it with his handkerchief, and put it carefully in his pocket.

We must return to our party, whose fortunes we have abandoned for a while to trace the devious ways of Mr. Cosmo Saltasche. Hogan continued to sit next Nellie, drinking in the light of her candid eyes, watching her clear profile, the lines of which were as fine and pure as

those of a Roman cameo, watching every stir, every movement—so unstudied, yet so graceful, so natural and so
fitting — listening to the laughing remarks, sensible and
straightforward, without a trace of worldly cunning or
arrière pensée in them. He had caught a glimpse ere now
of Diana Bursford, who was seated near, and who cast
now and anon cold watchful glances in his direction;
he had paid a visit at her house that afternoon, and had
quitted it steeped to the eyes in the flattery she so well
knew how to ply. He knew she expected, and that she
had a right to expect him to go to her; but Nellie's fresh
beauty chained him beside her, and Diana looked and
smiled in vain.

Hogan parted from Miss O'Hegarty's party at the door
of the theatre, leaving Dicky to escort them home. That
young gentleman, who was in high good humour, seated
himself in the cab beside his sister. Everything had succeeded with him; and he already, in his mind's eye,
grasped the fruit of his plans. He had overheard Mrs.
O'Hara ask Dorothy who that handsome lad was, and had
noticed Dorothy's pleased air in replying. He felt an
ideal half-sovereign in his pocket, as securely as if he
already possessed it. He waited patiently till they got
out at the door in Fitzgerald Place.

"Come in, Dicky dear; I want you one minute," said
Miss O'Hegarty, when the hall-door opened for them, and
the cook with a tallow candle (Peter, the independent, had
gone to bed) proceeded to light the candles on the hall
table.

"See, Dicky; pay the cabman, and keep the change for
yourself;" and she handed him three five-shilling pieces.
"You must have something for being so good and considerate."

Dicky's heart throbbed with delight; he quickly took
his leave, with many thanks for the liberal tip, and
bestowing eighteenpence on the cabman, buttoned up his
topcoat and strode off to catch the last train. Thirteen-
and-sixpence, exactly one-half of his subscription, he
counted into his drawer when he got home. Nellie and

his mother were good for five shillings between them, at least. He had a florin of his own; six shillings only remained to be got together; and he tucked himself up in bed, cogitating how to make up that deficit, more anxiously and eagerly than ever Chancellor of the Exchequer brooded over a shortcoming in his Budget.

CHAPTER XII.

"JACK CADE.—Be it known unto thee by these presents, that I am the besom that must sweep the court clean of such filth as thou art. Thou hast most traitorously corrupted the youth of the realm in creating a grammar school ; and whereas, before our forefathers had no other books but the score and the tally, thou hast caused printing to be used ; and, contrary to the King, his crown, and dignity, thou hast built a paper mill. It will be proved to thy face that thou hast men about thee that usually talk of a noun and a verb ; and such abominable words as no Christian ear can endure to hear."

MR. SALTASCHE, who had been obliged to go to London for a couple of days on business, had telegraphed to Hogan from the Westminster Palace Hotel that he must see him on Saturday, and desired him to engage seats for the theatre, it being a Command night, and to meet him at the Shelbourne Hotel at five to dinner. Hogan obeyed, being on his own side equally desirous to settle matters with regard to the Parliamentary business. After much and anxious consideration, he had determined to accept. The Bishop declined to interfere —saying that Hogan was as well aware of the risks as himself, and that, after all, it might be cheaper to try now than at the general election, when the Tories would certainly be measuring their strength against the present Government, and entailing thereby a larger outlay. So, not without misgivings, he gave orders to his broker to sell out his shares of Great Southern Railway stock, and lodged the proceeds in the bank to meet the expenses of his candidature.

At five o'clock he presented himself at the front entrance of the Shelbourne, and found his friend standing in the

O

hall, fresh and trim, and with a superb dark-red camellia in the lapel of his dress-coat.

" How do you do, Mr. Hogan ? I'm glad to see you. No, I'm not a bit tired ; too old a stager, I assure you. Come along : this way." And so, talking all the while, they followed a waiter into a comfortable private room, where a round table was laid for two. Mr. Saltasche had ordered a capital dinner ; the wines were the best to be had, the fish unexceptionable, and the *menu* carefully chosen. No word of business was uttered by either of the men until the last dish had disappeared. Saltasche threw himself back in his chair, which he had turned round towards the fire, and, pointing to the opposite end of the hearthrug, motioned Hogan to bring up his.

The barrister changed his seat, pushing up his wine-glass and plate, and Saltasche opened the ball.

" Well, Mr. Hogan, about the business we were talking of ; have you made up your mind ?"

" Yes, Mr. Saltasche ; I have decided to offer myself as a candidate for Peatstown. I need not tell you what a loss it will be to me if I fail."

" Don't speak of failure. Pshaw, man, you are per-fectly safe. Your attorney is——?"

" Mr. Muldoon. I mean, he will act for me, for as yet of course he knows nothing of my intention. I have pretty well decided the platform and address. Home Rule, absolute and unconditional ; clerical control of Education, Tenant Right, Amnesty, and—ah—oh, of course, the Holy Father's grievances. I think that's the whole list."

" By Jove, and a complete litany, too ! " said Saltasche ; and he grinned to himself as he pictured Lord Brayhead's face on hearing the last item of the programme. What a pill that would be for the "swaddling lord" to bolt ! " Well," continued he aloud, " of all your platform, you have not one solid, practical scheme : not one. Home Rule looks the only thing likely to raise a stir in the House. Clerical Education — won't hold water, that notion ; the Government cannot, without giving the lie direct to their own principles, grant a scheme such as

would satisfy the Cardinal. Tenant Right, or Fixity of
Tenure, is blocked too; at least, until the days of universal
suffrage, when the House will be full of Radicals and Reds,
and them only. I decline altogether to give an opinion on
Amnesty; a few blackguards more or less at large in society
is of no great account; but the *morale* of the army would
be injured by such a concession. And as for the Holy
Father's grievances, what! do you want to embroil the
Government with Victor Emanuel?"

"Bah! don't go dissecting me so pitilessly as that. My
conscientious opinion is that Home Rule for this country,
and Scotland too, would be very beneficial. The country
is really suffering by having everything drained out of it
to London. Absenteeism has swelled to a fearful extent;
you must see it yourself. People all flocking over to
London, and the very people who are most wanted here:
nearly all the brains of both countries are drained by the
capital. It won't end well; I promise you it won't.
And the evil consequences of it are already beginning to
show themselves. I cannot see why statesmen refuse to
entertain the idea. It seems to be too much the fashion
to smell treason in every Irish project. People overlook
the real good that lies beneath."

"Well, I don't doubt there is something in your views;
but, Mr. Hogan, what the people mean by Home Rule—
the people who are sending you to Parliament to demand
it for them—is a rather more highly-coloured article.
They want what O'Connell was always dangling before
their eyes—a fight. Then another set want, not a mere
Legislative Chamber, but separation and independence;
and that third class of Irish malcontents, the returned
Americans, and those whom they have infected, want a
Republic. I'll tell you, of all other things in the world,
what completely proves to me the impossibility of this
scheme is the opposition of the clergy to it."

"They have not opposed it," interrupted Hogan hastily;
"I know some priests who are in favour of the movement;
there are, indeed, a great number; but, like all sensible
men, they are waiting to see their way clearly before them."

"Ah! you will see in the long run. The priests don't oppose it now, because to do so would set the people against their nominees at the General Election. They may be wanting also to reserve it for a threat in case the Education Bill doesn't please them; but everywhere the Ultramontanes——"

"Now," interrupted Hogan again, "pardon me, Mr. Saltasche,—there you are falling into the cardinal error of the general Protestant public, in laying national agitation to the charge of the Ultramontane party. That party has no existence in Ireland. There are, of course, a few dignitaries and a few priests here and there whose views are identical with those popularly ascribed to Ultramontanes. But the reason that the clergy oppose the mixed system is diametrically opposite to that generally imagined —that is, the reason given by the English journalists."

"Humph! and now tell me what is this opposite reason?"

"In one word," returned Hogan, "proselytism; and that includes nationalism. Little wonder, indeed, that the people follow the priests to the poll! They were always the very purest patriots. Look what the priests suffered in old times for their flocks. The early Christian martyrs were never more persecuted and hunted; that is not forgotten yet."

"True, but *that is not any longer so;* and I think the clergy of the present day are rather trading on the reputation of their ancestors than taking any pains to earn one for themselves."

"That's as may be," returned the barrister. "You remember, Mr. Saltasche, that in speaking this way to you I do so as to one who is above all prejudice, party or religious."

"Quite so, quite so," assented Saltasche.

"People blame the priests for not accepting the purely secular education, and taking it upon themselves, provide religious instruction separate from it. But how could Roman Catholic priests depend on the secular books and secular teachers provided by a Government which made the introduction of some proselytising subject an integral

part of every educational scheme ever propounded, and, as
I told you before, looked upon this proceeding as one
calculated to win the allegiance of the natives as well as
their souls? There could not be found a means better
calculated than this blending of apostasy with treachery
to turn the people against it. The priests have acted with
admirable consistency."

"Ah! that's all over and past now. The devil of it is,
you won't let the hatchet be buried."

"Won't let the hatchet be buried!" And Hogan laughed
out. "Why, these things are always present to their minds;
they are never forgotten—never will be, either. They lie
behind this Home Rule question, along with the Land
question. It's long enough since the Tithe was abolished,
but the people will tell you stories of that time with as
much gusto as if it were yesterday. Tradition never dies;
faith, I think the older it is the better, like whiskey."

"They are incorrigible; and where are they to be got
at? Every door seems to be shut to improvement. The
famine, as the English *Times* said, solved a great difficulty:
not altogether. Ha! ha!"

"Not quite all;" and Hogan laughed too. "Emigration
did a good deal. By themselves the people now could do
nothing; there are too few of them. A mass meeting such
as O'Connell used to treat them to would be impossible
now."

"Oh, utterly, utterly. By-the-bye, do you count on the
support of the Bishop of the diocese? Can your interest
do anything for you with him? The contest is doubtful,
you see."

"I could not say. The Bishop does not count for much,
so much depends on the parish priest. If he favours Home
Rule, all's well. He may prefer that some one with local
interest and influence should get in. However, even if
Lord Kilboggan's nephew does come forward, I shall not
care. You see the family are unpopular—rackrenting
absentees! What hold they have over the priests remains
to be tried; but just at present I could get in very easily
on Home Rule alone."

" You think so," said Saltasche, nodding his head as if satisfied. " You will soon have an opportunity of trying, for I'm told there are no hopes whatever of the member's recovery. Try this Burgundy: very fine; perhaps you would prefer dry sherry. An olive, please."

Saltasche now lighted a cheroot, and began to smoke slowly and seriously.

" I called round at Mrs. Bursford's the day before yesterday," began Hogan, who was lighting his cigar at the gaselier.

Saltasche twisted his head on one side, so as to get a clear view unobscured by the smoke, and looked keenly at him. Then he turned his eyes towards the fire, and first exhaling a huge cloud, remarked indifferently, " Indeed; clever, stylish girl that. Did she settle with you about my charitable concert ? "

" Bah ! " said Hogan, " that question settles itself. I can't have anything to do with it. Impossible !—a Protestant affair ! "

" Pish ! to be sure. I forgot: how stupid of me ! How did you like the young lady ? "

" Very clever, charming girl ; very stylish indeed ; fine looking," said Hogan, quite warmly. He had been so plied with subtlest flattery by the practised Diana that his unaccustomed brain was reeling. How well he remembered the scene ! The half-light, the drawn curtain of blue brocade shedding a softening shadow on her blonde hair, the glowing hearth, the perfume, the softness and sweetness ; and the low coaxing voice and veiled eyes looking into his as if every word he uttered had a thousand meanings and his listener feared to lose a single one.

" Very highly connected family, that is." Saltasche, as he spoke, knocked the ash off his cigar. " Very ; they go into the best set, here and in London. The mother has immense influence."

Hogan, who seemed to have had some idea conjured up in his mind by his friend's last speech, only smiled in reply ; and after a few minutes spent in smoking silently, took his cigar between thumb and forefinger, and said to Saltasche,—

"Were there no brothers, eh? I fancied I heard Miss Bursford had brothers."

Mr. Saltasche pursed up his lips sententiously. "Certainly, my dear fellow; two,—no, three of them."

"Dead, eh?"

"Well, they might as well be. Two of them ran wild; they were all older than the girl. And one—well, for some particular and not very well-known reason—lives in New Zealand. He made a *mésalliance*, I believe. The others disappeared *in toto*."

"How very unfortunate for the family! It is surprising how many men go to the deuce nowadays. Among my contemporaries at college, I assure you I could count up a large proportion of black sheep, mostly among the Catholics too."

Hogan's mind, as he spoke, was running on a story he had heard that morning, of the death of a young friend of his own, or rather the son of a friend—a lad of twenty— who had "gone the pace that kills" for the last three years or so. How many men indeed had he seen fall by the way, even in the short measure of the road of life that he had travelled.

Saltasche, hearing the hall clock strike the quarter past eight, threw the butt of his cheroot in the fire. "Time we were off, by Jove! Mr. Hogan, shall we walk down?"

"Yes, if you please; it's a fine clear night."

They set out arm-in-arm, and turning down Kildare Street, walked smartly in the direction of the Hawkins Street Theatre.

"I must ask you to allow me to leave early—at least, as soon as the piece is over. I could not stay for the after-piece," said Hogan.

"Oh, by all means; do what you like. I don't think I'll stop, either. I am rather tired. Some rascals in London been trying to catch me out, rigging the market. I've settled them, though. I calculate to clear fifteen thousand by the operations I have arranged yonder; in a week hence, too."

"Ha!" said Hogan, drawing in a deep breath. A sort

of wonder, not unmixed with envy, filled him. A sudden
thought occurred to him. The twelve hundred pounds
lying at his bankers' : why not ask Saltasche to use it, at
a fair rate of interest ? The bank gave only three per cent
—nothing at all. Saltasche would think nothing of obliging
him, he was sure ; yet it was with a slight feeling of ner-
vousness he began.

"I—er—have a thousand or so in the Connaught Bank
at this moment. Mr. Stonelock sold out my shares the
other day. I lodged it to meet electioneering expenses.
It may remain there some months, perhaps."

Saltasche turned with a sort of bound, and his brown
eyes kindled with a sudden flash. "You'd like me to invest it, eh ? Of course, of course ; bring it to me to-morrow,
and I'll see if I can't put you up to a good thing with it.
Let's see : it must be invested where it can be got at easily,
hey ?"

"I don't mind telling you, Mr. Saltasche, it's pretty near
all I have in this world. I just make, altogether, by my
profession about three hundred a year, or less ; and my
expenses are large. Of course my income is increasing
yearly."

Saltasche's face had that quiet, unmoved look that tells
of rapt attention ; and a glimmer in his eyes—could Hogan
have seen them—denoted that this intelligence was a mark
added to his score.

"All right," said he, quietly. "There are plenty of
ways for a man like you to get on. You write, I know.
I have been thinking of starting a newspaper. Not here
—dear no ! In London. There is a firm in Sycamore
Alley, Stier and Bruen, with whom I deal largely ; and they
have been meditating that move for some time. You have
no idea what a help a well-managed, smartly-written paper
is in business. A circulation once secured, you can do
anything with it. You would be very useful as editor, or
nominal editor, with some practical, experienced man in
the background, until you get well started. Hey ? Thus
you see you have an independence clear, and a position,
moreover, as editor, second only to your membership."

" It looks remarkably enticing, I confess," said Hogan thoughtfully; " but I am not returned yet, and I am not sufficiently practised as a ready-writer to take such a post as editorship."

"Bah! Keep your hand in; it is an invaluable accomplishment. I had a great turn myself that way, now. Yes, by Jove, I remember the day when I could have turned you out an article in first-rate style—trenchant and clear, you know: I often lament that my time is so taken up. One sees a thing requiring an answer so frequently. The *Financial Review* the other day had some rot on 'Economic Values : the Comparative History of them.' He hadn't a notion of the true origin of *agiotage*. My fingers itched to reply to him; but time,"—and Mr. Saltasche shrugged his square shoulders,—"time I never have."

A sneer curled Hogan's lips. " Time, indeed," thought he: "that's all that's wanting, of course!" Then the sneer turned into a good-humoured smile at his friend's absurdity: " We all have our little weaknesses." Then aloud, " It doesn't take so long, I assure you: one knocks off a thing of that sort in an hour or so. I nev——"

" Er—ah! I daresay. You fellars that have the trick, er—practice, er—and *leisure*."

By this time they had reached the hideous gateway of the Royal.

CHAPTER XIII.

" Les rivières sont des chemins qui marchent, et qui portent où l'on veut aller."—Pensées de Pascal.

THE day but one after the evening in the theatre, Mr. Saltasche, towards three o'clock in the afternoon, leisurely descended the handsome granite steps of his office. He stood for an instant thinking, when he reached the lowest step; then, having felt in his coat pocket with one hand, he nodded as if reassured, and looked across to the cabstand by King William's statue. The jarvey whose turn it was, being at the head of the stand, to obey a signal jumped quickly on the "driving side" of his vehicle, and was speedily at Mr. Saltasche's orders. While waiting the arrival of his conveyance, the gentleman in question cast a scrutinising look over his own dress, and having buttoned up his perfectly fitting brown surtout and flicked a faint trace of dust off his boots with his white silk handkerchief, gave his hat a cock and jumped lightly into his seat.

" Where now, your honour?" asked the jarvey.

" Er—Kingsbridge; and take the far side of the river.

The car rolled quickly down Westmoreland Street, and threaded its way across the bridge, now densely thronged with traffic; and turning to the left, held on along the Quay. They passed the Four Courts rapidly; Saltasche looked keenly at the groups by the railings, but failed to recognise anybody. Park Gate Street was soon reached. Here he dismissed his driver, and turning to the left again, kept the highroad for a few minutes until he found the terrace he was looking for.

" Just what I expected," he muttered to himself: " dingy

lodgings. Let's see," and he vainly tried to decipher a half-obliterated inscription on the corner house of the row of little houses, seven or eight of which stood removed from the road by some forty feet of ill-kept front gardens.

He opened the gate of the third house, and walked up the long weed-grown path; as he did so he became aware of a pianist, evidently in the house to which he was going, practising with a vigorous hand noisy scales and exercises, and breaking now and again into great wild chords and *cadenzas*. His skilled ear detected at once a master-hand: no tyro ever struck so boldly, or with such finished precision.

His knock brought a dirty servant-girl, with smirched visage and hands so black and grimy that it was not without some misgiving that he entrusted his card to them.

"Poignarde is not at home," he thought, as he ascended the little narrow stairs after his guide. "I should imagine not, indeed; and my little beauty consoles herself with music pending his return."

"A gentleman, ma'am," said the menial, laying the card on the piano. Mrs. Poignarde ceased playing, and took it up between her fore and second finger.

"Did you say Captain Poignarde was out?"

Saltasche grinned as he heard the imperious tone of this question outside the door.

The servant, instead of answering, opened the door wide; and the gentleman with his sweetest smile presented himself. Mrs. Poignarde was not a whit embarrassed, and held out three fingers of her right hand, looking at her visitor the while with a blended expression of astonishment, greeting, and interrogation.

Saltasche took her taper white fingers and bowed over them.

"How do you do, Mrs. Poignarde? Did you get home safely on Saturday? Capital piece, now, was it not? You reached home quite safely? No cold? No annoyance? Such a long drive!"

All this and much more was uttered in the most suave, finished, courteous tone. The little lady in black, who was

anything but in gracious humour, was first amused, then
roused, and at last pleased and quite won to good humour
by the well-laid plan of attack. She smiled, and pointing
to an easy-chair by the fire, seated herself with her side-face
to the window nearly opposite.

"We got home very well. It was very stupid, though ;
and to add to my vexation, I lost my fan. I was so sorry
and put out about it ; and, of course, I have no chance of ever
seeing it again. It was my poor uncle Rodolphe's last gift."

Saltasche smiled quite pleasantly. "I think I can give
you some intelligence of it;" and he took a tissue-paper
parcel out of his pocket as he spoke, and unrolling it
leisurely, held up before her wondering eyes the ivory and
scarlet of her treasure.

She gave a little scream of joy, and rising hastily, held
out both hands to take it ; then examining it closely, and
holding up a broken scarlet ribbon, exclaimed,—

"See there : that went so, round my wrist ; something
must have broken or cut it, and I dropped it. How did
you find it ? And how good of you to bring it to me !"

"Do you remember getting into your cab?" said he.
"You must have let it slip into the folds of your dress or
mantle. I found it at my feet, under the colonnade.
Then the initials, you see, guided me where to bring it."

"How really good of you ! I would not have lost it for
the world ;" and she raised her fine liquid eyes with a look
of real gratitude full on his. "Poor Uncle Rodolphe !—
his very last gift to me ; and I never saw him again."

"You can't imagine how pleased I am, Mrs. Poignarde,
to be the means of restoring it to you. I had no idea," he
added, with a spark of curiosity in his look, "that, apart
from its intrinsic value, it was such a treasure. Captain
Poignarde is not in, then ?"

"No," she answered. "Eric is scarcely ever here ; at
least, scarcely ever after twelve in the morning.

"And you, Mrs. Poignarde, beguile your time with your
charming music, no doubt : I heard you just now. What
a magnificent touch you have ! Not at all a feminine one
—so strong and full." And he looked as if incredulous at

her small, fine fingers. "Do play me something," he added entreatingly; "I am so passionately fond of music."

She assented, after but little demur. Perhaps there was a particle of vanity in her doing so. She saw he was really eager to hear her; and feeling exactly in the humour for playing, she sat down carelessly and plunged into Mendelssohn's well-known Andante. Her piano was a Broadwood's cottage—one of the best make; and though now something worn, yet full and rich-toned. Her manipulation was splendid, and the rich chords and subtle variations of light and shade were brought out in perfection. She sat easily and unmoved—not a trace of self-consciousness or effort marring the perfect performance. Saltasche was astonished beyond measure. He, while listening with a perfect sense of enjoyment, leaned his elbow on the back of his chair, and deliberately surveyed the room; small, grimy, and shabbily furnished. On an ottoman lay Mrs. Poignarde's black lace bonnet and veil, her little silk umbrella stood in a corner, and a pair of wash leather-gloves lay on the top of some whitey-brown packages on the sideboard. An untidy, ill-kept room—just the dwelling-place of an ill-conditioned, ill-mated couple. The woman who would spend a day in a chamber of that ilk, must indeed be far gone on the road of despair and sullen indifference. Pipes and cigar-boxes were on the mantelpiece, and under the sideboard a little stack of soda-water bottles. Some ill-used looking books lay about; and on a footstool before the fire a hideous bull-terrier, with a black face, was curled up. Not a flower, not a work-basket, not a single trace of a lady's presence, beyond the piano and a pile of well-bound music-books, was there in the room. The keen eye of Saltasche noted everything; and then returned to the musician, now drawing near to the *finale* of her piece. Ere her fingers had touched the closing chords, Saltasche was beside her, and, seating himself on a chair at one end of the piano, he leaned his elbow upon it, and waited till the sound had died away.

"What a treat, Mrs. Poignarde!" murmured he; "how perfectly you play! That piece is simply superb. Your style is exactly French."

"I did take lessons from a Parisian," she returned, negligently running the right hand over arpeggio chords.

"It's a great charm, music; such a resource to you, too."

"Well, yes. At least," she added, "I expect it will be so one day." And she turned her head aside with a negligent, indifferent air, and then rose and went back towards her seat in the window.

"Oh, now, Mrs. Poignarde, will you not play me something more? Please do. I have heard from Mrs. Grey that you play Liszt's music so perfectly."

"Liszt's is too much for this little room."

"Will you help with our concert? Mrs. Grey must have told you of it. If you would only play a piece or two."

"Yes; Mrs. Grey has told me about it. But I do not care for playing in public. I don't know anybody here; I don't go into society at all." She turned as she spoke, and looked quickly down the road. "There comes Eric, you see, with that gentleman." And as she spoke she bent her head a little forward, and looked closely at the advancing figures. The result of this inspection was apparently displeasing to her; for a settled frown gathered on her face, and her lips curled impatiently. She rose and gathered up her music, after which she locked the piano. Saltasche, whom a glance out of window had satisfied as to the cause of the change of her expression, smiled half in pity, half contemptuously. Rising, he held out his hand, and said, "It is quite time I was back in the City, Mrs. Poignarde. I am very glad to have been the medium of restoring to you your property." He spoke slowly and deliberately, watching her face; for he knew she was dying to escape before Poignarde should enter the room.

She looked at him frankly, as if she divined his kind thoughtfulness, and held out her hand.

"I thank you very much indeed; and in token of my sincerity you may tell the Greys I will play at their concert."

He held her soft white hand in his an instant; not

venturing to press it, yet unwilling to let her go. Just then the swing of the gate was heard, and Poignarde's uncertain, heavy step on the gravel. She released her hand, and hastily picking up her bonnet, flashed one look, in which terror and excuse were blended, at him, and escaped off upstairs to her own room.

Poignarde entered the room. Glancing round with a sulky and stupid look, his eyes fell on the broker, who, quite at home, was reading a *Bell's Life* in an easy-chair.

"Hullo! Mr. Saltasche, eh? Glad to see you."

"I've been waiting for you, Poignarde. I came here on a double errand: to restore Mrs. Poignarde's fan (she lost it at the theatre on Saturday), and—ah—this to you, Captain." And as he spoke he handed a slip of gray paper across the table.

"I've had a run of luck lately," spoke the gallant officer, in a thick tone. "Hang it, man, when a fellow's got capital, the thing for him is to back the colour long enough; it's sure to come up if you just go on long enough. That's what it is: back the colour and stick to it. Keep at it," he muttered, nodding his head sapiently in the direction of his friend. "I say," he broke out suddenly, "you've not seen Adelaide—Ad'laide—eh! my wife, sir. She's locked herself in that beastly room of hers, I bet." And he rocked himself to and fro in his seat, staring fatuously at the bell-rope, and plainly calculating the exertion needful to make a lurch at it.

Saltasche rose, and stood between him and the fireplace, stroking his chin and looking critically, and with a smile on his lips, at the interesting figure of his client. It seemed to supply the key to a riddle rising in his mind; for he glanced once more round the room, and nodded his head slightly, as if acknowledging to himself the fitness of things in general.

"Day, day, Captain!" said he, making a move to go. "I must be off; business in town."

"Take somethin'?" stuttered the Captain, on hospitality intent. "Ad'laide, I say, where's that——?" and he gathered himself together as if for a plunge at the bell.

But Saltasche laid a heavy hand on his shoulder, and forced him down in his chair.

"I'll see you to-night, Cap.," said he, laughing. "Don't forget your—hey?—ah——" and he nodded towards the slip of paper lying on the table. "Bye, bye." "He shut the door quickly, and was gone.

"What a pair!" thought he to himself. "I wonder will Mrs. Grey be able to tell me anything about her. She must have something in her head when she works up her music like that. Why, it's something superb. She is a lovely creature, too—a perfect *artiste*." All the way back he mused on the queerness and incongruousness of the scene he had left. The mean, untidy room; the most sordid details of daily life obtruding themselves unabashed in every sense; and in the midst of it all, the determined, cold face, the slender, supple, black-robed figure of the musician—indifference and scorn on every beautiful line of her face—rapt, evidently, in her art, and bitter and cynical to all else. "She must have a history," thought he. "What a bitter look she gave at him coming in! And that fan, too—little vixen—she was pleased to get it back;" and he seemed to see the bright, glad look that flashed for an instant from between her white eyelids. And Poignarde: "Bet on the colour, and bet long enough." Saltasche grinned to himself as he remembered the tone and look with which this axiom was enunciated, and the appearance of the prophet himself: the bleared eyes, the trembling lips and hands, and the thick utterance. "Why in this world doesn't she leave him?" thought Mr. Saltasche.

There were reasons undreamt of by him. Adelaide Chrestien, for such was her (Mrs. Poignarde's) maiden name, had been the only child and heiress of a wealthy South American planter and merchant. On his death, which occurred when she was a very young child, she had been adopted by her father's brother, who had absolute control over her fortune. Mr. Rodolphe Chrestien never married; and his niece, his only living relative, was reputed heiress to his wealth also. She was sent to England to be educated at a first-class school, in a manner befitting her condition and prospects in life. Here she made the acquaintance of the family of a school companion; and when about sixteen, met at their house, one summer vacation, Eric Poignarde, then a dashing cornet of dragoons, —deeply in debt, for his was one of the fastest regiments in London. The youth cast his eyes on the Brazilian heiress—an interesting and beautiful young girl, with the reputation of a fortune of nearly a quarter of a million; and with the aid of his relation, the school-girl friend, a clandestine correspondence was carried on.

In about six months more, Miss Chrestien eloped with the now almost penniless Poignarde, who believed that she was entitled to her fortune in her own right. She, filled with romance, had never dreamed of telling him that her uncle and guardian had unreserved powers over the money bequeathed to her, and that all she possessed in her own right was five thousand pounds, which was hers by virtue of her mother's marriage settlement. However, the awakening came soon. Uncle Rodolphe, whom she had hoped to have won over in orthodox romantic fashion, had had ambitious designs for his niece, to whom he really was attached, and in whom centred all his ambition and hopes. Disappointed and furious on hearing of her marriage, he telegraphed some curt directions to his London agent, who, immediately on receiving them, sought an interview with the happy husband. Poignarde was informed that his wife's allowance would be paid quarterly, as heretofore, by the agents of Rodolphe Chrestien; and that on her attaining her majority the five thousand pounds would be paid over to her husband. The rest of Mr. Chrestien's money he intended to devote to the Public Works of Rio—the city in which he had amassed his colossal fortune. The agent added, as a piece of supererogatory information, that the fortune which Adelaide Chrestien would have inherited, had she shown a sense of duty to her relative, amounted to nearly two millions English.

Poignarde reeled home, sick with fury; he cursed himself, his cousin, his wife—everything. What a prize he

P

had missed! He had been swindled, he declared. The miserable five thousand would not pay his debts. Of course he was the victim, the injured one; her wretched situation in no way concerned him. He quarrelled with his relatives, at whose house he had met his school-girl wife; blaming them, with the short-sighted rage of disappointed egotism, for their instrumentality—innocent enough, in truth—in his downfall. He had to exchange out of the Guards, and getting a handsome sum of money into the bargain, he was enabled to settle his affairs; compromised with some creditors, paid one or two in full, and cheated the greater number. And then, having joined a line regiment, he took his wife, whom he began to treat with systematic brutality and neglect, to live in barracks with him.

She was too young to break her heart, and too vigorous of constitution to pine and waste in useless regrets. She retained her own piano, and at all times passionately fond of music, devoted herself to it now with heart and soul—inspired by the double purpose of one day making a living by it as a profession, and also as a present resource in the long hours of tedium and *ennui*, if not worse, that she had to spend by herself.

Poignarde drew her allowance and spent it; and had already, she knew, borrowed money at high rates of interest, to be repaid out of her five thousand pounds when it should fall due. So she had no hope but in herself; and worked and studied with a passionate persistency that astonished every one. Six hours a day was the minimum she allowed herself for practice; more frequently she sat at the piano all day long, with an interval for a walk in some quiet, unfrequented direction.

She and her husband hated each other with that persistency and thoroughness only to be found amongst married couples, and which hardens and grows with years of daily practice. It is a common enough mistake that people make when they suppose that time wears out inequalities of disposition and renders us less sensitive to the unpleasantnesses and peculiarities of the people with whom we live. Poignarde detested his wife more and more: every day, week, month, and year, added in intensity and bitterness to the store. And with her, the desire to be free, now that she had attained her majority and saw the last few hundred pounds vanishing in the same way as the rest —swallowed up by the usurers, and squandered in vice— became a passion too strong almost for endurance. Yet her plans were misty and vague. Friends she had none; Poignarde had an aunt and cousin in London, both elderly and respectable women; and she counted that when the crash came, when he would be forced to go to India or on some other foreign service, she might find a temporary shelter with them, and remain until she earned enough to carry her out to Rio, to plead her cause in person to Rodolphe Chrestien. Every letter she addressed to him had been returned unopened; but she felt sure he would pity her when once the true story had been told him.

Sometimes visions of triumphs in the musical world would pass before her over-worked brain; she fancied herself an Arabella Goddard or a Madame Schumann; and then she would dream of a public concert in Rio. She almost saw herself, dressed in white, the centre-point of a crowd of listeners,—everybody hushed and silent; the Spanish women, with their dark eyes bent upon her enviously and curiously, keeping even their feather fans immovable lest the faint rustle should cause them to lose a note; and amongst the throng, listening and watching, Uncle Rodolphe's hard determined face, with his white hair and wavy moustache, like the Emperor's. He, as one of the notables, though, would be on the platform and quite close: she would play to him and for him; and he would listen to her and forgive her, and take her away where Eric could never follow.

So she would dream over her instrument, hardly knowing what she did, and playing from that wonderful memory which only born musicians like her, who assimilate and make a piece a part of themselves, ever have.

With Poignarde she was silent and distant, and as much as possible avoided provoking any of his outbursts of brutality. When he commenced to rail at and taunt her, she opposed him by a silence which no utterance of his could induce her to break. She knew the end was approaching fast. The five thousand pounds had melted away to as many hundreds, though she was not as yet more than six months past her majority. Poignarde was utterly unable to stop drinking and gambling; both had become a part of his nature. Another year, she thought, would set a term to her punishment; and she worked harder than ever.

Saltasche reached his office again, shortly after four. Running up the stairs, he almost knocked against Lord Brayhead, who was coming down for the second time—having, with the fretful impatience characteristic of him, been twice within an hour to see if the broker had returned.

"I have been waiting for you, Mr. Saltasche," he began in an aggrieved tone; "I have an important message for you."

Saltasche quickly opened the glass-panelled door leading into his office, and held it for his client to pass before him.

"Mr. Wyldoates cannot live twenty-four hours; and I have a telegram to the effect that Lord Kilboggan will send over his eldest nephew, Theodore Wyldoates, the *attaché* at Constantinople, to stand for the seat in the Conservative interest."

"Ah! no matter, my lord. Hogan is the man: I shall have him in Peatstown the day after to-morrow—or to-morrow, if you like. And now about money matters. He has money; but of course your lordship is aware we are bound to do something. He is running a great risk—a very great risk."

"I will allow him to draw upon me for one-third of the expenses."

Saltasche gave his lordship to understand pretty plainly that he must be more liberal; that the Government would not assist Mr. Hogan; and that, the Dissolution being so near at hand, he could not afford to risk his capital. It was finally arranged that Lord Brayhead should pay two-thirds of the sum-total, and it was also stipulated that Mr.

Hogan was to be very discreet concerning the transaction : in fact, he was to be made, if possible, to understand that it was in the form of a loan, rather than anything else, that the money was to be forthcoming. After a long consultation—a consultation which the impetuous Mr. Saltasche vainly endeavoured to cut short—Lord Brayhead took his leave, in great anxiety and tribulation as to the success of his dubious venture.

Saltasche sent a messenger with a note to Hogan's lodgings, and betook himself home. He was eager to see Mrs. Grey, his neighbour at Green Lanes, to learn from her the history, if history there were (and if she knew it), of Adelaide Poignarde.

Mrs. Grey and Poignarde were in some remote way connected through his aunt and cousin the Stroudes in London; and Saltasche, confident in his own powers of suasion, calculated on hearing the whole story ere he was many hours older.

CHAPTER XIV.

" Why did I ever one brief moment's space,
But parley with this filthy Belial ?
. . . . Was it the fear
Of being behind the world, which is the wicked ?"

A. H. Clough.

STRANGE to relate, Dicky Davoren's sanguine expectations concerning his friend Orpen's speculation were fully realised. Mr. Orpen took fifteen to one against a horse which won the Churton Cup ; and the firm of bookmakers, on the Monday after the race, sent a cheque for sixty-five pounds, payable at the Bank of Ireland, to that gentleman. On Tuesday morning, therefore, Mr. Orpen's advent (he was not a resident student) was anxiously watched for in the precincts of Botany Bay. Mr. Gagan, and his friend and cousin Tad Griffiths, a youth who had been oftener on the verge of expulsion than anybody else in Trinity, stuck their heads out of window every two minutes.

At last Orpen, Mahoney Quain, and Dicky Davoren came in sight ; they walked quietly and decorously along, until they turned the corner and were 'out of sight of the crowd coming out of the morning lecture ; then the exuberance of Mr. Quain's animal spirits broke forth. Lifting Dicky over his head with both hands, he playfully gave him his choice of having his head knocked against the wall or the granite pavement. Dicky snatched off his tormentor's mortarboard, and shied it as well as he could, considering the disabilities of his position, down the path. The young giant was on the point of putting his threat into execution, when Dicky, seeing Orpen, who with his usual matter-of-fact, business-like way had walked on ahead, turning into the doorway leading to their destination, raised the alarm, "There's Orpen bolting with the money!" Mr. Quain, entering into the spirit of the suggestion with perhaps more completeness than its originator intended or wished, dropped his burden on the flags, and taking as many steps at a time as his long legs would compass, rushed up the stairs. Dicky followed, and they all burst into the room at once.

After an interval of horse-play, Mr. Orpen produced a bundle of notes, the letters which had been received from the bookmakers, and their statement of accounts. According to this document, the commission at ten per cent amounted to seven pounds ten; then some other items were alleged, in order to justify the retention of two pounds ten as well: in all ten pounds; which, deducted from the profits of the transaction, left sixty-five pounds (seventy including the stake) to be divided among the four subscribers. Mr. Orpen handed each gentleman a clean ten-pound note, then a five-pound, two one-pound notes, and a half-sovereign. Then ensued a general reckoning of scores.

Mr. Gagan had drawn largely in advance of the expected dividend. His Ulster coat hung in its accustomed place behind the door—a place, indeed, which knew it seldomer than did the shelves of the accommodating "bank." A gold seal-ring and pin formed conspicuous items of his toilette, and the bookshelves groaned under the unaccustomed weight of a complete set of medical and classical books. The box of tobacco on the chimney-piece was so full that the lid refused to shut down, and the fragrant bird's-eye overflowed around it. A new pipe was stuck in the rack above the chimneypiece, and bottles of porter, ginger-beer and ale for shandy-gaff; together with spirits and soda-water, in thoughtful deference to Mr. Orpen's advanced tastes, littered the apartment.

Mr. Gagan took out a battered pocket-book and a metallic pencil, and sitting on the table, began to tot up a column of very straggling entries.

"Hold your row, Mahoney, will you? Where was I? Yes, the fees, six pound ten; and 'taking out' my traps was two more; and, Orpen, what's your little bill—hey?"

"You know right well; so pay up, and look pleasant over it," was Mr. Orpen's answer, delivered in a jocular good-humoured tone, as of one already in possession of the amount.

Mr. Gagan responded by flinging three sovereigns and some silver on the table; then he counted the remainder and stuffed it in his pockets. Mr. Tad Griffiths was paid his small account by his friend Mahoney, who said, good-naturedly,—

"Where were you this age, Tad? You might have been in for this pot of luck if we'd only seen you."

Mr. Tad replied by a comical grimace.

"I had to keep quiet. Got in a ruction down on the Quay; and didn't they follow me half over the city? I never got in till next day at all, and I was watched for at the gates for nearly a week; so I just read up that blessed Hebrew for old what's-his-name. I say, Gagan, are these bottles here to be looked at, or are you bloated capitalists going to stand treat?"

The various drinkables were quickly discussed. Dicky Davoren, who had scant inclination for stout or ale so early in the day as twelve o'clock, nevertheless drank glass for glass with his more inured companions; and then various plans of amusement were broached and discussed. At last it was settled that they were to drive down on an outside car to Bray, and dine at the hotel, then return to town and visit the theatre (not the Royal,—a minor theatre, of not too good repute, was recommended by Mr. Orpen, and agreed on by the young gentlemen); and finally wind up with a thorough spree anywhere: in fact, to make a night of it. When these preliminaries had been arranged, Dicky begged for time to run out on some errands of his own. Orpen, who had no notion of losing sight of him while the seventeen pounds was in existence, cautioned him not to be long, or they might start without him. Dicky, who had very little intention of missing the

fun, hastened across College Green and plunged into a
dirty lane not far up Dame Street. Out of this he emerged
in a moment or two, carrying a large strap full of books
under his arm; then he disappeared into a hatter's, and
bought a low hat, which, with the books, he asked to have
kept for him until next day. He then, with unwonted
care, folded up the receipted bill, putting it carefully in
his pocket.

As he stood for a moment waiting to let a number of
carts pass before crossing the Green again, he became
aware of a hand laid on his shoulder. Looking up
quickly, he saw Hogan and Mr. Saltasche.

"Do you care to earn fifteen pounds, Davoren, eh?"
said Hogan, with a good-humoured smile.

"Yes; I've no objection," answered the youth coolly
enough, and wondering to himself if the floods of Pactolus
were not pouring themselves at his feet.

"Would you like to help in an election, eh? Will you
be sub-sheriff? There will be an election at Peatstown
directly."

"Peatstown! Oh! I know Peatstown. I have been
there: my father has a cousin, a big farmer there. I've
often been there with him."

"By Jove! have you, though?" Saltasche now struck
in. "Then write to him, Master—*Mr.* Davoren"—(he
corrected himself),—"and tell him you'll bring down your
friend the new member that is to be, and introduce him to
all of them." And Mr. Saltasche nodded at Hogan as
much as to say, "That is he."

"You know Mr. Muldoon's son, Ignatius?" asked
Hogan; "he will be a sub-sheriff too, and you could work
together."

"I shall be delighted," said Dicky; as indeed he was.

And the next day, when he returned home at midday
sick and weary, and with only seven pounds of the seventeen left, he thought over Mr. Hogan's proposal, and made
up his mind that the projected expedition would be very
desirable indeed. He felt miserable and ill, and crept up
to bed, avoiding Nellie, and never going near his mother's

room until late in the afternoon; then, after having bribed
a servant to procure him a bottle of soda-water, he felt
somewhat more comfortable, and concocting a lie about
having lost the last train and sleeping with a friend in
town, presented himself and told his story with cool assurance. His sister, however, followed him out and began to
question him.

"Where have you been? As for sleeping with Mulcahy,
sir, look at your eyes! You have been up all night, I do
believe."

"No such thing. It's biliousness. I don't feel at all
well."

Still she distrusted, and as a last resort asked him
sternly,—

"Where is the new hat you got seven-and-sixpence to
buy, some days ago?"

For answer he nodded at the hat-rack in the hall,
where the article in question hung. He had not forgotten
to carry it and his books back with him. Nellie retreated,
baffled, though by no means satisfied, to her mother's
room. After a time she was called downstairs, and going
into the parlour, found Dicky stretched on a sofa near the
fire and shading his burning eyes from the light with his
hand.

"Is that you, Nellie? I've a piece of news you would
like to hear." Seeing that she paid him no attention, and
was turning out of the room, he sat straight up on the
sofa. "Your friend Mr. Hogan is going into Parliament
soon."

"What do you say? Soon? And for what place, eh?"

"Yah! you'd like to know all about it," returned he
mockingly, letting himself fall back into his recumbent
position. "You wouldn't lend me that couple of shillings,
then, last week; so now find out for yourself, Miss."

"I really think you very mean to be taking all my money
from me, that way, Dicky! It's most unmanly; and you
never pay me back."

The youth made no reply, but taking a sovereign out of
his pocket, jerked it silently across the room in her direc-

tion. Nellie picked it up in utter bewilderment, which
increased when he jerked a second sovereign at her.
Then he sat up again, and watched her face and attitude
closely.

"Now, Miss Shylock, how much do I owe you now ?"

"You owe me money still; but never mind that.
Where did you get this ? and how ? Do tell me, Dicky."

"Never you mind. Am I to account for every penny
to you, please ? That's a joke ! Listen: if you don't tell
the governor on me, I'll let you keep that money, and—
ah—I'll tell you all Mr. Hogan told me to-day."

"I shan't promise: if I am asked I must tell; you
know that very well. And your conduct is scandalous. I
heard of your card-playing in Mr. Saltasche's stable, with
Jasper Grey and the gardener and coachman, and drinking with them. Are you not ashamed ? And how did
you get into the house ? Coming in at three in the
morning through the window. However, I have had that
nailed up, and a new lock put on the garden gate."

Mr. Dicky looked conscious and penitent—to outward
view, at least; but in reality he was meditating which
night his sister alluded to, because on one or two occasions
the company at the stable card-parties had numbered other
guests than those she mentioned. Who could have told,
he wondered. The coachman's wife, no doubt; she was
employed sometimes by Nellie, and had carried the story.

"Well, there's an end of that, since you've nailed up the
window," he growled. In reality he had used another
mode of ingress, and meant to use it again. "Now listen,
Nellie: Mr. Hogan is going to stand for Peatstown (didn't
you see in the *Enfranchiser* this morning the death of the
member, Mr. Wyldoates, at Paris ?), and he is going to take
me down as sub-sheriff,—worth fifteen guineas, let alone
the fun."

"Oh, I see," she cried, jumping to conclusions with the
usual feminine alacrity; "and you have been paid in
advance ! isn't that it ?"

A sudden flash of intelligence illumined Mr. Dicky's
rather heavy-looking eyes. It had not occurred to him to

combine the circumstances so neatly; but now he did not
scruple to avail himself of the junction so presented. So he
nodded a sort of Burleigh nod, and lay down again, feeling
quite sure his usual luck would carry the day.

The dinner passed off to his satisfaction. His father,
who was tolerably indifferent, except for occasional spas-
modic fits of severity, to Dicky's general conduct, asked no
awkward questions, and accepted the glib excuse without
comment; not that he was unaware that it was a lie, but
it did not suit with his temper at that time to investigate
or sift the affair. Another time, as his son well knew, he
would have encountered a torrent of questions, cross questions, and perhaps blows, for a comparatively trivial offence.
It all depended on the humour of the moment, and also on
the personal bearing of the delinquency. If anybody made
a complaint to himself of Dicky, and thus annoyed or
disturbed him, woe betide the lad! But anything that did
not concern Mr. Davoren senior (however remotely) per-
sonally, was passed over comparatively unheeded; unless,
as has been said, the escapade afforded an opportune vent
for the ill-humour of the moment.

After dinner Nellie slipped up to her mother's room.
Mr. Davoren went to town, as was his custom at times, to
amuse himself; and Dicky, disinclined for out-door adven-
ture or work, dragged a sofa up near the fire, and having
turned out the gas and put fresh coal on the fire (for not
being very well, he felt chilly), lay down for a sleep until
eight o'clock tea.

At about half-past seven a sounding knock at the door
startled him from his uneasy slumbers.

"It's that beggar Mulcahy; dear, oh dear! who the
mischief wants him this hour of the night?" And with a
cross, sulky face, he proceeded to push back his couch and
relight the gas. But when the door opened and Hogan's
face appeared, Mr. Dicky's humour changed, and he advanced to meet him, hiding his surprise under the hearti-
ness of the greeting.

"Good evening, Dick," said the barrister; "how are you,
my boy? I called to ask your father about letting you go

down with me to-morrow morning to Peatstown to help me
with my canvass, as you have friends there. Hey? what
do you say to it? Will your father allow you?"

"I'm sure he will; he is out now, and won't be in till
late: but wait,—I'll call Nellie down."

Dicky went up to his mother's room, and beckoned
Nellie out. She came out on the landing with her book
held open in her hand, and looked interrogatively at him.

"Come downstairs—quick," said he; "Mr. Hogan has
come about that business I told you of to-day."

"What! the election?"

"Come along," he whispered impatiently; "he wants
me to go down by the midday mail to-morrow."

"Wait an instant, Dicky, please," said she; and running
into her own room, she washed her hands and smoothed
her hair. No adornment did she permit herself: some
sort of proud instinct forbade that. Then she hurried
down after the impatient Dicky, and, with a heightened
colour, due partly to her haste and astonishment, partly to
consciousness (it is certain that Mr. Hogan ascribed it
entirely to the last), entered the room.

"How do you do, Mr. Hogan?" she said, advancing to
meet him. "I am sorry papa is out."

"I am sorry too," he said; "but after all, you can let
me know his decision to-morrow morning. Dicky, of
course, has told you everything about my intention. He
would be very useful to me; and my friend Ignatius Muldoon is also to be sub-sheriff; however, the writ is not out
yet, and until it is, and business has really begun, he does
not appear on the scene. I wish you would allow Dicky
to come down and canvass with me; he would be invaluable, knowing the place as he does."

"I am sure papa can't make any objection. You go
down to-morrow?"

"Yes; to-morrow, by the midday train from the Kingsbridge."

"We must telegraph to the Sheas in the morning,
Dick: you must, at all events, for I don't know them."

"Nellie seated herself, as she spoke, by the fireside,

opposite to a large easy-chair which Dicky had advanced
for Hogan. She looked exquisitely pretty; the firelight
played on her soft brown hair, and lighted up her clear,
fine skin and eyes. She looked so fresh, so rosy, and so
young: childish, almost, as compared with Miss Bursford,
to whom Hogan (alas!) had paid a third visit that very
afternoon. Miss Diana had also sat by the fire with him;
that is, she had reclined in the most graceful manner in a
velvet-covered low chair, and instead of allowing the flickering blaze of the coals to light up the hollows of her face,
had discreetly shaded it with a handscreen, used in the
most airy, coquettish manner, and from beneath the shadow
of which she had darted languishing glances now and again;
and when he spoke of himself, as our hero was slightly
addicted to doing, she would lean her chin in the palm of
her hand, and, stooping forward, concentrate her attention
on every syllable he uttered. It was very pleasant, very
flattering; but there "was something more exquisite still"
now, in watching, as he was doing, the colour come and
go, the eyes dilate and half-close with every word, and the
unconscious simplicity and naturalness of Nellie.

They begged Hogan to stay for tea; and he, nothing
loth, although he had promised to see the Bishop that
evening, remained. Then Dicky opened a door leading
into the drawing-room, and lighted up a round three-
windowed room, on the ground-floor like the parlour, and
looking out on the garden. There was no fire; but the
warmth from the sitting-room penetrated it. Here was
the piano; and Dicky, who could play pretty well, sat
down and dashed into a spirited waltz. Nellie seated
herself on an ottoman in the centre of the room; and
Hogan, taking an album off a table, placed himself close to
her, and began to turn over the leaves. Of course she had
to look at each as it presented itself; and Dicky, glancing
round, might, had he been so disposed, have made the discovery of the exact number of shades of difference between
the golden-brown of his sister's and the black-brown of the
barrister's hair,—the two heads being in the precise position needful for such observation. As for their conversa-

tion, it consisted of nothings, vain repetitions of already answered questions, opinions and judgments flattering and otherwise.

"I hope Dicky will be of use to you," said Miss Nellie. "I am glad he is going; then we shall know early how matters are progressing for you."

"Yes, yes," he answered. "I shall tell you that myself." And then, taking the half of the great photographic book that she was holding, he closed it, and stooping a little nearer, looked straight, with his keen gray eyes, now softened with an unwonted tenderness, into hers, and said in a low tone and quickly, for Dicky was crashing the *finale* of his waltz, "May I come and tell you my success?"

She could not trust herself to answer, but her eyes spoke for her; she glanced, half involuntarily, upwards, and then rose and went over to the piano. Dicky made her play a soft Schubert melody, that seemed like a pleasant dream after his wild, chaotic, though rhythmic dance.

She was a little distant with Hogan for the rest of his stay, which shortly ended. She felt frightened more than anything else, at present, and confused with a strange new sense as yet unknown to her. On his side he feared to have acted on the impulse of the moment, and tried to conjure up a new meaning for the startled though not displeased look in her eyes as she rose. They bade each other good-night ceremoniously. Hogan did not venture to press her hand when parting; but when down at the entrance-gates—whither Dicky, chattering like a pie, convoyed him—he turned and saw the dark tall figure in the doorway, the light on her graceful head, as she stood waiting to see him out of the gate and call her brother in, he looked admiringly, and waved his hand to her. A frank, pleasant laugh answered him; and, reassured, the young man went his way to town.

CHAPTER XV.

" SIG.—How now, my masters, have you chose this man ?
1st CIT.—He has our voices, Sir.
BRU.—We pray the Gods he may deserve your loves."
                                                Coriolanus.
" Behold, these are the tribunes of the people.
The tongues of the commonwealth.   I do despise them !
For they do prank them in authority
Against all noble sufferance."—*Idem.*

O'ROONEY HOGAN and Dicky started by the mail from the Kingsbridge terminus for Peatstown, a thriving market town and borough in one of the southern counties.   The route lay through a dreary, uninteresting line of country, —flat and monotonous when once the Dublin mountains were left behind.   And though the day was dry, a cold fog bounded the view from the windows.

Our two travellers talked and smoked for a fair portion of the time ; but at last Hogan drew a sheaf of papers out of his travelling-bag, and Dicky was obliged to content himself with a newspaper.   Late in the afternoon they came to a junction.   The mail train, having kicked off a couple of carriages, proceeded snorting and shrieking on its way to meet the American steamer at Queenstown, and the barrister and his companion got out to walk up and down for ten minutes ; then, after a short delay, the Peatstown train was announced, and scrambling in they found themselves advancing at a much slower pace along a cross line, bounded on each side by the bog.

The winter day was fast closing in now.   A tawny hue in the sky over the tops of a pine wood to the right showed where the sun was vanishing; a blue vapour rose from the dark pools where the peats had been cut; and here and there a tree, stunted and naked, held out bare skeleton-like limbs. Dicky opened the window a moment, and looked out, seeking some familiar landmark by which to guess the distance. But the cold mist and the still, lonely country outside were not inviting, so he shut it again, and stretched himself on the seat, well wrapped up, to try and doze. Hogan was not inclined to talk; he leaned his elbow on the cushioned arm of his seat, and mused for more than an hour in silence. In truth, now that he was away from Dublin, and that the lively, sanguine Saltasche was no longer at his elbow to goad him onward with his banter and encouragement, he felt a sort of reaction. Even the Bishop's half-hearted counsel and timid dissuasion, nerving him by its very bonelessness to more braced determination, now would have acted as a stimulant. He felt chilled and dull, and longed to reach their station, to get out and stamp life and warmth into his feet. Not a light could he see from the window. The sunset tints were gone, and blackness fell imperceptibly and swiftly over everything.

At last they slackened speed at a station not much larger than a cattle-shed; and Dicky, who had fallen asleep in his rugs, woke up, and almost jumped out, with sheer impatience. Before the train had stopped he was out on the platform in the midst of a group of frieze-coated men, and was shaking hands and exchanging noisy, hearty greetings with them. A rush was made in a moment up to the carriage, out of which Hogan and a porter were, by this time, pulling the rugs and bags.

"Mr. Shea, Mr. Hogan; Mr. Barney Shane, Mr. Hogan. This is Mr. Killeen: Mr. O'Rooney Hogan."

These and some more introductions were gone through by Mr. Dicky in such a hasty way that Hogan could not connect the names with the right individuals of the group of big men, all of whom grasped his hand and wrung it till the bones almost cracked. Mr. Killeen was the editor of the *Peatstown Torch*, and a very important personage; joining to his literary avocation the functions of weigh-

Q

master and butter-taster on fair days. The little crowd, picked their way with difficulty out of the station, which was only lighted by a couple of flickering oil-lamps. Behind stood in readiness an outside car with a fine bloodhorse in the shafts. Dicky and his cousin Shea mounted on the driving side, Hogan and Killeen on the other; the rest of the party brought their own conveyances. Then the man, having turned the horse carefully, sprang out of its way, and off they started at a tearing rate.

"Yer soul, Dicky," cried Shea, heartily, "but I'm glad to see you; the girls will all go mad with delight; we never thought of you till the holidays. You did well to send the telegram."

"You have a splendid horse, Mr. Shea," said Hogan, who was admiring the paces of the animal.

"He is. I sold him this morning to Lord Kilboggan's steward for ninety guineas; bred him myself. So I must be careful of him," returned Shea, who was looking out cautiously ahead. "We've five miles to go—four and a half to the town, and a half a mile beyond it to Mulla Castle."

"Mulla Castle!" Hogan smiled at the promising title. "Is the railway four and a half miles away from the town?"

"It is, indeed; and a cruel loss it is to us, dragging to it up hill and down dale as we have to. When these railways were made they paid small heed to the convenience of the people along the lines."

"Augh!" said Killeen, "Home Rule will settle everything for us; won't it, Mr. Hogan?"

Hogan and Dicky both laughed heartily. Meantime the car dashed on fast, splashing through water and over stones without ever slackening. No sign of light showed as yet, and not a sound, save the distant bark of a cur dog, or the ghostly rustle of the bare branches overhead, broke the stillness around them.

"Look out before you, sir," cried Killeen; "there's the river!"

The horse slacked an instant in a "soft" spot—a

perfect bed of mud and water at the foot of a rise in the road; and listening, Hogan could hear the swift running murmur of the stream behind the tall sedges that hid it from his sight. On a level almost with the top of the bank, and far below that of the road, he could now trace a row of wretched cabins. A faint gleam of light in one or two showed that the inmates had not all as yet gone to bed. But most of them were black and silent.

"Are they empty, then?" asked Hogan. "What wretched damp holes they must be!"

"Damp!" cried Killeen. "Wait, sir, till to-morrow. They are mere ruins. And instead of repairing them he's paying the people to come out of them till he pulls them down."

"Best thing to do with them indeed," said Hogan.

"No, sir," said Killeen; "it is not. The poorest dog-hole is better for a man than the workhouse."

"The workhouse: why that? Are there no other cottages?"

"There are not; and Kilboggan won't build them. He has to pay rates on them, and he'd rather see every one in the poorhouse than that."

"There are now twelve hundred in that workhouse yonder," said Killeen, nodding in the direction where the building lay, though the darkness did not permit it to be seen. "And there are scores of able-bodied men, and their wives and families. We'll show you the cottages he has pulled down. The people that have cabins here are letting lodgings. Yes, begad, sir, in those places we passed they get sixpence a week to let a man lie on the floor with a lock of straw or hay under his head,—men that could pay rent for a house, too, but can't get one in the place."

By this time they had reached the town itself. A good long main street, with comfortable-looking shops on both sides, flagged pathways, and a tolerably well-kept thorough-fare. The hotel, a large yellow house with green jalousies, and a high flight of steps, on which were lounging a number of people, stood at the top of the street. The

hall doors were open, and the light and brightness were
inviting. The Kilboggan arms were painted over the
door. At the first sound of the wheels a general rush
was made. All down the street the people sprang to
their doors, and a crowd of spectators thronged, curious
and open-eyed, out of the bye-streets and lanes. Every
one was on the alert. But Shea whipped up his horse,
and the sight-seers were disappointed. As they passed
the hotel, he stooped forward and called to a man,—

"Hurry them on, Jack. Father Corkran's above, and
he waits for no one." He pointed backwards with his
whip, indicating the other cars, which he had distanced by
a long stretch.

Hogan pricked up his ears at the name; and Dicky,
who heard and noted it too, turned to Shea with a
laugh.

"Father Jim's to be in it, of course? I bet you we'll
fight. Will Father Desmond be down?"

"Ay," replied Ned Shea, "and three or four more as
well; just wait till you see. Be easy now, Dicky, with
your tongue," he added, "and don't set 'Jim' against——"
and he jerked his head backward, indicating the candidate
behind them.

They now reached a low swing-gate, painted white. A
couple of men sprang, apparently out of the ditch, to open
and hold it. They passed through, and on to what was
like another road, only narrower than that which they had
left, and running through a field. After a minute or two
they turned a corner, and a huge square white house, well
lighted up, stood at the top of a wide field before them.
A little white railing ran on each side of the grass as they
approached, and marked off the sweep before the door.
As soon as the sound of the car was heard in the house,
the hall door was thrown wide open, letting out a stream
of light and noise, and mingled odours of all sorts, the
basis of which was turf smoke; and a crowd rushed out
to welcome the visitors. A half-dozen or more daughters,
some grown up and others as yet in the chrysalis stage,
seized on Dicky. Then they all bustled in; and in the

hall, where was burning a huge fire of peats, Hogan was introduced to his hostess, a comely matron, with an amiable, good-humoured face,—a Kerry woman, as evidenced by her accent, and with the fine dark eyes and hair so often seen in that favoured district. Hogan and Dicky now followed a barefooted girl up to their rooms, which blazing turf fires made agreeable and home-like after the chilly journey. Hogan made a speedy toilet, and had sat down to warm his feet, when Dicky appeared at the door of communication, operating on his head with a pair of hairbrushes all the while.

"Are you hungry, Mr. Hogan?" asked he.

"Well, yes."

"A good job: wait till you see the dinner you've to go through. Camacho's wedding feast was a fly to it. Hurry, and let's go down to the drawing-room."

"Drawing-room!" echoed Hogan, staring at him.

"Yes, drawing-room; and as good a piano as ever you heard, too. Bless you, man! do you know what Shea is worth?"

"Indeed I don't," said the barrister, who was asking himself whether he ought not to have brought down a dress suit.

"His parish priest told me, one time I was here, that he had every copper of eighty thousand—value for it, you know."

"God bless me!" said Hogan.

Then they went down to the drawing-room. A huge square room occupied the best part of the second floor. It was comfortably furnished, with plenty of stout rose-wood and velvet chairs and sofas. A couple of round tables covered with red cloths, and on which were candles not yet lighted, had a business-like air. The piano was well piled with music; and vases of paper and wax flowers, and those wool-work performances which indicate the presence of convent-bred young ladies just as surely as anything can be indicated in this world.

Mrs. Shea, gorgeous in a green silk gown, invited Hogan to a seat beside her, after presenting to him in their various

order about a dozen ladies, old and young, daughters,
aunts, and cousins of the house—all jolly ; and the young
ones good-looking and clear-skinned damsels fresh from the
convents, and on their promotion. A couple of priests
were present : a Father Desmond from the mountains, who
seemed with Dicky to absorb the attention of the ladies ;
and a heavy, but good-humoured looking curate belonging
to Peatstown. The great man, the parish priest himself,
had not yet come in. In a minute Shea, now dressed in
his Sunday frock-coat, which showed his wiry, active figure
to advantage, stormed into the room. He was a good-
looking man, sunburnt and healthy, with merry blue eyes,
and hair clustering in little curls over a white forehead,
that contrasted strangely with the tanned cheeks below it.
With him came all the stragglers : Barney Shane, a cousin,
a gigantic, wild-looking fellow in a shooting costume of
gray tweed ; Killeen the editor, oily and meek of manner ;
three or four wealthy farmers, big and rough and healthy-
looking ; and in the midst of the throng the redoubtable
Father Jim Corkran himself.

Mrs. Shea rose and presented Hogan to his reverence.
Her manner in doing so struck the keen-eyed barrister as
being somewhat peculiar; there was a faint shade of
trepidation in the tones of her voice, and she seemed to
look with a sort of nervous deprecation at the domineering
face of the priest, as if fearful of finding there some displeasure or disapproval. Father Corkran bowed, muttering
some half unintelligible words of greeting as he did so.
Hogan was standing on the hearthrug, having deliberately
chosen that position for the expected encounter ; and while
smiling blandly in return to his reverence's remarks, was
mentally taking observations, and making up his mind to
face the situation boldly. Mrs. Shea's manner had given
him unconsciously a valuable hint. The key of the position, her husband, must be secured at once, and pledged
irredeemably to his side. So while talking all round with
the off-hand, good-humoured way so peculiarly his own, he
ran his eye over the person of his adversary,—for such, he
felt convinced, was the *rôle* to be played by the parish priest.

A lubberly, coarse figure, bullet-headed, and with the prominent round forehead that tells of obstinacy and impetuosity, wiry black hair and brows which contrasted strangely with round light blue eyes, hard and ruthless, and with a fixed staring look most unpleasant to encounter, while the lips were scornful, and pursed out with pride and self-sufficiency. And with all this he was utterly devoid of dignity, either of manner or bearing. Those who feared him—and they were many—were servile and cringing before the bully ; but those who, like Shea and the richer class of farmers, were independent of his good graces, spoke of him, irrespective of course of his saintly office, with a freedom which showed that the reverend Father Jim was valued at his proper rate by them. Dicky, being an outsider and independent, used to have wordy tilts with his reverence, in which the youth seldom came off second best ; his cousin Shea, who had some private grudges against his parish priest, used to put Dicky up to many a sharp saying and innuendo that he dared not employ himself; and a bout between the two was a favourite after-dinner diversion at Mulla Castle.

Dicky, who had been hidden on an ottoman among a crowd of admiring girls, spied his old enemy on the sofa, and jumping up, advanced with a show of the greatest cordiality and affection to greet his reverence.

"Father Corkran—my dear sir!—and I not to have seen you till this minute ! "

Father Corkran stretched out a grudging paw. "Well, little divelskin, so you're here again, are you ?"

"Little !" repeated the youth. "By Jove, if I was as broad as I'm long I'd just fit your clothes—no more."

Before his reverence could think of a suitable retort, the dinner was announced, and Mrs. Shea demanded his attentions ; the pair headed the way,—the rest streamed after. Hogan took in Miss Shea, and Dicky seized a couple of willing damsels, who squeezed and giggled downstairs abreast. A good number of the women of the party remained upstairs, as the dinner-table only accommodated twenty ; and far more men than women sat down. A curt grace was pronounced by Father Corkran ; and then, as Shea graphically described it, they "saw their dinner." Hogan looked round him in undisguised wonder and amusement.   At the head of the table, before Mrs. Shea, was a boiled turkey as big as a sheep; at the foot an entire sirloin, perhaps forty pounds in weight, of beef. A boiled leg of mutton and turnips claimed Hogan's attention. Two dishes of fowls, a roast saddle of mutton, a boiled round of beef, a monstrous ham and a roast turkey, a meat pie and a chicken pie, occupied places before the gentlemen of the party.   Vegetables were handed round by red-cheeked smiling servant-girls ; and beer-jugs, sherry decanters, and magnums of good champagne were in constant request to wash down the solids.

"What a superb turkey, Mrs. Shea!" said Hogan: "is that one of your own rearing, may I ask?"

"It is, Mr. Hogan," replied the lady, who was carving with a skill and dexterity that evinced long practice.

"It must have taken a railway train to *draw* that fellow."

This somewhat technical joke was welcomed by the hostess with a hearty laugh ; but on the rest of the audience it fell flat.   Father Corkran, who sat opposite, grunted a note of approval, but never raised his head from his plate or relaxed his operations, the intensity and fervour of which brought beads of perspiration out on his bald head.   It was not the time for *jeux d'esprit*, as the barrister acknowledged when he looked round the table and noted the curious comportment of the guests, all solemnly engaged in the grand event of the day.   "If they take in solids in this way," he thought, "what will they stop at when it comes to the whiskey and hot water?"   So he wisely determined to lay a substantial foundation by way of precaution.   After about twenty minutes, Father Jim Corkran, who having been first on the road was the first to declare a halt, laying down his knife and fork, threw himself back in the chair and employed an interlude, or rather an armistice, of about five minutes in staring at Hogan.   He then resumed his avocations, but with somewhat less assiduity :

and in a minute or two conversation became general. In deference to the ladies' presence the company eschewed politics, and local affairs were discussed until the end of the second course. Then came a formidable array of glasses, hot-water kettles and whiskey decanters. Each man brewed for himself; and in a moment or two the founda- tion-stone of every real Irish political discussion was laid : every disputant was provided with a tumbler of whiskey punch. O'Rooney Hogan filled his own glass with a mixture as weak as he dared to brew it, and .instinctively girt up his loins for battle.

The moment was come. Ned Shea leaned forward in his chair, and looked all round the room. A silence unbroken, save for the clinking of busy ladles, reigned immediately amongst the guests.

" Your reverences and ladies and gentlemen—this is my friend from Dublin, Mr. O'Rooney Hogan, and I'm right glad to see him amongst us. I hope you will all join me in drinking his health and success to his cause."

" Hear, hear ! " went round the table heartily ; and all —the ladies, who were each provided with a wine-glass of steaming punch, included—drank to the toast. Hogan got up and bowed; and then, a little nervously, he made a short speech, expressing his thanks for his host's kind- ness, and concluded with a flowery compliment to his fair hearers.

After this, which was only the introduction, the ladies trooped off upstairs, and the real business began. Barney Shane, the stalwart tenant-farmer and cousin to the host, proposed, in a stentorian voice, the toast, " Success to the Cause ? " This was barely drunk when the· parish priest, who was now in fine fighting trim, planted one sturdy elbow on the table, and spoke in a loud grating voice,—

" I'd like to know, Barney Shane, and Ned Shea too, and Mr. O'Rooney Hogan,—I say, I'd like to know what's the cause Mr. Hogan, no offence to him, has adopted ! "— and he banged his great hand on the table, and flung him- self back in his seat awaiting his reply.

The glove was thrown. Shea and his guests turned to

Hogan with expectant eyes, solemn and inquiring ; and feeling that the hour of trial was come, our hero jumped to his feet.

"Gentlemen," said he, "I am now called upon publicly to state with what political views I have presented myself to the voters of Peatstown. When I proposed to myself the honour of representing you in Parliament, I was fully aware of the magnitude and importance of the great questions now agitating this Empire; and were I to hesitate in declaring my principles concerning them for one moment, I should feel myself deserving of your heartiest condemnation. I will therefore proceed to read to you my Parliamentary programme embodied in this." He held a strip of blue paper in his hand. "I may remark that this address will appear in all the Dublin papers to-morrow; and Mr. Muldoon, my agent, will settle with Mr. Killeen for the printing and distribution of the same throughout the country to-morrow."

Mr. Killeen's countenance now took a pleasant expression : he had been sorely vexed as to whether the printing of the election papers was to be confided to him or not.

"Come on to the address," interpolated the impatient Father Jim.

"Certainly, Father Corkran," was the bland reply ; and unrolling the strip of blue paper, Hogan cleared his throat, and in a fine full voice began as follows :—

"GENTLEMEN—The duty devolves upon you now, owing to the death of your late lamented representative, Mr. Theodore Wyldoates" (a scornful laugh from Barney Shane made itself heard at this point), "of electing a representative in his place. Never before did the task carry with it a greater responsibility.

"You are now called upon to determine whether the nationality of our country is slowly but surely to be crushed, or whether, the dark cloud of oppression having been lifted off, the glorious sunshine of freedom and emancipation is to be substituted, never more to be eclipsed. At this critical moment I offer you my services, and seek the honour of being your representative. In me you will find the most staunch of all the supporters of the principles of Home Rule. I will devote my energies and talents, such as I possess, to obtain for Ireland the most complete powers of self-government.

" I heartily concur" (here he raised his voice perceptibly) "in the views upon the Education question entertained by the prelates and clergy of my Church. In me they will have a sincere and energetic supporter.

" On behalf of the Tenant Farmers, I hold and maintain that complete fixity of tenure at a fair rent is not only the inalienable natural right of the tiller of the soil, but is for the mutual benefit of owner and occupier.

" I hold it to be the duty of every Catholic to sustain our Holy Father the Pope against a most unjust spoliation; and if you return me as your representative, my voice shall not be silent in his behalf.

" It is unnecessary for me to state that a full and com-. plete amnesty should be granted to all political prisoners.

" I ask you, in conclusion, to entrust me with the duty, as your representative, of endeavouring to carry into effect these principles—sanctioned as they will be, I hope, by your votes. If entrusted with your confidence, I pledge myself to accept neither office nor favour, and to devote my best energies to the welfare and prosperity of our country.

" Gentlemen electors,
" I have the honour to be
" Your faithful servant,
" JOHN O'ROONEY HOGAN."

The applause was a little flat, although unanimous; and Hogan felt it. He repented having read the address,—a speech is always so much better appreciated. He handed the blue paper across to Killeen; and clearing his throat afresh, began to speak, determined to regain the ground which he felt he had lost.

" Gentlemen, you have now my programme; and to-morrow, by Mr. Killeen's kind agency, it will be in the hands of every one in the town and district I have placed the portions of the programme in the order in which it seems to me they ought to come. First of all, Home Rule, the grand object for which every true Irishman is striving; then Education, pure and untainted by heresy and infidelity. Until we have the grand aim secured, néver" (and here he raised his voice), "never will the ground-down peasants, the plundered farmers, the Sainted Martyr, or the poor caged prisoners, have their rights,—never, till Ireland be once more a nation!"

A roar of enthusiasm greeted this peroration; the table was thumped by the excited listeners until the glasses rang again. When the tumult had a little subsided, so that his strident voice could be heard, the parish priest leaned across the table, and fixing Hogan with his hard blue eyes, in which sparks of anger now shone, began,—

"I see, sir, how it is with you: Home Rule is the horse you want to ride in on—eh?"

"Never mind, Father Jim," put in Dicky, in whose brain champagne and whiskey punch were beginning to hold divided sway; "what horses are you talking of now? If every man rode his own horse, you'd walk oftener than you do."

"Well done, Dicky! Yer soul, Dicky, ye had him then. Bravo the Dublin boy! More power!" roared the company, in high delight at the allusion to a well-known jockeying trick played by his reverence. Father Jim laughed too: he could well afford it.

"Go on up to the ladies, ye jackeen!" he roared back; "where are ye prating here? Go on, I bid ye!"

"Catch me!" retorted the boy with a grimace.

Father Corkran returned to his charge with the candidate.

"I was talking to the Bishop," he began in the pompous high voice people will assume when they mention their superiors, "the other day; and his lordship told me he doesn't understand this new go at all, at all. What's to come of it? and what do ye want, and what will ye do with it when ye have it? Peace and quietness, and every man look after his own; there's me ideas, and there's the Bishop's."

"You, and the likes of you," broke in Barney Shane, in a truculent voice, "that have nothing to lose, may prate of your peace and quietness, and every man look after his own. We'll look after our own,—and trust you to look after yours." Here an assenting shout almost rent the ceiling. "Look at me," he went on, smiting the table with a fist like Thor's; my lease will be out in two years' time, and what will that gambling blackguard Kilboggan give me? The key of the street! and I born and reared in the place, and my father and grandfathers before me;" and the big man's voice almost faltered as he spoke.

"Ay, and what will Home Rule do for that?" sneered the priest.

"I'll try," was the concise answer. "Ye have two years before ye," added he, turning to Hogan; "an' if it doesn't——" He finished the sentence by the significant act of spitting in the palm of his hand.

"Right, my friend," cried Hogan; "'Heaven helps those who help themselves.'" This man could bring twenty voters or more, perhaps, with him; and Hogan felt his cause was winning. All this time the punch was being consumed fast and steadily. Ned Shea, the host, drained his fifth tumbler, and running one hand through his fine curly hair, he stretched out the other to Hogan.

"I have a lease for a couple of hundred years," said he; "but ye have my support, sir, all the same. And there's success to ye again, Mr. Hogan!" and he filled out a bumper of raw whiskey and tossed it off.

"And mine! and mine!" ran round the table, as the guests followed his example.

The priests at the table said but little, except the curate of the mountain parish, who drank every toast and sentiment with the rest. Father Corkran, who was vicar-general of the diocese, had been to see the Bishop the day before; and none of them knew as yet what course was to be taken with regard to the election, and especially with regard to the new party cry Home Rule, so they were careful not to commit themselves in any way. As Ned Shea's guests, they were bound to respect his friend; but

they knew that Hogan was a loose fish of a Dublin barrister, who, of course, was doing the best he could for himself; and it rested with the Bishop as yet whether they
were to support him or not. They all, too, had a pretty
shrewd idea that the vicar-general had written or telegraphed to Nice, to the lord of the manor, for instructions
as to whether there would be an opposition or not, and
also concerning some other minor matters, important to
clerical interests. The Kilboggans had a stake in the
county—a vested interest,—and as well as Tories and
bigots, they were aristocrats; and aristocracy, and all
pertaining thereto, is dear to the clerical heart. And
naturally :—are there not orders and degrees of aristocracy
in the Church—cardinals, archbishops, bishops, parish
priests, and curates ? Father Corkran looked forward to
being a bishop one day; and every curate has his eye on
a fat parish. And though priests and people owed everything to the Whigs, in fundamental principles and in
reality the first-named are far more adapted to Toryism.
Home Rule had begun, somehow, too independently of the
priests. The Protestants were entirely too much mixed
up with it to please them. It seemed so unnatural, and
so opposed to all precedent, to see Tories, Protestants, and
gentlemen working hand in hand with the Catholic nationalists: it couldn't be sound socially or politically. And
now the Ultra party, the dregs of Fenianism, and those
vile returned Americans, who of late swarmed everywhere,
with their republican and democratic notions, were collecting themselves together under the name of Home Rulers.
Altogether, most of the clergy looked with distrust and
disfavour on the movement—as yet, at all events—for
they were careful not to commit themselves one way or
the other.

Father Corkran sat sulky and silent, brooding over the
turn events had taken. It was perfectly clear that every
man in the room was going to follow this adventurer to
the poll. In fact, the fellow himself was so sure of his
success that he was taking a cool, independent tone in
speaking to him—Father Corkran, the administrator !

And the Education Question, forsooth, was to be laid
aside till Home Rule and Fixity of Tenure was got.   It
was a new experience indeed; and what a pass things
must have come to, when a candidate might "cheek" the
parish priest! No doubt he felt safe, with this new dodge
the Ballot at his back.   However, beyond a sulkiness in
no way unusual or remarkable, his reverence showed no
overt hostility.   He dared not, indeed, tell the voters his
own opinion of Home Rule: would that he could!   The
"cloth" had always been national; and the country having
made Home Rule a national cry, the priests could not dis-
own it completely,—at least not yet, for the trump might
change, and pledges are awkward things.   The best thing
was to play out the present hand as skilfully as possible.

Ned Shea rose now, in obedience to a summons from
above stairs, and his guests followed him up to tea.   The
piano was open, and Mr. Dicky was seized upon by the
young ladies to play.   However, Mr. Dicky had something better in view; and when tea had disappeared,
seeing that Shea, Father Corkran and Hogan, with Barney
Shane and a farmer named Hara, had seated themselves
at one of the card-tables, he determined to follow their
example, and speedily organised a game of "spoil five"
with a couple of priests and Mrs. Shea.   One of the
daughters seated herself beside Dicky; and a mountain of
coppers having been produced, they speedily set to work.
At the other table a far more serious business was being
done.   Unlimited loo was proposed, and a shilling was
placed by each in the pool to begin.

"Looed for the amount now, and the rigour of the
game!" declared his reverence, who loved a "hand of
cards."

He was the first to infringe his own law.

Shea dealt; and turning to Father Jim, who was on his
left, he asked the formal question, "Will you play?"

Father Jim inspected his three cards, and answering in
the negative, dashed them into the middle of the table.

"You are looed, sir," said Hogan politely.

"No, I'm not," was the gracious reply. .

"You are looed," cried Barney in delight. "You threw out before the time; and it was yourself made the rule for the strict game."

"Pay down five shillings here this minute; pay down your money, and look pleasant over it,—come on;" and Shea held out the saucer in which the five shillings were.

There was no help for it; and glaring savagely at them, Father Jim gathered up the five shillings, leaving a half-sovereign instead. Hogan won the whole pool; so his reverence was consoled on seeing twenty shillings put down by the others. The stakes soon reached such a height that they proposed to limit the pool to two pounds ten, or in other words, the loo to ten shillings. It was anything but a quiet game: the eagerness of the priest, and the ferocity of Barney Shane, who glared at the others as if they were in a league to cheat him, and was far more watchful that they did not gain an unfair advantage than careful to play his own cards so as to win, were openly displayed. Hara was tricky, and on him Barney and Father Corkran concentrated their attention. Shea himself, too lazy and good-humoured to care whether he won or lost, adjured the rest to take things easy. Hogan was too much a man of the world to show much feeling one way or the other; he had intended to lose twenty pounds to Father Jim, but as things were going, he thought he might as well win as lose. The pool was a full one when the deal came again to Father Corkran; and the whole sum fell to his reverence's lot. Seizing the saucer, he emptied it on the table with a clatter that raised the ire of Barney Shane.

"It's easy seen," said he bitterly, "ye took care of yourself. Oh, begad, yes, I don't like to see the dealer walking off with everything that way."

"Don't ye, be me sowl!" was the scornful notice his reverence vouchsafed.

So they went on for an hour; until at last Father Desmond took Shea's place, to let him sing one of Moore's melodies to his daughter's accompaniment on the piano. Hogan had lost ten pounds—most of which had gone into his reverence's pocket. After a few more rounds, Hogan called Dicky over to his place. Dicky, who guessed that high play was going on, from the loud, excited talk that had reached him, obeyed gladly. The girls wanted him to come and dance ; but he refused, and they were left to the clumsy attentions of a couple of young farmers. They scarcely looked at Hogan, and answered him coldly when he addressed them ; with the fine instinct of their sex they divined him, and estimated his worth pretty accurately. " Leave him where he is, Mary," said one shrewd damsel to another ; " it's some grand Dublin lady, maybe a lord's daughter, he has his eye on ; leave him where he is ; he won't be much good to any one that gets him."

Then there was a rush to where Dicky was sitting— his high clear voice being heard in altercation with Father Jim.

" Have you any money—eh ? " he asked of the priest, who was angry at his joining the set.

" Have I ? " retorted he. " I 've more than you ever saw, or ever will, my Dublin slieveen."

" Do you know how to play loo ? " asked Dicky imperiously.

" Oh, faith, we'll try that ; so here's at you now ! " said Father Corkran, thoroughly nettled and slapping down the cards with fiery emphasis.

The luck was even for a few turns, but changed suddenly ; and Dicky won a couple of pounds in a breath. Another "hand " was played, and he again took the pool.

" Now, Father Jim, how do you like that, hey ? " And he stood up, holding the money in his hand, as if to move off with his gains.

" Look at him ! " cried Father Jim in pathetic tones, " Oh, look at him now—walking off with the poor priest's money."

A shout of laughter greeted this appeal.

" Ho ! ho ! how poor you are ! You got it easy, and it's gone easy," railed the youngster.

" If you ever worked half as hard in your life, you little Dublin jackeen ! " retorted his reverence.

R

" Worked !　With the knife and fork, you mean, I suppose ?"

" Yah ! you slieveen, you jackeen."　And then, with a funny change of tone, " Sure if I had any idea such a grand gentleman as yourself, Mr. Davoren," he continued, " was comin' down to our poor little place, I was talkin' to the Bishop, then, and the O'Gorman Mulcahy, and sure I'd have asked them round to ait a bit ov dinner with ye, so I would."

" And if I'd any *ideeah*," mimicked Dicky, " Father Jim, that you were intimate with such grand people entirely, I'd—I'd—never have won your money."

This gibe finished the fragment of patience left to Father Jim.

" Come on out of that here, an' divel sweep you for an impident small crumb of humanity.　Come on, and I'll play you double or quits."

Dicky, with a gambler's prescience, feeling himself in the vein of luck, threw down his money on the table. Barney Shane seized and counted it.

" Twelve pounds between Dicky and Father Jim!" shouted he.

A rush was made from all parts ; and facing each other, the opponents began.

" Two games out of three," said his reverence, " and cut for the deal."

Dicky's luck continued ; he won the twelve pounds, to the delight of the room; and Father Corkran went off home declaring the youth's company to be neither sound nor saintly.　After ten o'clock all the clerical party left. Shea caught the curate Desmond by the coat as he was going out of the room.

" Mr. Hogan and I will be in Ballinagad to-morrow in the afternoon.　I think we'll sleep at Barney's."

" Come to me for dinner.　I say, Shea " (he dropped his voice to a whisper), " it won't be a walk-over.　One of the nephews will be over at the end of the week."

" Sure !　By gad, the rogues have stolen a march on us !"

"I won't say for certain; but there's something. Don't let on I told you, Ned, for any sake."

Dancing began, now that the restraint of the priest's presence was removed; and it was late when our two travellers retired, with weary limbs and aching heads, to their much-needed repose.

CHAPTER XVI.

Jean Paul Richter says : "No man really believes his creed until he can afford to laugh at it."

NEXT morning, after a late breakfast, Hogan and his host sallied out and visited the farm and out-offices. The house did not show to much better advantage in the daylight. The plaster was rain-soaked, and in many places had fallen off altogether. There was no garden, although a fine southern slope at the left side of the house might easily have formed one. The farm-yard was unpaved, and the animals stood half-leg deep in pools of stagnant water and stable muck. The outhouses were new, and consequently in fair order, although the internal arrangements were so dirty and slovenly as to offend every sense. Wasteful, disorderly plenty seemed the reigning characteristic. Not so much as a rosebush or creeper against the walls spoke of the taste of the piano-playing ladies within, and the dairy, to judge by the smell which saluted Hogan's nostrils as he put his head in, was equally in need of a supervising eye.

Shea, having shown his fine cattle and horses, desired that the car should be got ready and brought round to the front door; and in a short time they started to visit the town.

Peatstown, taking its name from the bog on the skirt of which it is built, lay in a hollow. There was a good main street, and a number of smaller ones branching off it; but the greater portion consisted of rows of miserable cabins, which, from their position and sunken state, must be often almost under water. The people were wretchedly poor,

and the rags of the beggars, with whom of course the place
was swarming, were a perfect marvel in point of variety of
colour and texture. Shea drove straight to Killeen's place
of business, and alighting, penetrated with Hogan into the
editorial sanctum. There they found the presiding genius
of the *Peatstown Torch* smoking a short pipe and gossiping
with a couple of worthies of the town. These were presented to Hogan in due form, and, after a short conversation, in obedience to a hint from Shea, left the editor with
his new visitors.

"Father Corkran was in a while ago. It's well you
had me engaged on your side, Mr. Hogan," began Mr.
Killeen.

"What! there *is* to be a contest then; I thought all
along it was a false report," cried the barrister.

"A telegram from Nice this morning, upon my honour.
Mr. Theo. Wyldoates, him that's *attaché* at Constantinople,
is on his way; bedad, you'll have a pull for it, sir."

"Oh ho! But there is no fear of him, Mr. Killeen; the
family are very unpopular. Anyhow, Home Rule will
carry it. You can't trust the Kilboggans, you know."

"Father Jim has got the grant of land for the chapel,
whichever way it goes."

"He has, eh? has he?" said Hogan. "Well, if he be
worth his salt he'll get what'll build him a chapel house
too. Come now, Mr. Killeen, let us arrange our business,
for I must be away to canvass."

Then some business matters were entered into in refer-
ence to the printing and placarding of posters and hand-
bills. The charges for these astounded Hogan; but he
was wise enough to settle nothing beforehand, and only
stipulated that the figure should not exceed a certain sum.
He expected Muldoon to arrive by the evening train, so
they next went to the hotel to bargain for rooms for
election purposes, and to see what use could be made of
the ball-room at the hotel as a ballot office. Then Hogan
started on a canvass among the shopkeepers. Few of them
would promise anything, for fear of offending the priests.
They made some allusions to the Ballot, however, which

reassured the candidate. Shea indicated to him some houses into which it was useless to go, the inmates being employed by Kilboggan, or depending in some way upon the Castle. Agents were engaged and sent out to canvass; and Hogan, feeling that the farmers and outlying voters were the most important, and needed to be seen and talked to more than the townsmen, mounted the car and started towards Ballinagad, along by the river side.

The road was soft and dirty, and having been made in the old days when horse power was cheap and labour also, ran up hill and down dale with glorious indifference to the wear and tear of animal tissue. The vehicle was two-wheeled, as were all those they met; the reason of which became apparent when they reached the hilly ground. At the foot of every elevation lay a slough of mud, of various degrees of depth and consistency. No number of horses could have dragged a four-wheeled conveyance through it. The ditches at the sides of the road were full to overflowing; and watercress and other ditch-weeds grew over the footways. Gullies under the road led foaming streams to the river—already swollen and angry. Low-lying, marshy fields, over which hung a mantle of dark-gray fog, lay on both sides. The stunted hazels and alders, scarce rising above the level of the hedgerow, had every little twig hung with crystal-like pendants. A dismal, dreary country scene as man could behold, on a chill winter afternoon. It seemed almost a desert. Here and there, at long intervals, a cabin sunk below the road-level raised its brown indented roof in a sheltered corner. The thin blue reek of turf-smoke seemed to rise almost on a level with the face, while the cackle of the hungry geese wandering homewards through the mud pools, alone-broke the wide-reaching stillness. Seagulls rose sometimes out of a ploughed field as they passed, or a solitary heron or a curlew, uttering its melancholy shriek, flapped upwards from the river sedges. They crossed a bridge, and leaving the river behind, took an up-hill road lying for the most part through a wood. After emerging from this, they struck again on a broad highroad, and kept on at a swinging trot for nearly an hour.

"Eighteen miles altogether, Mr. Hogan," said Shea. "Yonder is Barney's house. We're into Ballinagad now."

They turned up a narrow muddy lane, and Hogan saw right before them a two-storied brick house, which looked very much the worse for time and weather. In front of the hall door, if the entrance deserved that appellation, was a huge pool of water; stepping-stones laid down in this showed that it was a permanent institution. Fowls of all sorts seemed as much at home in the house as in the yard, which was indicated by a ruined wall running out beside it to the left.

Barney appeared now at the door, and after hallooing to a man to come and take the horse, welcomed the travellers to his mansion, and led the way in. Pointing to the holes in the floor of the entry, he warned Hogan against putting his foot inadvertently in them, and related with glee how MacScutch, the agent, had twisted his ankle the day that he came up to inspect the state of the place. He led the way into the one sitting-room of the house— which, indeed, looked a great deal more like the robbers' caves to be read of in romance than a sitting-room in the ordinary sense of the word. There was no grate; and a perfect stack of turf was blazing on the hearthstone. A rickety painted table and half-a-dozen old chairs, in a fearful state of dilapidation, composed the whole furniture, save a broken sofa, one end of which was supported in a hole which had been made in the wall of the room apparently for that especial purpose, and which seemed the chosen home of a brace of fine pointers and a clever-looking terrier—all three of which were curled up on it. Daniel O'Connell, Robert Emmet in his memorable Hessian boots, and other worthies, graced the walls of the room. In every corner lay whips, saddles, bridles, and other implements of Barney's profession; for, although ostensibly a farmer, his sole occupation was horse-breeding.

This stalwart fellow had a dull, hoggish life enough; perched in such a weather-beaten eyrie all the year round. Unbroken in its sameness save when he started with some of his young stock for a horse fair or market, Barney's life was monotonous in the extreme. His profession was by no means an arduous one—it left rather too much idle time on his hands. He had no wife: the lease of his farm being almost run out, none of the match-makers around considered him worth their attention. Newspaper reading consumed most of his spare time. The *Enfranchiser* came down from Dublin daily; and he and a neighbour, a dairy farmer, subscribed for the *Daily Telegraph* between them. Every in and out of the Tichborne case was as familiar to Barney Shane as to any other newspaper student of the day, and filled up many a gap in the otherwise scant budget of gossip. He followed the fortunes of the Carlists with unwavering interest, identifying that particular party in some blind way with the Catholics and nationalists, and looking upon the Republicans with disfavour, as aliens and heretics. On wet days—by no means rare in his mountain district—Barney would retire to bed with a sheaf of papers collected from all parts (he never heeded dates), and read all day till dinner time. Dinner over, the pipe beguiled an hour; and then, having finished his dudheen, Barney would kick the dogs off his sofa and take a nap. He usually spent the evenings in some of the neighbouring farm-houses: or if disinclined to go out, would despatch one of the "runners" always hanging about his place to fetch a neighbour, or, last resource, the schoolmaster, to help to while away the long dull evenings.

Hogan seated himself by the fire, and looked round him with astonishment. The floor was bare, save for a plentiful covering of dirt, for it plainly had never been washed. The walls had at one time been whitened, but were now an indescribable dingy brown,—mud-coloured, indeed, they looked to be by the light of the home-made tallow candles which graced the table. A red-haired, barefooted girl brought in a clean though coarse cloth, which she spread; then a dish of ham, and three or four dozen fried eggs, tea, and bread and butter made their appearance; to all of which they did ample justice. Barney was hospitality itself, and forced the viands on his guests with right good will.

Ere the supper was half over, a horse's foot was heard
without; and the little curate, Father Desmond, having
alighted with no small diplomacy on a dry stone, and picked
his way through the pitfalls of the entry, presented his jolly
countenance at the door of the room.

"Ah! By the powers, boys, is it here I find ye? Ned
Shea, sure ye promised to dine with me to-day, and Mauri-
ade has lost her temper (aisy losin'—God help the finder)
entirely waiting for ye. Have you the news? Of course
ye have."

"Ay; Kilboggan's at his old thricks," said the master of
the house; "come on over here and sit down, Father
Dan."

"Where's Master Dicky?" asked Father Desmond, taking his seat. "Sure he ought to be with you, Mr. Hogan."

"I could not get him away from the ladies down there,
the little villain. It's soothering my voters he ought to
be, and not the pretty girls."

"They ought to make a counsellor out of that chap,"
said Barney. "The devil's own tongue he's got in his head.
Nothin' kills me but the cheeky way he walks into 'Jim.'"

"Ah! bedad then, boys," said Father Desmond, "look
out for Sunday, at last mass. 'Jim' is going to fire on ye.
Kilboggan will give the right of turf-cutting and the chapel
ground, and maybe a handful of money into the bargain.
The son is worse than ever—no hope of him for six
months; and Theodore, the nephew and heir, is to be got
in for certain."

"What's this right of turf-cutting?" asked the barrister.

"Faith, like many a more, it is giving us back a present
of what's our own," said Barney. "He stopped the turf-
cutting to the people along Sandy's Lane; and they always
had it. I'll tell you who knows the history and the ins
and outs of it,—Killeen."

Hogan made a note of the item, thinking he might make
capital of it.

"He took in the far common," continued Barney, "that
never was his at all; run a big wall round it, and dared
any one trespass."

" What's his income now ? This estate should be very
valuable," asked Hogan of the priest.

" Thirty-five thousand a year out of this county, sir.
Yes, and he doesn't spend as many pence in it. Neither
here nor in Dublin does that man leave one penny of his
money ; and look at the state of the town. The people
are literally bribed to go into the poorhouse. He wouldn't
drive a nail to keep a cabin from falling about their ears.
No ; keep them down, and down with them."

" Look at that, Mr. Hogan," said Barney ; " our money—
yes, ours ! the rents of the lands that ought to be ours—
carried out of the country ; and look at the place. The
people are fading off the land. The shop-keepers below
there are broke. There's less business doing through the
country now than ever was. It's the small people that are
the support of the business people ; and when they're not
in it, who consumes ?"

" To be sure," said Hogan. " He gives no employment
of any sort, either, I suppose ?"

" Divil a bit. Mary !" roared the host, " are you coming with that hot water and glasses ? I can tell you, Mr.
Hogan, when we get Home Rule we'll make a clean sweep
of absentees."

" Do you propose to confiscate their estates, or to put on
a tax ?" asked the barrister, who was making his punch.

" Oh, a tax—a smart tax," said Ned Shea. " Mr.
Hogan, what way is that you're making your punch ? Ah ?
come on, now ; a half-glass."

" A tax, wisha !" sneered Barney. " I'd tax him : strip
him clean and bare, as he stripped many a one, and let the
State take all his lands—the Protestant villain and
swaddler !"

" Swaddler he is ; no doubt of that," said Father Desmond.

" Well," replied Barney, " and look at Father Corkran,
below there, maintaining a Protestant foreign tyrant against
Mr. Hogan here."

" Yes, indeed : a priest sending a Protestant into Parliament—it is very strange," said the candidate. " What can

we expect that Englishman to do for you,—if he were a Catholic, even ?"

Hogan always insisted on displaying this special virtue when in presence of any of "the cloth."

"Bah! Catholic or not, English is enough," growled the host; "but for English Catholics, sure there'd be no Protestants at all."

"Right, Barney; and if English Catholics in the time of Elizabeth had done their duty to the Religion, the Spaniards would have triumphed and England would be Catholic to this day. Lord Howard and the rest of them were, what they always were, cringing to the sovereign— the earthly sovereign—and neglecting their Spiritual Ruler, who had the first claim on them."

"Ah! come now, Mr. Hogan," said Ned Shea, "soldiers are bound to fight for their flag; I can't give in to that."

Father Desmond only laughed good-humouredly. He had some experience of electioneering talk in his day, and was inclined to take the candidate's professions with a grain of salt; he guessed very shrewdly that this ultra-religious zeal was put on for his especial benefit, and that if he were absent Church interests would be relegated to a secondary position in the discussion. Still, his was not a very high-pitched standard. Such as it was, Hogan, although he did not reach it, came as near doing so as any one else going; besides, he opposed Kilboggan, which was the recommendation. He took a slip of paper out of his pocket, and handed it to Hogan, saying,—

"I had to go round about the place to-day, Mr. Hogan, and those names are promised to you; and here are a few you would be as well to call on. Do you see? I am thinking, though, we should call a meeting down there in the schoolhouse, and let them all come in—say on Friday night (this is Wednesday); then, Saturday night, have the meeting down below in Peatstown."

"I must be in town on Saturday," said Hogan. "Could you collect your men for to-morrow night and let me know?"

"I'll send out a couple of gossoons across the fields in

the morning," said Shea. "Why not? Time's precious, and the writ is out already."

"I'll tell you who'll vote against Father Jim, anyhow," said Barney : "Hara's brother, Tom Hara of Beerstown."

"Bedad, he will," said Father Desmond.

"Why is that, pray, if one may ask?" said Hogan.

"Well," said Barney, nothing loth to tell the story, " one night at half-past ten Father Jim was going home from a dinner ; and passing Hara's house, he saw a light in the windows. He was afraid there was some fun going on that he knew nothing about, so he ties up the horse to a rail and in with him into the house. Well, he brought the whip with him, and nothin' would serve but he hits Hara a crack of the whip, and, says he, 'What has you out of bed this hour of the night? Go 'long to bed, you vagabone, you.' Hara caught the whip from him, sir, and he bet him down the boreen till he broke it on his back. Devil a lie ; and well done to him too ! "

"Ah ! but 'Jim' had it off him in the end," said Ned Shea. "When Hara's haggard burned down that autumn, didn't 'Jim' say from the altar 'twas just the price of him for lifting a hand against the priest?"

"*Pishogues !* " returned his cousin scornfully, "sorrow a more."

"Well, I heard a good story from Father Tom McCollumby the other day," said Father Desmond.

"Tell us that, Father Dan ; it's sure to be good."

Father Desmond cleared his voice, took a sip of toddy, and began in a dry solemn way,—

"A friend of his, a priest, was hearing confessions one Saturday, and a boy came to him and said he had a rale bad sin on his mind. 'Well, me good boy, come on wid it,' said his reverence : 'sure we all must be forgiven ; so what is it now?' 'Augh den, your riverence, I do be always sayin', Be the Holy Father.' 'You do?—that's very bad, me boy. Now, how often do you be sayin' that? do you say it twiced a day?' 'Oh ! begor, an' I do, an' more your riverence.' 'Do you say it twenty times a day, me good boy?' 'Augh ! begor, an' I do ; an' more than forty times a day, your riverence!' 'This is very bad indeed, me good boy. Go home, now,' said the priest, 'and get your sister to make you a bag, and hang it round your neck; and every time you say, Be the Holy Father, drop a little stone in it, and come here to me this day week.'

"Well, that day week his reverence was hearin' as usial in his box, and he heard an awful noise in the church, so he looked out ov the dure; and what does he see but his penitent, an' he draggin' a sack up the body ov the church! 'Tady Mulloy,' says he, 'what do ye mane be sich conduck as that in de church?' 'Shure, yer riverence, says the fellow, 'dese is all the Be de Holy Fathers, an' de rest of um's outside in the dray.'"

"Well," said Ned Shea, when the laughter which greeted this anecdote had died away, "I think Father Corkran's story every bit as good."

"Come along with it, then; I haven't heard it," said his cousin Barney.

"There was a Kerry priest," began Ned Shea, "and he had the fashion of hearin' confessions wid a slate an' pencil; an' he'd write down every sin, an' the price of it opposite. Well, one day a big mountainy fellow came to his duty, an', says he, 'I bruk a man's head last Hallow-eve.' 'That's ninepence,'' says the priest. 'I cut the tail iv Larry Kelly's cow.' 'That's a shillin': oh, begob, a shillin' that is!' and down it went on the slate. 'I murthered me wife twice.' 'That's thruppence,—go on.' 'I kilt an Orangeman.' 'Whoo!' says the priest, rubbin' out everything; 'that clanes out all the rest.'"

Much laughter greeted Ned Shea's contribution; and the evening wore on fast, amid stories and talk. Barney drank a fearful quantity of whiskey punch, related over and over again his pet grievance against Kilboggan, shook hands and vowed eternal friendship for and awful threats alternately against Hogan if Home Rule did not see him righted ere the two years' lease was out. At last they separated. Shea and Hogan were conducted to their beds in an upper room by the girl, and lost no time in bestowing themselves for the night.

A pleasant warmth pervaded the bedroom from the wood fire in the chimney. Shea stopped a great clock that was ticking loudly in a corner; but just as they were sinking to sleep a peculiar noise was heard in the kitchen beneath them.

"May I never," said Shea, sitting up in his bed, "if Biddy isn't making butter this hour of the night! I heard her tell Barney she'd churn, as the butter was out."

Sure enough, they could distinctly hear the thud of the dasher below. The servant, after her hard day's toil, was now setting to work at nearly one o'clock at night of her own accord to make butter for their breakfast.

"We ought to stop her; it's too bad, by Jove," said Hogan, who indeed was actuated more by fear of being kept awake than by consideration for the weary girl.

"Lord, no, man! don't do that," said Ned Shea; "she'd rather than not, and it wouldn't be gracious."

Hogan resigned himself to sleeplessness for the night, or the better portion of it; and while admiring the hospitable thoughtfulness of the poor handmaid, wished in his heart she would take it into her head that a night's rest was of more importance to the guest whom she delighted to honour. Not so, however: the dasher went on pitilessly; the monotonous sound ceased at last, and Hogan was able to follow the example of Shea, who, less sensitive of nerve, had long before sunk to sleep.

At about eight o'clock they rose and went to the pump where the master of the house usually performed his ablutions. Refreshed by the cold water, Hogan enjoyed his breakfast—a repetition of the supper of the night before, except that there was no punch; and directly afterwards they sallied forth to business, accompanied by Barney. The morning was dry and clear; and the sun, a welcome and rare visitor, lighted up the landscape cheerily. The grass seemed greener and fresher, the larches' silver bark and the red coats of the pines glistened and glowed after the rain; and behind, at the foot of the hill, the river shone like silver between the rows of tall bulrushes. They pulled up on the top of a hill; and away to the left, just at the bend of a distant wood, Hogan saw the smoke of the railway engine curling upwards, and just a faint echo of its rattle reached his ears. Shea pointed him out several of the farm-houses they were to visit, lying at different points of the landscape before them: bare, ugly buildings, the plastered walls looking hideously discoloured by the rain. The great straggling ditches were overflowing, pools of rain-water lay on the fields, and came up almost to the doors of the houses.

"It's a terribly bare spot; wretched-looking! Have these fellows no leases? or what is the reason they have so little care of their places?"

"All tenants at will," returned Barney; "and if they were only to let MacScutch know they ate a good dinner, he'd be down on them and raise the rent in no time. It's their interest to be as poor as they can, and to look poor and miserable,—let alone to keep up a decent appearance. They're afraid to buy manure lest he should find it out; and that was always the way with these people."

"They have no capital to farm with?"

"Not a penny. See, there's Daly's house below,"—and Shea pointed with his whip to a long thatched house on the brow of a slight eminence opposite to them. "Daly married a girl with a fortune of six hundred the other day; well, instead of putting that in the land, he gave the two sisters two hundred each and portioned them off, and then the old father and mother got two hundred for their share in the farm and place. That's the way down here; they'd never think of spending their money on stock, or putting it in the land at all."

"The two hundred the sisters each got will no doubt go in the same way."

"Exactly the same way: 'tis the custom. You know it wouldn't be fair for the son to get everything. He has the land, and then the money he gets with the wife fortunes off his sisters; they have a right to their share as well as him."

"But would it not be better to put that money in the land, and——"

"It is to have the rent raised on him; and who'd take the sisters off his hands, either? These men never marry without a fortune. Ah! Daly's a queer chap," said Barney: a real clever fellow. He had a deal to do in the Fenian scare. Sure, he was a head-centre, and in prison too; he had to run to America. Wait till you see the place where the rifles that came from America were hid, and the old still in the haggard. Sure, he used to make four or five gallons of whiskey in the week."

"And was never found out?"

"Never. He gave it up, though, a while ago. You see he thought to make money on it; but all the neighbours round about used to be sending for a pint now and a quart again; an' so, begad, they all got it in a neighbourly way. Pat Daly was never the fellow to refuse them. So where was the good of wasting money and time, for them to have it to drink with their potatoes and buttermilk?"

"Not a very profitable business, certainly."

The horse now turned into a deep muddy lane, that led up the slope to Daly's house; and after a quarter of an hour's splashing and climbing, they found themselves before a broken gate. The house, beside which lay a stable-yard, ill kept and ruinous, like all the rest, was a long one-storied thatched building, that, had it been at all well kept or orderly, would have been comfortable and pretty to look at. The windows were broken and the thatch out of repair; and a grassy slope, the lie of which would have delighted a gardener, before the house, was abandoned to the tender mercies of a lank pig and her family, who had wandered out of the farm-yard. A couple of half-fed dogs, which were roused from their sleep under the hedge, now set to barking with all their might and main.

The door of the house flew open, and a tall man, about thirty-five years of age, dressed in a smart suit of gray tweed, made his appearance. He wore a moustache and "goatee," like a Yankee, and used an immense number of Yankee idioms in his speech: in fact, but for the native brogue underlying and cropping up every now and then, he might almost have passed for a New York loafer.

" Now, Daly, this is Mr. Hogan—our member that is to be, please God," was Barney's introduction.

Mr. Daly at first thought of simply bowing, but remembering the usage of his adopted country, he held out a dirty hand, and honoured Hogan's with a prolonged shaking.

" Most proud to be acquainted, sir. Are you calk'lating to stay long with us in our part of this country, sir?"

Hogan explained his visit, and apologised for the necessary shortness of its duration. Mr. Daly, who grew more and more Yankee in his accent as he resumed his self-confidence, led the way into the parlour, first driving out a couple of hens which had got in and were perched on the end of an old horsehair sofa. Hogan heard a scamper and rustle as he entered, and guessed that something else besides the poultry had received notice to quit. The floor was of clay, which certainly harmonised well in colour, and in other ways too, with the furniture and fittings. At one end of the room was an old square piano, open, perhaps with a view to showing that it really was a piano, and not another article of furniture; its small size and peculiar shape being calculated to give rise to doubts on the subject. At the other was an old-fashioned spindle-legged mahogany buffet, curiously inlaid with brass and bits of carved wood, but so thick with dirt, so encrusted with the dust and grease of ages, that it was only where the chance rubbings of passers-by had prevented extraneous accumulations that the original material could be seen. On this was placed, *mirabile dictu*, a gilt French clock under its glass shade—a paltry, vulgar thing, worth possibly some thirty shillings, and of which the hands were fixed in stock immobility; perhaps, like its owners, too full of dignity and pride to do an honest day's work. On the walls were the prints to be found in every cabin—O'Connell, Robert Emmet, and a few of the hideous daubs Germany sends broadcast over the world, under the names of some of the more prominent members of the calendar of Roman saints. Over the fireplace, begrimed and smoky, hung a sewed picture, representing St. Patrick issuing from a magnificent Gothic church, the purely pointed style of which would have

S

delighted the heart of Ruskin and Pugin. This, with the cushions on the sofa, were the handiwork of Mrs. Daly—a "lady," and of "shuparior edgication," as denoted by the same productions. The chairs were horsehair, like the sofa; like it, too, the majority of them were broken. The fireplace seemed a wilderness of papers, broken bottles, and ashes. A stale smell of punch and tobacco hung about the place; and on the chimneypiece was a suggestive looking row of glasses—most of them *minus* the shanks. Even Barney Shane's bachelor den was less forlorn and hopeless looking than this.

"Wal, sir, be seated. I'm proud to see you." And Mr. Daly, after handing the most trustworthy-looking of the chairs to his guest, took up a free-and-easy bar-room sort of attitude on another. As a travelled man of the world, he assumed at once a superior tone with Barney and Ned Shea, meaning to impress them with his powers of conversing with the Dublin gentleman, and to establish himself at the same time in a proper position as a man of great political influence and experience, home and foreign, in the opinion of the member.

"Very bad weather for spring operations, Mr. Daly. Your sowing must be backward," began Hogan.

"We are behind, sir. I opine we'll have a real moist time all raownd. Country's most depressed at present, except as to politics, sir; we're pretty lively on politics just now. Home Rule's a-going to shake up the Britishers. Make the Government a fine darned fix there, hey, Barney? The Fenian scare won't be a patch on this."

"Ha, indeed! You are a Home Ruler, then, Mr. Daly?" Hogan was rather puzzled by the fellow, and scarcely knew where to begin.

"I should think I was: yes. Consid'able some, I am. Only the programme isn't quite so clear laid down as what I'd wish. However, sir, I guess that'll turn up all right. I hope it won't be long till we see a real Irish Republic: no half measures; the whole hog or none, that's my idea; and——"

"Ah! Come on now, Daly, wid yer stuff. Do you

imagine Mr. Hogan is come to listen to your rubbish ? A Republic, and a New York government — bah !" Ned Shea was the speaker, standing with his broad back against the chimneypiece.

"Why not ?" said Barney. "Wouldn't Kilboggan be worse than any government ? Ireland for the Irish ; and no English thieves of landlords carrying the money over the sea to spend it."

"Right you are, Barney ; and isn't everything, whiskey and beef and potatoes and all, going over the sea instead of being kept here for our use ? Wait till we're up in Dublin, till you see the stopper we'll clap on exportation for them—yew bet."

"And where'll I get the price for my fat stall-feds ?" said Ned Shea. "Bedad, Daly, 'tisn't you and your Fenians and Home Rulers will give me my money for them, like the Liverpool salesmasters."

"And how about the clergy, Mr. Daly ?" asked Hogan.

"The clergy, Mr. Hogan ? what about them ? The clergy have changed their tactics entirely. They were with us in '48 ; but in this last—the Fenian affair, you know— how scandalous their conduct was ! They proved themselves utter renegades—mere truckling aristocracy worshippers. They want nothing ; and what do they care for our patriotic aspirations ? Their influence is gone. I bet my life, sir, I have more influence in the town this moment than the parish priest ; and this Ballot business will do for them entirely. It's a real grand system, sir ; and the landlords are equally defeated by it. Why, in America, sir,——"

There is no knowing where the loquacious Mr. Daly would not have dragged the conversation, had not the appearance of Mrs. Daly, in her Sunday silk dress, interrupted it. She was older than her husband ; and had been a pretty woman, but was now slatternly and unhealthy-looking. Her manner to Hogan had an assumption of familiarity and equality somewhat unpleasing, were it not for its ludicrousness. She affected to be cool with Shea, because his wife had declined her acquaintance, though

both families could be "traced up" to an equal height in
point of pedigree.   She apologised for the absence of her
" servant" (such people have always servants), and going
to a press in the wall, produced a blown-glass decanter of
whiskey, and another of highly-coloured sherry.   Then,
holding the glasses up to the light, she discovered that they
had not been washed since the last time they were used ;
so, in the most natural manner, she stepped into the bedroom ; and reappearing with a very dubious-coloured, but
unmistakable bedroom towel, proceeded to rub the glasses
in it.   Hogan's gorge rose at the sight.   Shea, who was as
alive to the manœuvre as he, winked at him meaningly, as
if encouraging him to an inevitable duty.   It was of no
use.   Hogan begged for a cup of milk instead ; and the
hostess, good-natured and hospitable, however "clarty,"
granted his request.   In return, Hogan held it his duty to
be agreeable, asked after Mrs. Daly's uncle, the parish
priest of a southern parish, for whom he had once conducted a case ; hoped to have the pleasure of meeting her
at Kingstown in the summer ; invited the husband to
attend and speak at the meeting to be held at Ballinagad,
and engaged him as agent and canvasser at once.   The
conversation became general then ; and after a short time
the visitors rose to go.   Hogan, struck by a sudden thought,
invited Daly to dinner at the Kilboggan Arms ; and after
a flourishing exchange of civilities, they again mounted the
car and began to thread their way down the boreen.

    " That's a queer chap, now, isn't he, Mr. Hogan ?"
asked Barney,—" a very clever fellow entirely ; if Pat Daly
'ud only mind himself, what's to hinder him going into
Parliament, now, eh ?   Can't he speak beautiful ?"

    " Arrah, Barney, man," cried Ned Shea, " for God's sake
what are you talking of at all ?   That dirty blathering fool,
—ah !—him in Parliament ?   You wouldn't take the glass,
then, Mr. Hogan ?" and Ned Shea, now fairly out of ear-
shot, laughed loud and long.   " Well, that's a fine lady-
wife for you !   Now you see Irish pride, Mr. Hogan.   I
suppose you never saw the like of that in Dublin yet.
Well, well ; and now, do you know, Pat Daly threw over

a nice, smart, sensible girl, with a fine farm of her own, just because Miss Burke, of Limerick, was better family and had an uncle a parish priest. Ay,—right well you know it, too, Barney Shane, and yet you'll believe in him !"

"I give in to you there, indeed, Ned," returned Barney.

They held on now, up hill and down dale, through mud and water, on their round among the farmers. Everywhere Hogan received promises of support ; everywhere he heard the same complaints of Kilboggan—the people all leaving for America, the little country shopkeepers ruined, the small farmers sold out, the farms knocked together or "squared," and let to those who could pay the heavy fines exacted, no leases renewed without fines, and all the money carried off to London and spent out of the country. Double wages to servants, and no servants to be had. The graziers and dairy-farmers were all sub-letting grass and cows to a factor, who put in his own servants and took all the work off the owner's hands, paying so much rent per cow. This left the farmer little or nothing to do ; and the spare time, it may be imagined, hung rather heavily on his hands. For all these evils Home Rule was looked to as the panacea. How, or why, they never troubled their heads to ask. It was the new shibboleth which was to succeed Fenianism, and to do all that Fenianism had left undone ; just as Fenianism was to wipe up the tears of the young Irelanders or the Phœnix party—the fatal legacy of unrest and discontent that seems entailed on the Celt. Grand qualities these two : the first elements of progress in every nation, when turned in the right direction. Instead of setting themselves to hew a channel for these tempestuous waters, the would-be guides invoke the negative qualities beloved of Philistines from all time : common-sense, and content. What has common-sense done for the world ? and what has not content left undone ?

It was Hogan's first exploration of the country parts of his native land ; and he was astonished beyond measure at the Irishness of everything. He had seen Boucicault's plays ; and, like many of the audience, believed the charac-

ters to be the usual stock Hibernians that people the
dramatists' brains — evoked ready - made with as little
trouble as are the costumes out of the property - man's
wardrobes ; but here he might see Miles na Coppaleens and
Shauns the Post walking by the ditches, dressed in the
frieze coats, brimless hats, and knee-breeches so familiar to
theatre-goers.   The dirt, the carelessness, the merriment,
the overflowing genuine hospitality,—all were present.
Everywhere they went they had to take their glass of
whiskey, which in the poorest place was always forthcoming, and drink to the toast of Home Rule. It was late in
the day when the horse's head was turned homewards ;
but Hogan did not grudge the time or exertion, for he felt
his cause was gaining.

On arriving at Mulla Castle he found a bundle of letters.
A telegram from Saltasche told him the stale news that
Wyldoates was on his way home, and might reach Kilboggan Castle next day.   The Bishop, as usual, sent a long
epistle full of warnings and cautions.   The Mother Superior
of St. Swithin's scolded him for not coming to see her
before leaving, and desired him on no account to omit to
claim relationship with her in speaking to the Sheas, some
of whose children were in her school.   Hogan sat down
until dinner - time to write letters, business and other.
When he came down to the drawing-room, later on in the
day, he found his host standing by the fire with a serious
expression on his face.

"The priests are all gone to dine at Chapel House.
That means a settlement of plans, Mr. Hogan.   By this
time they're all ordered to canvass for Wyldoates,"
began he.

"Whew !" returned the barrister, walking up to the fireplace ; "that's the way now, is it ?"

"Ah ! you have no chance with them, sir.   You see,
Father Corkran's chapel is too small and too tumble-down
entirely ; and he wants that patch of ground off the main
street that's Kilboggan's to dispose of, and Jim won't be
given that for nothing.   And then, too, the Quarries would
be shut against him.   Ah ! it's a bad job—a bad job."

"Would no other plot of land but that lot suit him?"

"No: or he pretends not. Moreover, he don't like Home Rule—damn the bit. He knows well the Home Rule the people here are thinking of is just a regular Republic. In Dublin 'tis a sort of a Federal Parliament, with one of the Queen's sons for Lord Lieutenant, and a grand court and the rest of it. But, faith, 'tis a congress they want in this part; you can see it for yourself. Hear Daly."

"Do you mean to say that the priests and their candidate will carry the day against Home Rule? What! with the Ballot?"

"Bah!" put in Killeen, the editor, who just then came in; "not at all, Shea. Their back is broken, for good and all. I met Father Jim coming down street; and you might light a match on his face when I told him Wyldoates would be out in the cold. That's where he is, sure and certain, Mr. Hogan."

"Never fear, Mr. Killeen; but we have not a man to spare: recollect, over-confidence is very dangerous."

Knowing the indolent, easy-going fellows with whom he had to deal, Hogan determined to stick to that as his motto. They went down to dinner—a somewhat quieter repast than that of the evening of their arrival. Dicky turned up in time, having been out canvassing, in company with the two best-looking daughters of the house.

Mrs. Shea was rather low-spirited; she had met Father Jim, and he had passed by without pretending to see her.

"Didn't see you, Margaret, hey?" said her husband; "wait till to-morrow, or next day, and he'll stare at you and never see you. I know him."

"And he's invited to dine at the Castle on Saturday. The housekeeper was down to the hotel; all the party are to stay there, and they're as busy as bees. Dear me!" sighed she wistfully, thinking it might be better that Ned had sided with the great folks. She felt confident that "The Castle" would win. It seemed so natural: grand folks, in Mrs. Shea's mind, had always a sort of divine right on their side in everything. Moreover, the mere

fact that the priests were acting in the opposite interest
gave her an uncomfortable sensation. Nothing went right
or well that they opposed or disapproved. How could
it? And she began to conjure up in her own mind all the
dismal stories she had ever heard: Hara's haggard burnt
down not six months after he quarrelled with his clergy;
Mr. Magrath, of High Park, who married the Protestant
lady and drank himself to death within the year; Biddy
Flannery, that would marry the Presbyterian sergeant, and
had a deaf-and-dumb baby, and never held up her head
after. It was tempting Providence, clearly, with "foot
and mouth" raging in the very next county; and she
determined to send a pound to her sister, the nun Mary
Columbkille, of the Poor Clares, for such "intentions" and
prayers as could be had for the money.

CHAPTER XVII

THE meeting of the voters announced to take place was held in a sort of large room over a schoolhouse, but now rented by the landlord of the rival hotel to the Kilboggan Arms, and used by him for various purposes—some of them, indeed, if report be credible, not calculated to bear the light of day in a political sense. There was an entrance through the tap of The Harp; and this was thronged by an unusual number of customers. All of these, having drunk their glass in the bar, slipped through a door opening into the yard of the public-house, and crossing it, found themselves at the entrance to a long, low room, dingy and cobweb-hung, having a sort of raised platform at one end.

Long before the hour the voters had been gathering in knots of three and five; and when Ned Shea and his cousin Barney, with whom was the accomplished Mr. Daly, boiling over with excitement and energy, arrived, the big room was nearly filled. Daly leading the way, they shouldered through the crowd up to the platform. Beside it stood a young fellow with a pocket-book in his hand, in which he was evidently writing down the names of those present. Barney looked round and round until he caught sight of some one particular person in the corner; then he leaned forward and caught the sleeve of the reporter.

"Do you see Finlay, the teacher, beyond?" he whispered. "Put down his name, my boy."

"Well, well, now; and he has just asked me not to do that same," answered the reporter, looking up with a puzzled stare.

"You'll do it, ma bouchal," was the quiet reply of Shane;

and there was a glitter in the look he turned on the young man that impelled him to unquestioning obedience.

The person whose name Mr. Shane was so anxious to have thus honoured was a member of the body of national-school teachers. He had been appointed by Father Cork-ran; and like most of his class in the Catholic provinces of Ireland, held his wretched situation entirely at the will of the priest, and was liable to be turned out at a moment's notice. As a matter of course, he lived in a state of abject submission to the whims of his patron; and instead of holding a position inferior only to that of the clergyman in public esteem, his very scholars despised and looked down on him as no better than a servant. Shane knew he was a creature of the parish priest, and that he had come to the meeting unknown to his master, or had been sent to it by him as a spy. Therefore his action as above related.

In a very short time the room was filled by the big frieze-coated men; and Ned Shea, who had been counting them as they entered, advanced to the front of the platform. Striking his ground-ash stick on the floor, he looked round the room. In an instant perfect silence prevailed; and he began in a loud clear voice:—

"Boys—I don't need, I suppose, to tell you for what purpose we are assembled here. You know what Mr. Hogan wants of us; and you know Kilboggan. The Land Tenure we'll never get without Home Rule first; and to get Home Rule is now the heart's desire of every Irishman, whether he owns one sod of land or no. I have a lease for a hundred and ninety-nine years, and he can't touch me; but it's not so with ye. An' what do ye look forward to, an' what do ye expect to get for the money ye put in the land?" ("Compensation, wisha!" interpolated an old farmer in a tone of concentrated bitterness). "That's not enough. As for trusting the word of this London fine gentleman, that's come over now with his palaver, we know the Wyldoates breed too well for that." A laugh followed this; and the blackthorns and ground-ashes were grasped tighter in the great brawny fists of their owners. "But for Father Corkran he would not have a chance.

He's against Home Rule, so he is; and he's always, like plenty more of the clergy, played into the hands of the landlords." ("Ay, did he,—true for you, Shea.") "Home Rule doesn't seem to suit the clergy at all: why I can't tell; but from the first I see they're against it,—or if they're not against it, they're not for it—they think we ought to demand the University first. Well, I say, let those that want the University ask for it; we have no call with that; and those that have call to it don't seem to care. We want Fixity of Tenure and Home Rule; and it's to Mr. Hogan and men like him we must look, and not an absentee like Kilboggan, that's draining every penny out of this country to spend it in London and France, and all them foreign parts."

A burst of applause followed Ned Shea's deliverance; and he sat down to make way for his impetuous cousin Barney, who stalked up to the extreme front of the platform and with one hand under the tails of his great frieze cothamore, and a sardonic grin on his florid countenance, began:—

"Father Corkran condescended the pleasure of his company to dinner at the Castle yesterday. Oh, begor— thruth I'm spakin'," he added, seeing the surprise on the faces of the "mountain'y" people, to whom this important political item was news. "And," continued the orator, turning his face in profile to the audience, and looking out of the corners of his blue eyes with an inimitable expression of drollery, "the new chapel will be purceeded with immadiately." A chorus of laughter showed that his intelligence was fully appreciated. "And the weather bein' so bad for canvassing, 'tis likely his reverence will have his new covered car home soon. Faith, boys,"—and here Barney dropped the sardonic bantering style, and turned full front to the audience,—"if this goes on, in a very short time his reverence will be indipindint of weddings even." ("Easy, Barney—be easy, now!" remonstrated his cousin.) "Everything," roared the speaker, "that he can grab for himself; an' the country can go to the divle! He has sold the votes he can command to

Wyldoates just as you or I'd sell a bushel of spuds; and
let him, too—let him sell the beggarly wretches he has his
paw on; but he'll not get a vote out of Ballinagad."
("No, no—not one!" resounded from the hearers, and
an indescribable din of excited shouting and tramping
deafened Barney for a moment.) "Stand up for your
rights, boys, and let them see there's life in Peatstown
yet! Never heed sweet words or promises; be warned
by Morty Sinnot." (Morty Sinnot was a farmer who had
been evicted shortly after an election; notwithstanding
the promises of the *candidate*, on which he foolishly relied,
and which the *member* found it convenient to forget.)
"And leave Father Corkran where he is. I wish him joy
of his chapel and his ground; he may build the house—
let him take care lest another man live in it. The days
are gone by when the soggarths stood up for the cause.
They got the Protestant Church turned out, but they have
not got the money; and there's the last of them. They're
afraid of Home Rule; they're afraid to lose the little
beggarly cringing importance they have, in this way of
politics, with the landed gentry. 'Tisn't for us they're
working now,—'tis for themselves. I always said it," he
shouted: "as long as the soggarth by rowing in our boat
suited himself and his own aims, he did it; but now we're
pulling in opposite directions entirely."

"You're wrong now, Barney," spoke a shopkeeper, in
the crowd. "The priests are working for us when they
are working for Catholic Education. And the Catholics
ought to have a college as good as Trinity. Why should
a man be forced to send his son among a swaddling crew,
or go without college education altogether?"

"Augh!" replied Shane; "there's lots of Catholics
talking and pretending, and all the time their sons are in
Trinity College, and they'd rather put them there than to
any Catholic university. Hasn't Father Corkran got his
own nephew there? Answer me that! Sure every great
man we have got his education in Old Trinity; and it's
proud of her, Protestants and all, we ought to be. Where
did O'Connell and every one of them larn what they

knew? Answer me that! Look at Wyldoates himself—
a Trinity man. And Father Corkran supporting them.
Arrah! where's the use of my talking at all?" he burst
forth in a fit of uncontrollable excitement; "Home Rule
and O'Rooney Hogan for ever!"

Then came Mr. Daly, the ex-American; and he, assum-
ing his very best Yankee accent for the occasion, dilated at
length on the merits of the Ballot system; "high-falutin"
as his speech was, he did some good by explaining the
working of the machinery, which he illustrated on the wall
with a piece of charred stick, and by following the programme laid down for him by Hogan. Others succeeded;
most of them detailing their own grievances, all declaiming
against their landlord, and vaunting the universal panacea,
Home Rule.

CHAPTER XVIII

"On ne voyait, à la naissance de l'église, que des Chrétiens parfaite-
ment instruits dans tous les points nécessaires au salut. Au lieu qu'on
voit aujourd'hui une ignorance si grossière, quelle fait gémir tous ceux
qui ont des sentiments de tendresse pour l'église." — Pensées de
Pascal.

PEATSTOWN, we have said, was built on the river, and consequently lay low in a hollow flanked by hills, or, at least, what were hills by courtesy, for in reality they were very modest eminences. The main street of the town lay parallel with the river, and was a continuation of a road that led straight up the high ground past the parish chapel and the graveyard, which sloped to the very edge of the highway—from which, by just leaning a little forward over the railings, you could read the inscriptions on the weather-stained tombstones. The road, however, ran on direct and straight; and of course soon parted company with the erratic stream, which bent and twisted at its own unstable will, past meadow-land and fallows, corn-fields and bog, far off to the west, to lose itself at last in the broad bosom of the Shannon.

On the river side, as you went towards the chapel which crowned the height, and looked down on the sleepy little town, stood a long, low, slated house, built below the road level, with brass-barred windows, and a hall door, to enter which, you descended a couple of granite steps. At the end of this house, and behind it, ran a garden, whose low, moss-grown wall overlooked the stream at the back—the brawling of which came pleasantly in the open windows in summer time, and mingled harmoniously with the song of the bees at work among the lime trees and the lavender hedges. Dead creepers overhung the walks, and long withered arms of clematis and jessamine stretched themselves down to meet the flood plashing by below. The garden was laid out in terraces; and big white vases full of geraniums, pinched and blackened by the frost, stood exactly at each corner of the prim gravel walks. In the centre was an arbour—arches of wood-laths crossed, covered with ivy and creepers, in which stood a plaster-of-Paris Madonna, sadly weather-beaten and discoloured, chipped and cracked. Hens and chickens roved through the garden, picking up a supplementary and scanty diet among the weed-grown beds; and a surly terrier, chained to an old wooden box, lay with eyes fixed in hungry expectation on the kitchen door.

It was nearly half-past nine; and Father Corkran, the owner of the house, having finished breakfast, seated himself by the window with the *Peatstown Torch* for a quiet couple of hours, before proceeding to the chapel to preach the mid-day sermon. He had scarcely got half-way through the very first column when he started violently, and turned over the page, and began to read and count a number of names printed in a double column. He threw down the paper before he had finished, and going to the fireplace, rang the bell furiously. A little girl opened it, and looked timidly in.

"Cattey, did you see the schoolmaster go up to the catechism yet?"

"No, sir."

"Call down to his house this moment, and bid him to come up to me, and not to lose a minute. I'll put a stop to this work. This wretched insect!" he growled; "to think of his audacity!"

Then he walked over to a press in the wall, and unlocking it, took out a thick memorandum book, which he unclasped. He seated himself then at his desk, and turned over the leaves until he came to a page on which were two columns of names; before some of these there were crosses in red ink affixed. Then, taking up the paper again, he

proceeded to copy down a number of additional ones from
the list of those who attended the Thursday night's meeting. Some of the names—among them Barney Shane's—
were already included in his reverence's own collection;
and to these he affixed a red-ink cross, or a second one if
they were already so decorated. This list of sinners kept
Father Corkran's memory green; and whenever opportunity
served, he found a means of paying off the offenders on his
own account, or, as he would call it himself, of being the
instrument of Divine justice or vengeance. If a lease
expired and the tenant prayed for renewal, a word from
Father Corkran went a long way with the agent in either
direction. If a bill was due at the bank, his reverence
was well aware of the fact, and the manager was sure
to abide by his advice. Then, if the farmer was turned
out, or the little shopkeeper sold up, the general verdict
referred the catastrophe to Providence, whose inscrutable
ways and means were never questioned. The tenant-
farmer or the little huckster, had " *gone against the priest ;*"
and, as is well known, that sort of conduct is " *unlucky.*"

His reverence had scarcely finished his task and replaced
the memorandum book on the shelf of the press, when a
knock at the door announced the arrival of the person for
whom he had sent.

"Come in," said Father Corkran, in a short gruff tone,
flinging himself into his easy-chair by the fire as he spoke,
and turning a scowling face full on the new-comer.

The national schoolmaster was an insignificant looking
man of about thirty years of age, shabbily dressed, and
with a nervous expression of eye. He entered timidly,
with his hat in one hand and with the other fumbling
with the lock of the door. No salutation of any kind
was exchanged.

"What's this I hear, sir? Is this your name at the
meeting at The Harp on Friday?" and his reverence,
pointing with his index finger to the newspaper, seemed,
threatening as was his tone, to be willing to admit that
there might be some doubt on the question—that his
senses might be playing him false.

The schoolmaster's eyes drooped submissively before the angry glare of his patron, and he answered, "It is, your reverence."

"And how dare you,—you !" he thundered, with concentrated scorn, "attend any meeting without my permission and approbation ? "

"I didn't think it any harm, sir," was the deprecating answer.

"If ever you presume to attend any such gathering, or to busy yourself with anything of the sort again, without first consulting me, I'll turn you away on the spot, mark my words," and he shook his forefinger threateningly. "Begone now !" and pointing to the door with the gesture he might have used to an ill-behaved dog, he dismissed the terrified schoolmaster, who, glad to get off so lightly, took himself away as fast as possible. He was too well used to his ruler's tyranny to mind such outbursts ; and his only feeling was one of thankfulness that Father Corkran had not selected the schoolroom to humiliate him in the presence of his scholars, as he was in the habit of doing.

Last mass was unusually well attended this particular Sunday ; it being known that Father Corkran had been in treaty with the Wyldoates faction, a manifesto from the altar of more than usual interest was accordingly expected. All the parishioners of any standing were in their accustomed places ; and when mass was finished, the kneeling crowd at the sides thronged up to the rails of the altar almost simultaneously, so eager were they to hear the declaration. The usual prayers after mass were totally unheeded ; and all eyes were fixed anxiously on the sacristy door. After some five minutes' or so expectation—for Father Corkran was above mere punctuality—the sacristy door swung wide open, and the parish priest, clad in black soutane (no alb), walked forth.

He ascended the steps of the altar, and stood with his back to it, looking steadily for some moments at the people before him. His unusual vestment, the wrathful frown on his face, all were pregnant and ominous of indignation

T

pent up, and ready to burst forth. A pin might have
been heard to fall; and the heart of every listener beat
faster, whether in expectation, dread, or defiance. After
this impressive pause, he began, in a distinct and delibe-
rate tone, grating and hideous to the ear:—

" It was not my intention to address you to-day on the
subject that is, no doubt, uppermost in the minds of all
of you: I mean, the election. But circumstances have
occurred that make it necessary I should deviate for your
guidance " (he emphasised these words) " from that purpose. There are times when it becomes a duty—and I
will be the last to shrink from a duty, however painful,
which a man owes to himself and to others " (here he
paused an instant),—" I mean that he should speak out
when he will be criminal if he remain silent. As I said,
I did not intend to address you at all on this matter,
foolishly confident as I was that no one else would take
on my place—would have the *brazen audacity* to attempt
to influence your opinions. There are, it seems, in this
town "—(these words were hissed out with all possible
bitterness)—" ill-minded, ill-conditioned men who have
determined to go on presuming on my forbearance as far
as I will let them. And lest the simple, honest, disinterested electors should be led astray by disturbers of this
class, I have resolved to expose their schemes.

" You have two candidates soliciting your votes. Now,
there never was a time when Irishmen were more urgently
called upon to send honest, upright men to Parliament
than the present. A great deal has been done for Ireland
in the last few years, and a great deal more remains to be
done. The incubus of the Established Church, which was
supported by the *plundered revenues* of the Catholics, has
been got rid of. The honest, hard-working farmer has
obtained some measure of justice, which must be still
further complemented by Fixity of Tenure before he can be
secured in the fruits of his toil; and there still remains
the great question of religious Education for your children.

" To those rulers who have given us so much, it is, then,
that we are to look for more; and we shall best show our

gratitude by sending in a fit and proper person to co-operate with them in their good works—one who will have your interest at heart, not his own, who will not make promises without meaning to keep them, and who will not offer himself to this minister or to that for the highest penny. We hear a great deal of what is called *pay*triotism—bless the mark!—these times: well, I think myself as good a patriot as any of these fellows who shout 'Home Rule,' 'Ireland for the Irish,' and the rest of it—all blatherum. 'We'll have no one but a Home Ruler, says Mr. Barney Shane and Mr. Ned Shea"—(immediately every eye in the chapel was turned full on the Sheas' seat, to the consternation of the family). "There are good Irishmen and bad Irishmen; and I prefer any day a good *English*man, who belongs to a family traditionally good, because, therefore, we have the greater security that he will be good himself—to any place-hunting, pettifogging blackguard who calls himself an Irishman. The candidate who has a fortune and position—who commands the respect of ministers, and is at the same time independent of them —has in this fortune and position a guarantee of his fidelity to his principles, and is therefore the one entitled to our support.

"Mr. Wyldoates, I do not hesitate to say, is that candidate. He has a fortune, and can despise office; so he is not likely to throw you over for a paltry situation—the price of a vote adverse to your interests. He is pledged to support your just demands: and to give you a sample of what he is prepared to do for you, the right"—(here his voice was raised, and directed towards the side-aisles) —" the right of turf-cutting will be conceded to the Sandy-Row people." (Murmurs of applause.) " And moreover the lot for the building of the new church is promised, and a donation of one hundred pounds already given; and the works will be at once commenced.

"I don't need to tell you that where tradesmen are employed at high wages, as they will be, their money soon finds its way to the pockets of the grocer and baker and butcher, and of course the publican. Mr. Wyldoates does

not go in for Home Rule—that mischievous, iniquitous
agitation, the work of a few political desperadoes who
have broken up the Liberal party in Ireland, retarded Mr.
Gladstone's wise legislation, and done more harm to their
country than all its enemies.   What would they do with
Home Rule?   Sell it again, as they did before.   They
know that their project is a sham ; and they are not even
of one mind as to the form that sham is to take.   Some
call it Home Rule, others Federation, others Repeal.   Have
nothing to do with schemes or schemers, till you know
more about them.   Be warned!"   Then looking at a
paper he held in his hand, he continued, after a pause :
"This is a requisition that has been presented to me,
asking me to convoke a meeting of the parishioners to
choose delegates to send to the meeting on Wednesday.
Some very wise people in their own estimation have
thought fit to propose this county meeting, for the purpose of determining whether the adoption of the Home
Rule programme shall be the test of qualification for our
future member.   I see no obligation for your sending
delegates at the bidding of these self-constituted authori-
ties.   If any movement of the kind were to be made here,
I think *I* (his anger rising to apoplectic pitch) ought to be
the best judge of its necessity.   But there are *some* people
for whom nothing is too hot or too heavy, the devil is
so busy with them.   They are the black sheep, who, if
allowed to go on unchecked, would soon infect the whole
flock.   Let them not, or their abettors, push me too far.
I have put down disturbers before.   I have peeled the
skin off them, and I'll do it again."   (Here Mrs. Shea
left the church, sobbing hysterically.)   "Is it to them you
go for advice or assistance in any extremity?   No : to
your priest.   Whose influence in every way is oftenest
asked for?   Mine.   'Men may come and men may go'"—
(his reverence, we may be sure, was ignorant whence he
drew his apt quotation),—"but who have you always?
who have you at the last?   Your priest, the true shepherd.
Go not with the hireling.   You have known men in this
parish who went against their priest ; and you have your-

selves seen their fate: swept away like the froth of the river!" (Frightful groaning from the side aisles.) "And as the true shepherd knows his flock, and his flock know him, *I* shall mark out the black sheep, and *remember* him among you who does not heed my voice."

Then, after a genuflection at the foot of the altar, the parish priest returned to the sacristy. The people dispersed; the men crowding together—some laughing, some indifferent, a few frightened; the women for the most part in consternation, and foreboding the advent of the general judgment at least—one or two of them, defiant and reckless, maybe revengeful, cackling shrill sedition from beneath their blue hoods, the cynosure, the while, of their more impressionable sisterhood. In spite of the cold drizzle of rain falling without, the crowd delayed a long time in the churchyard, intensely excited by the parish priest's heavily shotted defiance, the women recalling to each other, with fearful groans, all the terrible "judgments" that had heretofore overtaken rebels to his reverence's authority, and connecting Hogan in some vague way with the enemies of the Church, scientific, politic, and other, who were condemned in general terms diurnally in the *Enfranchiser*, and in particular, and by name, three or four times per annum in the pastorals. At last they scattered, some home to the town, some by car or on foot away to the hills, murky and cheerless in the all-encircling gloom.

CHAPTER XIX.

"Look, where the holy legate comes apace
To give us warrant from the hands of Heaven,
And on our actions set the name of right
With holy breath."

King John.

ON Wednesday evening Mr. Wyldoates, whose aristocratic and slightly imbecile countenance bore traces of the fatigues of his long journey, was lounging in a deeply-cushioned easy-chair in the library at Kilboggan Castle, spending a bad quarter of an hour in company with the family lawyer, Mr. Hanaper, who was also Crown Solicitor for the county, and Mr. MacScutch, the agent and manager of the Kilboggan property. They were waiting the arrival of Father Cork-ran ; and Mr. Wyldoates, whose very soul was weary, was yawning fearfully. He had brought down a select couple of friends from Dublin ; and these gentlemen were occupy-ing their leisure in looking over the billiard-room and its appurtenances. Their entertainer considered himself per-fectly victimised in being forced to spend time on such humbug as canvassing. Not a creature in the county : no hunting ! Not a horse fit to ride in the stable ; nothing but a hack or two of MacScutch's. This last discovery was enough by itself to put him in a rage. "Like his considerateness," he growled, thinking of his relative. It was hard work talking to these legal gentry while pool was going on in the left wing of the same house ; and Mr. Wyldoates made them feel all his ill-temper.

"What's this fellow's name that's down here ? Has he been here long ?" he asked of his agent, in an insolent. impatient tone.

"Mr. Hogan, a Dublin barrister; he has been here since Wednesday, driving all over the place canvassing. The hill people are all promising him, I'm told."

Mr. Wyldoates was in the act of growling a curse in reply to this intelligence, when the door opened; and Father Corkran, resplendent in a black velvét waistcoat, crossed several times by a huge gold chain, appeared.

Mr. Wyldoates rose immediately, and putting on his grand manner, advanced to meet him.

"My dear Father Corkran, you are most kind."

"How do you do, my dear sir?" replied his reverence, with equal warmth.   And the two gentlemen, who had never seen each other in their lives before, shook hands in the most cordial style.   "I wish you every success in your venture."

"Thanks," replied the ex-dragoon.   "But you see this —ah—lawyer fellow has got the start of me."

Mr. Hanaper, a stout, tall man, with gold spectacles, glanced up an instant at the speaker in a manner that betrayed surprise, and was meant to convey a warning, and then resumed the study of the list in his hands.

"Oh dear me! never think of that," said Father Corkran in a most confident tone; "he has been busy among the farmers; but the town is ours—our stronghold, quite—if my advice is followed."

A discreet personage clad in black here glided in, and announced dinner, between two bows to the arm-chair in which Mr. Wyldoates' puny figure was almost hidden.

They all adjourned to the dining-room—Mr. Wyldoates leading the way with evident pleasure.

It was a grand chamber; panelled in black oak, and hung round with family portraits. The glittering silver and wax-lights were reflected in the mirrored buffets; and a fine epergne filled with hot-house flowers, camellias, heaths, and delicate ferns, formed a delightful *point de mire* in the centre of the table. The chairs were of antique oak and stamped leather, with the crest of the Kilboggans in raised work on the backs. The mantelpiece was a superb block of marble inlaid with *lapis lazuli*, and most beautifully carved. There was no grate; the logs burned in the picturesque, old-fashioned style on the hearthstone. The velvet curtains were closely drawn, and the room heated to the exact pitch.

Father Corkran's face beamed with delight and exultation. He was placed on the right-hand of the host, who exerted himself creditably, and did the honours of the table with an easy grace and assiduity. The two gentlemen who had accompanied him down from Dublin made their appearance hastily by the side door, from their tour of inspection. A rapid introduction was gone through, and they took their seats near each other, keeping up an *ex parte* conversation during dinner.

"What cook have you?" asked Mr. Wyldoates abruptly of the butler, turning over something on his plate as he spoke, and eyeing it with evident disfavour.

"Kilboggan Arms, sir," returned the man deprecatingly.

"Good Gad!" said Wyldoates, turning to Mr. Hanaper, "the place is literally falling into ruin. Telegraph to the Bilton for a cook immediately," he added; "and, Kelly, be sure you desire them to send a good one. This is truly abominable. Papillon and Germaine, are you able to eat anything?"

The two gentlemen hastily uttered disclaimers and assurances, and went on with their dinner, apparently thoroughly contented with it. Mr. Hanaper, who seemed utterly unconscious of this episode, employed a short interlude in scrutinising the reverend Mr. Corkran's lineaments; then, clearing his throat, he in the most unctuous tones asked,—

"Father Corkran, you are, I believe, vicar-general of this diocese, under Bishop Gogarty."

"I am, sir; I have that honour."

"Indeed! and how is his lordship?" went on Mr. Hanaper, in the tone of a family doctor. "I had the pleasure of meeting him on a former occasion, nearly thirty years ago. It was on the occasion of Colonel Bursford's election for the county. Do *you* remember?"

This "do *you* remember" was a fine touch, and full of

subtle flattery. It was a statement by implication that the good vicar-general was not old enough to recall the events of nearly thirty years back. He was as old as Mr. Hanaper—every day; but then the latter was Crown Solicitor for the county, and had reached the top of the attorney ladder, whereas the mitre and crozier still haunted the dreams of the parish priest.

"Remember it! dear, yes. Bishop Gogarty held my parish then." Here a little half-sigh said plainly, "Would that he held it still!" "Con. Delahunty came forward to oppose him. Fifteen hundred the colonel paid him to retire. There's no harm saying it now."

"None, indeed; they're both dead. We have lived to see a great change, my dear sir—a great change indeed!"

"And we'll see a greater yet, I'm certain. Things are come to a pretty pass indeed." And his reverence swallowed a piece of sole *au gratin* with a snort.

Mr. Diesele, a little dried-up man, too intensely Orange to care much for his reverence's company, looked sympathisingly at his client, who was wearily toying with the food on his plate.

"You seem very fatigued, Mr. Wyldoates: have you travelled straight on?"

"Yes; straight on from Nice, anyhow. My uncle telegraphed to me to come on, since the Reform have put forward this cad so suddenly. Otherwise I shouldn't have moved until—the fourteenth." It plainly required an effort of an unusual kind for him to remember the date.

MacScutch, a northern, deeply tarred with the same brush as the little Diesele, conversed with him in low tones.

"What's that you're saying, MacScutch? This Hogan's a barrister in good practice, hey? Don't believe you," said Mr. Wyldoates, who had caught up some fragment of their speech.

"Dear, yes," hastily interpolated Father Corkran, seeing his way to a certain effect. "Mr. O'Rooney Hogan is a barrister of standing. I assure you he distinguished himself on several occasions; and he goes into the best society

in Dublin.   I must do the young man that justice, though
I don't care for him myself.   Of course we all know what
his motives are in going into Parliament."

"I should think so—scum !" Mr. Wyldoates' lip curled
contemptuously.   "What a business this Home Rule is
turning out for these fellows !   The Irish bar have always
gone in on the stalking horse of national politics."

"Softly, my dear sir," said Mr. Hanaper, in his oiliest
tones, but with a sneer on his face; "what has the English
bar had to do with politics ?   I think our men could show
cleaner hands than the big-wigs over the water, past and
present."

Mr. Wyldoates turned abruptly to the attendant.

"Coffee in the library ! and, Kelly, see that there's a
good fire.   Germaine, were you at the levee ?   I did not
arrive in time.   If I had I'd have gone, I think."

"Yes, of course," replied Mr. Germaine quickly.   "Everybody was there.   His Ex'cy was talking to me about my
mare.   Would I enter her for Fairyhouse ?   I said I thought
not ; but would save her up for Punchestown.   Sells
better always, you know.   He's looking remarkably well."

"Oh, ah ! he loves a good horse, does his Ex'cy," put in
Mr. Hanaper, who, as a solicitor, was debarred from the
honour of attending Court, but who relished "Cawstle
gossip" as keenly as anybody else.

Mr. Germaine, feeling himself the central personage for
the moment, surveyed the speaker through his eyeglass,
and then went on in a slightly raised tone,—

"I was out with the Ward Unions on—ah—Tuesday;
and Betty Martin was awfully fresh.   I was taking her up
a lane between two hedges, when I heard a horse coming
up behind us, as if wanting to pass me.   I didn't feel like
letting him ; for Betty Martin doesn't follow very kindly.
So I just hallooed, ' Keep off, will you ! this horse kicks.'
' Do pray go on, then,' said a voice ; and I turned, and by
Jove, it was his Excellency himself.   I believe you, I
cleared the road."

Everybody listened with the most profound attention :
even Wyldoates' languid countenance put on a glimpse of

intelligent appreciation befitting the stirring incident which the gallant hero had related about six times per diem since its occurrence.

" How did you find the billiard-table ?" he asked, as the party rose and moved towards the door.

" Oh, capital—capital. Are you going to try it ?"

" Well, I'll join you there directly. You can smoke here, if you like."

The two remained in the dining-room, and the rest returned to the library. Wyldoates locked the door, and drew the heavy curtain before it. "Father Corkran," said he, with an air and tone so business-like and decisive that it astonished the others, "let us come to an understanding. This Home Rule candidate is to be trusted for nothing, but to fill his own pockets."

" That's as may be. I don't know. You see his party have a swinging majority. My dear sir, the Whigs hold the country, and will do so for—oh, who can say how long ? The Tories are nowhere ; they are dissolving every day more and more."

" This means," thought Wyldoates, who was astute enough in some matters, "that I had better come down with something handsome on the nail. His reverence prefers a bird in the hand—hum. Now, Father Corkran," he added aloud, raising his drooped eyelids and looking steadily at his reverence, "as to Home Rule, why, we are Home Rule too. Hanaper, give me my address."

But Father Corkran, with a knowing sort of laugh, declined to read the address. Clearly, he was not to be blinded that way. "Mr. Wyldoates," said he sturdily, "leave all that flummery there. Exert your influence with your tenants, and procure the co-operation of those who can manage the town votes." And Father Corkran threw one leg over the other, and leaned back in his chair with the air of one who had said his say.

" Oh dear, yes," returned Mr. Wyldoates, with a grin ; " see here, Father Corkran, we are prepared to go to great lengths, I assure you."

Then the solicitors stepped into the discussion ; and the

lot of ground was indicated on the map which was most suitable for the new church ; and finally Mr. Wyldoates, after much preamble, signed a cheque which was filled up for him by Hanaper, and handed it ungraciously enough to his reverence, who, discontented with the amount, received it to the full as ungraciously, and stuffed it into the capacious pocket of his velvet waistcoat without acknowledgment or thanks beyond a surly bow.

The business over, he left almost at once.

" Well," yawned Wyldoates, " that's done ; and if he is not with us he won't be against us. You published the decision about that Sandy Row right of turf-cutting, hey, MacScutch ?"

Mr. Wyldoates then vanished to the more congenial society of the billiard-room, where his friends Germaine and Captain Papillon were playing.

CHAPTER XX.

" HOTSPUR.— * * * Sometimes he angers me
   With telling me of the moldwarp and the ant,
   Of the dreamer Merlin and his prophecies ;
   And of a dragon and a finless fish,
   A clip-winged griffin and a moulten raven,
   And such a deal of skimble-skamble stuff
   As puts me from my faith.   I tell you what :
   He held me but last night, at least nine hours,
   In reckoning up the several devils' names
   That were his lackeys."

                                    King Henry IVth.

HOGAN had not honoured the meeting at The Harp with
his presence. He found it unnecessary to do so. The
people seemed entirely on his side ; and the Home Rule
epidemic having seized upon them with such hold, the
illusory promises and threats of the Wyldoates faction
were not accounted much, either by him or by his clients.
He was tired of the work, too, and gladly alleged an
engagement in the Four Courts to justify his leaving by
the midday mail on Friday. He left Dicky Davoren
behind—to carry on the work of canvassing, ostensibly ;
but shrewdly suspected, at the same time, that the young
gentleman's exertions would not go far to swell his lists.
For various reasons, Hogan avoided all encounter with the
parish priest. He knew that the good-natured curate,
Father Desmond, was on his side ; but not wishing to
compromise him in any way, he kept out of his way too.
The Sheas accompanied him to the railway station—Ned
Shea trying hard to make the candidate promise to accept
his hospitality on his return for the grand meeting to be

held the following week. But Hogan declined the offer
with sincere gratitude and equal determination. He saw
clearly that his hostess was miserably uncomfortable on
her husband's account; and divining pretty accurately the
nature of the declaration to be expected from Father
Corkran on the coming Sunday, he wisely resolved to shift
his quarters to the hotel; alleging to the Sheas, as his
explanation for so doing, that it was a more convenient
situation. He promised to be back in time for the meeting,
but had grave doubts within himself as to the advisability
of going to it and of making a speech of the Ultra hue that
he would be necessarily obliged to in order not to fall out
with his too-ardent supporters. These and many other
thoughts he revolved in his mind, as he lay back in the
cushions of the railway carriage. It chanced that an ocean
mail had arrived that morning; so the train was filled
with Americans on their way to Dublin from Queenstown.
Hogan's compartment was crowded with them, discoursing
nasal depreciations of everything they could see from the
windows. He got into conversation with one of them—a
little gentleman, with a funny round body, somewhat reminding one of a spider's, and with curiously attenuated
legs. The likeness did not end there, as Hogan acknowledged to himself ere long. The little Yankee was a
species of intellectual spider, sucking dry the brains of
every one he could entangle in the web of questions which
he seemed to emit and weave round the hapless victim as
easily and skilfully as any member of the *arachnidæ*.
There was no getting out of it: every plunge landed one
deeper in. Hogan vainly tried to exchange parts, and
with his barrister practice opened up sidings and new
issues beyond counting. The little man was great on
figures. He asked the "population" of every "town," as
he persisted in calling the stations at which the train
stopped—some of them five or seven miles away from the
place from which they took their name. He popped his
head out, in this thirst for information, at a wooden station
on the edge of the bog, and hailing anybody on the platform, asked at large—

"Say, stranger, what's the name of this city?" Every one stared.

"Hey? what's the name?" Then, getting impatient, "I guess it ain't big enough to have a name of its own."

"Oh yes, it is," retorted a big cattle-driver who was seated on a railing, smoking his pipe; "an' it's got a popilation of its own—two millions."

The American shut up the window with a burst of derisive laughter, and sitting down, slapped his leg, and said, good-humouredly,—

"The gentleman thinks he's made a real fine joke now." Then he went to the subject of national schools, and drew Hogan into an elaborate explanation of the working of the system. The train passed a peat-condensing manufactory as they went along; and he made a man who had got in after Hogan tell him all about the process. That done, he returned to his first victim, and got him on the geological formations of the different counties they passed through. Hogan's knowledge was speedily exhausted, to his own surprise quite as much as that of the American, who told him that his own countrymen, almost without exception, were thoroughly "posted" in those matters. A priest who, out of curiosity, changed his seat to hear what the eager-looking little man was saying, was then swept in, and made to tell all he knew about cattle-breeding,—the sight of a field of fat kine having suggested the topic. The American wanted to know what were "black" cattle, and why the south of Ireland was noted for that particular colour. He was told by the priest that the cattle alluded to in the old Irish historical writings were always spoken of as being black, and that it was supposed that the original tribe of cattle—possibly those imported by the first colonists, who were Milesians—were black. The American was delighted: this kind of information was especially to his liking. He knew very well where the Milesians originally hailed from ; he had been there.

"Been in Asia Minor ! Dear me ! " said his reverence admiringly.

"Yes, I've bin all over—bin everywhere and I fully

bullieve, sir, that all cattle was black in the beginning. I
mean that God created 'em so—I dew ; for when I was in
Palestine I noticed all their cattle was black. Yes, sir—
that just proves the whole question most clearly ; and they
told me in Palestine they'd bin always just so."

"Hem !—You spoke the language ? " asked Hogan, in a
curiously constrained tone.

"No, sirree—didn't take time. Can you tell me, sir,
what is the prevailing notion here just now on this Home
Rule ? "

It is not very—ah—easy to say. Society is divided on
that subject——"

" Society ? Ah ! but I don't mean society, sir ; I mean
the people."

"Well, a good many of them go in pretty strong for it
—just as strongly here as you may have noticed among a
certain class of them in New York, now. I suppose the
extreme democratic party there favour the scheme, do they
not ? "

Not a question would the American answer ; he had
come out to take, not to give—that was perfectly clear ;
and Hogan, amused beyond measure, but with a little irri-
tation mingled with his sense of the absurdity, resigned
himself to the tender mercies of the little vampire for the
rest of the way. However, at Portarlington, where they
stopped for refreshments, and where the American, telling
him if he " wasn't thirsty he had ought ter be," insisted on
his taking a drink, he contrived by a clever manœuvre to
get a seat in another carriage, and to scribble some pencil
notes to have ready for the mail on reaching town.

One of these notes reached Miss Nellie Davoren next
morning at breakfast time. She opened it quite unconsciously, thinking it some mere business letter ; but when
she glanced over the few lines, written in a bold hand, as
clear and easy to read as large print, and saw the signa-
ture " J. O'Rooney Hogan" at the bottom, she was so
startled as to be surprised in her own mind at herself.
She left the room quickly, as if to go upstairs to her
mother ; but in reality she ran into her own chamber, and

seating herself in the window, drew out the wonderful letter, sorely crumpled in the pocket into which she had thrust it in the agitation of the moment.

She set herself to con every word, line, and sentence. No address—only a date; and scribbled with pencil.

"DEAR MISS DAVOREN,—I have had to run up to town for a few days. Dicky remains behind, and has commissioned me to bring back a small fowling-piece belonging to Mr. Shea. I shall call for it on Monday, if not inconvenient to you.—Very faithfully yours,

"J. O'ROONEY HOGAN."

Not much, after all—very little indeed. And this inconsistent damsel, who had been so astonished to receive a letter at all from her admirer, found herself wondering he did not say more when he was about it. But then, if he is coming on this absurd business, he no doubt thought it better to keep all his news to tell it in person. And a bright rosy colour flew up to the young lady's face as she reflected on the fact that this gentleman—a barrister, on the point of becoming a member of Parliament—was coining such a ridiculous excuse for calling to see her. What would Dorothy say? And she got up and stood before the mirror, and smoothed back her ripply hair, thinking what she should say to him and how receive him. She forgot breakfast altogether, until a maid put her head in and awoke her young mistress out of the land of day-dreams, by demanding a second cup of tea for Mrs. Davoren. Then she ran downstairs again, and took her seat at the table. She had finished her own breakfast, and having given the maid what she asked, she remained sitting quite still for a little time, feeling with one hand in her pocket the letter which she had received.

Certainly she had not expected it. He had asked leave, that night that he came out to see Dicky, to come and see them again, and to tell them the news of the election and all his adventures in the south; but he had not said a word about writing. And she went over in her memory every word and look of his, as in truth she had often done

U

since that memorable evening. She ended by making a resolve in her own mind—a resolve that, to tell the truth, was but a half-hearted one—that she would treat his note literally, and take the visit as purely and simply a matter of business. Dicky very naturally wanted the fowling-piece; and what more natural than that Mr. Hogan should offer to bring it to him? In fact, it was just like Dicky's carelessness not to write for it himself. Then she went out to the hall, and looked at the gun, hanging, with the fishing-roads and other things of the kind, at the end. It wanted cleaning sadly. The thought flashed into her head that perhaps she ought to have it sent to Mr Hogan's address. It would certainly save him the trouble of coming out; and he must have so much to do. Then the note was again read over : " I shall call for it on Monday." This was Saturday morning; there was plenty of time; and she certainly would have the fowling-piece put in order and sent to Mr. Hogan's office. And with this Spartan resolution Miss Davoren went to the kitchen, for her usual morning consultation with the cook; this over, she busied herself with sundry and various household duties until midday; then she usually went to her mother's room, to sit with her and read aloud, or sew if the invalid were inclined to sleep. In the afternoon she might have to see a visitor, if such chanced to come their way, or to practise; or take a walk if inclination or the weather tempted. She generally spent Saturdays in town; she was wont to go to confession at Gardiner Street chapel, where most of the Dublin young ladies congregate on that day. Then Dorothy generally expected to see her at two o'clock to lunch; and so the whole day, from twelve until late in the afternoon, was usually spent in the city.

This Saturday would be a busy day with Nellie. She had to be ready in time for the one o'clock train, and it was nearly twelve when she had finished her morning tasks. However, she reached Gardiner Street by taking a cab across town, and, after an interval of preparation, an obliging friend, a sister penitent, gave her her "turn" at Father O'Hea's box. The chapel was very full: it was the Saturday before the first Sunday of the month ; and the rows of benches drawn up at the sides of the innumerable confessionals were all crowded—as usual, in the proportion of ninety-nine women to one man.   Girls, school-girls, young ladies, young-old ladies (the most pious of all), and old ladies, thronged and squeezed and elbowed, and cast looks like daggers on every daring wight who presumed to borrow a "turn" from some one near the box, instead of waiting patiently at the tail of the long files on each side until all who had come before her were "heard" and had taken their departure.   The Raffertys and Mary Brangan were high up, and smiled amiably at Nellie. Mary Brangan was rather downcast in manner, and when Nellie had taken her place beside her whispered in doleful tone,—

"I wonder is Father O'Hea in good - humour to-day. Oh dear ! what'll I do if he's not ?   I've got such a confession pain."

"Have you ?   Oh, dear ! do you get them ?   I never do."

"Laws ! don't you ?   I've been dancing fast again : what'll I do ?   Say a prayer for me that I'll find him good-humoured.   Oh ! I'll be killed.   Last time I got it awful from him ; he said if I did it again he wouldn't give me absolution."

All this Miss Brangan whispered under her fingers, which she held so as to turn her voice into her neighbour's ear.   In her other hand she held a huge scarlet-and-gold-bound "Key of Heaven," stuffed full of holy pictures and markers.

"I don't think fast dancing a sin ; and my confessor told me if I didn't I needn't confess it.   I don't think it is, at all." ·

"What ! did Father O'Hea tell you that ?   Then I won't confess it, either !"

"I have more than one reason for my opinion, Miss Brangan ; and besides, I never was bound, as you were, not to fast dance.   Now, please do not follow my example : I'm sorry I told you. "

" You needn't. I have to go out a great deal ; and
what's the use of going to a dance and sitting still ? And
besides, I hate quadrilles. Oh laws ! there, he's called off
now to the house. We'll have to wait an age."

A man-servant had crossed the chapel from the door
leading to the priest's house, and, tapping on the confes-
sional, called away the confessor to see some one who had
sent for him. The double row of penitents cast disappointed glances after him, for they would probably have to
wait an additional hour or more. Miss Brangan looked
rather relieved ; she turned to Nellie and whispered something in her ear ; then both ladies rose, and leaving their
prayer-books on the seat in token of their return, passed
out of the main door and down the steps into the street.

" We may as well wait here awhile," said Miss Brangan,
drawing a long breath. " I'm expecting to meet a cousin
of mine. Did you see Miss Rafferty and young Mr. Dooly
on Sunday? They were on the Pier ; and I'm told the
mar'ge is to come off after Lent. I met them all at the
ball last night ; and oh, Miss Davoren, that gentleman—
what's his name ? the young bar'ster, I mean—Mr. Hogan,
was expected, but he couldn't come. Ah ! wouldn't you
have been sorry if you were there, eh ?"

" Not a bit, Miss Brangan. I can't imagine how or why
I should."

" Don't be vexed : I know he admired you greatly. I
met him a while ago, sure—I nearly forgot to tell you (this
with a palpable exhilaration of tone and look)—walking
in Nassau Street with a lady. She was beautifully dressed
—oh ! be-yeu-tifly: navy blue silk and pale blue ; and
she'd lovely golden hair. She wasn't young, though, at
all."

" Ah ! was there an old lady very like her, and dressed
in sealskin and black ?"

" Yes, exactly. They were Protestants, I'm sure ; for I
could hear their accents, and they looked like it."

" No doubt," said Miss Nellie, quite carelessly. She
divined at the first word, almost, that Miss Bursford was
the beautifully dressed lady—the pale, blonde girl whom

she had met at Cousin Dorothy's. Walking with her!
the very same day that——. And she determined now
that that gun should be sent, without fail, on Monday
morning to his office. Diana Bursford—beautifully dressed:
and she pictured Hogan's pleasant face smiling into hers as
he walked beside her; proud, no doubt, to be seen with
Miss Bursford. Why not? and the girl's cheek grew the
least shade paler for an instant only. She dismissed the
envious thought from her mind (it was merely envious)
without an effort, and not without a twinge of self-upbraid-
ing for having harboured it.

Miss Brangan's cousin came up now, accompanied by
Miss Eily Rafferty and the pious Miss Doyle. The young
ladies entered into conversation.

"Mary Doyle!" said Miss Brangan; "what are you
comin' for to-day again? Weren't you at confession on
Wednesday?"

"Yes; but I wanted to ask Father McQuaide's leave to
employ Miss Feathers, the dressmaker; she's a Protestant,
you know, and I couldn't think of giving her anything to
do till I knew whether he'd approve it."

"Listen, then," said Miss Eily Rafferty; "here's a
wrinkle for *you*, Mary Doyle. Did any of ye hear this
story? Mother Paul told it to mamma last day she was
visiting at St. Swithin's. There was a young lady, a great
friend of her own (so now it must be true), livin' on the
Laracore Road, just out that way a bit towards Green
Lanes; and she was most anxious to get settled. Do
ye mind how a nun never says 'get married,'—it is
always *settled* they call it—ho! ho!" and Miss Eily
giggled irreverently. "Well, the girl began a novena to
Saint Joseph; and the ninth day, when the novena was
done, and nobody turned up to marry her, she flew in a
rage, and says she to Saint Joseph, 'Old boy, you've been
here long enough,' says she—'and out you go!' An', me
dear, what do you think but she opened the window, and
she hurls the imidge plump into the street! 'Tis a fact!
Well, a gentleman was passin' by, an' he saw the white
thing fallin' down, an', me dear, he caught it, and he came

up and knocked at the hall door. Well, her mother was
in the hall ; an', of course, the least thing she could do in
mere politeness was to ask him in. Then, the girl she
comes down, an', me dear, her mother introduced her, an'
they were married in a month. So now !"

"Laws !" said Mary Doyle, opening her eyes and her
mouth as far as they would go.

"Musha, then !" said Miss Brangan the sensible; "I
think they were badly off for men in that house. I
wouldn't be her—no ! indeed ! Would you, Miss Davoren ?"

But Miss Davoren was laughing too much to be able to
answer the question ; and after a few minutes' delay, the
party separated and repaired to their respective confessionals.

When Nellie got away it was too late to think of going
to Dorothy ; moreover she did not feel inclined for the
long journey across town ; so, having made some necessary purchases, she returned by one of the afternoon
trains.

The Sunday passed uneventfully. A note came from
Miss O'Hegarty to ask why she had not seen Nellie the
previous day, and to announce that she would call on
Monday. Nellie was glad of this for several reasons :
firstly, she wanted to see Dorothy ; and secondly, her
presence, and the stir she always created when she came,
would prevent any mental tergiversations or useless regrets
on her part, such as she knew herself liable to fall into,
once that the white heat of determination had cooled
down,—and which she determined to strive against.

So on Monday morning the gun was sent, with a polite
message of thanks, to Mr. Hogan ; and Miss Nellie went
through all her duties with a somewhat unusual vigour.
Lunch was prepared for Dorothy; and two hours' vigorous
practice at the piano concluded by two o'clock, at which
hour that lady was expected. Whatever delayed her, it
was half-past three ere she appeared. By that time Mrs.
Davoren was asleep, and could not be disturbed ; so Miss
O'Hegarty seated herself in the dining-room with Nellie.

" I couldn't get away any earlier, my dear. Peter is in one of his tantrums—says he'll leave on the first of next month; and he spent two hours this morning packing his trunk. Really, I'm wearied with him."

Nellie with difficulty restrained a laugh. Peter gave notice, on an average, once a fortnight; but the idea of the trunk-packing was something extraordinarily ludicrous —the trunk, according to Dicky, being a pure myth. Dicky had once upon a time penetrated the garret where this wonderful piece of furniture was kept, or was supposed to be kept; and declared ever after that the trunk was not in existence, and never had been, any more than Mrs. Gamp's Mrs. Harris.

" Why don't you take him at his word, Cousin Dorothy? I would, and have done with him. You would get an excellent servant for his wages."

" 'Deed, my dear, I think I will. Mrs. Hepenstall has often wanted me to take their man Kirk; they want to do with the page-boy only, now that they have him trained and in on their ways, she says. How she could endure a gammon (*gamin*) of that sort about her, I don't know. I'd just as soon take in the organ-man's monkey. He's English, too."

" She brought him over with her, then ? "

" She did; and indeed she was telling me after she got him, that she was lecturing him one day on not allowing anything to be wasted, and how she'd value him if he was economical. ' Waste, mum,' said this page-boy; ' lor, no, mum : sooner than 'ave anything wasted, I'm sure I eats till I nigh busts.' The Hepenstalls wanting to get rid of the man looks as if they were not getting on all too well. Poor Charlotte !" sighed Miss Dorothy, " she has a fast husband, I fear. What are men coming to now-a-days ? I was at the Griffiths' the other day ; and she looked that miserable and woe-begone ; their son in college is a dreadful boy, and Judge Griffiths such a nice, steady man. It is incomprehensible to me."

" It seems to me very clear indeed, then," said Nellie, a little sharply. " Boys are allowed to do what they like

and go where they choose.   From the day our Dicky
went to school he has been his own master altogether; and
indeed, he refuses to tell even where he has been when he
comes in.   He goes out in the morning to college; he
does'nt come back till dinner-time.   In the evening he
goes out again.   Mamma and I scarcely ever see him at
all; and he won't go with me anywhere hardly, except
by the greatest coaxing.   Papa never minds anything, you
know."

"Well, you see, my dear, he's getting to be a young
man now; and they won't be controlled and questioned.
Boys must all go through that stage: it makes them hardy
and manly to be left to themselves; and then they learn
the world."

"Learn the world!   Well, Cousin Dorothy, look at all
the young men who learn the world.   Tad Griffiths is
learning it.   His eldest brother killed himself in the
process, no doubt.   And there is young Grey, the clergyman's son here, who enlisted last year, after getting himself expelled from college.   The Miss Greys have not one
of their brothers to take them about.   They say they
can't get them to go into society; they hate girls, and it's
all humbug, and slow.   Every night they are out; never
in their father's house except for meals."

"It is a fact," said Miss O'Hegarty thoughtfully.   "In
my time men were just as wild—wilder!   Look at the
stories of their doings!   Somehow they didn't begin so
young then, whatever's the reason; and it was a different
kind of wildness.   Practical jokes, and fighting, and hard
drinking, and that.   They have a quieter style of sowing
their wild oats now-a-days; and, indeed, it is a deal a more
mischievous one.   Fashion, my dear,—it is the fashion."

Fashion was the final court of appeal with Miss O'Hegarty
in all doubtful cases, and by its decisions she abided faithfully.   She never troubled herself about their justice;
expediency with her was the equivalent.   She was not in
the habit of looking deeply into things; indeed, she seldom
stirred the surface at all, and pronounced off-hand judgments on the first aspects of cases with a dogmatism and

decision truly wonderful. We must do her the justice to say that this rule did not hold good in politics. She never relaxed a fibre of her Toryism, and had not a whit of that latent chameleon nature which becomes apparent in people even of the best set, on the changes of administrations. All Whigs were Radicals with her. The hybrid Conservative-Whig and the Liberal-Tory were impossibilities, and as such ignored and scouted.

"By-the-bye, Nellie, to-morrow I'm going to a concert for this Asylum. Mr.—ah—what's his name?—that great friend of the Bursfords, Saltasche—has found out some splendid *pianiste*, an officer's wife, living up somewhere near the Park; and he and his friends have taken her up. It's a Protestant affair, but if you like I'll take you; I can easily get tickets."

"No, thank you, Cousin Dorothy; I could not go. You know we are forbidden to attend any of those entertainments. Tell me, is her name Poignarde?—a very young, pretty woman? I think Dicky spoke of having met her with the Greys."

"Yes, that's the very name. I never do remember those foreign names; but I'm told her playing is something divine. The husband is a fearful scamp; and the Greys are very kind to her. You might as well come, child."

Just as Nellie was about to reply a loud knock at the door startled her. Mr. Hogan's knock!—she thought it must be Mr. Hogan's knock; and in spite of her efforts to remain composed, she could not prevent her surprise showing itself.

"Who's that, Nellie?" asked Miss O'Hegarty sharply. "Had we not better go into the drawing-room?"

"I know who it is; at least, I am sure it is Mr. Hogan. He was to call here for something to take down to Dicky in Peatstown; and—and——"

But by this time they were at the door of the room, and further explanation was impossible. There indeed stood the candidate for Peatstown, looking as bright and fresh as possible. He was presented to Miss O'Hegarty, and bowed low to her, recognising the lady who had been

Nellie's chaperone at the theatre the evening they met there.

Cousin Dorothy guessed intuitively the whole affair, and was more cordial than was her wont, considering who her new acquaintance was. She seated herself on an ottoman, and scanned him as curiously as politeness would allow.

Nellie began in a slightly nervous tone.

"It was too—too much trouble for Dicky to burden you with his gun, Mr. Hogan. I sent it to your office this morning. Did you get it?"

Had Miss Davoren's cousin not been present, Mr. Hogan would have said the truth—that he did receive the gun and the message between ten and eleven o'clock; but, with his usual caution, he reflected that the admission would certainly entail the inference by the clever-looking old lady, whose gray eyes were fixed upon him so scrutinisingly, that he had come to pay a visit to the young lady of the house. So he answered composedly,—

"No, Miss Davoren; I had left before its arrival. I did hear since, indeed, that my servant had been looking for me with a message of some kind." And this mendacious gentleman looked at her to see if her expressive countenance betrayed any disappointment. On the contrary, she looked intensely relieved—and was so too. She dreaded being rallied by Miss Dorothy; and she had also some undefined dislike to being talked of in connection with any man. However proud she might feel, the idea that Miss Brangan and her set should ever discuss her, as they were now discussing other girls, was unbearable. Her dislike of the particular kind of current small-talk known as "chaff" was something morbid in its intensity. Hitherto it had been very easy for her to avoid the bantering of her friends, for she found the ordinary "young gentlemen" of her acquaintance so uninteresting that even the simplest conversation was difficult; and they, however they admired her, were afraid to show any marked preference to one so cold and distant in her manner.

Miss O'Hegarty, having surveyed him well, now began to speak to the young man.

"I see by the *Beacon* that you are standing for Peatstown in opposition to Lord Kilboggan's nephew."

"Yes. I am contesting the seat in the Liberal interest," he replied, a little pompously.

"Does your canvassing go on well?" asked Nellie anxiously, and a little cordially, as if inclined to counterbalance the old lady's patronising tone.

"Oh yes, so far satisfactorily. It won't be a very close contest. I have had hard work; but I think the most wearing part of the work is the journeys up and down by rail. I had an American—a most extraordinary man, a perfect question-machine—for travelling-companion on Saturday. He did so annoy me."

The old lady smiled mischievously. "Was he catechising you on your political creed, Mr. Hogan? What tiresome creatures one does encounter in travelling."

Her first allusion to his affairs was coupled with the mention of the *Beacon*—a paper which had recently made a savage onslaught on the Home Rulers generally, and on the progress of the Peatstown election and the candidate and his platform in particular. Hogan was keenly alive to the implied sarcasm of the second speech; but he ignored it by a literal interpretation, and replied quite unconsciously,—

"Well—ah—he did not confine himself to any one subject. The number of questions was fully paralleled by their diversity: he went from statistics to topography, geology, and zoology—everything that possibly could be dragged in; and kindly informed me that I was greatly behind his countrymen, insomuch that I was not conversant with the mineral productions of Tipperary."

"Are they not wonderful creatures, now?" said Miss O'Hegarty. "Perfectly wonderful! I never could endure them. One meets such a dreadful set of them abroad."

"Ah! well; but you don't find better-class Americans, Miss O'Hegarty, making themselves so objectionable. You mustn't take the shoddy specimens as representatives."

"Nonsense!" replied Dorothy, with a most aggravating

air of superiority. "They are all alike: isn't it a Republic ? Manners must be the same with everybody where there are no class distinctions. They have no aristocracy. Fine dress seems to be their sole idea of refinement. Faugh !"

"They have an aristocracy of intellect," put in Nellie.

"Nothing of the sort, child," said Dorothy, almost angrily. "What literature have they, indeed ?"

"They have ours—which they take without paying for it," laughed Hogan.

"They've none of their own," continued Miss O'Hegarty. "No, none. What great poets or prose writers have they ? They can't call Longfellow a national poet. There is no American epic—no history——"

"Epic, eh ? Well, I think the real American epic is Barnum's autobiography. The genius of the nation is best expressed in that. Ha, ha !"

"What is Dicky doing ?" asked Nellie ; "and when may he be expected home ?"

"Well, Miss Davoren, he is canvassing : that is, he takes pleasant country drives with the young ladies of the house, and seems to do a great deal of work indeed. He is remarkably clever."

Miss O'Hegarty, with whom her young relative was an especial favourite, smiled on hearing the encomium pronounced by Hogan ; and in a pleasanter tone of voice asked him when he was to return to Peatstown.

"To-morrow. Then I do not come back here until after the election."

Miss O'Hegarty would hear nothing of the election. She casually brought in the name of a prominent Conservative peer, as being interested in the result, on account of his cousin the candidate—showing that she was retained on the other side. So the conversation shifted to indifferent topics ; and after a stay of twenty minutes he rose to go. He felt sorry he had not sent a note acknowledging Miss Davoren's attention, instead of coming in person. However, when Nellie placed her hand in his, and looking straight into his eyes, thanked him—a little

tell-tale colour dyeing her cheeks the while, and a brighter
light shining in her fine eyes—for his kindness and attention, he thought that, after all, his visit had not been
bootless; and he pressed her hand ever so little as he left
the room. He had accurately gauged her before—that is,
as much of her character as it behoved him to know: to
wit, that she was not, like most of the other women of
his limited acquaintance, business-like husband-hunters,
admiration-mongers,—turning, like sunflowers in quest of
every ray, their beauties to all eyes. Neither could it be
said of her, as a witty Castle aide-de-camp said of some of
the Corporation ladies, that she bore "the mark of the
Beast." Her face and style were eminently Protestant:
even in London society, he thought to himself, there could
not be found a trace of "Dissenting appearance" in her.
Good blood!—her mother came of the Rathbone and
Desmond families: nothing like it! And Mr. Hogan
reflected with great self-satisfaction on his own maternal
ancestor, that royal prince of the ninth century, the founder
of the O'Rooney family. Not, indeed, that he had ever
cared to claim the kinship; he had rather affected to
laugh at the idea; but of late he had noticed the tide
seemed to be setting in favour of such appendages. The
Raffertys had got home a genealogical tree from Sir
Bernard Burke; the Ryans wrote themselves O'Ryan;
and Donnell, the retired wine-merchant, who bought Lord
Ramines' patrimony, insisted on the prefix Mac. There
was great talk of the septs and tribes; and sundry extinct
peerages seemed to be only waiting for moneyed claimants
to come forward. Hitherto he had overlooked the fact
that his ancestry might be of service. His profession and
his success had sufficed as a patent of respectability; but
the pedigree would undoubtedly be an addition indirectly,
for as the Bishop had often told him, "The only chance of
respect and consideration from the Protestants, you being
a Roman Catholic, is to let them see that you have both
from your own people." So he determined that the chief-
tain Rhuadne, and that the ruined Castle Rhuadne, near
Tara, should both be skilfully introduced as a background,

so to say, to the representation of the family O'Rooney—the composition, consisting only of the Bishop and himself, seeming a little bald and crude. It was not an absurdity; it was a means to an end. He had set to build a mansion to himself; and he had fixed the top stone of the building first,—a well-paid and lofty Government situation, to be the reward of Parliamentary services,—to render which services a seat in Parliament must be attained, which seat in Parliament must be obtained by——any means. "*De minimis non curat Lex:*" he used to repeat that quotation frequently to himself,—not that he derived much mental comfort from it, or that he distinguished very clearly the difference between the broad elastic margins of the Lex and the close, fine-drawn distinctions of the inner tribunal, which he much seldomer invoked.

As he drove back to town, he debated within himself the desirability of calling on Miss Bursford. He had, indeed, sent her a note from Peatstown, to say that everything was going on well with him,—a note couched in such terms that neither answer nor acknowledgment was needful, but which had nevertheless been answered; and it was this answer that made him hesitate as to paying her another visit.

"Better leave it till we go to London," thought he. "Safer—much safer, and more to the purpose;" and he did leave the visit till then.

CHAPTER XXI.

"HAMLET.—You would play upon me; you would seem to know my stops; you would pluck out the heart of my mystery; you would sound me from my lowest note to the top of my compass, and there is much music, excellent voice, in this little organ, yet cannot you make it speak." *Hamlet.*

"WELL, Cousin Dorothy," said Miss Davoren after the departure of Mr. Hogan, "shall we go back to the other room. Perhaps I ought to go back and see if mamma is awake."

"Never mind, my dear, yet a bit. And so that is your friend, Mr. Hogan? Quite a nice, gentlemanlike man." And the veteran turned round her wide gray eyes full on Miss Nellie's ingenuous countenance. "Diana Bursford,— what was she saying? She's met him, I know, somewhere."

"He knows Miss Bursford. I heard he was seen walking with her the other day." This was ungenerously said; but when an ostrich is minded to stick its head in the sand it is never too particular.

"Humph! walking with her indeed! Diana really goes to the fair with absurdity now-a-days. Surely she knows the man is a Romanist. Absurd!—and she is ten years older than him. Where did you meet him?"

"I told you, Cousin Dorothy: at the Rafferty's ball."

"Oh, ah! last November. Dicky or you were telling me. I know now, to be sure; that Saltasche man has brought him out."

"That Saltasche man" was one of Miss O'Hegarty's pet aversions. When she took a dislike to any one she was

sure to make the fact known by the very way she pronounced their name; and as the disagreeable cognomen
passed her lips now, her thin nostrils curled, and her
under-lip shaped the word ominously. "Depend upon it
they are chums—birds of a feather. I never could endure
these mere adventurers."

"Adventurers, Cousin Dorothy!" Nellie's eyes opened
wide. "Why, Mr. Saltasche owns a splendid place just
behind us; and I have heard papa say he was worth fifty
thousand pounds. To be sure, he is not Irish—or at least,
he is only a half foreigner? And surely you do not consider Mr. Hogan that? You don't include him?"

"Tush! my dear, you don't understand. Of course Mr.
Hogan is not one in the sense that Mr. Saltasche is; and,
indeed, if he is an adventurer in any other sense, it is quite
as much other people's faults as his own."

Miss Nellie, indeed, was far from following the working
of her relative's mind; and she was content to leave the
speech a mystery, and not to beat her brains over the
solution. She quite understood Miss Dorothy's carpings
at Diana—their bearing was plain enough; but the criti-
cisms on Hogan were surely uncalled for. She saw no
flaw in him.

"I forgot to mention that Dermot—Dermot Blake, my
nephew—has been heard of. He has been away since he
was a lad; travelling ever since he left college. Did you
ever see him, Nellie?"

"No; I think I heard you speak of him, and that he
was to be home when he was five-and-twenty."

"Yes; though indeed it's ten years now since he was
five-and-twenty. I never was on terms with the Blakes;
however, he'll be home next year. That will be a catch
for somebody: three thousand a year! He's at the Cape
now."

But Nellie was staring into the fire, thinking of some
one who was far from Dermot Blake and the Cape, and
wondering should she see him again, and when. How she
wished Dorothy would go up to her mother's room, so that
she might think over his coming, and the manner of it, and

everything, quietly by the fireside! Dorothy had been so stiff and so sarcastic; but what was the use of thinking of that? It was always her way.

"Dermot is like the Blakes," Dorothy talked away: "tall and brown—fine man, and such a good, warm-hearted fellow! Who will he marry? The accumulations—at least, the accumulations there ought to be," she added in a dubious tone, "would clear off the estate entirely. He ought to marry money. Yes, he ought to marry money."

"Ought he?" repeated Miss Nellie, dreaming still, and seeing in the wood-ashes in the grate a droll likeness of Mr. Hogan in his barrister's wig.

"Run away, and see if your mother be awake, child; I must be going," said Cousin Dorothy, pulling out the great diamond-set watch that had belonged to Desmond O'Hegarty, the last of the family. "Dear bless us!—a quarter to six. I'll be half an hour late for my dinner; and that Peter like a fiend already. I declare: the martyrdom I undergo with that creature! There, the other day, I told him to go and get himself a new hat; and just as he always does when I desire him to buy himself any new things, he comes and asks me, ' Will I get a hat to fit meself or to fit anybody, marm?'—as if he was thinking of leaving, you know. So says I, 'Oh, you'd better get a hat to fit anybody, Peter,'—never meaning him to take me up; and the ojous old wretch goes and buys a hat as big as a wheelbarrow, just to spite me: so he did. To see him yesterday, with it rattling about on his head, it would vex a saint, it would. Talk of Job, indeed! I'd like to have set Job up with a couple of family servants of the real old style! Dermot Blake, now, he and Peter always got ,on together; perhaps when he settles down he'd take Peter off my hands. You have no idea how smart Peter can be! I declare now, I don't know anybody would suit Dermot's house so well."

"That Saltasche man," as Miss O'Hegarty scornfully styled him, had not been idle since we last saw him. He had skilfully extracted the somewhat biassed, if comprehensive, history of her relatives the Poignardes from Mrs.

Grey. They were not relatives in the strict sense of the word—merely connections. Poignarde, indeed, was scarcely a creditable appendage to any family; and his strange wife, however beautiful and talented, was so cold and reserved and odd, that the clergyman's wife, busy and worn with her large and troublesome family, had neither time nor inclination to make friends with her. Mr. Saltasche had managed very cleverly, as he did always, to impress Mrs. Grey with the belief that he was desirous to secure the services of Mrs. Poignarde as *pianiste* for the concert in which she had a particular interest; and he sent his sister, a lady somewhat older than himself, who managed his house and always lived with him, to call on Mrs. Poignarde with Mrs. Grey. This point secured, he devoted himself, heart and soul, to make the charitable undertaking, as it was called, a social success. Mr. Saltasche set great store on popularity, and prided himself on holding the most amicable relations with everybody, irrespective of creed or class. He had all that off-handed, ready way of talking and giving, that goes so far with the lower orders of Irish people; and the labourers and poor folks of Green Lanes exalted him to the very highest pitch. If his swarthy countenance appeared in the window of a train, every porter made a dash at the door of his carriage. His parcels found a score of bearers to fight for the honour of carrying them; and the jarveys could see no one else beckon until Mr. Saltasche had selected his conveyance. His dinners were pronounced to be the acme of perfection; and the company was always as well assorted and selected as the *menu*. Strange to say, nevertheless, it was in his own immediate neighbourhood, precisely where he expended his best efforts and a vast income to attain the good-will of every one, that his enemies were keenest. There was a class of Protestants—not the best set, nor the second set, but still a very respectable and old-established faction—who stoutly denied Saltasche's supremacy, and would have none of him, "A half-foreigner," "a fellow come from God knows where," "a mongrel:" they even declared him to be a free-thinker. And one gentleman, who, on the strength of avowed atheism, had acquired a sort of reputation for general information, if not erudition, imparted, under the seal of secrecy, to his most particular friends his opinion that Saltasche was a Comtist.

Whatever he was, he was able to snap his fingers at the clique the night of the concert, when the schoolroom, hung with red cloth and decorated with splendid exotics from his own hothouses, was crowded with the *élite* of his friends—Lord Brayhead, the Bragintons, Bursfords, Hepenstalls, Wyldoates—military men innumerable—in attendance on the pretty O'Haras and Dillons. Everybody was in full dress; and the best amateurs in Dublin had been secured as performers. The prime mover, although ostensibly only one of the committee, Mr. Saltasche was everywhere at once. He received Lord Brayhead at the door, and conducted him to the place of honour—a red velvet chair on a raised step beneath the platform, oppressively close to the singers and musicians, but still in sight of all the audience and most conspicuous in every way. Beside his lordship were chairs occupied by his relatives the Misses Braginton and the rest of the daïs company. A glass door led to a room where the performers were congregated together. A singing doctor, high in favour at the vice-regal court, and a lawyer who had "fiddled himself" (so the story went) into a fine position in the law courts; a tenor captain, and a basso major, both from the Linenhall barracks; a buffo singer of rare excellence, by profession an attorney; and a number of ladies all congregated together, talking, humming airs, and otherwise killing time until the bell rang for the commencement. Such was the assemblage that greeted Mr. Saltasche's pleased eyes as he dived through the glass door to muster his company.

"Everybody's in now. Stukely, my dear boy, you lead off. Chorus! everything's ready. Where's Mrs. Poignarde? Is she here?" His eyes had already satisfied themselves that she was not.

"Mrs. Poignarde has not appeared," said Diana Bursford; "but I think I heard some one come into the outer hall just now."

Mr. Saltasche sent off the first detachment to sing a glee, and passed quietly out by the side-door to see if Mrs. Poignarde had come. In the dressing-room he heard a stir, and tapped at the door gently.

No answer. He turned the handle and looked in cautiously ; the gas was half turned down, and the brilliant well-piled fire filled the room with a mellow, fitful light. On a footstool drawn close to the grate he saw a slender figure crouched, holding out both white-gloved hands to shield her face from the glare. A long wave of white froth-like texture streamed backwards. She looked like some fairy visitor in the ugly room, with its prosaic rows of benches and map-hung walls.

She never moved. He bent forward, and then closing the door, advanced quietly.

" Mrs. Poignarde ! I half imagined you were deserting us at the last moment."

' Ah ! did you ? " and she stood in a moment erect before him. " No, no ; I came with Miss Saltasche. But why did you think that ? Because I am not there. I don't want to go with them. To play well I need to be quiet—to think ; so I stayed here until my turn came. Do you mind ? tell me : do you ? Tell me : do you ? " she repeated, in a sweet half-tone, lowering her voice almost caressingly, and looking at him from beneath the drooped white eyelids. There was a charming dependingness and timidity in the tone and look—something so different from the reserved coldness of her usual manner—that it went straight through him like a flash. A bright light came in his eyes, fixed on hers searchingly and triumphantly.

" You will do as you please. You know very well it is for you to command us all." And he leaned forward and touched the gas jets above their heads, letting a broad glare of light fall upon the slender figure beside him. She looked exquisitely lovely—so white and graceful : the long robes falling in soft wreaths behind her gave a look of height and dignity to her figure. A narrow gold collar clasped with a diamond circled her throat ; and the soft plaits of her hair, dressed in defiance of the fashion,

hung low on her neck, contrasting with its ivory whiteness.

He longed for the moment to come when he should
walk out past the crowd with her on his arm, and appro-
priate to himself all the praise and delighted raptures of
the audience. She was his property, a gem of his discovery ; and they were indebted to him for the treat. He
would take her, after her first piece, to Lord Brayhead, and
present her to him as a personal friend of his own and a
distinguished *artiste*, needing only his lordship's approval
to stamp her as one of the first stars of the firmament.
The Bragintons would patronise her, or try to do so, and
burn their fingers in the process ; and every one would be
on the *qui vive* to know who she was.

She did not seem to hear what he said ; she had turned
aside, and was thoughtfully looking into the fire, remembering, half-sorrowfully, half-bitterly, the last time she had
played before an audience, at the breaking-up of the school
in Kensington. It seemed only yesterday : the hot July
afternoon, the trees waving outside ; the close room, and
all the people ; and Eric Poignarde, then a dragoon officer,
bowing before her, the South American heiress. That was
a fatal day indeed !

The transient flush of excitement that had come upon
her when Mr. Saltasche entered the room had died away ;
and the old bitter, constrained mood, like an ever-present
sense of soreness, returned. She repented her promise,
and wished herself, were it possible, back in the dingy
lodging at Inchicore. What had she to do among these
staring strangers—curious and indifferent, if not scornful ?
She hated them already. Stupid, cold wretches : what
were they to her ? And she turned round impatiently,
only to meet the ardent eyes of Saltasche still fixed upon
her. Suddenly he remembered himself, and looking at his
watch, said,—

"Tell me, Mrs. Poignarde : what would you like to do
—to remain here alone, until I come for you ? or will you
join the performers ?"

"I shall remain here," said she decisively, "if it is

possible ; pray don't let me keep you." She spoke petu-
lantly, and he had no choice but to go.

In a few minutes he was back : it was her turn to play :
and taking his arm, she passed out of the glass-door and
up the steps into the concert-room.

A buzz ran round immediately, and curious heads were
bent forward. Opera-glasses were in requisition. "Is it
Miss Bursford ? No ! no ! A mysterious *prima donna*,
imported by that Monte Christo of a Saltasche specially
for the occasion. Foreign, of course. Jewess. The
colour is Jewish—that dead white, you know."

So the knots of men leaning against the door and the
walls murmured to each other, until the musician, seating
herself at the piano, struck into one of Liszt's most
masterly compositions. Saltasche had taken care that the
instrument should not be unworthy of the performer.
The extraordinary difficulties of the composition seemed
nothing to the lissom white fingers, that flew over the keys
and produced such wonderful depths of tone with so little
apparent effort. The charm of the instrument and a sense
of her own power, produced in her an unwonted exhilaration ; and she played with a fire and spirit that astonished
even herself. Saltasche was in an ecstasy. He refused to
allow her to play an *encore*, and led her up to the noble
patron to present her to him before the whole room.
Sundry spiteful tongues were silenced by this planned
manœuvre. A chair was forthcoming beside one of the
Bragintons ; who immediately commenced, after polite and
approving thanks, a characteristic conversation.

"How *enormously* you must have practised ! You do
play so exquisitely : quite as well as Lady St. Elmo.
Don't you think Mrs. Poignarde plays quite as well as
Lady St.——"

"Oh dear, yes ; quite," returned the lady addressed,
who had never heard the performer in question in her
life. "Exquisite touch, and such—such—ah—*expression*,
you know ! How you *must* have practised, Mrs. Poignarde !
All day long, no doubt ?"

They all dwelt upon the same theme, so anxious were

they to depreciate the too obvious merits of her achievements. By making it appear that she owed her proficiency merely to time and study, it would seem to prove that the same efforts on their part would have brought them up to her level. That was all that was necessary, of course.

" Oh yes," she answered, frankly ; " I should be quite ashamed to tell you how much I practise." She read their thoughts perfectly, and flashed an amused look at her mentor, standing near. He appreciated the situation, and said, approvingly,—

" Spoken like an *artiste,* Mrs. Poignarde ; the general thing with ordinary performers is to try and make us believe that they never touch the piano at all. I never could see how the value of their music was affected by the statement."

" Never believe them," she said : " I know better ; there is nothing in the world that requires more work · than— playing,"—and she looked at the ladies with a smile at her own quip.

His lordship put on a solemn visage. He loved music no better than did the great lexicographer ; he was old-fashioned, too, and had serious doubts as to the becomingness of ladies excelling in anything. It was not quite consistent with his prejudices ; he had a dim idea that these sort of things were marketable commodities, bought and paid for, and that it was *infra dig.* for a lady or gentleman, as such, to meddle with professional pursuits. Although he had written a polemical work himself, he considered writing scarcely allowable ; however, the appearance of certain of the nobility in print had of recent years rather unsettled his convictions on the subject. Then he was not sure who the musician was. She might have been a governess, or some " person " obliged to support herself. So he deemed it right to qualify his approval.

" Do you consider that music in itself repays or justifies the expenditure of so large a portion of our allotted time ?" —and the long sheep's-face inclined sideways towards her. " Is it not open to question whether we are justified in encouraging trivialities that pass with time itself ?"

Mrs. Poignarde looked at him, opening her wide brown eyes in genuine astonishment. She understood not one word of what he had said; but she divined in some way its import, from the edified expressions assumed by the women—the Bragintons especially. Miss Blanche seemed to be offering internally a thanksgiving that she, too, was not a musician. Mrs. Bursford came to the rescue.

"Do not overlook the parable of the talents, my lord," she said, with her sweetest smile; and a graceful gesture of the woman of the world towards Adelaide Poignarde implied a patronising compliment to her, and at the same timed showed that she meant the discussion to be closed.

Scriptural allusions of this kind were perfectly admissible, and, indeed, were the predominant tone of the conversations of his lordship's *entourage*.

Some sudden thought made Saltasche watch the expression of his *protégée*; and he could have shouted with laughter on reading, clear as print, on her candid brow, utter unconsciousness of Mrs. Bursford's allusion. A song now occupied the attention of the circle; and Mrs. Poignarde had time to make up her mind as to her surroundings. What did they mean? That stupid old creature! —she felt sure she could not sit patiently in the room with him and these women. She understood them a little better, and determined to disobey her mentor and play *encores* for spite. She looked critically at them: Mrs. Bursford and Mrs. Hepenstall were neutrals; the little yellow-haired lady making such *moues* and *œillades* at the men, whom she was plainly keeping by main force around her, need not be counted either, although she did look vicious when she found her attendants' eyes wandering to the strange lady in white. The Bragintons looked mischievous. Old?—yes, they were old, and made up very palpably indeed: rice-powdered, and with stippled-up eyebrows. And she ran her eye critically over those points, unnoticed; for their cousin, Diana Bursford, was singing in a quartette, and they could not spare a look, so eagerly were they listening for a flaw in the performance. She saw them exchange a smile and a glance at a badly-executed shake; and when the singers had retired, she said, tentatively,—

"Very nice song. I admire Mendelssohn so much: that lady in blue has the best voice there—so well trained !"

"Indeed ! You think so ? " The speaker was clearly disappointed. " The lady in blue will be glad to hear *your* opinion."

"Mrs. Poignarde," said Mr. Saltasche, "now, your turn will come again directly. Let's see : what is it ? ' Woelfl's *Ne Plus Ultra* sonata,' " he read from the programme. "Very fine : but what do you say to substitute something lighter ? What do you think ? Come ; you have a large *répertoire*, you know."

This proposal fell in with her humour completely ; and she played a set of German waltzes so as to call down a storm of applause. She played three pieces before she left the piano,—finishing with a transcription of the " Flying Dutchman," by Liszt. Saltasche led her back to the waiting-room, amid a storm of applause.

"Give me my cloak: I am going," she said, peremptorily.

"Oh no ! Surely not yet. You will play in the second part ? Please tell me what has annoyed you,"—and he looked at her searchingly. She answered his eyes, as usual, listlessly and indifferently ; the flush of excitement was gone.

"Nothing has annoyed me. I'm tired of it—that's all; and I hate those people. I don't want to see them again, any of them. Now let me go home."

He took her hand in his, and bent forward as if she were some wayward child.

"I only want to please you. You will do exactly what you like. Command me : but will you not tell me who has offended you ?" He came nearer still, and looked entreatingly at her.

"I'll tell you about it another time, if you'll only let me go now. I am stifled in this place. No ; I won't let you send for the brougham, or disturb your sister. I'll slip up

to Vévey House by the side-door. I'll find it easily enough,
we came out that way."

When she got out into the night air, she drew a long
breath of relief. It was bright and clear, and she could
see far up the road under the dark lattice of the branches.
She glided quietly along under the windows, through which
came the voices of the singers distinctly ; and passed unobserved through the groups outside. A dark hood and
cloak covered her dress ; and rejoicing in her escape, she
walked quickly up the side lane leading to the garden door
of Saltasche's residence.

She found the entrance without difficulty : a green door
half hidden in the ivy, which grew luxuriantly all over the
walls, and formed a winter shelter for innumerable birds.
As she shut the door behind her, a couple of the feathered
inhabitants awakened, fluttered out helplessly, for a
moment, in the darkness, but quickly returned to their
resting-place. There was not a creature in the grounds,
and the house could not be seen for the evergreen trees
and shrubs of the plantation. The green-houses had a
cold, ghostly look in the moonlight ; and a tiny breeze
swept the dead leaves on the hedges with a shadowy
rustle. She felt uncertain which way she should take, and
she stood still for a moment, fancying that some sound
might guide her to the house. She heard none ; and as
she looked around, her eyes fell on a rustic seat under an
ash tree, whose long dry stems swept the ground. The
whim entered her head to seat herself there for a few
minutes. It was opposite the door, and there was every
probability that some of the people of the house would
pass. So she picked her way across the turf, and sat down
to rest under the weeping ash. It was not cold—the night
was only refreshingly cool ; and everything round was
clear and distinct as in the daylight. She threw back her
hood, and let the breeze play on her brow, heated still, and
drew long breaths of the night air. She leaned back in
the seat, and recalled the concert-room she had just
quitted, and the applause she had won. A vision of
another concert-room, and another concert—that for which

she was always preparing, in the theatre of Rio—rose before her mind's eye. One more year, and she would be ready. If she could only get to Paris, to study a little under the great masters there! How these creatures applauded! but they were no test; and her lip curled scornfully. She longed to try her powers among the acknowledged stars of the musical world.

"Nearly as well as Lady who? That woman was talking of some player." She thought over the names of all the musicians she knew. She surpassed all the private ones she had ever met; but her experience was limited—as limited as her ambition was boundless. Now she heard steps in the lane without; in a moment the latchet clicked, and the unmistakable figure of Mr. Saltasche presented itself at the door. She never moved, in the hope that he would pass on unheeding. Not so: he perceived her almost instantaneously, and crossed the grass.

"How imprudent of you! I half feared you would do this. Why not have gone into the house?" He seated himself beside her. "Every one is speaking of you. Your playing is the most wonderful ever heard; and I have been credited with bringing over a pupil of Rubinstein or Von Bülow."

"What! do they not know who I am?" And she turned sharp questioning eyes upon him. "Is it possible? I thought from the manner of those ladies——"

She had betrayed herself; and he was quick to seize his opportunity.

"What could you think? They don't know you at all. And moreover, they need never. Mrs. Grey——"

"Ah! then *you* know my history," she cried impulsively. "Mrs. Grey has told you all. Be it so, then!" And she rose to go: indignant and angry. All her blood revolted at the idea that the history of her early years was in the mouths of the women whose cold, envious eyes she now saw bent in scorn upon her. She was nervous and sensitive to a degree. She inherited, with her French blood, a morbid dread of ridicule, among other less questionable endowments; and the knowledge of her own fatal mistake

was an ever-present torment to her. To get away from it
was her dream—the hope of her life. Everything that
could remind her of it she banished out of sight ; and yet
it seemed to dog her footsteps everywhere. She bitterly
regretted having yielded to the entreaties of Saltasche and
Mrs. Grey, and vowed in her own mind that she never
would see either of them again.

"Dear Mrs. Poignarde, listen to me for one moment.
You mistake ; you do indeed wrong me. See : let me
explain."

He took her hand entreatingly ; and she, but with a bad
grace, consented to sit down. Watching her closely, he
went on.

"You cannot have imagined me capable of intruding
without a particular motive into your affairs. You blame
Mrs. Grey wrongly—believe me. I do know your history,
but not from her. Your husband and I have had business
relations together ; and long before I had seen you I had
learned from his connections in London Captain Poignarde's
history. It was necessary. Mrs. Grey has said—will say
—nothing. Believe me, Mrs. Poignarde, you attach a
foolish importance to mere trifles."

She did not reply. Her face was pale, and a strange
contracted look came about her mouth. As he finished,
she raised her eyes and looked at him, with a wondering,
mournful gaze.

"Trifles !—mere trifles ! Ah ! that is all you know."

She clasped her hands together, and a shudder passed
over her frame. The momentary weakness passed away ;
and she rose again to her feet, possessed now of but one
idea—to make her escape, and never return. He, reading
every thought, stood before her and barred the way.

"I tell you, Mrs. Poignarde, I know all,—all ; believe
me, for Heaven's sake ! I am indeed your truest friend.
Do you imagine me ignorant of your sufferings, your aspirations ? I can help you, and I will. Let me."

She looked at him in amazement and distrust, and a
wild hope shining in her eyes.

"Listen," Saltasche went on rapidly. "Your husband

is on the brink of ruin. What are you to do when the
crash comes? I know what you would do; but without
assistance you are powerless. Is it not so? You have no
friends, and his people take part against you?"

A mute gesture of despairing assent was the reply.

"Trust to me, Mrs. Poignarde; let me be your friend,
your guide. We are of the same race; my father was a
Brazilian. I will stand by you if you will only trust me,
believe in me. A new life will open its doors to you, and
all the past will be blotted out. Adelaide, speak!"

She did not reply, but she did not try to remove her
hands from his grasp. Everything had become dark suddenly, and she felt a cold chill creep over her. The bare
arms of the trees tossed menacingly in the breeze, and the
rustle of the evergreens seemed so loud as to drown his
words. He picked up her hooded cloak, and wrapped it
round her. His hands were trembling, and his eyes met
hers with a troubled, wild look: taking her hand, he placed
it in his arm, and they walked a few steps onward, neither
knowing where, in silence. He stopped suddenly, and
faced her.

"Before returning I must know your decision. Will
you accept my offer? Adelaide, poor child, will you refuse
to let me help you? Look at me, Adelaide! Say only
one word."

She placed her hand, cold and trembling, in his; and
the two stood for a' moment immovable and silent under
the shadow of the beeches. Saltasche could not speak;
his face was as pale as hers, and his heart beat so as almost
to choke him. He drew her hand again beneath his arm,
and holding it still, they reached the green gate.

"I must go back: I shall be missed. And do you
return to the dressing-room, to the fireside there. If you
do not wish to play again, you need not. It must be
quite time I were back. You are content now? you
accept my guidance?" And he looked into her beautiful
eyes eagerly and triumphantly.

"Yes, I am content, if you will help me—to go home."

He raised her fingers to his lips, and pressing a kiss on

them, left her abruptly and returned to the front hall.
He gave his coat and hat to a servant of his own who was
standing at the main door; and entering quietly and unobserved, joined a knot of talkers at the side for a moment
or two. By degrees he made his way up to the top, and
to his own seat near Lord Brayhead.

"You have been away, Mr. Saltasche,—out?" said some
one, inquisitively.

"I have," he answered, composedly. "I was called
away a little while ago. I see I didn't lose much time,
though. You have not told me how you liked the *pianiste*,
ladies."

He was instantly overwhelmed with opinions.

"Peculiar-looking little person—quite foreign style.
Foreign style of playing, too," said Mrs. de Lancier, meaning thereby to convey a depreciation.

"So *very* good-natured; gives any amount of *encores*,"
sneered another, who, had the musician refused *encores*,
would have declared her to have but a limited stock.

"Is she professional?" inquired the noble patron.

"Dear, no! an officer's wife, and belonging to a noble
Brazilian family. Noble, I assure you. She was at one
time reputed heiress to a couple of millions!"

So Mr. Saltasche enhanced the rarity of his black swan.
The gentlemen were less critical, and their admiration was
hearty and sincere. Several pressed for introductions;
but he refused them, saying that Mrs. Poignarde had
declined positively—in fact, had stipulated that she was
not to have her privacy intruded upon. She in fact
declined all society. So he managed to put them off.
Everything went off well. Lord Brayhead expressed himself delighted with the performance; and Saltasche, after
accompanying his friends to the railway station, to see
them off by the last train, returned home feeling that he
had accomplished a good evening's work. The Fates had
surely been propitious to him; and he trusted that, now
the foundations of his plans were so well laid, no awkward
hindrance would intervene to frustrate their success.

He lay for an hour in a comfortable easy-chair by his

dressing-room fire, dreaming over his interview in the pleasure-grounds with Mrs. Poignarde. Rousing himself at last, he was about to go to bed, when a ring at the front door startled him. He guessed its import, and hurried down. At the door stood his confidential clerk Johns.

"A telegram, sir; and delayed by some accident nearly two hours. I brought it on, for fear anything might be wrong."

Saltasche had mastered its contents before the clerk had finished speaking. They ran as follows,—the message being from Dicky Davoren at Peatstown:—

"Poll declared. Hogan eight fifty-seven, Wyldoates two thirty-one. Everything right. Coming up to-morrow."

CHAPTER XXII.

" O sacred hunger of ambitious mindes,
  And impotent desire of men to raine !
  Whom neither dread of God, that devils bindes,
  Nor lawes of men, that common weales containe,
  Nor bandes of nature, that wilde beastes restraine,
  Can keep from outrage and from doing wrong,
  Where they may hope a kingdom to obtaine."

The Faerie Queene.

IT was with a strange feeling of elation and pride that
Hogan leaped from the railway carriage at Kingsbridge, to
receive the greetings and congratulations of his friends,
who, headed by the Bishop, were drawn up in waiting on
the platform. There was a larger number of them than
he had expected ; indeed, a great many who before had
ranked as mere acquaintance had lately enrolled themselves
among the ranks of his best sympathisers.

Every one had been taken by surprise ; and the un-
expected exaltation of the young barrister was ascribed by
most to the discrimination of the constituents, who so
seldom alight on the wrong man or pass over deserving
merit. The mystic letters which Mr. Hogan had now
appended to his name stand for a great deal more than is
commonly supposed. The politicians in general were
delighted—taking his return as a proof of the depth and
sincerity of the national feeling ; and sundry well-known
and tried warriors set to burnishing their armour for an
assault on the Parliamentary fortress on the very first
opportunity—shrewdly judging that if a nobody like Hogan
had won his spurs thus easily, there must be golden prizes
to be had for the trying.

The Bishop and some other influential friends had written to the candidate, offering to get up a public dinner—a banquet, in short—as a token of affection and esteem; but this had been declined by our hero, whose intention it was to get to London immediately, and to work. Mr. Saltasche and Lord Brayhead were positively waiting for his parliamentary services; and the railway bill was in actual danger. So, on the plea of want of time, he nipped the project in the bud.

Dicky and the Muldoons, father and son, dined quietly with the member at the Shelbourne. The party broke up early; the Muldoons being the first to leave. Dicky took himself home to Green Lanes, and the Bishop and his nephew were left alone.

"Well, John," said his lordship gravely; "now, can you give me any idea of the bill?"

"I cannot, sir; it will be heavy,—far heavier than I thought. Although some expenses were *nil*, the very ones I least expected—for instance, your old friend Father Corkran——"

"Ay; he went against you, I know."

"Yes, utterly. Had it been any other time, and only for the extraordinary misconduct of the landlord, and this agitation, I'd have been swamped. As it is, the Ballot accounts for a good deal. One of the priests worked very hard for me."

"One, hey?—who?"

"Father John Desmond, the curate of Ballinagad. The parish priest was dead against me—frightful man: won nearly ten pounds off me at cards, and denounced me the Sunday after. The Bishop was opposed to me, I think."

"Ah! 'Twas hardly worth his while to interfere; you see, it's not long now you'll be in, for all the money and the trouble." And his lordship groaned discontentedly.

"No matter, sir, no matter;" and Hogan shook his head determinedly. "I go to London on Tuesday, to take my seat. I don't know when I'll be back. Let me see. I must run to and fro a good deal. I don't want to let go my practice altogether, you know."

Y

"Ah! John, I wish you had stuck to the practice a little longer; it's the surest card—it is indeed."

"Yes, sir, I know that; however, 'nothing venture, nothing win.' I should be a thundering fool not to take the ball at the hop. There is not a doubt on my mind that I'll be re-elected. No, no, my lord! the Liberal Government is rooted as no Government ever was before in the country. Why, it is ridiculous, on the face of things, to imagine they could ever be upset. They monopolise all the talent of the century—all the learning. There are only a couple of Conservative papers in London: that is very significant, sir."

"As for talent and learning, that is trash—mere trash. It's votes that does it. To every *talented* voter, how many fools have you? And as for newspapers, divel a bit I ever believed in newspapers—never. And another thing the Liberals have done, with extending the franchise here. Mark you this. Everybody has it, and so nobody values it; the better classes don't care for the trouble of voting: it is no *class privilege* now, as it was once upon a time; so the power is passing into the hands of the rabble—that is, comparatively speaking I call them rabble."

"That will be only temporary,—must be, sir. We have the example of New York before us in that matter; and, after all, as Saltasche said the other day, the utterances of this country in politics are scarcely responsible yet. You must not forget that we are young,—yes, sir, young, in political life—inexperienced." And Hogan drank off his glass of wine with the air of one who has decided everything.

The Bishop sighed gently, and shook his head with a little gesture which signified plainly that, while yielding to the persuasive tongue of his nephew, he reserved his own convictions on the subject.

The next day, in Sackville Street, Hogan met, at the corner of a street leading to one of the chief railway stations, Miss Davoren and her brother, walking together towards the bridge. He had a spare half-hour, he found, on consulting his watch; so he accosted them, and all three walked on together.

"I ought to congratulate you, Mr. Hogan," said Nellie, looking up almost shyly at him. She felt the least bit in awe of him now. "You had a wonderful triumph."

"Yes. I am astonished at myself. I ascribe it to luck, and to my friends—and assistants," he added laughingly to Dicky.

That young gentleman had the grace to blush a little.

"There wasn't any need,—there wasn't, positively. They're all gone mad on this Home Rule."

Dicky had been talking to the aristocratic Mr. Orpen in the train that morning, and his views on Home Rule had undergone considerable modification at the hands of that mentor.

"Gone mad! Tut, tut! you mustn't speak disrespectfully of my standard, my dear fellow!"

Dicky only laughed, and turned off short into the college gates, which they had reached. Hogan had an appointment with Saltasche in the Green; but it wanted nearly twenty minutes of the time, and he thought to himself that he could not do better than spend the interval in the company of Miss Nellie, whom he never remembered to have seen looking more beautiful.

"In what direction are you going, Miss Davoren?"

"Fitzgerald Place: to Miss O'Hegarty's."

"Ah! the lady I met at your house some time ago. Do you know, I had been thinking of running out on Monday in that direction again."

She only looked at him, and said hesitatingly, "Yes."

"Yes," he repeated. "Did we not agree I was to come and tell you all my adventures: eh?"

Nellie did not even look up this time; but her cheeks flushed a little. He watched her well.

"You wouldn't care to hear about it all, though?"

"On Monday," she replied, with a little tremor, "we shall not be at home. Dicky and I have to go to a place beyond the Park, to pay a visit which it is impossible to put off."

"Oh me!—and Tuesday I go to London. Is it not too bad, now? Let me see;" and he stood still, as if to turn back.

Nellie looked up hastily, as she turned, to see if there
were any trace of displeasure or misapprehension of her
meaning in his face. In reality he was thinking that it
was as well she had declined his visit ; he was pressed for
time. After all, though he knew he was in love with her,
it was safe to be prudent. So, conscious of having the
advantage, he held out his hand.

" It may not be good-bye ; but, wish me well, won't
you ?"

He was cold-hearted by habit, if not by nature, and
fenced round with caution and foresight ; but there was
something in the beautiful eyes which met his now that
put calculation to flight, and it was with a very different
feeling that he murmured, as he pressed her hand,—

" Good-bye, and God bless you : you will hear from me
soon."

Then he turned abruptly, and walked away down the
street as fast as possible, heedless of everything and every
one he passed, and seeing only her face and the bright
transformation that came over it as he spoke to her. He
almost wished he had remained a moment longer. It
might be a long time ere they met again ; and he fell into
a gloomy train of undefined foreboding most unusual to
him. What reason there was for it he could not have told ;
but certainly he was not in his customary equable, sanguine
mood. The reaction after the excitement and over-work
of the last month had, no doubt, set in ; and he felt, in
spite of himself, languid and depressed. The day was
heavy, no sun illumined the long rows of sombre tall houses,
and a light gray fog hung over the trees in the College
Park. It made him think of Peatstown, and his weary
drive through the hills. Mud, cold, wet, and desolation ;
these four words summed up his principal impressions of
the place. He recalled Barney Shane's dwelling on the
hillside with a shiver of disgust. What an experience, to
have passed a night in such a hovel ! Let them say what
they would, he considered he had earned his prize.

Hardship of any kind was antipathetic to Hogan's
nature. That which was soft and easy in life he clung to.

He could work hard ; but if he did, it was not as men do who work for the love of working and for the love of their calling. He worked hard that he might the sooner play. There was a strong tinge of the peasant nature underlying all his polish : the ingrained hatred of work, the fatalistic indifference engendered by a social and religious system of long and complicated standing, the curious reverence and love of power and authority peculiar to those who have been oppressed. All this old leaven worked under the super-imposed layer of training and culture. On the maternal side he had inherited good blood, or the legend of it ; whereas the Hogans had neglected to preserve their family record. He had his cleverness from his mother ; and, as often happens when such is the case, his mind ran in rather a feminine mould. There were some parts of his character, at all events, which were not what the world calls manly.

He reached Saltasche's office nearly ten minutes late, and sauntered up the stairs with a sort of defiant leisureliness. He thought he would take a slightly independent tone with his friend now. Just as he reached the door, a man running downstairs from an office on an upper story hailed him.

"Hollo ! that you ? Mr. Hogan, allow me to congratulate you, my dear fellow !" And the gentleman, whom indeed he hardly knew, shook his hand violently.

He was a noisy, chattering attorney of the money-lending class, who knew everybody and everybody's business, and who was a most notorious liar.

"Thank you, Stamps ! Can't stay a minute," returned the member carelessly.

Stamps seemed gratified with this much notice, and darted upon the handle of the door to open it for Hogan. The member passed in, nodding his acknowledgment. Slight as the incident was, it was nevertheless a tribute to his new dignity, and sufficed to put him in good humour again. He advanced to the fire, apologising to Saltasche for his delay. There was the least shade of consequence in his tone, which his friend's fine observation did not miss. He laughed pleasantly, and pointed to a chair opposite.

" You got a stunning majority, didn't you ?   No fear of a petition, eh ? "

" Not a whit.   They couldn't do it.   Anyhow, it would not be worth while wasting powder on.   They'll wait until I try it again.   I take my seat on Tuesday evening."

" You do ?   Do you know anybody in London ? "

"Scarcely.   I have been promised letters to people there."

The Bishop, indeed, was procuring him letters of introduction to sundry Irish Catholics in London—people whom Hogan ungraciously vowed never to go near.

" I'll see about that.   Hem ! Mrs. Bursford and her daughter are going over for the season.   You will do well to call upon them.   Mrs. Bursford has a relative in the present Government.   I'll find out their address and send it to you."

Hogan murmured his thanks.   He was astonished at this intelligence ; and vainly tried to recall some foreshadowing of it in his conversation with Miss Diana.

" Now, of course," went on Saltasche, "those prospectuses can be issued.   I have two or three here waiting your name ; and you will be able to save me many trips to London about getting the slate companies floated, and this mad old fool's railway company too.   He'll ruin himself at that yet.   By-the-bye, there's something nice to be made on the Patagonian Loan.   The stock is now at ten shillings ; but on Thursday it will be stated that the United States have offered to buy Patagonia.   So I am wired from Washington.   You can imagine how that will start the prices.   You will be in London on Wednesday.   Stier and Bruen, of Cole Alley, Mincing Lane, do most of my commissions.   Suppose you give them a call ?   I'll write in the meantime to them about you."

" Very kind of you indeed ; but there's a little hindrance in the way.   I have no money."

"What ! ten shillings even ? "

" Not a *sou !*   It's very tempting, though."

" It's a sure thing.   You see, all they want from you would be a deposit for cover, in case——; but in this instance, except as a form, that would not be necessary. I introduce you. You understand me."

But the barrister had, in fact, never given his attention to the Stock Exchange science. So Mr. Saltasche was obliged to explain the modern system of betting on the differences, or "selling short," as the process is called in the land of its birth.

Hogan was dazzled by the talk of his companion. That transactions involving millions could be carried on by men who were comparatively penniless, seemed an absurd impossibility. Saltasche, however, was able to give him chapter and verse for his assertions, and told him the names of many plutocrats, with the history of their successful operations.

Then they adjourned to lunch, and a bottle of champagne threw an additional tinge of rose-colour over everything. Hogan quitted his friend in a state of bodily and mental exhilaration more unusual to him still than the fit of blues under which he had laboured in the forenoon.

CHAPTER XXIII.

" But by record of antique times I find
That wemen wont in warres to bear most sway,
And to all great exploites themselves inclined
Of which they still the girlond bore away ;
Till envious men, fearing their rules decay,
Gan coin straight lawes to curb their liberty.
Yet sith they warlike arms have laid away,
They have excelled in arts and pollicy,
That now we foolish men that prayse gin eke t'envy."

Faerie Queene.

DIANA BURSFORD determined to go to London as soon as she heard of Mr. Hogan's success at Peatstown. She had indeed been considering the desirability of such a move for some time previous to that event. The family friend, Mr. Saltasche, having told her mother that his *protégé* was likely to be in Parliament ere long, Miss Bursford kept the contingency in her mind's eye. London was decidedly the best ground of operations ; and, after all, leaving Dublin in the middle of the season was no great hardship—to her at least. For her mother, who loved her native city, and detested every place else except Florence, it would certainly be a grievance. But the old lady was used to travelling ; it was by no means the first time they had pursued an eligible *parti* across the water ; indeed, their cousins, the Bragintons, had a story to the effect that Diana had followed a man to Naples, and that he only escaped her by putting to sea in a friend's yacht.

She wondered, as she planned the expedition one day at her toilette, what romantic legend these amiable people would concoct. She was certain they had not a glimmering of idea that there was a man in the case this time. This season, and indeed for a good many seasons before it, her name had not been coupled with that of any one; so that they would have a difficulty in finding a groundwork on which to base their edifice of fiction.

As for arrangements, the house could be shut up,—which was a pity, certainly, at the time of year when houses were most in demand. What could be done with it? The new lace curtains only a month put up, and everything in such order! Miss Bursford laid down her hairbrushes, and began to think that she had heard that the O'Gorman Mulcahy and his family were in furnished lodgings in Clare Street, and that they were looking for a house. What a delightful arrangement to offer theirs! The Mulcahys were paying thirty guineas a month, and had all their own servants. She was quite certain her mother would be glad to get them to take her establishment off her hands. Then she put the finishing touch to her attire, and sailed leisurely down to luncheon. She found her mother in the dining-room, waiting for her; and the two ladies sat down together. When both had been helped to mutton broth, Diana broke the silence, saying, deliberately and coldly,—

"We were speaking of London, mamma; if we go we had better go soon."

She had broached her intention for the first time the previous day at breakfast, and it had not been alluded to since.

Mrs. Bursford paused in the act of raising her spoon to her lips, and breathed a sort of little resigned sigh.

"To London? Well, yes; I suppose so, indeed. But really, Diana, when you consider the young——"

"I know, mamma," her daughter cut her short, with a tone and expression which Mrs. Bursford had long learned to know. "What I wanted to say to you was this: the house is to be shut up, is it not?"

"Of course it will have to be shut up. What else can be done in the middle of the season? And the new lace curtains and the drawing-room carpets. What good have we had of it, after all the trouble ?" And Mrs. Bursford took an aggrieved expression, nearly lachrymose.

" Don't you think the O'Gorman Mulcahys would take it ? They are paying thirty guineas a month for three rooms in Clare Street ; and they have not place for their servants : they have to lodge them elsewhere. It would save us a great deal of trouble."

" I don't like the idea at all of letting my house. Miss O'Hegarty never would allow any one into her house that way ; she always shuts it up when she goes away, no matter for how long."

" Stuff, mamma ! Everybody does that sort of thing nowadays. The Helys have let their place in Carlow for the shooting season repeatedly. The Hepenstalls are trying to let their house in the Green for a year. Lord Brayhead, if you want an example now, has let his London house in Curzon Street to Mr. Wickers, the member for Lincoln, for the London season only."

" Let his London house, has he ? The Bragintons will be so furious,—not that that makes much matter, one way or another."

" Now that we have settled to go, we may as well go and see the Mulcahys about it."

" I don't like the idea of the Mulcahys at all. They are so careless and dirty, and their Connaught servants are so destructive. I forget what they had to pay in their last lodgings for mischief ; but it was really something terrible."

" Well, tell them about it, and send them to a house agent to deal with. Then they're responsible for every-thing they injure."

" House agents require such a heavy fee—five per cent."

" That wouldn't come to more than two or three pounds ; and the Mulcahys will do more than that much mischief."

" Ah, no, Diana ! it looks some way too business-like,— and with friends too, now."

" Please yourself, mamma. But they can have the house by this day week, you know."

" By this day week ?" Mrs. Bursford groaned as she finished her mutton broth.

She made no audible objection, though ; for between her and her daughter there had been of late years a tacit agreement that Diana was to lead in these arrangements. It saved the old lady a great deal of annoyance afterwards, if it did entail present trouble and fatigue ; for if matters turned out as Mrs. Bursford had got into the way of expecting them to turn out, Diana could not blame her. And Diana's temper, however well managed and kept in hand, was latterly becoming a trial.

" Dermot Blake is coming home, Miss O'Hegarty was telling me, from New York; he's there now. She does not know when."

" Yes," said Diana. " He has been in China and San Francisco, and—all round the world. He always was a queer creature ! "

"She think's it likely he'll marry and settle now,—he's thirty-five." Mrs. Bursford as she said this looked at Diana in a sort of exploring way over the rim of her tumbler of water, as if to see whether the information took any effect on her.

But Diana, though fully conscious of her drift, hardly even seemed to hear. Ten years ago, Dermont Blake and she had had a passage of arms together ; and she knew perfectly that she had no hopes whatever in that quarter. Her mother knew of this, too ; and it vexed Diana that she should have forgotten, or should act and speak as if she had forgotten it. But Mrs. Bursford was always expecting miracles. She knew some woman whose lover, having thrown her over and gone off to Timbuctoo, came back after twenty years enormously rich, and married her there and then ; and it would have seemed to her almost the natural order of things that Dermot Blake and Diana should marry in the same way.

Diana had finished, and was thoughtfully smoothing the salt with the spoon. She was a little vexed with her mother ; and if she had had time and leisure to think over the grievance, it would have led to one of their not unusual scenes. She had other food for thought, however; for she was meditating taking some new dresses with her. It was cheaper to get them in Dublin, and she recollected a letter from a friend in London, giving some information as to the newest fashions and cuts, which she considered much more explicit and satisfactory than the engravings in *Punch*,—which, indeed, presented a finished whole, but left details and ways and means over-much to the imagination..

"We must go round to the milliner's, too, this afternoon, when we have settled with the Mulcahys, mamma; I want a couple, at least, of new dresses. I'll get a bonnet when we can go to Madame Tripotte's."

"Dresses! why, Diana!"—and now Mrs. Bursford's voice had a ring of real sharpness and authority in it,— "it's impossible. Pray consider what you have had this year already,—and our journey. I cannot do it."

"The fact is, mamma, I suppose you have been sending money to Jervis again."

Then there ensued a scene, and Diana came off victorious.

Jervis was Mrs. Bursford's youngest son, younger than Diana, and a ne'er-do-well; living somewhere,—nobody knew where, and, save his mother, nobody caring. Hopelessly idle and untrustworthy—and clever. He could act well; but manager after manager dismissed him for insubordination and unsteadiness. He could play the piano and sing; so he picked up a queer livelihood in music halls, betting and billiard-rooms, and such places; doing odd jobs for odd people, and liked by every one. He had all sorts of accomplishments, and not one single capability. He was always his mother's darling, and the terror of Diana's life; she fancied that any day Jervis might turn up and demand to live with them. Indeed, he had done that already. One winter that Mrs. Bursford was at Boulogne, the amiable Jervis dropped in with a carpet bag, and remained until his behaviour forced his mother and sister to fly the place. Just at present he was at Monaco; where Diana fervently hoped he might be induced to remain until her

London visit was over; and where his mother was quite reconciled to have him stay, because Monaco was such a nice place for his delicate chest in this severe season.

When their dispute was over, and Diana had fumed and threatened until her mother had been brought to promise that she should have whatever she needed, and to give a sort of undertaking that Jervis was to be left to his own resources for some time to come,—an undertaking which Diana well knew was not to be depended on,—the ladies sallied out on their double mission; which, ere the day was done, was accomplished to the satisfaction of one of them at least.

CHAPTER XXIV

DICKY DAVOREN, on the day after his return from Peatstown, when he left his sister and Mr. Hogan at the front gate
of the college, dashed straight up to the rooms of his friend
Gagan. Him he found sitting in consultation with Orpen ;
and both of them appeared delighted to see him,—Mr.
Orpen especially was most cordial.

"Dav., old boy!" he exclaimed, "how are you ? I'm
glad you've got back all safe. How have you got along
ever since ?"

"Blooming! Morrow, Gagan; hollo! 'such an eye as
you have! Who knocked up against you ?"

Mr. Gagan's eye had a suggestive green and yellow
tinge all round it; he put up his fingers and stroked it
tenderly.

"One of those 'bom'nable Corporation lamp-posts. Put
everywhere but where they're wantin'; so they are. And
I, never expecting it, fell foul of one of them as I was
coming home from a 'small and early' in Ramines'. It's
a shame, it is!"

"So it is," assented Orpen; "he was promenading round
one special lamp-post for two hours,—and that's a memento
of the happy meeting. Was it a policeman severed you
from the object of your affections, Gagan ?"

"None of your chaff! Davoren, what were you doing ?"

"Didn't I tell you! Hogan—you know him—was
standing for Peatstown, and he gave me a sub-sheriffship ;
worth a nice pile of money, let alone the fun."

"Fifteen guineas. I had one last winter," observed
Orpen, thoughtfully.

" Have you got the money yet, Dick ?" asked Gagan.

" No; not yet. What have you been at since ?"

Both gentlemen grinned, and looked at each other.

" We hav'n't exactly been tearing our hair in sackloth and ashes for your departure. No; ha! ha! I'm cleaned out; dead beat. So's Tad. So's Mahoney. So is *not* Orpen."

" Why, Gagan, your Ulster is there yet. And—no, the books are gone!"

" 'The shelves are still there; but the books, they are gone," sang Gagan, parodying Moore. " I'm going over to bank the coat as soon as it's dark. Dick, will you come in to-night till we have a small game ? Grey is coming; and we'll go to Wilding's rooms. He has a piano, and we'll have a musical tea."

" And a highly moral and restricted rubber," added Orpen, winking to Gagan. " Come on, now; there's one striking, and we'll be late for moral philosophy."

As they went downstairs Dicky asked where was Mahoney Quain.

" He'll be in to-night. I say," said Orpen, confidentially, " Mahoney's going it just now with a pretty housemaid of his mother's. I met him walking with her the other night—in Summer Hill. By Jove, he is—h'm;" and Orpen winked and grinned suggestively.

" You don't say so ?"

" Yes, I do. That fellow is fool enough for anything— ass!" And Mr. Orpen straightened himself up with a look of superior wisdom that greatly impressed his companion.

" What style of a looking girl is she, now ?" asked Dicky, with a would-be knowing air.

" Oh—um!" said Orpen, as if he found a difficulty in selecting terms which would accurately describe a fascinating housemaid,—" a lively, pretty-faced stump of a girl."

" Not genteel, even, I suppose ?" said Dicky, critically.

Orpen looked at him with an expression of mild contempt, and continued without otherwise seeming to hear.

" She writes letters to Mahoney; copies them off from

a Polite Letter-Writer—invitations to balls, dinners, everything, straight out,—fact, for I've seen 'em. Sh! here we
are, now. Last one he got from her was a letter of advice
about a promissory note,—begad, yes."

The lecture over, Mr. Orpen linked his arm under his
young friend's and carried him off to a billiard-room
situated close to the college, in a by-street. Under the
billiard-room there was a bar, where anything to drink
could be had at public-house prices.

Dicky had not been in a billiard-room to play before.
He had several times accompanied his father to a billiard-
room on the other side of town; an establishment of much
better standing than this, and where he had seen some fine
players. He had never had a cue in his hand before, and
felt quite ashamed when he saw Orpen, having taken off
his coat, chalk the end of his cue in the most natural way
possible. Orpen and the marker, a red-nosed, dirty man,
played a game first. They offered Dicky the mace to try
a stroke or two with, as a beginner; but he declined
rather sulkily. It was stupid enough, sitting on a raised
form by the wall looking at them; and he began to think
what he should do. Presently a thought struck him.

"I'll have a drink, Orpen—hey? What will you have?"

"I'll get it, sir; in a minute, sir," said the marker,
who seemed to be imbued with new life on hearing this
proposal.

He left the room; and Orpen, coming over to where
Dicky was lounging, said, in a half whisper,—

"When he comes up with it—ah—tell him to go and
get one for himself; it's the way in this sort of place, you
know."

Dicky despatched the willing Mercury this time on a
still more grateful errand; and when he returned, affairs
wore a very different aspect. The marker, having knocked
the balls into position, called Dicky over.

"Now, sir; this is a very nice stroke, sir. What do
you think you'd do in my position, sir?"

"Why, go in between, and pocket that red ball."

"Precisely, sir. Why, you couldn't have settled it more

accurately if you were—'scuse me, sir—an old hand.
Would you like to try the stroke, sir? Take my cue."

Dicky knocked the red ball into the pocket with ease.
The marker was loud in his praises. Such steadiness of
hand—fine eye! The gentleman only required a little
practice to become a bang-up billiard player. After a
while Dicky found himself obliged to stand treat again;
and when the time came to go, he found he had actually
won a couple of shillings from Orpen—who, most un-
accountably, though he could hold his own against the
marker, was obliged to confess himself unable to stand
against some of the tyro's strokes. They said they would
call again soon; and the marker, a most good-natured
poor fellow, offered to give the strange gentleman the use
of the table any time he liked to drop in, when there was
nobody using it, for a little practice.

Dicky stepped out into the ill-smelling lane feeling in the
highest good humour with himself. It was not every one
that developed a talent for billiards; he knew that very
well, without the marker telling him. Mahoney Quain
could not hold a cue in his hand. Lots of fellows could
never strike with the right degree of force. Mahoney was
unrivalled at football and racing and wrestling, but he
never did anything, except betting on the game, at billiards.
Tad and Gagan were no good either,—not a bit. When
they got to the corner of the lane, where it debouches into
Brunswick Street, Orpen, who had no fancy for being seen,
was for drawing back cautiously until a group of people
just passing had gone; but Dicky, heedless of the pull at
his sleeve, blundered on, and his companion had no choice
but to keep up with him.

"What hurry are you in—you fool you! Couldn't you
have waited an instant to let those Smyths go by, eh?"

"Eh?" repeated Dicky, quite unconsciously, and turning
in surprise. The expression of Orpen's face explained
what was wrong. And all in one minute he became aware
of the reasons why they should not be seen. For the first
time he realised the exact significance of what he had been
doing. Gambling and drinking! And that, too, in broad

z

daylight, in a low public-house, when he ought to have been reading for his grinder. A frightened look came into his eyes, and a sort of idea rose to his mind of atonement —of remaining at home that evening, instead of going to Wilding's rooms.

"I must go to the train. Orpen, good-bye," he said.

"I'll see you to-night ?"

"Well, I think not ; I think I'll have to stay at home. I've lost all this afternoon, you see, and old Chute——"

"Pshaw! what a flat you are. Why, Wilding invited you specially. Every one will be there. Are you afraid, young one ?"

He saw what was passing in Dicky's mind, and he determined to reassert his mastery at once.

"Afraid! no, I'm not." Dicky resented his mentor's tone. "By-the-bye, too, I cannot come to-night. I forgot entirely—I'm obliged to remain at home, positively : very sorry."

His tone was perfectly sincere ; and Orpen thought it better not to press the point. He was sure that the next evening would do quite as well. He knew with whom he had to deal, and that Dicky's conceit and desire to be thought a man by his new friends, all of whom were older than himself (Orpen was twenty), would soon bring him back if he had any notion of breaking with them. He was a fish that required a little playing ; and Mr. Orpen's practised hand could do that patiently and well until the time came to gaff, and land him high and dry.

CHAPTER XXV

HOGAN'S affairs seemed almost to settle themselves, so smooth and clear had the path been laid down for him. He had called, on the day after his arrival in London,— the first day of his Parliamentary career; for he had only taken the oaths, and his seat among the Liberal members, the night before—on the stockbrokers in Cole Alley, and had been received with great courtesy as the friend of Mr. Saltasche. Mr. Stier, the senior member of the firm, had shaken hands very warmly with him. He was a Hamburger, with a broad fair face and yellow hair and eyebrows; and spoke with a very elaborate carefulness as to accent and grammar. Bruen, the other partner, had made all his money in California. He was a quiet man; silent of manner, and courteous, but very observant.

"And how is our friend Mr. Saltasche?" began the senior partner in a purring tone of voice. "Ah, we are always so glad to meet his acquaintances. You know Mr. Saltasche very well, Mr. Hogan?"

"Yes, very well—we are fast friends. He wrote to you?" Hogan wanted to get to business at once; but the Hamburger was not to be hurried.

"Ah! I have known him for years—years. In Vienna —he was once settled in Vienna—Prince Metternich was a very good friend of his; but, ah!" and Mr. Stier purred a sigh as he opened an enormous volume on his desk. "Bruen, too, knew him. Mr. Saltasche dealt enormously one while in Paris. He was splendidly settled there; and what friends he makes everywhere! Prince Gortschakoff, he says nobody knows everything like Mr. Saltasche; he

corresponds with him. And the ex-Emperor of the French,
—he, too, received Mr. Saltasche at the Tuileries; one
time, I am told, he could have married a princess. Yes,
indeed !"

"Why didn't he ?" answered Hogan, bewildered. He
knew the standing and wealth of the speaker, and because
of them he felt bound to believe him ; he had before heard
some wild talk of Mr. Saltasche's acquaintance with the
great ones of this earth, but had paid but scant attention
to it.

"Why did he not, you say, Mr. Hogan ? Well, my dear
sir, princesses are princesses ; but to plain business men
they are something more—they are white elephants. I
would not like a white elephant : should you, Mr. Hogan ?
Ah !"

The barrister laughed. "I must be away to my work.
Mr. Saltasche wrote to you, did he not ? And I have to
settle for the shares—the number I mean to take. What
are they to-day—the Patagonians, I mean ?"

"Patagonians—whew !" said Mr. Stier, raising his eyebrows in pleased surprise. "Bruen, where is that list ?"
His partner looked at the quotation as he handed it, and
then fixed his keen black eyes on Hogan.

"Ten—ten shillings : nearly the price of the paper
—ah !"

Two hundred was the number he had originally intended
to take, but some greed suddenly seized upon him ; he
wanted to grasp with both hands.

"I will take two hundred. Stay—make it four," he
added hastily : "that will be the full amount of this
cheque, two hundred pounds." He handed a cheque for
that amount, signed by Lord Brayhead, to Mr. Stier, who,
with his mouth drawn up as if he was going to whistle,
nodded his head as he looked at the writing.

"That is right,—quite right. Now look, Mr. Hogan,
will you touch these ?" And he handed over a sheet of
papers, blue, pink, and green ; lithographed chiefly, and
highly decorated and got up. Hogan glanced at them,
then at Mr. Stier, who was sitting up in a high desk

smiling amiably over his spectacles, and looking like nothing but a great yellow cat.

"Well, not to-day, thank you, Mr. Stier."

"Ah! I wish you would take some of those, Mr. Hogan. I wish you would, indeed. You see, everything Mr. Saltasche touches, it turns into gold."

"Luckily for Mr. Saltasche. I didn't know he had the gift of Midas." Hogan thought to himself that his friend's gift lay rather in his skill in watching other people's alchemy, and stepping in just at the moment the transformation began to work, and before the anxious operators became aware of it themselves.

Mr. Stier had never heard of Midas.

"He has gifts; yes, he has many gifts. But then, he is over-bold; sails very close to the wind sometimes, and sometimes he misses great *coups*,—ah, great *coups*" (pronounced "goups").

"Now, Mr. Hogan, we shall see you often in the City; is it not so? We shall work much together. Some new companies, directorships—ah, yes. This railroad, Bruen; Lord Brayhead's railway. You know the ground."

Then Mr. Bruen came forward, and Hogan was made to relate in a very short time all that he knew of the projected railway: the line of the country, the distance from the coast railway, the population of the district it was to traverse. Mr. Bruen asked questions very rapidly indeed, and his keen eyes seemed almost to anticipate the answers. Hogan found they knew everything about the Parliamentary business, and their object in questioning him was to see what chance of ultimate success the railway as a *bond-fide* venture might have. Mr. Stier uttered a great many "ah's" during the process; but from neither of the gentlemen could Hogan in the least divine his real opinion.

When the great subject of the newspaper was mooted, Mr. Bruen knew just the man to manage the business. His antecedents were not satisfactory; he had been dismissed from some half-dozen offices for every fault save incompetence. It would never do to have this man's name appear, so Hogan agreed to be nominal editor; and the

City article was to be written in Stier and Bruen's offices, under the supervision of those gentlemen. The City article, as it was nominally called, was in reality the leader. A well-written, spicy—political or Parliamentary, according to the season—essay certainly filled the first column or two. Then came the *résumé* of the financial operations of the day, the heads of which were collected, and handed to Hogan, who rough-hewed them into shape, and submitted the crude sketch to the real editor for the final touching-up. This financial article, which was ostensibly devoted to exposing the snares of the "long firms" and bubble companies with which the City swarms, was a perfect study of art. Saltasche and Co. were adepts in the science of throwing water on drowning rats. Peruvian Mines, Tammany Rings, Panama canals, and *hoc genus omne* were slashed with a bitterness and personality that never failed to attract readers. A sort of record was kept of the antecedents of prominent operators; and at a critical moment this *dossier* would be published and sent broadcast over the country. The effect on the public may be imagined. Of course the beautifully pure and disinterested motives of the *Beacon* were plain on the face of it. Cato, the censor, was a schoolboy compared to Saltasche, whose diatribes against manipulators were as edifying as any pulpit oracle. How the information was obtained, where the queer stories came from, nobody knew. The expenses of the *Beacon* were very large ; for in spite of a good circulation and plenty of advertisements, the returns were little more than the outlay. It was a peculiar style of paper altogether, and rather a novelty in British journalism. Mr. Saltasche might be credited with having invented it ; in reailty, that versatile gentleman had only borrowed from America one or two of the worst features of its Fourth Estate.

Hogan undertook the political article on condition that his name was not divulged. He had already had some practice in this line, and possessed a fine gift of literary imitation. He could reproduce the style of the *Times* or the *Telegraph* to perfection ; and whenever his cruse was exhausted, there was always some clever hack, who for a consideration would dash off a bright, gossipy sketch, to fall back upon. Thrice a week a serial story from the gifted pen of Mrs. Stryper appeared. Poetry, save of the Pasquin *genre*, was eschewed. There were no foreign correspondents. The Press and Reuter's agency supplied a broad-sheet of telegrams to compensate for this deficiency. There was a first-rate theatrical critic, who blamed and praised to order. There was no literary critic : that department was under the management of the printer's foreman, who reserved a half-column for hire, and who had charge of all advertisements.

CHAPTER XXVI

" La vraie poésie d'un tel amour, c'est la chanson de Printemps, du Cantique des Cantiques—poëme admirable, bien plus voluptueux que passionné. Hiems transiit, imber abiit et recessit. Vox turturis audita est in terra nostra. Surge amica mea et veni."

Ernest Renan.

IT was an April afternoon, soft and warm, for the east wind was gone. There had been showers all the morning, but now, between three and four, the sky was perfectly clear. Everything smelt sweet and strong after the rain. Rows of wall-flowers—brown, yellow, and streaked—gave out bitter-sweet odours; tufts of yellow primroses and double lavender primroses, tall pale narcissi bending their faces inwards, stiff-necked in their modesty, filled the air with most delicious incense. The apple trees had on charming pink robes; and the tomtits took a thousand impudent liberties among the blossoms, cutting somersaults, hanging head downwards, and celebrating the warm weather with uncountable antics.

Beyond the garden hedges the chestnuts had the faint transparent green shade to be seen for a few days only, just while the leaves are peeping out of their brown sheaths, and the flowers are hidden altogether in a tiny knot in the centre. From the wood came the voices of the nesting birds, shrill and clear, and echoing all round.

> " The ousel-cock, so black of hue,
>   With orange-tawny bill ;
>   The throstle, with his note so true ;
>   The wren, with little quill."

Had one the gift of Solomon, it were a pleasant employment on such a day to go as a spy among the feathered people, and learn what they all were saying. Just like ourselves, no doubt—making love and making mischief, and using their charming voices in various unpleasant ways. Solomon must have had but few illusions; and that which we rejoice in as a charming idyl, or madrigal, was to him but a dispute as to right of way, an ejectment suit, or a vulgar connubial quarrel.

There was a walk, hedged by espaliers, which ran across the garden, and divided the flower-beds and greensward from the plots of vegetables. It was edged with box, trimly cut; and between the box and the row of espalier apple trees were quantities of sweet-smelling spring-flowers and herbs. Up and down this walk, slowly, and often standing quite still, in earnest converse, walked our friend Nellie and Mr. Hogan.

Nellie was paler, and looked taller than when we last saw her; taller, because she had grown thin. Hogan also was changed; his eyes had lost the bright, confident expression of old, seemed both darker and larger than before, and the bluish lines under them told of hard work and late hours. At the same time he had improved. A certain priggishness of look, a little condescendingness of tone, and an over suavity of manner, had given way to a simplicity and naturalness, not unstudied, perhaps, but far more pleasant and becoming.

"I do think you might have written me a line, if only one, Miss Davoren. It was very hard of you," he was saying.

"You did not ask me, Mr. Hogan. And what could I have to tell you that would interest you?"

"Ah, you don't know that. My dear Miss Davoren, tell me, is it not pleasant to come out here into this delightful garden, after the close heat of a crowded room, among the flowers you are fond of—that you know and tend? Believe me, a letter from you here to me in London—stifled, and tired with work and talk, and disagreeable strange people—would be just as sweet and refreshing.

And I longed for such a letter, just as you might pine for this spot if you were—say, in prison."

Nellie did not answer; she only looked at him timidly and searchingly, as if fearing to find in his eyes the contradiction of his words.

"Is your life, then, so disagreeable ?" she asked, after a pause.

"Disagreeable ! no, decidedly not. One must take the rough and the smooth, you know ; and if a man goes into Parliament to work as I have done, he must not expect to have it all skittles and beer, as the saying is. It's too much of the one thing, though—the opposite of skittles and beer. There has been a deal of heavy night-work this session—private bills, and all that rubbish."

Amongst the rubbish, Lord Brayhead's scheme was included ; we may be sure it was not one whit nearer to being settled than ever.

"And the Home Rule question ? Have you been working at that ? Is it any nearer being settled ?"

He laughed and shook his head. "It is not even licked into shape yet ; and I'm not the man to do that. I wonder what my Peatstown friends are about ? There are a couple of gentlemen there who have their eyes upon me. One wants a farm, and the other wants a republic ; and if they don't get them by means of Home Rule,—which, by-the-bye, is to be got first,—ere two years are over, I am a doomed man."

"A pleasant prospect truly. Dicky has told me enough about Peatstown."

"How is my friend Dicky distinguishing himself in college ?"

"I don't know, indeed. Really, I hardly see him except at meal-times ; he might as well live there always. It is wonderful to me how he likes to be always away. I'd get tired soon of that perpetual amusement."

"Perpetual amusement ! ah, ah ! So that is the way with him. Well, all boys seem to be inclined that way. There are very few workers now. I don't know how it is."

"He never opens a book. Of course he has his studies ; but if you were to see the story-books he buys ! I assure you he reads those 'penny awfuls,' and novels that one would imagine a servant, and a servant alone, could care about."

"Yes, that's the way ; most boys are the same. I recollect them well enough. After all, a taste for reading requires to be cultivated ; and they have not yet taken that into account in our universities. There is something absurd in a man being able to read the Greek and Latin classics, and knowing and caring nothing for his own. However, there are more absurdities than that remaining to us from the monkish founders."

"I don't like the university system at all. I don't see why a number of young lads should be shut up together in a sort of barrack—it is that—if they are to live at home, and if they are intended for family life ; it is not a good preparation for it. And Dicky has got so rough since he went there, and so independent ; he won't tell a thing about himself, or answer a question ; he is utterly changed."

"Ah, he'll change back again, never fear. It is not possible he could be rough to you—he or anybody. I never had a sister," Hogan continued, after a short pause, and changing his tone. "You have no idea what a loss it is to a man—one is always different from other men, somehow."

"I can fancy that ; for girls who have no brothers are very different from those who have. I fancy they are always more companionable to men, and understand them better when they have been brought up with men. They are more sensible, too."

"It is a great improvement to the brothers, anyhow. Yes, I have missed many a thing in this world, I think. I hardly remember my home, and I have had to fight my way single-handed upwards, without a friend, even."

"You must have been lonely," said Nellie, looking at him sympathisingly.

"Yes," said he ; "I've often thought how I'd like, when the day's work was done, to have some one—some one like you "—and he turned to her—" to talk to me and advise with me—to be my rest and my consolation, my good angel."

She did not answer, but her heart beat fast and faster; she met his eyes one moment, but the look in them brought a hue like that of the apple-blossoms to her cheek.

"Tell me, Nellie: would you be that to me—could you? You don't know how I think of you; how I long for the day when I shall be independent—*when I can* ask you to be—to be something nearer still. Not yet; but soon. I wouldn't bind you, Nellie,—I could not, fairly; but tell me, dearest Nellie,—don't take away your hand,—tell me you'll promise to do nothing—to take no step without telling me. You do?"

A look gave her promise; and he went on.

"You'll trust me, and confide in me; you'll write to me?—and I'll write to you—I'll tell you everything. You'll be my Egeria, my goddess! Dear child, you don't know how happy I am—how grateful I am to you! Why are you pale?—surely you are not afraid? Nellie, dear, I go back to London with a new heart. I'll work harder than ever; and in the summer, dear—in August we'll meet. Shall we not?" and he took both her hands in his.

"Let us go in, please; we have stayed too long. No! please don't keep me. Yes, I'll remember to write. I will, indeed—I promise." Nellie was trembling and pale. She felt very happy, and also not a little frightened; and she almost wished he were gone, that she might run away up to her room to think of it all in quiet.

They returned to the drawing-room, entering by the glass door that opened into the flower garden. Here Dicky was found with his friend Orpen, who had called ostensibly to get a book of his (in reality to make an appointment); and Hogan was obliged to take his leave. Nellie did not like Orpen, and she was glad to excuse herself and get away. When she reached her mother's room, she sat down again in the window seat where she had sat and thought over her first meeting with Hogan. Then it was a dark winter afternoon; and she remembered well the sunset, into whose clouds she had woven doubting, half-hearted fancies and day-dreams,—which she had confessed to herself were but day-dreams. How quickly it sank and faded! But now it was different, and spring, with all its light and promise, seemed really to have come —not merely into the land, but into her heart and her life. She opened a little latticed pane, and let in the song of the thrushes and the smell of the new leaves and buds; and she felt as if, like the birds, she could have sung for joy; like them, too, she wove and built an ideal future—an ideal home; heedless of enemies, of coming change and storm, or the sudden malice of cruel, unrelenting fate.

When Hogan left Nellie he proceeded by a cross road, leading past Green Lanes, in the opposite direction from the Davorens' house, to Mr. Saltasche's mansion, where he was to dine and spend the evening. He sauntered along leisurely; and it was just ringing six when he reached the entrance gates. The house was built, although situated on a large piece of ground, close to the road, which it faced. The high wall, however, prevented it being easily seen. There was nothing remarkable in the façade. It was a large square stone house, overgrown with vines, and every window had a majolica box filled with flowers. No *parterres* before the house,—only a green, close-cut grass plot. The hall was filled with pyramids of flowers in pots, among which were a couple of fine statues. The drawing-room was a large room opening into a superb conservatory. A Persian carpet covered the centre of the floor, only the rich mellow oak of which showed itself wherever Indian matting and snowy sheep-skins and queer embroidered rugs were not. The hangings were of maroon velvet; and the walls of the room were stained a pale oak colour that set off the fine pictures,—some of which were hung up, while others stood on easels. A carved black oak cabinet, and a couple of chairs which matched it nearly enough, although they came from widely different places, stood at one end. Portfolios of etchings—some of them more valuable than Saltasche ever owned to his most intimate friends—were lying on the table. A veiled virgin of Marochetti's, bronze figures of beautiful workmanship, beautiful vases of hot-

house flowers, were judiciously bestowed wherever a dark
background served to set off their fragile beauties. A
splendidly executed intaglio portrait of Saltasche, and one
of his sister, Miss Saltasche, by the same sculptor, hung on
each side of the fireplace. The various mementos of foreign
travel which people bring home with them were not wanting; but all of them were uncommon—of form and
material which commended themselves at first glance to
the connoisseur. China hung here and there in quaintly-
arranged groups on the walls, and was reflected in the
mirrors, and an old chased silver flagon and cups surmounted a cluster of strange foreign weapons with hilts of
every shape, and some with jewels sunk in them. The
windows all looked out on the pleasure-grounds; and a
tempered light came through the curtain of flowering
creepers hanging before the conservatory door. A sweet
and heavy odour filled the room, partly from the flowers
and partly from the Russian leather folios and books.

Hogan sat down in a low easy-chair, and ran his eye
round the room. The curious and artistic arrangement
was lost upon him; but he could judge that everything
was of the richest and best of its kind. He thought it
odd, and out of the way, that there should be no carpet;
and he put down this, to him a defect, to the foreign tastes
of the host. There was no piano either to be seen; it was
in a smaller room at the side. Mr. Saltasche considered
that the piano spoiled the general effect, and had it kept
in a smaller room, divided from the other only by a velvet
curtain.

In a moment three ladies entered by the conservatory
door. Hogan had met Miss Saltasche before, and shook
hands with her cordially. She was a stout, sombre-looking
woman of fifty, who must have been handsome in her
youth, for she had magnificent eyes, and features that were
regular, if rather coarse. She never dressed, as the saying
goes; holding, with her dissenting notions, that fashions
and jewellery were carnal indulgences. A ruffle of Flemish
lace at her throat and wrists somewhat relieved the plain-
ness of a heavy black silk; which, in these days of fur-

belows and flounces, was Quaker-like in its simplicity. Her hair, plentiful, however streaked with gray, was gathered up under something that was not a head-dress and yet not a cap. She was quite without style or *ton;*—"Dissenter, every inch," would have been Miss O'Hegarty's comprehensive summary. And yet one would hesitate before saying she was not a lady. She was an admirable house-keeper, and there was nothing in the way of needle-work that she could not do. She made lace—real Brussels point, sending to Brussels for her materials; she had embroidered the chairs, table-cloths, and curtains of the drawing-room in the most beautiful manner,—the designs having been made by her versatile brother.

Hogan had never met the other two ladies. One was Mrs. Grey, a faded woman, with a troubled, careworn face; the other was Mrs. Poignarde, looking more beautiful and interesting than ever. He recollected directly where he had seen her before—at the theatre, that night with Sal-tasche; he remembered, too, with a smile, how struck his impressionable friend had been; and now he took a good look at her while they sat waiting the arrival of the master of the house. She was not his style at all; but still, she was a beautiful woman. He did not like her manner,—it was too indifferent; and he watched her replying in mono-syllables to Miss Saltasche's cumbrous attempts at conversa-tion,—scarcely raising her eyes, as she spoke, from the little bouquet of pale white primulas she had brought in with her from the conservatory.

Hogan left his chair, and sat down nearer to her; he was curious to hear her speak, and wondered could he find any subject that would interest her. After a commonplace or two, he asked directly,—

"Are you long in Dublin, Mrs. Poignarde?"

"No: eight months. I was for six weeks in Cork, before that."

"And which city do you prefer? Dublin, I hope."

"I hate both!" she said curtly, ignoring the second clause of his question.

"What a pity!" Hogan spoke in a condescending,

half-chaffing tone. He knew something of her history
from Saltasche, and had seen her husband. He felt sorry
for her misfortunes, certainly; but mixed with the com-
passion was a tinge of something akin to contempt.
Worldly people, with the best intentions, have always a
shade of that running through their charities. "What a
pity!—and why so? Our climate is it, or ourselves, now?"

"Ah! your climate—ugh! Your winter is a torment
—always present, almost; and your summer, a disappointment."

"That is almost an epigram, Mrs. Poignarde. And
ourselves?"

"I don't care for Irish people," she answered bluntly.
"What I have seen of them, with an exception or so, they
bore me." As if to point this more, she went through a
semblance of a yawn, barely opening her mouth, and
drawing down her chin and up her eyebrows. It was
rather a becoming grimace, and he admired it as much as
he did her coolness. Then she pulled over a book, and
opened it leisurely. Scarcely had she done so when the
door opened, and in came Mr. Saltasche. The hand that
held open the cover dropped it—very suddenly, Hogan
thought; and as he rose from his chair, he noticed a
quick glance, full of meaning, flash from her eyes to those
of Saltasche. Then they all went to dinner. Miss Saltasche took the head of the table; Hogan sat beside Mrs.
Poignarde, who took no notice whatever of him. After
they were seated, the reverend Mr. Grey came in, apologising for being late. The synod had detained him. The
conversation at dinner ran wholly on Church matters.
Hogan was amused at his friend's ready sympathy with
the victims of Disestablishment, and his acquiescence in all
the doleful forecasts of the clergyman.

"The country parts will be reduced to a sad state. The
clergy gone, and their influence removed, the gentry, you
may be certain, will be more of absentees than ever. How
are the lower orders to be dealt with?"

"You admit absenteeism to be an evil, then?" asked
Hogan.

"Certainly I do. I had a parish in the south, and the landlord resided almost all the year round on his estate,— Sir ——, a most excellent man. You have no conception how the poor people improved. They kept their cottages in good order; he built out-offices and pigsties for them, and encouraged them in keeping little gardens. You might almost fancy yourself in a really English village. They had flowers in their gardens and in their windows. They kept themselves cleaner. In fact, it was wonderful, when you compared them with the tenants on the other estate."

"All owing to the landlord's encouragement and assistance; his daughters, too, worked very hard in that parish," added Mrs. Grey.

"Well," said Hogan, "I have seen something of Irish country villages; and it is deplorable that the landlords don't reside, for ever so short a time in the year. In English counties it is so different. The 'great house' can do so much. If the young ladies of the landlord's family would do in Irish villages what they do in the English ones,—refine the poor by their example and presence, teach them to make their houses a little more human-like, raise them out of the barbarism they are now sunk so hopelessly in,—the good would be incalculable."

"It is not merely the poor who suffer by absenteeism," said Mr. Saltasche; "but the better classes in country towns. The doctors, and their families, attorneys, agents —all that class—lose immensely. These people, for want of stimulus and example, I suppose, too, sink below their own level. They have nothing to look up to, and they require that. They do indeed. We all require it. Even here in Dublin, what would become of manners, refinement —society, in a word—if it were not for the Court, wretched little travesty that it is."

A faint smile played on Mrs. Grey's lips, as she recollected that the speaker was disqualified from attending the same wretched little travesty.

"There have been projects of abolishing the office of Viceroy," said Hogan; "and I can't imagine, were it so,

2 A

that manners and refinement would utterly vanish from
Dublin with it."

"I daresay they will do that," said Mr. Grey, with a
most melancholy voice. "It will be another step in the
direction of abolishing all traces of order and decency,
paving the way to revolution and destruction. Unhappy
country !"

"Take some strawberries ! Out of my forcing-house ?
Yes, they are, Mrs. Poignarde," Saltasche said ; then in a
lower key, "This is so tiresome to you, is it not ? Have
you shown Mrs. Poignarde the greenhouses, Elizabeth ?" he
asked, looking at his sister.

"Yes ; but not the fernery. We could not get in."

"Ah ! you must see that by-and-bye. I have some new
ferns."

A glance swift as lightning followed. She interpreted
it, "I have something to say to you."

Some hours later, after tea, he led her out into the conservatory off the drawing-room. The doors remained open
between. A swinging lamp hung in the centre from the
dome ; and under a great tree-fern, the leaves of which
grew to the roof, and then bending back, hung down so as
to make a sort of arbour, were wicker seats. All round
were tires of beautiful flowers: creamy yellow roses, curious
broad-leaved geraniums, trumpet lilies—scarlet, yellow,
every brilliant hue—relieved by the cool masses of ferns
and the background of dark stephanotis and passion-flowers,
climbing behind on the sides and hanging down in graceful
wreaths from the roof.

"Sit down here one moment," he said, drawing forward
one of the low chairs.

She seated herself, and leaning her elbow on the arm of
the chair, rested her chin in her hand and turned her eyes
upward, wide open and impatient, full on his.

He seemed nervous, and almost avoided their gaze.

"We mustn't stay here long," he whispered, glancing back
at the open door of communication. "Your husband was
with me to-day, and he has drawn another couple of hundred pounds. That leaves in my possession only one

hundred of his now. I hear he is laying heavily against a horse."

"Bah! Is this all?" she interrupted, scornfully; "have you brought me here for this? Say the last penny of our money is gone, at once—the sooner the better, too. I am weary for the end: I am indeed." And she clasped both her hands in her lap despairingly.

"Let me counsel you, Adelaide," he whispered close in her ear. "The end cannot be far off. Poignarde cannot succeed at book-making: he drinks; and that science, as they call it, requires a clearer head than his at the best of times."

"I know," she answered, and turned away her head listlessly. "I thought we were going to the fernhouse."

"Wait one moment," he said; "I forgot something." Then he went back to the drawing-room, and taking a taper, lighted it. He returned with it to the conservatory, where she was, and said in a loud voice, "Follow me, if you please, Mrs. Poignarde; I am going to light up the fernery." He opened a door leading into a peach-house. They passed through this, and entered a labyrinth of rock-work, all overgrown with beautiful and rare ferns. Clusters of maidenhair and queer foliage plants filled every nook. There was a fountain in the centre, and its tiny cascade fell into a pool in which gold fish glided lazily away to hide from the light under broad hart's-tongue leaves. Gold and silver ferns, silvery mosses, all glittered when he lighted little lamps fastened here and there. Some of these were placed so as to shine through the red-veined leaves of the begonias, which looked like curious beetles of mammoth size. Mrs. Poignarde looked round in delight and wonder. He extinguished the wax taper, and there was now only the pale light of the coloured lamps among the leaves. A damp, faintly acrid perfume filled the air, and the dripping of the little fountain was the only sound. Saltasche took her by the hand, and led her close to one of the lights.

"Now," said he, "look down there." Outside, in the clear twilight, she could see across the garden to the pleasure-ground, and to the weeping ash tree, now in full leaf, where he and she had sat that night two months ago.

"You remember ? What did I tell you then ?—to trust me, and me only, and to call upon me when in need. I know your wretchedness; but the end has now come. To everything——"

"But—but he may win. Then he would have enough to go on for a long time."

"He will not win ; he will be utterly beggared. He may have to leave the army ; then he won't want to keep you with him. He will let you go where you like, and where can you go, now ?"

"And I will go to Rio,—back to Uncle Rodolphe : he will receive me, I know. You will help me to do that, will you not, Mr. Saltasche ?" and she raised imploring, tearful eyes to his, which were turned away. "Help me to go back home."

He looked at her pitifully, holding her hands in his without replying to her question, wondering to himself how she would bear the news that was waiting for her at home—the news of the death of Rodolphe Chrestien, the merchant-prince of Rio Janeiro, which had been telegraphed to him from London that evening. To-morrow it would be in the papers ; no doubt the agent had written to her the bad news too. Saltasche had a kind, sympathetic heart, however lax he might be in morals ; and he felt sorry for the pain this friendless creature was to undergo, even though it furthered his own plans.

She could not see his face clearly ; but she could see his eyes bent upon hers. A strange light seemed to shine in their depths ; and it seemed to her as if he were smiling. Could it be that he was mocking her ? She drew her hands away with a violent effort, feeling that she could have bitten her tongue with rage for having yielded to such weakness ; and with a look that was defiant and frightened, she made a sudden turn to go. With one step he was before her, and barred the path with his arm.

"Let me pass, Mr. Saltasche, at once."

"Hear me. You will know why I say nothing ; you

will indeed,—soon—too soon !" Something in his tone reassured her, and at the same time gave her to understand that there was something behind ; and she looked at him as if for an explanation.

He walked beside her to the door. There he stopped for a moment, and said to her in a low, meaning tone : " You will send for me, won't you ? You will look on me as your best friend."

"I may easily do that," she answered, despairingly, "for I have not a friend in the world."

" You have *one !* Go now, go ! We shall be missed."

In the drawing-room they were discussing parish affairs. Miss Saltasche, by her brother's directions, took a strong interest in the schools and charities of the neighbourhood. If she had her own will, she would have attended a queer little Bethesda in a lane off the village main street ; but with Cosmo's aristocratic proclivities, that was out of the question, so she was forced to content herself with the tepid ministrations of the Reverend Wilmington Grey.

Hogan was yawning over a book of exquisite etchings, which his untaught eye could not appreciate. He was wondering to himself how anybody could draw such ugly faces and figures, and what on earth was the use of putting pots and pans in a picture.

"Ah! you have that, have you? Some fine bits there," said Mr. Saltasche, leaning over him. "See Ostade signed under that horse. Do you like pictures ? Come over here. That, now : where do you think that came from ?" and he pointed to a picture hanging on the wall. "That is one of Jordäen's best pieces ; that picture was stolen at the sacking of the Palais Royal in Paris in 'forty-eight. It is invaluable. This frame, look " (and he turned to another picture), "that is more than two hundred years old. Fact: that is a Poussin."

"The bust ? Yes, that Veiled Virgin : Marochetti's. He did it for me. Clever idea ? Yes ; but it's a mere trick—a mere trick."

And so talking, he led Hogan round the room until they came to the door. He stopped a moment, and taking a cigar-case out of his pocket, held it up, calling to the clergyman,—

"A cigar, Grey?"

He was answered, as he expected, in the negative; and then, with Hogan, he went out to the garden.

"I had a word to say to you before you go," he began, as soon as his cigar was lighted. "Lord Brayhead is very irritable about this Bill. You see it is an unpleasant position——"

"Most confoundedly so. I wish to God I had never heard of it. It is utterly impossible and ridiculous to expect to get a day for it, with the present crush of business. Unreasonable! Does he think that not only my own, but the business of the country, is to stand still for his crotchet?" There was a little too much heat in Mr. Hogan's tones. He knew very well that only for this crotchet he would not be in Parliament at all, and, moreover, that the six hundred pounds which Lord Brayhead had contributed towards his expenses gave his lordship a real claim—not the less real because it could not be openly avowed—on his services.

"I was talking to him about it on Saturday; and he seemed very angry at the session being lost. He counted on you to attack it at once, you see. I think you had better see him and explain matters."

"I'll give him back his money, and be done with him."

"Softly, Mr. Hogan," said Saltasche, in a cold voice that Hogan had not heard before. "You cannot throw us over in that fashion. And we have reason to complain of the way you have done the work. The night the motion was made by Sir Harry Vane you were not ready to answer the objections brought up by Duffield on behalf of our opponents; you failed, also, to make that point about the mineral resources. In fact, you have not attended to the business."

Hogan's cigar almost fell from his lips. The sudden way in which Saltasche had identified himself with Lord Brayhead, the tone and manner he had assumed, all took him with a shock as if a bucket of cold water had been thrown over him. He quickly realised the position, however. He acknowledged to himself that he had not done his utmost for the Bill: it was hard to strive and work for an absurdity; and knowing the accursed thing to be an absurdity, he had treated it so as to deserve his lordship's censure. But that Saltasche should pull him up, and identify himself with "the old fool," was, for half a second, incomprehensible. Then he remembered the tuft-hunting proclivities of the man—remembered what the Lord Brayheads were to him, not merely in society, but in business —and he almost wondered at his ever expecting anything else. And then, too, he had got his price: he was a member of Parliament, and he had realised nearly five thousand pounds, or saw his way clearly to realising that sum, by the good offices of Mr. Saltasche. He acknowledged all this; but he remembered, too, that there were considerations on his own side: he had helped Saltasche and Stier and Bruen to float many barques on the financial ocean that were intended to sail very close to the wind indeed. But what of that? (and he tried to put his own share in those ventures out of his mind). Hundreds of men in better position would do the same—were only too glad to get the chance. He comforted himself with precedents—prompted thereto by something of the same sheeplike instinct as Mrs. Bursford. Perhaps he had caught the trick from her. He was a good deal in her company of late.

"I am obliged to confess," replied Hogan, "that more might have been made of that occasion; and, though I don't offer it as an excuse, I must tell you that when public opinion and your own judgment are against a thing, it is difficult to work it up."

"That is not to the purpose," Saltasche went on— speaking now, however, in his own tone. "See him tomorrow, and make the best case for yourself that you can. On no account give him to understand you think his project hopeless; mark that, please."

"It is notorious, in the House and out of it, that he is doing it for a spite against the Broad-gauge Company. What do you say to my offering to refund his money?"

" You will please yourself as to that. Considering that his lordship could have got some one else to do as much, and also " (here Saltasche spoke with emphasis), "that the obligation does not rest there, your course should be obvious."

Hogan, as he walked home that night, made up his mind to see Lord Brayhead and eat humble pie. It was the first time, and the savour of the dish was not pleasant.

So unpleasant was it that, as he left Lord Brayhead's presence the next day, he almost swore he would throw up the whole thing and go back to his practice—the practice which he had despised, and which his uncle the Bishop had declared to be the safest and the surest in the long run. He had always been independent before; and now—— well, he had got what he bargained for, and this was part of the price. Lord Brayhead had spoken to him as he might have done to his servant-man. As for Saltasche, whose tone in speaking to him rang through his ears still, and affected him just as a bad taste does one's palate, Hogan hoped soon to be able to throw over that flunkey. On the whole, he went back to London in bad spirits.

CHAPTER XXVII

"Der Mensch erwatet oft einen Kelch mit Necktar, und er kriegt eine Prügel suppe, und ist auch Necktar süss, so sind doch Prügel um so bitterer ; und es ist noch ein wahres Glück, dass der Mensch, der den andern prügelt, am Ende müde wird, sonst könnte es der andere wakrhaftig nicht aushalten."—*Heine*, " *Reisebilder.*"

THE Bursfords had taken lodgings in Clarges Street, Piccadilly. A large drawing-room, with two windows facing the street, and one bedroom, formed their whole accommodation ; and for this they paid a sum so high that were it not that she had the O'Gorman Mulcahy's rent of the house in Merrion Street to fall back on, Mrs. Bursford would have rebelled outright. As it was, Jervis' supplies were necessarily cut off.

It was an afternoon late in the month of May. The windows were open, and the air, though close and warm as it is of a London May day, smelt pleasantly of the mignonette and musk in pots in the balcony. Mrs. Bursford was lying on a sofa by the wall. She was weary and exhausted ; an extensive shopping expedition had occupied her and Diana all the forenoon, and they had not long returned. Miss Bursford was sitting in the window, busily trying to read the debate of the previous night in the *Times*. She had taken a great interest of late in Parliamentary business.

She felt too tired to wade through much of it, however ; and presently, lying back in her chair drowsily, she let the paper slip out of her lap and on to the floor. The rustle seemed to startle Mrs. Bursford : she raised the cushion on which her head was resting, and said,—

"Diana! you might give me Miss Saltasche's letter. I had not time to read more than a page of it this morning."

Her daughter unlocked a desk and handed the letter, a voluminous epistle written in a crabbed hand. Then she returned to her seat; and Mrs. Bursford put on her spectacles and began to read it aloud, with comments interpolated.

"Her brother is coming over next week, to the Westminster Palace Hotel. He always goes there. 'That unfortunate little Mrs. Poignarde'—do you remember, Diana? the pretty foreign-looking little woman who played so well at his concert—'she has lost her uncle, a very wealthy merchant, whose heiress she was to have been: left all his money in charity, or something of that sort. I gather from the Greys that her marriage had displeased him. Mr. Saltasche managed some money affairs for the husband, —a sad scamp, it seems: he tells me they are almost penniless. She expects to have to teach for her living.' Dear, dear! I suppose it was the knowledge that she would have to come to that at last that made her practise ·and study as she did. I always thought there was something out of the way in her playing so well."

"Oh! quite," assented Diana. Then Mrs. Bursford went on, —

"She says she has heard Miss O'Hegarty won't go away anywhere this summer. Her nephew, Dermot Blake, is to be home in July or August: he means to go to Blakestown direct."

"August, is it now?" said Diana. "I thought we heard June, or May. He'll marry and settle, no doubt. I wonder will it be one of the Haras or Dillons? They will be on the *qui vive*."

"Won't they, though?" said Mrs. Bursford. "I should not be one bit surprised if they packed back to Kerry for the summer instead of going to the Rhine, just because he'll be there."

"The Taylors, too: they have money now."

"They'd need it. What a chance they have of him!

Dermot will marry some pretty face,—that's what he'll do. Let Dorothy do all she likes."

" Lady Brayhead thinks of Biarritz, and will take one of her nieces with her. She thinks it probable Miss Braginton will accompany Mrs. John Braddell to London for a while."

"Oh !" said Diana, turning round in her chair.

"She was furious when she heard of the letting of the Curzon Street establishment. I saw she was bent on getting over, by crook or by hook," said Mrs. Bursford, folding up the letter and putting it in her pocket. "And now she has just foisted herself on these Braddell people. I do wish——"

But the wish was never spoken; for Mrs. Bursford's glance fell on the clock on the chimneypiece, and she started up.

"Half-past four !" she exclaimed. "Diana, I forgot to tell them that we wanted afternoon tea. I'll ring for the servant."

" She has taken up with the Braddells because of their widowed brother-in-law—that's just it," continued the elder lady when the order had been given. "The O'Gorman Mulcahy has gone back to Mayo, and has made no sign. Pah ! the creature ! I am glad Mr. Saltasche is coming over—very glad. I feel uneasy about those Leadmines shares. From what Mr. Hogan says——"

"Pray, mamma, on no account let him imagine that Mr. Hogan is your authority : now please remember that Mr. Saltasche may be quite unaware that Mr. Hogan knows so much of our——knows we hold those shares, I mean. And then things take such sudden changes in the City: they were thirty-eight yesterday, and to-day they are thirty-seven and one-eighth. That is nothing extraordinary." Miss Bursford evidently had been studying something more than Parliamentary business.

At five o'clock Hogan came in, looking pale and tired, and very hot. Diana rose to welcome him, with quite a pretty fuss. A long reclining chair, with soft silken cushions, was placed in the shade by the open window,

where the air could come in but not the sun. A footstool
seemed to present itself of its own accord to his feet, which
were weary with the hot glaring walk up Piccadilly. After
the heat and dust without, the cool room was delightful.
It was not like a lodging : if it was, it was a different sort
from his rooms in Bloomsbury. There were quantities of
pretty trifles scattered about. Diana had taken the trouble
to pack all her knicknackeries and carry them across with
her. The O'Gorman Mulcahys must have found a bare
drawing-room when they took possession. Books, maga-
zines, china, and pots of flowers gave it a cheerful inhabited
look ; and Miss Bursford, in a charming cool dress of white
and blue, all the harsh lines softened and toned down by
the judicious half-light, moved gracefully, on hospitality
intent, about the room.

"What may we expect in another month—in the dog-
days ?" said Hogan, laying back his head in the chaise-
longue, and watching Diana's gliding movements lazily
from under his half-shut eyelids.

A confused dull hum, a faint echo of the thoroughfares,
came in from the street with the perfume of the flowers.
The change was so complete, that he felt almost as if in a
dream. Then the servant came in with tea. A round
table on three legs, holding a miniature tea-tray, was
brought forward ; a funny little round teapot, shaped like
a melon, with a leaf for a lid and some twisted silver
tendrils for a handle ; cups of different sizes, shapes, and
colours, but all of them pretty and quaint,—Miss Bursford's
thin white fingers moving amongst them gracefully, if a
little fussily.

"I assure you, Mrs. Bursford, you might get a sunstroke
to-day in Pall Mall quite easily."

"I daresay, indeed. I was out this morning : it was so
fatiguing. I am sure it will end with a thunderstorm.
There are always thunderstorms in London at this time of
year. Diana, you always put too much sugar in my tea."

Hogan rose and fetched back the teacup, to have the
fault rectified by the pouring in a little more tea. Mrs.
Bursford was sitting in the far window, in her own easy-chair.

" Now," said Diana, all smiles and graciousness, handing him a cup of tea delightful of fragrance.

He laid it on the gipsy table.

"I am too far away," he said, looking at the cumbrous chaise-longue and the footstool. "This will be a short cut ;" and he lifted the little table and its load a good foot nearer to his place. Diana placed her chair nearer, and laughed.

"You are fond of short cuts, I think," she said, with a trace of meaning in her tone. "I like them too, but I lack the power, somehow, of foreseeing short cuts. What a world of time and trouble it saves ! It is a real talent." She said this with an affected emphasis—an italicising of eyes and voice that implied homage and admiration.

He smiled a kind appreciation as he sipped his tea.

"What is there new to-day ?" asked Mrs. Bursford, from her arm-chair.

"Really very little. Judge Conolly is dying. They speak of Serjeant Guages as his successor. Conolly did not hold it long."

"No ; and Serjeant Guages is old : sixty-eight, they say. He has need of a rest, indeed."

"That, and the new theatre, and the financial scandal, are about all the news going. Lord Featherhead has advanced fifty thousand. Miss Babillon's salary is to be, according to some people, two hundred a week. Her dressing-room is a marvel : satin and point-lace hangings in all the shades of blues. He is having her picture painted as ' Queen Too-loo-loora,' by Fleshynge. I'm told it's to cost eight hundred guineas. And she is to appear on the first night in a new burlesque written for her by Lord Featherhead and Tom Titt."

"Especially Tom Titt, I suppose ?" said Miss Bursford. "What idiotic puns he makes ! When is his novel expected out ?"

"Quite soon ; it is nearly all stolen from Ernest Feydeau, and some other French writers. By-the-bye, Mrs. Stryper is bringing out another : that woman must work night and day. She makes money by it, too : advertises so daringly.

Her last dodge was to present copies gratis to all the public
reading-rooms and mechanics' institutes. Then, of course,
their acknowledgments appeared in the papers, and were a
first-rate advertisement. I am told she will get a thousand
pounds for this. The plot is certainly strong—a mother
and daughter in love with the same man. By-the-bye, she
is in a fury just now. Some Yankee got a letter of introduction to her, and was asked to dinner. And what did
the fellow do but write an account of her, and her house,
and her dinner, off to a New York paper!—described
everything, to the pattern of the plates. Everybody is
talking of it."

"What was the financial scandal?" interrupted Mrs.
Bursford, a little impatiently.

"A merchant,—City man—absconded with a large sum
—a hundred and twenty thousand, they say: gone to
Spain. There is no extradition treaty, you know, with
Spain. Such a foolish thing of anybody that is 'wanted'
to leave London! It is the safest place of all, if they
would only think it."

"Had he speculated?" asked Mrs. Bursford.

"Yes, and had made money; but he had been implicated
in some unpleasant business likely to injure his standing, and
people fought shy of him; so he thought it better to be off."

"Dear me!" Then Mrs. Bursford picked up the stitches
in her tatting, and dropped out of the conversation. Diana
quitted the tea-table, and seated herself opposite Hogan in
the window, well back from the light, among the shadows
of the curtains.

"You did not speak last night, then?" said she, in a
reproachful tone. "I was *so* disappointed this morning."
The blonde eyelashes drooped pensively for a moment.

"You were looking for the report, eh?" said he in a
lazy tone. "Ah! I had thought of saying something on
that Enlistment Bill. The subject did not interest me,
though; and I had had a hard day's work in the City, so
was glad to doze in my seat. It is a good quality of mine
to be able to go to sleep in all sorts of odd positions and
times—that is, after midnight."

"The Duke of Wellington and Napoleon could do that too, I have read." Diana related this admiringly, just as if she saw in it some additional links in the chain of analogy she had wrought in her own mind between these heroes and her swain.

"Saltasche, by-the-bye, prides himself greatly on his likeness to Napoleon," said Hogan, smiling. "Have you noticed that?"

"Dear, yes: he dresses the part, too. He has a picture of Napoleon: some people say he had it painted from himself. He can give a very good imitation—that is quite his weakness; and he is very susceptible to flattery on that head."

"I hardly supposed he had a weakness," laughed Hogan: "we all have. That mania for imitating great people is very common. What a number of fat men prided themselves at one time on being like O'Connell! It always dies out after a while. I think almost every short swarthy man imitated Napoleon more or less. I know another who has his photograph taken in jack-boots and a sort of hunting costume—with his arms folded, of course."

"Mr. Saltasche has a little too much colour," said Diana.

"Well, a little. It is very vexatious, though, when you are presented with a photograph and asked deliberately, 'Who does that remind you of?' Of course you don't know. Then when you are informed sulkily that it is *considered* so like the Duke of so-and-so, or Prince such-a-one, you can't help showing surprise. There is an old gentleman here who dresses exactly like Prince G——, and will do so to the end of time, because he was once mistaken for him. His head has been completely turned ever since."

"I quite believe it. People are so silly. In Dublin I know several people who persist in copying exactly his Ex'cy's dress, whiskers, and way of brushing his hair. I know a girl who was perfectly crazed for a season or two because she had been told she was like Lady H——. People went so far as to say that she had been saluted in the street in mistake for her. But that I doubt: she never was so good-looking."

"Mr. Saltasche, I mustn't forget to tell you, will be here on Monday morning," said Hogan, looking at his watch. "I must be in my place early to-night." Hogan had not yet got out of the trick, common to most new-made M.P.'s, of regulating their daily lives in accordance with the exigencies of the House, and of continually talking of the same. "There will be an effort made by some friends to get that wretched Railway Bill on its legs again. Ah! ——" and he sighed heavily.

"Is it so hopeless, then?" asked Miss Bursford, with a charming show of interest and sympathy.

"Hopeless?—indeed it is. That's not the worry, though." He spoke unguardedly, and heedless of the look of sharp curiosity that suddenly shone in her eyes.

"Oh dear!" sighed the lady, clasping her hands with affected vehemence, "if I were only a man! What a glorious career one could carve out! Don't you admire that saying of Napoleon's, *La carrière ouverte aux talens'*? To think that any man with talent and—ah—energy can raise himself! There is really something most fascinating to me in the aristocracy of intellect."

This was kindly meant; but there was something in it that jarred Hogan. Self-made men may be divided into two classes—those who have advanced themselves by intellectual achievement, and that other large class, of whom the immortal Whittington may be taken as the type, and with whom we are all familiar. The last are usually proud of their own success, and fond of reverting to their humble beginnings: an amiable weakness, which society has always condoned on the ground of its supposed stimulating effect on youth.

It is strange, but true, that the contrary should exist among the "aristocracy of intellect." This seeming anomaly may be accounted for by the fact that Intellect is not yet recognised as the ruling element of society. It is so in reality; but the multitude bow before money. Money excuses, gilds, ennobles everything; whereas if a clever man be poor, it is dangerous for him to advertise his cleverness,—people almost instinctively button up their pockets. A successful clever man has very often a sort of apologetic air.

Hogan was no exception to the general rule. He was a self-made man, and by no means of the best stamp. He was morbidly sensitive as to his origin—maybe from some conscientious motive, after all—and he could have well dispensed with Diana's lavish incense of this particular attribute. It was not in the best taste. But it must be allowed for the lady that she was unversed in the peculiarities of the specimen just now in hand. She was only feeling her way. He too, seeing clearly her motive—for he was quick of perception—in his masculine vanity was inclined to overlook the offence. So he smiled a mixed approval, and rose to go.

Diana accompanied him to the door with an expectant look, which he had not the presence of mind to ignore.

"Good-bye, then; I'll see you again shortly. Let's see, —this is Monday: Friday, in the afternoon; yes."

It was becoming his habit now, when leaving Clarges Street, to fix the day and hour for his next visit. He had fallen into the practice quite insensibly. Having called once and found them not at home, Diana had declared it to be perfectly insupportable that a "Dublin friend," as she was pleased to style him, should run the risk of a tiresome long walk for nothing. Mr. Hogan really *must* tell them when he was coming. No! she would not hear of his confining himself to Tuesdays—their at-home day: he must come whenever it suited him. The idea of tying down a member of Parliament, a public man, to a certain day or hour! Absurd! he *must* name his own time; and so on.

Hogan smiled on seeing the pleased, triumphant expression that kindled in her face.

"Oh, by-the-bye," said he, "I'll bring that book of poems you were speaking to me about. 'Love is Enough:' is that it? Yes, I have ordered it."

"You are really too kind," she murmured, with effusion. "You will come on Friday, and bring me news of all your achievements? Good-bye: *au revoir*." And a languishing

2 B

œillade accompanied the parting hand-shake. He pressed
her fingers just a little. It was impossible not to acknow-
ledge such persistent, such flattering efforts for his good
graces in some way ; and, clumsy novice that he was, he
could think of nothing else. It was pleasant, indeed, for
Hogan to be able to drop anchor in such a quiet, refreshing
haven, after the heats and burdens of the day! He felt
this keenly : and he liked the flattery, the attentions, and
caresses of the siren. It was soft and pleasant, and we
know his tastes lay in that direction. How or when it
was to end he never asked himself.

As he walked down Clarges Street to the corner of
Piccadilly, where he meant to take a hansom to drive
home to his dinner, he jotted down a hasty memorandum
of his engagement for Friday, and dismissed all thought on
the subject from his mind. After Friday there would be
another day ; and there might be a second visit to the
Royal Academy, or a flower-show or concert, or, maybe,
another book of poems. Then he thought of Nellie and
her coy shyness. And in the almost midsummer heat of
Regent Street, amid the noise and crowd and dust, there
rose to him a vision of the garden walk in Green Lanes :
the trees in blossom, and hung with little glistening rain-
drops after the spring shower, and the timid girl, with
apple-blossom cheeks and downcast blue eyes, who had
walked beside him there.

CHAPTER XXVIII

"Apemantus.—Heyday ! what a sweep of vanity comes this way ?

    *   *   *   *   *   *

Var. Servant.—How dost ? Fool !

Apem.—Dost dialogue with thy shadow ?

Var. Serv.—I speak not to thee.

Apem.—No ! 'tis to thyself—come away."—*Timon of Athens.*

THE afternoon of a fine day, early in June. The various approaches to the "Palace Gardens" were unusually thronged with people, on foot or in carriages. The Rose Show of the year was being held, and everybody was in haste to get in. Their Excellencies were to be present, and as the weather was perfectly fine and warm, hardly a ticket had been left unsold. At one of the entrance-gates —not the principal one—stood Mr. Saltasche, evidently on the look-out for some one. He never quitted his post of observation, though innumerable people of his acquaintance passed in, and many gorgeously-dressed ladies smiled gracious encouragement to him to escort them. Dicky Davoren passed, with his sister—taking off his hat gravely as they went by, in return for Saltasche's careless nod. The Brangans and Raffertys, looking like full-blown peonies of various startling colours, were attended by Bishop O'Rooney and a couple of young lads : gentlemen of their persuasion are not generally burdened with much spare time, and their young ladies are left pretty much to themselves until after business hours. There were abundance of military men—recognisable, as a rule, by their well-cut clothes and "set-up" air ; a sprinkling of professional men ; and a large number of country gentlemen up for the Cattle Show, slouching of gait, freckled of countenance, and de-

liberate of movement. All these passed Mr. Saltasche in
crowds. At last a cab drove up, and Mrs. Poignarde,
dressed in light mourning and looking paler and thinner
than before, accompanied by her husband and a lady whom
Saltasche did not know, got out. He advanced to meet
them, his eyes sparkling with exultation.

"I am so pleased you have come. My sister and Mrs.
Grey are in the tents : we shall follow them. How do you
do, Captain ?"

"My cousin, Miss Stroude, from London : Mr. Saltasche."

Saltasche bowed to a middle-aged, pleasant-looking lady.
After a moment or two, they joined the stream that was
flowing towards the tents. Poignarde was dumb, as usual,
and Saltasche speedily found his sister and introduced the
stranger to her. Miss Saltasche was busy with a note-book
and pencil, taking down the names of the finest plants.
Mrs. Grey was talking to people near her.

"Have their Excellencies come yet ?" asked Mrs. Poignarde.

"I do not know," replied Saltasche. "As yet I have
seen no one. We must have your opinion," he added,
turning to Miss Stroude with bland bow and smile, "on
our horticultural efforts. After Kew and the Crystal
Palace this must seem very poor to you."

"Are you exhibiting anything ?" asked Poignarde, who
for some reason or another seemed trying to be agreeable
and talkative.

"No, not this time. I had some things at the last show,
and got a prize—I believe for a tree-fern ; but the plants
were so injured that McKie would not allow me to send
anything to this."

"Your ferns are very valuable, I believe ?" continued the
Captain.

"I was offered a hundred pounds for a tree-fern, McKie
tells me. I know it cost me more than that," said Mr.
Saltasche, laughing.

"You have a Scotch gardener, then ?" said Miss Stroude.

"Yes ; I dare not gather one of my own flowers, he is
such a tyrant. The dream of his life is to compass a blue rose."

"A blue rose!" she repeated. "What an absurdity!"

"Everybody has his hobby; and that is McKie's. I believe my sister encourages him in it—just out of policy, you know."

Then Miss Saltasche fell into rank beside Miss Stroude. Poignarde seeing a brother-officer outside, slipped away to join him; his wife and Saltasche made the tour of the tent side by side.

"Come and see the geraniums," said he. "I want to show you Lord Brayhead's collection of plants."

They made their way across the grounds to another large tent, not yet thronged with people. They stopped for a moment before a beautiful pyramid of scarlet blossoms, which seemed to send out a glow of warmth all round it. The reflection shone in her long brown eyes, opened wide in admiration. Her exquisite oval face, framed in soft wreaths of hair and the black tulle of her mourning bonnet, looked like marble in its paleness. He was watching her.

"Tell me," he said in a low voice, "how has it been with you since? How have you decided now?"

"He is arranging an exchange. His cousin, Miss Stroude, is staying with us. She has come over here on some business, and has been very good, after her fashion. She says she will procure me teaching in London."

"Teaching? You! Surely not!"

"Yes; she wonders I have not tried long ago. It would be so easy, she says, with my talent and proficiency. She did not know the plan that I have been building on for years. And now that has all vanished, it seems to me I am indifferent to everything. What does it matter?"

"It does matter," said he brusquely. "You are talking nonsense. When does Miss Stroude leave you?"

"She is going down to Westmeath to-morrow. She will be back in a short time; and she spoke of my going over to London with her, if he can manage to settle his exchange in so short a time."

"Settle nothing," breathed Saltasche, in a low fierce whisper; "leave things as they are. I'll find you some-

thing pleasanter than teaching. You, indeed! Mind—
promise nothing."

She looked up at the strange tone, and a faint shell-pink
tinged her cheeks when she met the greedy eyes bent upon her.

"Let us find our people now," said he. And they retraced their steps towards the first tent. It was not an
easy matter to get on now. The viceregal party had arrived,
and the usual mobbing was going on. It was easy to dis-
cern their whereabouts. One had only to follow the pushing,
struggling *queue* that extended behind them. Every one
who had ever been presented bowed as they passed; and
his Excellency's unfortunate hat seemed to be only put on
his head to be taken off again immediately. They got back
to the rose-tent with difficulty, and found their party collected at the entrance.

"Oh, here you are," said Miss Saltasche. "We want to
see the fruit. Which tent is it in? Come with us, Mrs.
Grey. Lord Tenbrock is exhibiting some. You will like
to see that, of course." Lord Tenbrock was one of the
patrons of the Greys' parish.

They all filed off in the direction of a small tent, towards
which the crowd seemed also to be rushing. The viceregal
party having completed their scamper through the floral
section, were now inspecting the strawberries, giant cabbages, and onions, of the fruit and vegetable department.
On the way they encountered Mrs. Hepenstall, Mrs. de
Lancier, and some attendant military men. They greeted
the Saltasches and Greys very cordially. Mrs. Poignarde,
who was walking beside Saltasche, raised her eyelashes,
and timidly looked for a recognition. Mrs. Hepenstall, a
very frisky matron, and her friend of the auricomous hair,
looked blankest forgetfulness. Their military attendants
cast admiring glances at the slender, white-faced little
woman in black. One of them knew Saltasche, and commenced a lively conversation with him, in the hope, evidently, of drawing her into it. Saltasche, generally com-
plaisant enough in this *genre*, listened and answered stiffly;
and the two groups swept asunder presently. He looked
at her archly.

" You are complimented highly to-day, you see. I had
a great mind to introduce Captain du Maurel to you. I
wonder would those ladies ever have forgiven me. See :
here come their husbands !" A couple of well-dressed,
fast-looking men passed. (" Good-day, Lancier ! Day,
Hep. !") " The near man belongs to the little fair woman.
He won a bet of fifty pounds yesterday : rather a droll one,
too. Backed himself for two ponies to drink a pint of
stout out of a soup-plate with an egg-spoon, while Mr.
Duffer of the —th walked round Stephen's Green. Did
it, too."

" Oh ! was it he ? I heard Eric talking of that last night.
It seems to have caused great excitement."

" Immense. I believe it is a cousin of Du Maurel's or
Lancier's (I forget which)—Mr. Sharpsye—that owns the
Derby favourite this year."

" Bah ! Talk to Captain Poignarde of those matters ;
he is sure to know. I hate the very name of horse."

" What 'm I sure to know, eh ?" growled a well-known
voice behind them. The Captain's voice was thick and
his eyes watery. He had evidently been paying a visit to
the refreshment stall.

" I was saying to Mrs. Poignarde that Sharpsye, who
bought Skyscraper from Lord Bentinck, was a cousin of
one of those men who have just passed us."

" He is a cousin of Du Maurel. Made all his money by
knife-handles. Fact ; Sheffield man. I say, that reminds
me, I want to say a word to you. What are we stayin'
here for ? Just look at these cabbages ?—indeed I won't,
ma'am. These old women are fit for anythin'. Come on
outside and leave them. Selina Grey will pocket some of
those onions yet. Came from Tenbrock's ? Oh ! that's
what's the matter, is it ?"

So speaking, the Captain elbowed his way out. Saltasche,
after a look at her, followed him. When they got outside,
Poignarde shook himself as if relieved.

" I say," he began, " it looks nice and quiet over there ;
what do you say to cross over and have a weed ?"

They left the crowd and passed over the grass sward to

a comparatively deserted alley bordered with lilacs and laburnums all in full blossom. Entering this, Poignarde lighted a cigar and seated himself on a bench.

"I have been told," he began, "of a real sure thing." He stopped to give a long puff at his cigar. Saltasche's eyes kindled with impatience.

"Derby, eh?" said he quickly. He knew perfectly well what the fellow wanted; and he was in a hurry to get back to his friends. He looked at him with a sort of impatient disgust. The sodden countenance and pimpled nose, and the insolent, patronising air, never appeared to him more sickening. A wretch not worth a penny if his creditors were paid—on the verge of ruin, and yet swaggering and boasting to the last.

"Derby! Yaas, that's the ticket." And he nodded his head sapiently. "Stand to win three thousand this minute." Saltasche blandly smiled, as if quite pleased and not at all astonished at this news. "I say," went on the Captain, "I'll put you up to a good thing. Rattler is to be 'pulled.'" And he looked all round cautiously among the stems of the lilacs, as if some listener might be crouching to gather the words of wisdom that fell from his lips. "Don't let that out. I have it from the stable direct. I've laid heavily against him. Skyscraper's the horse. Yes, sir. Du Maurel even doesn't know; he'll come a cropper—ho! ho! Will you put anything on it, eh?"

"Er—no; much obliged to you, Captain. My business is enough for me. I never cared for 'horse politics,' either; never had time, you see: all that requires time and attention."

"'Tention! By Jove, I should say so. The sums I have had to pay for tips, now!" he added, reflectively.

"More than that, it really takes such foresight, calculation, and arrangement to win—er—you know. It would be quite beyond me—quite;" and Mr. Saltasche smiled agreeably at this avowal of his own incapacity.

"I daresay," assented the other patronisingly. "I think I'll have to ask you to let me have that hundred."

"Impossible!" answered the broker, sharply and decisively. "I could not realise it for a week to come. I can give you fifty, or eighty, to-morrow or the day after, if you like. I am told," said he, "you intend to exchange to India."

"Yes. The ——th sails July 2d; and in case—ah ——I'm only thinking about it," and he looked at Saltasche with a half-grin. "I don't want that generally known, you see; it ain't settled."

"Thursday next, the day after the Derby," said the broker sententiously, "you'll know for certain."

Poignarde nodded, and throwing away his cigar they strolled back to the crowd. Lady Brayhead and her nieces the Bragintons had appeared on the scene. They walked about patronising everything and everybody. The flowers were compared disadvantageously with those of the London *fêtes*: nothing to Kensington, not to speak of the private collections of their titled friends.

"Begonia? Yes; nothing to Lord Fraisefeuilles, is it, Blanche? Do you remember the table vines at dear Lady St. Elmo's? How do you do, Mr. Saltasche? Lord Brayhead? No, he is not here. Oh! you saw him in London the day before yesterday? Did you meet Diana and Aunt Bursford?"

"Oh yes, several times. I called in Clarges Street. They are looking uncommonly well, and go out immensely. The day I saw them, they were going to afternoon tea at the Under Secretary's, and to Mrs. Ware Hawk's concert in the evening."

Miss Braginton's complexion took a green shade, and her black eyes glittered viciously. Just then she caught sight of her friend Mrs. Braddell, escorted by a great fat country gentleman with a band of crape round his hat. She dived into the crowd to secure her prize; but when she came up with them she found Miss O'Hegarty had caught Mrs. Braddell in conversation, so she was obliged to wait an instant. She stared blankly at Nellie Davoren, who was leaning on her brother's arm, and on whom the stare was lost—for Nellie did not recognise the little lady in the pink silk bonnet, whose eyes seemed glancing in every direction. At last Miss O'Hegarty noticed her; and she was obliged to come forward—against her will, for she would much have preferred waiting until the coast was clear.

" Miss Braginton, how are you ? and where's your sister ? When did you hear from Diana ? She is enjoying herself in London, I'm told. Any amount of gaieties and beaux."

At the last word a smile curled Miss Braginton's lips that was edifying to see.

" I'm glad to hear it," she snapped out.

" Oh, indeed, then; but I have heard of her at the National Gallery, and somewhere else—Kensington Gardens —with a very devoted squire indeed. Fact, I assure you." And Miss O'Hegarty nodded her head significantly.

"Pray, who is it ? Come now, Miss O'Hegarty,—pray now; you *are* too bad,"—and Miss Braginton put on all her force of smiles and affected implorings, for the benefit of the widower, who was standing close by.

Nellie recognised her now: she watched the little lady's contortions with a sort of curiosity. She, too, had heard Miss O'Hegarty's insinuations; but she never dreamed that she could mean Mr. Hogan—Hogan, from whom that very morning she had received a letter, which was in her pocket now, and would be carried about with her until by dint of constant reading she would know its contents off by heart. She turned and said something to Dicky; and they both left Miss Dorothy to her friends, and went outside to speak to the Raffertys, who were now accompanied by Mr. Mulcahy. The Bishop was walking with Mrs. Rafferty. He gave a long look at Miss Nellie, remembering her perfectly well; and she, too, looked at him well and long—not for any interest she took in himself, but just because he was Mr. Hogan's uncle.

The day was beautiful, and it was pleasanter outside than in the tents, where the crowds of people and the heavy odours of the flowers made it very oppressive. Nellie felt in high spirits, and laughed and talked with Mr. Mulcahy until that youth felt utterly bewildered, and Miss Brangan, who looked upon him as her property because he had come with her party, bent her black brows in displeasure.

"Look out there; there's Mr. Saltasche: do you see him, Nellie?" said Dicky. "He's speaking to his Ex'cy, I declare." The whole group turned their heads in the direction indicated.

"I didn't see the Lord-Lieutenant yet," said Miss Brangan, in a discontented tone; "let us go over and try to get near that tent where they are now."

"Oh no, don't! They'll be going now directly, and we can watch them pass out of the gate," cried Dicky.

But Miss Brangan would not be satisfied with this. She was determined to inspect their Excellencies just as she had inspected the other attractions of the *fête;* and she dragged the party over to that part of the grounds where the vice-regal party now were. Dicky gave Nellie a pull and a meaning glance.

"Let them go—and deuce go with them. Pack! Here come Orpen and Griffiths; I'm delighted they're gone."

Mr. Orpen engaged Nellie in conversation, while Mr. Tad Griffiths whispered hurriedly to Dicky,—

"Are you coming to-night? Orpen said you were afraid to."

"Afraid, eh? We'll see. I'm short of cash, though. Has he settled who is to be in the collection for the Derby?"

"Yes, ten of us; it's twenty-five shillings each. Listen; they say Mahoney's married to the housemaid. Lord!— fact! Did you ever hear of such a fool? Big idiot! Mulcahy said he'd join too. Is all your money gone?"

Dicky nodded. "I'll manage it, though. Who else is in?"

"Wylding, he is going it: he told me this morning he had his mother's Indian shawl, his own and his brother's dress suit, and a whole heap of books, in pawn. And the fun of it is, they're invited to a dance next week, and the dress suits will be wanting,—ho! ho! Isn't that a joke? Moreover, there's a nice row already: you see his father locks the hall door every night, and the keys are carried upstairs. Well, my brave Wylding hops in and out by the dining-room window; there's no area round the corner. And if the cook didn't see him and tell on him! Such a scrummage! And now, if this other little game is found out it will be a nice job altogether."

Just then Miss O'Hegarty appeared, having followed Nellie and Dicky.

"How do you do, Mr. Orpen? I hope your mother is better. Nellie and Dick, their Ex'cies are gone; I think we ought to be going. Nearly six o'clock! dinner will be ready before we are home. Come along, dears. Nice gentlemanly lads, those are, Dicky," she went on as they walked towards the gates. "I am glad to see you choose such nice improving companions: that young Orpen is so quiet and refined in manner."

A grim smile passed over Dicky's rather haggard face; but he did not endeavour to disillusion her.

"Who were those people you were with, Nellie?"

"The Miss Raffertys and some of their friends," answered Nellie a little absently.

"Ah yes: R. C.'s; I guessed as much. Their toilettes decidedly bore the 'mark of the Beast,' as Mr. Wyldoates calls it. Wonderful,—it's wonderful; but one recognises them always. Do walk faster, children. Peter will be so furious."

CHAPTER XXIX.

A JUNE morning in College Green. The Bank stood out clear and bright; the scarlet uniforms of the sentries and the white and blue wings of the pigeons gleaming in the sun, might, by a fanciful eye, have been taken for flowers set against the gray stone background. The strawberry sellers were crying their wares, and a flower-girl or two with a basket of pot roses and mignonette, scented the air as they loitered by. A blue haze shimmered in the sky; the smoke curled up in thin, transparent reeks. The awnings were all drawn down before the windows; and the day promised to be intensely hot.

Mr. Saltasche, driving over to his office from the terminus, seemed to find it so already. He lay back in his seat languidly, resting his elbow on the well of his car, and holding a newspaper so as to keep the strong sun out of his eyes. He reached the office in Dame Street, and ascended the steps slowly, nodding mechanically in reply to the greetings of some men who were standing in the lobby. He walked over to the window, and looked out. High over head, in the centre of the street, the telegraph wires ran; he followed their course with his eyes, and noted where they connected at the Commercial Buildings, and then went on again to the newspaper offices, to the Corn Exchange, and across town.

"Humph!" said he, almost aloud, "another couple of hours, and everything will be decided." Then, after a long glance up and down the street, he turned round to his desk. It held a goodly pile of letters and telegrams; and he seated himself to his morning's work. An envelope

caught his eye directed in a lady's hand—large round
English handwriting. He opened it quickly: it was from
Mrs. Poignarde, and had been sent by hand.

"DEAR MR. SALTASCHE—Eric has just had a telegram
from London about the race, and he is in a terrible state.
He has left with some men, in order to hear the result as
soon as possible.   C. P."

He tore this into tiny atoms, and sat for an instant
debating whether to telegraph to her or not. "Useless,"
he decided; "I'll go out directly the news comes." The
next letter that engaged his attention was one from Mrs.
Bursford, asking him to sell out her shares in the Leadmines Company. This he disposed of quickly, scribbling
her an intimation that he would see her in a few days, and
asking her to postpone her decision. He meditated a
decisive *coup* with that scheme shortly, and had no intention of allowing her money to be taken out of it yet.
Then came telegrams from Stier and Bruen, one after the
other. The Patagonian bubble, which they had inflated at
his bidding, had burst with great report; ruining some
people outright, maiming others, but leaving a fair sedi-
ment of solid profit in the hands of the dexterous manipulators. Saltasche grinned as he finished the letter, written
in German, of Mr. Stier. This letter enclosed a draft of a
prospectus—not in the German language—of a new company. Lord Brayhead was chairman; Mr. Hogan, M.P.,
was also a distinguished member of the board; Messrs.
Stier and Bruen, and other great lights of the City, figured
prominently. There is no need to go into the details:
every inducement, social and political, joined to the promise of ten per cent, seemed to invite the speculator.
Two hundred and fifty thousand pounds were required;
of this more than one-half was already paid up. Ten per
cent!—and the Bank of England only paying two! Mr.
Saltasche half closed his eyes, and ran over in his mind
the names of possible subscribers: the reverend Mr. Grey,
who had lately commuted, and in consequence borrowed
some capital; old Dillon; Mrs. Bursford had some money

in Five Twenties. He remembered quite a number. There was that "Tract Distributors' Orphans Society," the meeting of which was to be held the same day at one o'clock, to receive the bequest of the late Mr. Fuzelle— seven thousand pounds. Then he ran his eye over the prospectus again, made some corrections, and prepared it for the post. He did a great deal of business that his clerks knew nothing of; the gas stove by the fireplace destroyed all traces of his private correspondence, and burnt paper told no stories.

So the morning passed away. At a quarter to one he touched the bell. His clerk appeared.

"Johns, the meeting is at one to-day, is it not?—the 'Orphans Board,' I mean?"

"Yes, sir," replied the clerk; "at Morrison's Hotel, at one."

"See here," said Saltasche. "Go over to the Buildings, and as soon as the telegram of the race comes in copy it down accurately, take a car and follow me to Morrison's; give it into my own hands, do you hear? No one else's: and don't delay."

Then Mr. Saltasche put on his hat, and stepped down into the street. He kept on along the shady side, ex- changing gracious salutations with every one. He met a great number of men hurrying towards the offices, eager to hear the news of the race—some indifferent, and only sympathising with the excitement of their friends, and some pale and anxious. A cigar shop by the College was crowded with loungers—well-dressed men, trimly shaven and brushed, with fatuous, vacant faces that always somehow seem to lack a feature until they are furnished with cigar or briar-root pipe. They filled the doorway and steps (fortunate he who secured the doorpost to lean against), watching the passers-by with interested looks, and now and again dropping a languid sentence. Poignarde was on the step, his face turned toward the Dame Street side, his pipe of course between his teeth, and feeling, thanks to an unlimited number of drams, in tolerable spirits. Still an observer might have noted a paleness betimes, in spite of

the bravado ; and there was a pinched, drawn look about
his lips.

"There's a fellow goin' down there," he said to a man
beside him, "wins a sweep every year.   Every year for the
last five he's won a hundred and fifty sovereigns.   Fact !"

"I hate sweeps," was the laconic reply of Captain Du
Maurel.   "Hallo ! good morning, Mr. Saltasche !" cried he,
stepping down to the pathway to greet that gentleman as
he turned the corner.

"How do you do ?   Morning, Poignarde !" returned he,
nodding to the group in general, and yet to each member
of it in particular.   "No news yet !   When *does* the telegram come in ?   Do you stand to win, Du Maurel, hey ?"

"I hope so," laughed Du Maurel, a handsome little man,
with rosy cheeks and merry black eyes.   "I've backed
Rattler, and Poignarde has laid against him."

Poignarde tried to smile, pulling the ends of his moustache ; but Saltasche noticed the pale lips beneath it and
the contraction of his brows.

"Dear me !" said Saltasche, shrugging his shoulders, "I
can only say I hope you'll both win."   Then, with a nod
and a significant smile, he passed on.

"I say,—do any of you fellows know if he has any
money on the event ?" asked Du Maurel, striking a match.

"Too many (puff) irons in the (puff, puff) fire," Poignarde
made answer, oracularly : "deep old boy !"

"The innocent get-up of him—that white waistcoat and
the everlasting rose !   He's a character, ain't he, now ?
Awful clever man."

"Clever !" put in a third man behind.   "Gad, you don't
know half.   Mephistopheles was a child to him.   He's
been everywhere—is richer than Crœsus.   Edgerton Cathcart, of the Dragoon Guards, says he used to be at the
Tuileries constantly ; the ex-emperor was awful chums with
him.   He corresponds with Gortschakoff——"

"Draw it mild, now, I say.   As for Cathcart's stories,
such a liar as that, you know——" and Captain Du Maurel
scornfully puffed out a great mouthful of smoke.

"It's not Cathcart alone says it.   Theo. Wyldoates, of

the Embassy, told me also; and Metternich himself dined with Saltasche in Paris."

" Rot !" was the Captain's comprehensive reply. " Poign., my boy, do you believe all this ?"

But Poignarde, lost in anxious thought, did not even hear the question.

The " deep old boy" strolled along leisurely to his appointment at Morrison's—to all appearance calmly indifferent to everything save the serene beauty of the day; he nodded smiling recognitions to every one of his acquaintance whom he met. Nothing of his bearing betrayed the consuming anxiety within him. He took his seat at the window of the room where the meeting was to take place, no one having yet arrived, and looked out musingly. Opposite was the College Park, and a fresh smell from the grass and the new-leaved trees crossed the asphalte and dust of Nassau Street. A game of cricket was going on; and he could see the lads at play between the branches of the trees.

He was not long left to his meditations. All the members of the board entered together, and business commenced. Some sort of sick heaviness came over Saltasche suddenly, while speaking; he leaned back in his chair at the table, feeling almost overcome. The heat of the room was stifling, his temples throbbed painfully, and it was with difficulty he roused himself to follow and take his part in the business going on. How he longed for the sound of the car drawing up at the door! He was too nervous to look at his watch, so strained his ears to catch, above the din of the streets, the chiming of one of the town clocks. He felt sure it was past one; and the telegram was expected at one. The chairman was reading a report; and his prosy commonplaces fell upon Saltasche's ears indistinctly and drowsily, like sick-room voices to a worn-out patient. There seemed a lull at last below. A long line of dray carts ended, and he could again catch the voices of the cricketers shouting to each other at their play. He could hear the rattle of a car now, coming towards them. No; it went by. He wiped the perspiration off his brow, and leaned back in his chair.

"You seem very warm, Mr. Saltasche," said a gentleman beside him, looking at him pityingly.

"Indeed, yes. I feel the heat intensely to-day." Then with a strong effort he overcame his weakness, and sitting up, threw himself into the work energetically. When the quarter-past rang out, he scarcely heeded: the excitement had passed, and he was cool and impassive again. If an hour had yet to elapse, he could have borne it patiently.

He neither heard nor felt the door open; and when Johns, leaning over his chair, put the whitey-brown envelope in his hand, he showed no emotion whatever.

"Don't mind us, Mr. Saltasche. No apology," said the chairman, anticipating him politely.

Saltasche bowed, and rising, turned to the window as if for light. The bit of paper torn from the clerk's notebook needed no unfolding. The names of three horses were scribbled on it, one over the other in a column, and Sky-scraper was not one of them.

Ten minutes concluded the meeting; and Saltasche, who scarcely seemed to feel the ground as he walked, hurried back towards his office. As he turned into College Green he met Captain Du Maurel, who had been with Poignarde in the cigar shop. His sparkling eyes and pleased face showed that the result had not been displeasing to him. Saltasche stopped.

"Captain Du Maurel, might I ask you——?"

"Certainly, certainly," hastily interrupted the young man; thinking that his questioner could have but one idea in his head, like himself. "Rattler first, Mayfly second, and Oswald third."

"Thank you," returned Saltasche, with a mixture of surprise cunningly blended in his tone. "Might I ask you where is Captain Poignarde?"

"Oh, perhaps at Blunt's; it's most likely, poor devil!" and away went the lucky gambler, walking jauntily, and feeling immensely proud of his wise selection.

Saltasche ran into his office for a moment; and then, with as little delay as possible, hired a car, and was soon bowling along towards the Phœnix Park. He reached the

Poignardes' lodgings without much loss of time. The windows were wide open, and he could hear her at the piano as he crossed the green before the house. He knocked gently at the door, and passed the servant, who indeed knew him well enough now, saying to her that Mrs. Poignarde expected him.

He knocked at the door, and on hearing her answer entered. She jumped up with a startled look from the piano, and stood for a moment as if bewildered. Evidently she had not expected a visitor; for she was dressed in a long white dressing-gown, and her hair, fastened in a bunch with a ribbon, hung down her back. Then she recollected his possible errand, her face flushed for an instant, and she advanced a step or two towards him.

"Your news! You have come to tell that——"

He took her hand and led her to a chair in the window, facing the light, then seated himself near her.

"Poignarde, as we anticipated, has lost everything," he said abruptly.

A paleness came about her lips, and the pupils of her eyes seemed to dilate as she looked at him, but she said not one word.

"This does not come unawares?" he said, affecting a surprise he did not feel at her apparent equanimity. He saw well the blank chill of despair that had taken hold of her.

"No, no," she replied, with an effort to control her voice; "I have been always expecting it, and pre-pared——"

"Prepared to do what, Mrs. Poignarde?" He leaned forward, grasping the arm of her chair, and looking into her eyes with an intense gaze. "In twenty-four hours you must be out of this: his creditors will be here. I have discovered that he owes money to the Jews. He may get off—may effect an exchange to India; but you—you?"

"Gertrude Stroude will receive me, and she will place me in a school to teach. Oh me!" she broke into a wail of despair,—"how different from what I had hoped!"

"Do you know what that is? Have you realised the

life that is before you? Were there not governesses at
the Kensington school? Do you remember them? And
to remain there, I suppose, until Poignarde sends for you,
to begin this"—and he glanced with a sneer round the
squalid room—"this over again? That is what your
friend, his friend rather, intends for you."

"No!" she cried wildly, springing from her chair.
"No, no: have I not suffered enough? Why must I
expiate his wrong-doings too? Oh, heavens! India!
India with Eric,—and after all I have undergone? Never!
never!" She threw herself on her knees, and buried
her face in the cushion of the sofa, moaning with sheer
despair.

For one moment Saltasche did not move; he watched
her every breath. He had chosen the shaft with care and
judgment, and now, having aimed and sent it home, was
minded to let it rankle in the wound awhile.

Presently she rose, and pushing back with both hands
the locks of hair which, loosened from the fillet, clustered
about her face, turned her wistful eyes on him.

"If I could only be sure of escaping from him, I don't
care about the rest. I remember well the governesses at
school; theirs was a wretched life indeed, but not so bad
as this—oh, no!"

"If you go with Miss Stroude to London, she will never
lose sight of you until she sends you to India with or after
your husband. Rest assured of that."

She turned ashen gray, and clasped her hands together;
drawing near to the open window, through which the
murmur of the river came distinctly, she pointed to where
it glittered like a broad silver band in the sunlight, gliding
fast under the narrowing banks towards the bridge, where
the dark still pools, flecked with cream-like froth, showed
the depths that lurked under the smiling surface.

"If it comes to that," said she, "I have a choice: a
way lies there,"—and she turned her eyes upon him as she
spoke. He had risen, and was beside her; so near that
his breath was on her cheek.

"Adelaide, there is another way! Listen to me. A

way out of all this misery and wretchedness, once for all,
to freedom and happiness, far off from every tormentor.
Leave them, my darling ; leave them with me ! In twenty-
four hours you are lost for ever to them, and they are
blotted out of your existence."

Her eyes grew larger and larger as he spoke, and a flush
came and went upon her cheek. She raised her hands to
free herself from the arms which clasped her as in a vice.

"One moment, for God's sake ! I stifle !" she gasped.

He opened the door and the window wide, and placed
her chair in the current of air. She opened her lips and
inhaled it greedily. He knelt beside her, and took her
hands, burning and trembling, into his, and showered kisses
on them.

"Will you trust me, dear ?" he whispered. "Adelaide :
O God ! will you kill me with suspense ?" He let his
head fall upon her knees. She raised it with a sudden
movement, and looking into his eyes with a despairing
gaze, murmured,—

"Leave me for to-day ! leave me ! I must think. This
is too sudden ; and——" here her eyes fell on the open
door, and with a startled gesture she bade him close it. He
did so, and returned. "This is too sudden," she repeated.

"No !" he interrupted, almost fiercely. "You have
seen, known long enough, my love for you. Come, Adelaide, I have nearly a hundred thousand pounds I can
realise. We will go to Italy when you choose, my goddess,"
—and he lifted the great coil of brown hair off her neck
and kissed it.

"Wait—wait only one day !" she pleaded, breaking from
him. His face darkened ominously.

"Child," said he, "you don't know what you say. Look
at my risk ; consider the step I am taking,—not that I
speak of that," he added, hastily, "but I want you to think
before you leave me in suspense. I must make my arrangements at once. Adelaide, give me one word of assurance.
Pity me, dear." And he knelt again before her, and took
her hands in his. "Say yes, Adelaide, darling—just that
one word."

Like a little bird before a hawk, or a child fascinated by a serpent, she trembled and faltered, powerless to resist the whirlwind of entreaty and passion that Saltasche poured forth. He read assent in her eye before it was spoken by the quivering lips, and leaping to his feet he seized her in a fierce embrace.

"Go away," she cried; "for God's sake go away! I have said yes; is it not enough for you? Leave me."

"Yes, I'll go—to work for you: I'll see you soon again."

Saltasche judged it well to leave her. He did not fear that reflection would alter her resolution; not a doubt of his success ever crossed his mind. She would remain dazzled and stunned for awhile; then Poignarde would appear on the scene—drunk and brutal, no doubt. That was the only thing needful. As for Miss Stroude's influence, he counted that as nought. The humdrum existence of her well-ordered English home, where even any excess of piano-playing was perhaps interdicted, would have little charm for her. The pear was perfectly ripe, indeed, he concluded, as he drove back to town, and all that was wanted was to give the tree the least possible shock. Now to find this Poignarde, and send him home. Then to business. Some of those letters he had written must be destroyed. Stier and Bruen must be stirred up. He had realised handsomely on the Patagonians; but there were Colorado mine shares which must be inflated by some means or another before he could consent to part with them. The Trans-continental Railway, too: some French fellow was blowing on that promising scheme in the *Phare de la Loire*. He could lay his hands on sixty thousand, as it was. If the Leadmines scheme were energetically worked, and Stier and Bruen's last company (Mrs. Bursford must invest in that),—it would require three months at least before he could get together all his money,—with care his sixty thousand might be doubled. Thus he planned and schemed as his car drove on—foreseeing events with the sagacity of a master-brain, and meeting them, combining and arranging. By the time he had reached his office his whole course had been struck out.

Not so with her.   As soon as he left the room she threw herself on the sofa, with her hands clasped above her head, and shut her eyes in dazed bewilderment.   What had happened ?   What was going to happen ?   Everything seemed to whirl round and round in the room.   She was weak and exhausted with excitement and want of food— for she had eaten nothing since the previous night; and the reaction set in now.   She lay still, feeling numb, almost cold, until little by little she realised the scene just enacted.   Eric had lost all and must go to India, and she remain in London and teach for her living until he could send for her, to begin over again the wretchedness and torture, the drunken excesses, the scenes that were so terrible to her, the degradation and misery.   "Never ! never ! never !" she repeated, almost in a frenzy, and she rose from the sofa and walked to the window.

She could see away over the river to the mountains, where the gorse was yellowing in the sun.   A sweet smell came on the breeze, the tall elms in the park were swaying gently at its will, and the white blossoms fell like summer snow from the hawthorns.   She longed to be out in the open air ; the hideous little room never felt so stifling. She went into her bed-room and hastily plaited up the long coil of hair, threw off the dressing-gown, and put on a thin black stuff dress.   A coarse black straw hat completed her toilet, and she started at a quick pace across to the Park gate.   The sentry, sweltering in his uniform on the hot gravel walk, stared at her as she walked fast by, with her white face and wild eyes.   She never heeded the sun pouring down on the wide dusty path.   She passed the People's Garden, with its flaring *parterres* of yellow and scarlet, and the ponds where the swans were gliding lazily among the reeds and water-flags.   She turned aside at last into a solitary thicket of hawthorns, and flung herself on the grass.   A wide green stretch lay before her ; and beyond it, hiding themselves from the sun in a distant glade, she spied the deer.

At her back the city lay seething in the heat.   The domes of the Four Courts and the Cathedral glistened like mother-of-pearl, and a blue veil of gossamer-like sheen danced before her eyes. Summer had begun to reign in earnest. The great spikes of the chestnuts were fast stripping, and the ground was white and yellow with their scattered glories. The air was filled with the bitter-sweet of the fading hawthorn, and down in the orchard by the river-side the apples were swelling among the leaves, where it seemed as but yesterday she had marked the clusters of white and pink blossoms. She lay back against a tree-trunk, and opening her lips, drank in the balmy air; and taking off her hat, let it play on her throbbing temples. How beautiful it was, and how calm and still! Almost insensibly the excitement passed away, and she was able to think calmly and to consider her position.

She was to be pitied indeed—a wretched, friendless creature, passionate and sensitive, with a past of terrible memories, and only now recovering from a blow which had shattered the dreams and nullified the labour of years. Disappointment seemed to be her lot. It had been so from the beginning; would it be so till the end? She asked herself the question with a sort of despair.

Gertrude Stroude's alternative was hateful, and she could not endure the cold pity which had prompted it. She remembered well, at the time of her marriage, how Miss Stroude, in common with the rest of Poignarde's relations, had testified her disappointment and chagrin at Rodolphe Christien's decision. They had all espoused Poignarde's side; not one of them had felt for her. She clenched her hands with revengeful determination. Were it only in opposition to them she would dare this. She had accepted, and she would keep her word. She secured a brilliant, happy life for herself, and punished everybody. Gertrude Stroude would condole doubly with Eric now, as she did when he brought home the news from Uncle Rodolphe's agents; but she would never have a chance to sneer at her, and insinuate how dear Eric was neglected, and his comforts not attended to, and relate stories of other people, the point of which stories was meant for her. Bah! all that was done.

Then she felt stiff and cramped with sitting so long on the ground, and she got up and shook herself. She leaned against the tree and took a long look round her. She could see the soldiers lounging, with their red coats loosened, in the shade by the lake. The deer were tossing their antlers restlessly, tormented by the flies; and the drone of the bees at work in the blossoms over her head was the only sound she heard. Her eyes felt tired and dazzled; she had brought no parasol, and her headache returned. To get back home, and lie on the sofa with the blinds pulled down, seemed to her now the most desirable thing. Besides, there might be a message from Mr. Saltasche; or Eric might have come home; so, creeping along the shadiest paths, she retraced her steps.

When she reached the door the servant put a telegram into her hand, saying that it had come nearly half an hour ago. She went up to her room, and first throwing herself on the sofa, for she was thoroughly exhausted, she broke open the envelope. As she guessed, it was from Saltasche; but the contents were so startling that she jumped off the sofa. It ran as follows: "Pack up everthing, and meet London mail in Westland Row this evening; on no account fail. Poignarde will be there."

It was nearly four o'clock, so she had not much time to lose. She rang for a cup of strong tea, and having drank it and bathed her aching head with cold water, she went to work with a feverish energy, and long before six everything was ready for the route. Then she ordered a cab, and lay down until it was time for her to leave the house.

CHAPTER XXX.

MESSRS. Stier and Bruen, and their friend and colleague Mr. Saltasche, were very busy for a while. After the collapse and disappearance of Captain Poignarde from Dublin, the creditors of that gentleman, whom he had so cleverly eluded, threatened and blustered, but ended by doing nothing. Military swindlers are very common; and unfortunate tradesmen have only to grin and bear their losses, for any attempt to obtain redress only entails loss of custom; and they have always the resource of making their honest customers pay for the dishonest ones. So, after a few days, the not uncommon episode of an absconding military defaulter was forgotten.

Mr. Saltasche, by some strange coincidence, was in London now almost constantly. His friends in Cole Alley were quite astonished to see so much of him. They marvelled, too, at his anxiety to push on the new company so fast. He seemed to want funds, for he insisted on selling out a quantity of railway stock, which, according to the brokers' advice, would have been worth more money if he chose to wait some weeks longer.

"He must have been losing money in something we know nothing about. Ah!" said Stier, shaking his yellow locks.

His partner rubbed his chin thoughtfully. "I do not think that," he replied. "I saw yesterday a superb statue he ordered from Rome for his sister; it cost a great deal. He is always buying things. Yesterday he was at Christie Wood's and bought more china; his lodgings are full of packages directed to Dublin."

"Ha! he was always like that—spending fast always. He has some great *coup* preparing, and is realising for some big thing."

"Humph!" returned Mr. Bruen. "He is getting all his money together—that is clear; and he is not to be depended on. This Lord Brayhead and he are together now a good deal. What sums of money he is spending on that scheme! He has an engineer and staff at work. He will begin everything before he gets the Bill. How many of those shares does Hogan hold now?"

"Ah! he is well into the boat," grinned Stier: "everything. Leadmines (very soon we must sell that venture); Honduras Bonds; Trans-continental. He is clever—that young man. I do wish I knew Saltasche's scheme; he has one, I am sure." And Mr. Stier went off to the Stock Exchange.

Mr. Saltasche, we may be sure, did not take his good friends into his counsels altogether. It would have been highly prejudicial to his interests to do so just now; for he meditated nothing less than carrying off the funds of a couple of the companies which they had started with his co-operation. He was head and chief in reality; and having purchased an immense number of shares, and induced a great many people of his acquaintance to do the same, he found no hindrance offered to his lodging the money in Bank in his own name. There was nothing out of the common in that. Stier and Bruen might look dubious; but he knew very well their anxiety was to surprise his plan and try to share the profits. They would be very clever if they surprised *this* plan.

Poignarde and his wife were in lodgings for a few days. They had selected a dingy street in Soho. Saltasche lent the Captain some money, and the exchange was in process of being effected. In ten days at the furthest he was to sail from Falmouth. Mrs. Poignarde was to accompany him thither, and then betake herself to Southampton and the Isle of Wight, where a widow lady had offered her a situation as companion. Such was the plan arranged for the ill-starred pair. Mrs. Bursford, who had it at first hand from Saltasche, wrote about it to his sister and Mrs. Grey. People asked but few questions indeed about the Poignardes. Mrs. Grey was in her heart rather relieved that they had sunk below her horizon. Few people knew them, and fewer still cared for them. So the meagre account of their final arrangements was allowed to pass unnoticed. Miss Stroude was angry and offended at their having neglected to inform her of their intended departure. She too felt relieved to think they had disappeared for good, and was disinclined to give herself any trouble about them. Her feelings altogether resolved themselves into an indistinct sensation of thanksgiving, and hope that the ne'er-do-well couple might never turn up again.

CHAPTER XXXI

" 'Nichts in der Welt will rückwärts gehen,' sagte mir ein alter Eidechs. 'Alles strebt vorwärts, und am Ende wird ein grosses Naturavancement statt finden.' "—Heine, " Reisebilder."

BETWEEN three and four, one scorching afternoon in the last week of June, Hogan, walking at a rate that seemed almost suicidal in such weather, turned the corner of Cole Alley, and abruptly plunged into the office of his friends Stier and Bruen. There was a cane chair unoccupied in the window, which had been left open to admit such air as might be going; and Hogan threw himself upon it. Mr. Stier, who was standing with his back to the chimney-piece, his hands stuffed far down in his pockets, turned half round and just looked at the new comer. The worthy Hamburger's face expressed the most intense perplexity ; his spectacles were pushed up high off his forehead, and the white-eyelashed eyes blinked in bewilderment.

"Well, Mr. Hogan, you have no news, I see. Ah !"

"None. Lord Brayhead believed Mr. Saltasche in Dublin. I have seen his friend Mrs. Bursford, too. They know nothing. His sister is the only person who could tell us, I daresay."

"Ah ! His clerk knows nothing—not even where to forward letters or telegrams. Bruen ! Bruen ! I say."

Mr. Bruen murmured something, and finished directing a letter which he was engaged on. That done, he left his desk, and advanced to the front of the office.

"Bruen," said the senior partner, " it is likely that Miss Saltasche could tell us something."

"It would be well," said Hogan, " for some one to see

Miss Saltasche.   A personal interview would be advisable,
would it not ?   You must settle, too, about the City article
in the *Beacon.*   It was very lame yesterday and the day
before."

This was accompanied by a look which evidently conveyed some suggestion to the gentleman to whom it was
addressed.   The partners nodded to each other, and Mr.
Stier replaced his spectacles upon his nose.

"Will you go over to-night ?" asked Mr. Bruen of
Hogan.

"No.   In the first place I must be in the House.
Secondly, I am acquainted with Miss Saltasche; and under
the circumstances, I think a stranger would be the best.
Yourself now, Mr. Bruen ?"

"H'm," returned Mr. Bruen, thoughtfully ; "I suppose
I must.   I shall have to hurry; it is just four o'clock.
I'll come back to-morrow night.   How to do,—go straight
to her house from the train, and surprise her, hey ?   She
used to know all his business : a clever woman !   I do
not believe he is gone—absconded, I mean ; certainly, if
he has, he has left nearly two-thirds of his money behind
him."

"He has ! do you say ?   But why has he gone away,
and where ?"

Hogan was very pale.   He had taken off his hat, and
was wiping his face with his handkerchief.   He had been
so stunned at the news of Mr. Saltasche's disappearance
that he had been utterly unable to reason or think over
the bearings of the affair.   He had dined with the missing man two days before he left the Westminster Hotel.
They had walked down the street together—Saltasche on
his way, he said, to the Haymarket.   Hogan vainly tried
to remember any hint of his intended movement in their
conversation together.   His memory was a blank ; there
remained to him only a vague recollection that Saltasche
had been in unusually high spirits.   The dinner had been
excellent : champagne—particularly good champagne—
had accompanied it.   He bit his lip when he remembered
that item, and acknowledged to himself that the last bottle

might have had something to do with his lack of memory. The barrister was a moderate man ; but he was one upon whom temptation and opportunity were not lost. He certainly never "exceeded" at his own expense. But there are men who for three hundred and sixty-four days will eat and drink moderately at their own tables, and on the three hundred and sixty-fifth will deliberately make themselves very ill at a public banquet. And there are men of unblemished character, and high commercial integrity or credit, who think it no sin to cheat a railway company by travelling first-class when they have paid only for second-class accommodation, and by travelling as often as they can without paying anything at all. The most moral and upright have their pet sins, their "mental reservations," while outwardly subscribing to the Decalogue. That last bottle of Giesler's dry Monopole !

"If we knew that," answered Mr. Bruen quietly from his desk, "I should not have to go to Ireland to-night. Tell me where this lady lives—the directions."

Hogan briefly indicated the route, and engaging to meet Mr. Bruen at Euston Terminus the morning of his return, took his leave of him and the senior partner, and set his face westwards in very bad spirits.

At the very moment that this conversation was being held in Cole Alley, Mr. Saltasche was seated in a shady avenue of Versailles beside Mrs. Poignarde.

No one would have recognised him. A silky moustache of glossy black shaded his upper lip, and joined to an imperial on his chin, utterly altered the whole character of his face. His hair was cropped in the scrubby fashion peculiar to Frenchmen. A frilled shirt, diamond studs, and a red tie, gave him the look of a Parisian *gandin* of the second order. Nor was his companion unchanged. Her rusty black dress had given place to a costume of rich silk and lace of the richest description. Her bonnet, placed far back on her head, lighted up the masses of rich hair and the creamy pale tints of her face and neck ; in one jewelled hand she held a parasol, the handle of which

was solid gold and coral. She turned it round and round
in her hand, looking at it indifferently; *ennui* expressed
itself in her very attitude.

"I wonder what they are thinking in Cole Alley," said
he, reflectively. "Hogan will be in a nice fright. How
Stier and Bruen must be puzzled! How well managed it
was!"—and he chuckled. "The idea of my seeing Miss
Stroude on London Bridge as I went to the boat."

"It was droll," she observed. "I had quite forgotten
when she was to return."

"I don't believe," said he, turning round and surveying
her critically, "that she or anbody would recognise you
now. You are changed for the better, my dear,"—and he
smiled with a sort of approving air of ownership and
patronage. She saw this and winced, though she smiled.
Already the golden chain was beginning to gall her. The
Dead Sea apples she had coveted for years were turning to
ashes and bitterness. She was thoroughly tired of Saltasche. She did not understand him : her intellect could
neither follow nor appreciate his. She listened to, but
soon lost the thread of his discourse, when he enlarged and
expatiated on his schemes. Sometimes, when he had read
to her articles out of the *Beacon*, which he managed to
procure in Paris, her attention would wander miles away,
and the voice fall on her ear unheeded; then, folding up
the paper, Saltasche would launch out into histories of the
people of whom he had been reading, and she would listen
in bewilderment—vainly trying to recall what had gone
before. The theatre every night, concerts, every kind of
public amusement, filled the time. A huge grand piano
was bought, and she played more than ever; still time
hung heavily on her hands, and she hated the red velvet
and gilt of their grand apartments as fully as she had ever
done the dingy room at Inchicore.

"I flatter myself," continued he, "that my get-up is
perfect; but I must soon think of laying it aside again. I
shall have to return to London in a week at the latest."

"Have you thought of what excuse to offer for your
disappearance?" she asked.

"Oh yes, rather," he chuckled; "that won't take long. I am sending to-night a notice to be inserted in the *Beacon*. They are to believe in London that I was in Naples negotiating about the new Sicilian railway with the Government. What do you say to go to Naples, since you do not care to remain here? If we start to-morrow, I may have time to place you in a villa of your own. You can amuse yourself during my absence. I had better not send to the *Beacon* after all: no use blowing on the affair too much. I see Prince D'Istria's villa at Baia is advertised. We'll look at it together; and I will get all my pictures and things packed and forwarded." Then he looked at his watch. "Now, Adelaide, we dine at six; let us be moving."

She rose and took his arm, and they walked along the alley towards the gate, on the way to the railway station.

"How long do you expect to have to remain?" asked she.

"In Naples, do you mean? A day or two, at the most, is all I can stay—to my sorrow!" And he looked into her eyes with an expression of sorrowful anxiety thoroughly real.

"And you will return?"

"Need you ask, dear one? I will not delay an hour—no, not one that I can help."

As they reached the *gare* a crowd of people were passing out from a train just arrived,—deputies, clerks, business men,—scarcely one that did not bestow a passing tribute of admiration on the beautiful woman beside him. Saltasche drew himself up, delighted beyond measure; he appropriated every glance from the black eyes of the Parisians. Two men, one of them dressed and got up like a *jeune premier*, cast admiring looks into the carriage where Saltasche and his companion had taken their seats.

"*Est-elle belle, est elle jeune. Ciel! quelle mise!*" said one, rolling his eyes in the vain hope of attracting her attention.

"*Le vieux c'est le père; il la ressemble,—hein?*" returned the *jeune premier*.

Adelaide threw herself back in the cushions of her seat, and pulling the folds of her skirts close to her, relapsed into a moody silence until they reached Paris.

CHAPTER XXXII

" Ich muss dich nun vor allen Dingen
Zu lustige Gesellschaft bringen,
Damit du siehst, wie leicht sich's leben lässt.
Dem Wölke hier wird jeder Tag ein Fest :
Mit wenig Witz und viel Betragen
Dreht jeder sich im engen Zirkeltanz
Wie junge Katzen mit dem Schwanz ;
Wenn sie nicht über Kopfweh klagen,
So lang der Wirth nur weiter borgt,
Sind sie vergnügt und unbesorgt."—*Faust.*

CAPTAIN ·ERIC POIGNARDE, formerly of the 2d Dragoon
Guards, formerly of the —th Regiment, and now of the
—th Line, with a detachment of which he was enjoying,
in Her Majesty's ship *Ramchunder*, the amenities of the
Bay of Biscay on his way to India, was by no means the
only person whom the Derby "event" had affected in-
juriously.

Mr. Gagan's rooms were the scene of a melancholy
committee-meeting on the afternoon of the fatal day.

Mr. Gagan, looking remarkably anxious and ill-at-ease,
occupied the window-seat. Tad Griffiths sat astride of one
of the three wooden chairs—his arms folded on the back
rail and his head resting disconsolately on them. Orpen,
whose impassive countenance preserved its equable expression under all circumstances, was sitting at the head of the
ink-besmeared table : beside him Dicky, his eyes fixed on
the open page of a memorandum-book, in mournful silence.
Mr. Wylding, who had been admitted to the subscribers'
fund on the last occasion, was smoking the fireside, with
his boots resting on the top bar of the grate.

"A blessed go, I call it, and no mistake!" spoke Gagan: "two pounds gone in a crack like that."

"Two?—ten pounds!" roared Tad; "and what on earth's to become of me? I've pawned my Sunday coat, and every blessed book."

"You're easily managed, you noisy beggar!" returned the gentleman by the fireside. "Look at me: I have Charlie's togs and my own in the bank, and a whole load of the governor's law-books (he's on circuit), and my mother's Injun shawl. Oh Lord! what'll I do at all, at all?"

"And me," said Dicky,—"I've boned the fees, and it's the second time; there are two sets owing now," and the boy almost sobbed. "If I hadn't been cleared out at that billiard-room, I could have paid both a fortnight ago."

Orpen looked at him with a sneer of contempt.

"Bob Aubrey owes a whole year's fees, you little flat, and he's not one bit afraid."

"Aubrey's father is a clergyman, and he'll be let down where I won't; he's got friends here. What am I to do? what am I to do?"

"I say, Gagan, have you got any whisky? I do believe this little softy is sick."

Gagan nodded sulkily at the cupboard, and continued tattooing on the window-pane. Orpen fetched out a black quart bottle and a tumbler, and administered a dose of raw spirits to Dicky.

"Look here!" said he, sitting down; "we must do something,—it won't do to have a shindy just at present. Mahoney, you see, has rather blown upon us a little. Did you hear of his doings, Wylding?"

"No; what's that, now?" asked a couple of the lads together.

"Well, some friends of the family discovered that Mahoney and the housemaid were spending a deal of time in each other's company; and it's been discovered by the family that they've been married this month or two. So my bold Mahoney is to sail for Australia next Monday, with his *sposa*."

"I knew another fellow did that sort of thing," said

Wylding, with a grin. "Do you remember Jack Leonard
that went to Oxford? They say he missed a fellowship
examination on purpose. Awful clever chap: he's a reporter in London now."

"I'll tell you," said Orpen, reverting to the first part of
his previous speech, "what must be done to stave over
this time. We must club and do a bill. I know a money-
lender."

"A bill!" echoed the company, terrified. "Oh! oh!"

Orpen shut up his red pocket-book with a snap, and
moved as if to rise from his chair, saying distantly,—

"Please yourselves: what is it to me? I'm not in
difficulties. Look at Davoren, owing two sets of fees.
Aubrey has been warned by Dr. —— that his name will
be taken off the books in three days."

"You said just now he wasn't afraid," interrupted Dicky,
hotly.

"Neither is he afraid; 'cause he's always drunk, that's
why. Wylding, you'd better be looking out, too. I want
that four pounds for my tutor, if you please."

"I tell you what, boys," said Tad, lifting up his head
for the first time; "come on and settle the bill notion at
once; it must be done. How much will it have to be
for?"

"Eleven pounds for me," said Dicky, drawing a deep
despairing sigh in spite of the whisky.

"Six will do me; I'm going to be economical," said
Mr. Wylding, taking his feet out of the grate and coming
over to the table.

"How will six do you, I'd like to know?" asked Orpen,
insolently; "you owe me four, and you have all those
traps in pawn."

"So as you get your four, Judas Iscariot, what's that to
you?" was the gracious answer of the gentleman, as he
poured himself out a dram of spirits.

Mr. Orpen took no notice; he continued writing down
the several amounts in a column of his pocket-book. Then
he added them all up.

"Five-and-thirty pounds. Now, see here: this must be

divided ; we'll make two bills, say of twenty pounds each.
And then there'll be the interest—forty per cent. That'll
be, let me see, eight pounds on each bill."

"Sixteen pounds to pay! O Lor'! we can't ever," cried
Dicky.

"Per annum, you idiot; for a month or two it's only
the twelfth of that," hastily added the financier.

"Must be done," said Tad, lighthearted and impecunious
ever. "We have had one blow-up, and will have to be
good boys for a while, till that jackass Mahoney is forgotten."

So it was settled that two bills, one of twenty and the
other of fifteen pounds, were to be drawn. There was a
slight difficulty as to whose name should adorn them—
none of the boys save Orpen having reached his twenty-
first year—and Orpen declined positively to take them out
in his name. After much debating a person was found—
the keeper of a saloon frequented by the lads—who for a
consideration agreed to appear as the drawer of the bills.

Mr. Melchisedech insisted on having a month's interest
in advance, and the bills were drawn for two months.
Dicky received his share, and gave a note of hand for the
amount to Orpen, as did also the other lads.

Relieved from present anxiety, Dicky Davoren speedily
forgot his narrow escape, and spent the half-sovereign that
remained to him of his ill-gotten money with his usual
spendthrift carelessness. Tad Griffiths had fifteen shillings
left, after settling his little bills, and he proposed to Dicky
to have a night's jollification.

"Where's the use of troubling?" said Mr. Tad, in an
offhand tone. "If you get in a hole your governor will
only have to stump up, you know. Enjoy your life while
you're young—that's my notion. Something's sure to turn
up before two months, you know ; and Melchisedech can
be got to renew. Lor'! I don't mind one fig."

Thus this philosopher discoursed. And Dicky, whose
mind was relieved from the terror ever haunting it of
Dr. ——'s notification being sent to his father, jingled his
shillings in his pocket, and yielded himself to the glamour

of his friend's tongue. So instead of going home to dinner,
he and Tad took an outside car and drove to a billiard-room
near the canal.   Here they remained for a couple of hours,
betting on the game and occasionally taking part in it.
Betting they found to be the more lucrative.   Tad had
some experience, and knew whom and when to back.
Some officers from the barracks were playing.   There was
a stout English major, who seemed remarkably skilful, and
whose play was certainly a study; betimes, in the beginning of a game, he made strokes so grotesquely bad that
even Dicky laughed at them; then he would collect himself and do astonishing execution.   They left this at six
o'clock, having won about five shillings between them.
Mr. Griffiths proposed dinner, and named " The Brander,"
near Hawkins Street, as a satisfactory place.   Then, of
course, another car was hailed, although they could have
walked the distance in fifteen minutes; and they were
speedily set down at the door of the restaurant.   The
brazen-faced barmaid bestowed a nod of recognition on Tad
that filled Dicky's soul with envy.

"Now, what 'll you have, gentlemen ?" asked she.

"Dinner.   We're going to dine," replied Dicky, with an
important swagger.

"I'll take a glass of sherry—*dry*," answered Tad, with
nice discrimination.   "Try one, Dick : give you an appetite."

"*Pale* for me," returned Dicky, not to be outdone.
"Will you take a glass for yourself, my dear ?"

The barmaid grinned as she filled both youths' glasses
out of a decanter of Hambro' sherry, and her own out of a
private decanter of burnt sugar and water.

"Now, what have you got for our dinner ?" Dicky
shouted to a waiter.   "Lobster ?—eh ?"

"Lobster, sir ?   No, sir; there's nothing at all in the
house except a cold shoulder of mutton, sir."

Dicky and Tad made a grimace of indescribable contempt
and disgust.   Tad swore audibly.   There was no help for
it, however.   Presently the cold shoulder of mutton made
its appearance, flanked by a dish of such potatoes as are in

vogue at these establishments—hideous to see; and greens which had been cooked in the early morning, and were now made presentable by the simple process of dipping them into boiling water. Beer was ordered by Tad, and sherry by Dicky. When the waiter returned with them, the last-named young gentleman, fixing him with his eye, demanded, in an offhand tone,—

"Where's the currant jelly?"

"Currant jelly, sir! For what, sir?" asked the waiter, respectfully.

"For this mutton, of course: do you imagine I'm going to eat it without?"

"We don't furnish currant jelly, sir."

"You don't, eh? Is this an hotel?"

"It is, sir; it's the Brander Hotel, sir!" The waiter was indignant.

"You call this an hotel, do you? and you expect people to dine without the proper sauces and condiments—eh! do you? Fetch me red currant jelly at once."

"Divle iver I see any one ait such a thing!"

"You didn't!" returned Dicky, in a tone of withering contempt. "Well, allow me to tell you, my good man, I never saw any one dine on cold mutton without it in all my life."

"Faix, I did often then, sir—begor did I," said the waiter; taken in, however, by the authoritative manner of the youth, he went out and returned with a pot of currant jelly, of which Mr. Davoren showed his appreciation by eating it clean out. He refused most positively to pay extra for this item when their bill was brought—telling the waiter coolly that he would charge for the salt next, and reminding him sarcastically that he had omitted to notice the mustard which the other gentleman had consumed. The other gentleman looked on, meantime, with semi-drunken gravity. Dicky carried the day. He profited by a moment of irresolution on the waiter's part to consign him to the warm regions, and throwing the amount of the bill—ten shillings—on the table, hooked his arm into Tad's and left the restaurant triumphant. The carman,

who had waited outside, informed them gratuitously that it
was very dry weather.   Tad jerked him a sixpence, and
nodded in the direction of the bar they had just left.
Having refreshed himself, the jarvey came out in high good
humour and suggested to the gentlemen to take " a breath
of fresh element out towards the Park." They agreed ;
and what with the drive and the theatre and supper afterwards, there remained of their joint twenty-five shillings,
and their winnings besides, only a few coppers in Dicky's
pocket when his considerate friend helped him into the
railway carriage on his way home.

" Good-night, ole f'ler," said Mr. Griffiths, after a prolonged handshaking.   " Never mind, I shay.   Get in a
hole, you know, gov'nor'sh 'bliged help sh'out again."

Dicky thanked him with effusion.   Somehow the idea
did not seem at all so reassuring next day.   The brilliant
and comfortable perspective sketched by his friend Tad
melted away almost altogether ; and there remained only
the deadening sensation that he owed eleven pounds since
the day before yesterday, and was twelve shillings further
off being able to pay it than he had been last night.

CHAPTER XXXIII

" Truth may perhaps come to the price of a peril that showeth best by day, but it will not rise to the price of a diamond or carbuncle that showeth best in varied lights. A mixture of a lie doth ever add pleasure. Doth any man doubt, that if there were taken out of men's minds vain opinions, flattering hopes, false valuations, imaginations as one would, and the like ; but it would leave the minds of a number of men poor shrunken things, full of melancholy and indisposition, and unpleasing to themselves."—*Bacon.*

" IT's the most unaccountable proceeding I ever remember to have heard of. Disappear in broad daylight, without ever giving notice to anybody, leaving one in such suspense ; and then a newspaper paragraph like this informs one of his whereabouts ! Do let me see that *Beacon*, Mr. Hogan. Are you sure it is he ?"

The speaker, Mrs. Bursford, who was seated in her easychair, stretched out her hand for the newspaper which Mr. Hogan had just brought in.

" Where is it ? Oh yes :—' Mr. Saltasche has had an interview with Signor Minghetti, and has quitted Naples *en route* for Vienna.' Well, well, it must be he : and what has he been doing in Naples ?"

" Or what is he going to do in Vienna ?" said Hogan, laughing. "That gives me very little concern, so that he reappears here, I can assure you. What a fright I did get, to be sure ! You know our friend Mr. Bruen went over to Dublin one night to see Miss Saltasche. She laughed at his fears, but at the same time could give him no information. They knew nothing about him at his office at all. At the same time, neither Johns, his clerk, nor Miss

Saltasche seemed to care in the least, or attach any importance to his disappearance."

"Elizabeth Saltasche knows him better," said Mrs. Bursford, drowsily. "How fearfully warm it is, to be sure!"

Miss Diana was leaning back in her chair, fanning herself with a blue and gold fan. "Fearfully warm!" she echoed.

"Just allow me," said Hogan, taking the fan from her. "How I should have enjoyed this last night in the House! Is it not awful to keep us in town this way? It will soon be over now, thank goodness!"

Diana smiled faintly, half closing her eyes under the vigorous breeze of the fan. She was not by any means in a hurry to leave London. She had now been there nearly four months, engaged in the struggle, and success had not as yet crowned her efforts. All her forces had been drawn up, and she had been sitting round the fortress, which had as yet given no tangible sign of surrender. Saltasche had deserted for the nonce; but he was to return, and she hoped to press him into the service for the final attack, ere the rising of Parliament should necessitate a retreat.

"How long have you to suffer now?" she asked, in the faintest die-away tone.

"Hum—another fortnight, I daresay, will see me nearly out of it. I'll go to Scotland, I think, for a few weeks. When do you mean to go? or do you remain till the end of the session?"

"We're going to Devonshire, to some friends near Exeter. After that, we thought of Blankenberg or Trouville for a while."

"Ah! Lady Brayhead is at some of those places now. By-the-bye, I met your cousin Miss Braginton in Regent Street yesterday. I was speaking to her. She said she would be here shortly to see you. She is staying with Mr. John Braddell, the member for Blankstown."

"I knew she was in London," said Diana, coldly. "Indeed, mamma, did I not say at the Academy the other day that I was sure I had a glimpse of her in the crowd? I wonder when she will be here."

"You were at the Academy, then? Did you look at the picture I recommended you to? Whom did it remind you of?"

Mrs. Bursford was gone out of the room. The door and windows stood wide open, and a pleasant current of air came from the balconies, which linen awnings kept fresh and cool for the flowers. Hogan felt more disposed than usual to-day for an æsthetic flirtation. The weight of anxiety had been removed by Saltasche's telegram to the *Beacon;* and although some things had gone seriously wrong in the City, he trusted that the return of their leader would set matters right again. So he disposed himself comfortably in the cool chaise-longue—thinking that an hour's pleasant, if idle conversation, would do no harm.

"I could not fancy. The portrait of Miss Babillon, the actress, do you mean?" said Miss Bursford, in reply to his question.

"No: Enid. Don't you remember Enid—that scene we were reading? Where is the Tennyson?"

He rose and fetched a large illustrated Tennyson from a side-table. Of course, from the special passage it was easy to digress to various others. Diana opportunely recollected several bits she "did not understand." Now, for two people to read out of a book it is absolutely necessary that they should sit not merely on a straight line with each other, but close together. Diana was really looking very well and even pretty that day. Warm weather suited her; and under its influence the wintry tints of her complexion had disappeared. A charming dress of silver-gray and blue silk set off her golden hair to perfection; and of course it was merely to hold the great awkward Tennyson that Mr. Hogan turned round that unfortunate chair of his in such a way that both their backs were turned to the drawing-room door. So it was, anyhow. And the explanations had barely lasted a short twenty-five minutes—only one piece had been dissected, and its abstruse and hidden signification brought to light; the second was in process of treatment, at a very much slower rate, and in a very much lower tone of voice than we would imagine necessary—

when a brace of exclamations simultaneously struck on the students' ears, and caused the valuable drawing-room-table, Doré-illustrated, Tennyson to slip from their fingers and crash down upon the ground.

"We have not disturbed you, I hope, Cousin Di. ?" said Miss Braginton, with beaming looks advancing to embrace her relative.

"God bless me, Mr. Saltasche! You back? Why?" And Hogan's astonishment fairly swallowed up and overcame his embarrassment. He was not deficient in *aplomb*, and managed to brave the quizzical, half-contemptuous eyes of Saltasche, and the triumphant, condescending significance of Miss Braginton's with fair success. Diana, whose very lips had turned white with mortification, speedily chose her *rôle*. She cast a meaning glance at her mother, who had entered, utterly bewildered, to find who the visitors were ; and assumed that air and tone *de circonstance* supposed to be peculiarly becoming to and indicative of the state of betrothal. So she kissed the extreme corner of her cousin's cheek, shook hands with Mr. Saltasche without raising her drooped eyelids, and sank back in her chair with a lassitude plainly referable to and caused by the same interesting and critical conjuncture. The amiable Miss Braginton hastily ran her eye over Diana's dress and general equipment,— both of them fortunately calculated to bear out the impression which was desired to be conveyed by her manner. "Engaged" was her mental comment. "Engaged, no doubt. At last !"

"Yes, Aunt Bursford ; I am in London, enjoying myself—oh yes, ever so much ! They've brought the carriage over. I haven't seen either of you in the Park since I came."

Of course she had not. The Bursfords had no carriage to appear there in.

"Well, no ; we have not a carriage this season of *our own ;* and—ah—of course we have been asked to join the Bradwardines ever so often, but really three girls in a carriage is too much ; and—ah—besides, the Bradwardines, you know, are *hardly* in our set."

Now Miss Braginton's boast was repaid with interest—
the John Braddells having been in business; but indeed
the lady scarcely heard the insinuation, she was so busy
taking notes of Diana's intended. "Not more than four
or five and twenty, quite plain-looking, and nothing of
manner or style. Diana just looks like his aunt." She
was already composing a letter home to Dublin.

"Are you going out at all, Blanche?" asked Diana, who
had taken a good-natured, patronising tone. "Mamma,
are we not going to Lady Clanronald's at-home on Friday?
We could quite easily get a card for Blanche."

"Well, if she'd care for leaving her friends. You know
she is staying with the Braddells; and—ah—I *couldn't*,
you know, ask dear Lady Clanronald for cards for them."

"Pray don't speak of it, aunt. I don't think Amelia
would in the least care for the Clanronalds. You see they
are in such a mixed set—*Roman Catholics*, and that sort of
creatures."

Diana gave a sort of little jump.

"Lord G——!" Mr. Saltasche had been talking rapidly
to Hogan for the few moments occupied by this little interlude; and now, having occasion to use that nobleman's
name, raised his tone unconsciously, as people will do when
they have to mention a name with a handle to it. Silence
was imposed on the ladies—not a bit too soon, for Miss
Braginton's blackberry eyes were gleaming ominously.

"Lord G——," continued the speaker, "was exceedingly
pleased with the intelligence; and he told me just now
that the Government will take up the matter immediately.
The English shareholders will be especially favoured in the
scheme."

"You have been seeing Lord G——, then?" said Diana
in awestruck tones, and heartily glad of the *divertissement*
thus afforded. Miss Braginton almost gaped with astonishment.

"Yes, I've been over to Naples, to talk to Minghetti, an
old friend of mine. I dined with him two days running
at the Ministry: delightful man! How are Lord and
Lady Brayhead, Miss Braginton?"

"Oh! very well, thank you. My aunt is at Biarritz with my sister. Lord Brayhead is at Claridge's Hotel."

"I must be away: I have appointed to see the Whip at the Reform Club," said Hogan. "Miss Bursford, good-morning. Good-morning, Miss Braginton," continued Hogan, bowing over the tips of that lady's gloves, tendered in the stiffest manner. In spite of himself there was some significance in his glance as he took Diana's hand, which she gave with an affectation somewhat unusual, and for which he was at a loss to account.

"*Au revoir, donc!*" She bowed and smiled as consciously as she could.

"Are you at home this evening? I'm coming up after dinner," said Saltasche hastily to Mrs. Bursford, but looking at Diana. Of course they were at home; so Saltasche followed Hogan, leaving the ladies to their own agreeable reflections.

"How on earth"—Hogan broke out when they found themselves in the street—"did you reach London at the same time as your telegram?"

"Bah!" replied his companion, airily; "I had left Naples two days before that was sent. I was in Paris, and telegraphed to a friend in Naples to forward that. Vienna was a mistake: I never said anything about Vienna. Then you see I was operating on the Bourse; and the rise in those Transcontinentals brought me over. By Jove! that won't do. I have to deliver on Monday, and they have gone up twenty. I have some slips here from the Paris papers yesterday; and I met a fellow who has let me into the scheme; so I think the *Beacon* financial article to-morrow will bring those shares down with a run. At all events, I stand to lose fifteen thousand by those fools Stier and Bruen."

"How is that?"

"Bah! hogs!"—and Saltasche shook his shoulders with a grimace of disgust. "Going over to Dublin, and shaking my credit there, with his nonsensical talk of my disappearance: damned egotist! Nothing like those Germans for egotism. I'll pay them for it. I must have a paragraph

for the Dublin papers now on Sicily and its mineral resources, and the new coast railway. I shall capitalise
shortly, and invest in land around Palermo."

"It's too hot to be walking," said Hogan, in a peevish,
impatient tone. In truth he felt his head spinning. So
they stood for a moment till a hansom approached.

"Now," continued Saltasche, "for a man to write up
this Sicilian affair. Jones, I suppose, will be glad of a
couple of pounds; and you must go to work now. I'll
drop you at Temple Bar. Here"—and the energetic
gentleman drew out a roll of papers and handed them to
Hogan—"I have marked what is necessary. Write it up
concisely; in a solid style, mind; and let me see it when
I call between six and seven this evening. I shall be
going up town again then. By-the-bye, am I to congratulate you and Miss Diana?" And Saltasche faced round,
with a movement as sudden and abrupt as his question,
and peered gravely into his companion's face.

"Dear no!" returned Hogan, with a sickly attempt at
a laugh; "not at all. Oh dear no! you are quite in
error."

"H'm, h'm!" said Saltasche, with a shake of his head;
"I must say I thought so. I can tell you Miss Braginton
gives you credit for it too. Hum—yes, indeed—it looked
very suspicious; uncommonly so. Here we are now,"
said he, stopping the cab at Temple Bar. "Goodbye:
half-past six I'll see you. I'm going to give these Cole
Alley blockheads a rating."

Hogan turned up Chancery Lane to Holborn; and Mr.
Saltasche went on his way down the Strand.

He grinned when he thought of how easily Hogan and
the women they had just left had swallowed his lie about
Minghetti and G——, —G——, whom he had never laid
eyes on in his life! "Nothing like a name: nothing in
life! If I'd said the secretary, now, or mentioned any
understrapper, I wager one of them would have made inquiries about it," thought he. Then he nodded amiably
to a Dublin broker, who was standing at the corner of
Farringdon Street, talking to a couple of men. He ob-

served the astonished look that came over the broker's
face as he returned the salutation, and also the pull he
gave his companions to look in his direction. He took out
his watch. Twenty minutes to three : just time to go and
show himself on 'Change. So he dismissed his cab at the
Bank, and crossed over to the Exchange. To a great
number of men he was unknown, of course ; but he found
numbers of curious, questioning eyes turned upon him as
he entered the crowd. Mr. Stier came forward a little
shamefacedly. Saltasche held out his hand with his usual
bonhomie, and plunged straight into business talk. He
transacted some business, too—making loud bids for some
condemned Peruvians, which had the effect of drawing
some more eyes upon him. Presently his Dublin friend,
whom he had passed at the corner of Farringdon Street,
entered, and made up straight to him.

"Hollo, Stonelock, how are you ? I've just come back
from Naples."

"Laws !" said Mr. Stonelock; "Naples, were you
now ?"

"Ran over to have a talk with Minghetti, my old
friend, about the new Sicilian line we're starting. Lord
G—— has promised me this morning that he'll have it
taken up in no time."

"God bless us all, man !" was all Mr. Stonelock could
say.

Then another man came up, heated and panting.

"I say, Saltasche, this is most infernal, I say,—the way
the *Beacon* has attacked the Mutual Combination Assurance
Bank. In three days, I declare to Heaven, the stock has
gone down to five-and-twenty ; and I bought at sixty.
Those infernal newspapers will kill all enterprise in the
country, I say."

"Why, the *Daily Rattletrap* is running ' Combinations '
down a month back."

"No, it's not : that's been stopped ; the manager is
paying fifteen pounds a week for advertisements." And
the warm gentleman, after exchanging a knowing wink,
plunged back into the din.

" Scandalous state of affairs—'pon my soul it's scandal-ous !" said Mr. Saltasche : "the idea of any newspaper blackmailing that way. Stonelock, is it not audacious of the *Beacon*, now ?"

" Yankee notions, my dear boy. The manager of the Diddlewhey manganese works refused to pay the *Rattletrap* ten pounds a week for advertisements ; and now see where they are. That Chaffinch, the editor, blew on the whole dodge. Sharp fellow that !"

" Fifteen pounds a week ; ten pounds a week. By Jove !" thought Mr. Saltasche, " I'd soon have Mr. Hogan's salary clear at that rate ;" and he began to consider to whom he could send a danger-threatening "proof." " Must be done by Chaffinch, though. Hogan would not like that sort of thing—oh no, no !" Then Mr. Stier came out of the Bedlam again, and taking Saltasche's arm, led him off towards Cole Alley.

CHAPTER XXXIV.

"A rock-surrounded bay,
Whence fronting headlands at the mouth outrun,
Leaving a little narrow entrance way,
Where through they drive the vessels one by one."

Odyssey.

It was a hot Sunday afternoon in August. Every particle of mica in the granite boulders and granite dust of Kingstown Pier glowed like molten silver. The harbour was like a mirror: not a ripple disturbed its surface; and every yacht seemed double, so clear was the reflection, in the water, of the brightly-painted hull and rigging. The tide was out, and the seaweed on the pier wall scorched and blackened in the heat. A tiny breeze that breathed but fitfully had enticed some few pleasure-boats out in the bay, and there held them captive, their white sails drooping, waiting its good will. Seagulls crouched languidly on the shady side of far-out rocks, left bare by the tide; and children in their Sunday clothes cast longing eyes at the pools where the little crabs were running about; and the sea anemones, hid under the tangle, were shrunk to the merest points of red jelly. Howth shimmered in a hot, blue haze; and the white villas that dot its sides shone in brilliant relief against the tawny fields of corn. The eye turned with a grateful sense of relief from the painful glare of the water to the masses of dark green foliage that lined the coast towards Dublin. The hottest and most exposed portion of the pier was that selected by the promenaders. Up and down, to and fro, moved the crowds, as if in search of something. All the motley population of a watering-

place joined to the contingent of Sunday people from the
city. Country girls, high-coloured of complexion and ap-
parel ; strangers, tourists, English and American, from the
hotels ; priests, up from the country for their summer
vacation, came down in scores from their boarding-houses
and lodgings. Father Jim Corkran, from Peatstown, with
a gorgeous black velvet waistcoat, swaggered about, casting
as he did so sharp glances in the direction of the Misses
Shea, of Mulla Castle ; one of whom was reported to be
engaged to be married to a prosperous wholesale dealer of
the Metropolis. Father Jim, strange as it may sound, after
his "denunciation," had been reconciled with the Sheas for
some time. Ned Shea was amiable and careless, and his
wife had little difficulty in bringing about a reconciliation.
Father Jim's "bark," as the saying goes, "was worse than
his bite." He prided himself on his peaceful, forgiving
disposition ; moreover, he was a member of that large class
who never have any difficulty in forgiving themselves.
The fact that there were three daughters in the house,
with fortunes of fifteen hundred pounds each, had no
doubt something to do with it. Father Jim was by no
means too well off, and could not afford to have the percentage on so considerable a sum of money "go past"
him. His parish, though wide in extent, was neither
populous nor rich. Eviction and emigration had wofully
thinned out the class of small farmers, who form the main-
stay of the prosperity of the priests, as they do that of the
country at large ; and he was obliged, like his *confrères*, to
supply the deficit in his income by taxing the wealthy few.
Five per cent is not an uncommon fee. It is almost the
rule when the woman's fortune is under five hundred
pounds ; when it exceeds that sum, a special arrangement
is made between the priest and the bride's family. This
custom, unknown in any other Catholic country, is of comparatively recent origin. Formerly, it was usual to send
round a plate piled with cake after the wedding feast; and
the guests each took a piece, and laid down his subscription,
—which formed the marriage fee. Forty years ago, when
there was a wedding every week where there is not one now

in the year, this mode was found to suit very well; but
with altered circumstances the priests have found it necessary to discontinue it.

Father Jim presently fell in with Ned Shea, who had
come up with his family from the country, and whose sunburnt countenance was turned first on one side, then on
another, staring in bewilderment at the crowds.

"How are ye, Father Corkran? I heard you were at
the sea. Did ever ye see such a power of people get
together? I did not think Dublin held half that number.
Where do they all get the dress? Bedad! the missis has
run a bill with what's-his-name, that has me nearly foun-
dered. Faix, only the hay was so good, I'd rebel."

"Ha, she has, eh? Who do you think passed me there
above, but that precious member of yours, Hogan! Be
jabers, yes! and here he's coming down. Look at him,
Ned Shea; fat and well the rogue is looking. Look at
him now and the day he came to Peatstown, with not as
much flesh on him as would bait a mousetrap. I was
talking to his uncle, Bishop O'Rooney; and begad, I don't
think he's content with the lad at all."

"No, now! why's that?" asked Shea; like all country
people, greedy for news.

"Augh! musha," replied his reverence, shaking his
ponderous shoulders, "he thinks he's giving up his practice
entirely, and has taken to newspaper writing. Rale low, that
is; but, as I say, take care the practice hasn't given him up,
ma bouchal. Here, he's coming over to talk to you. I'm gone."

Suiting the action to the word, Father Corkran hastily
mounted a flight of stone steps leading to the upper walk
of the pier; where he joined a party of bucolic Churchmen,
who, leaning against the wall, were sunning their fine red
faces, and enjoying the view.

Hogan, on seeing Ned Shea, dropped Saltasche's arm,
and advanced to meet him, with the greatest urbanity.

"My dear Shea, how are you? and why the deuce didn't
you let me know you were coming to town? Where are
you staying, and how are the family?—Mrs. Shea blooming
as ever, I hope?"

Shea wrung his hand with a will, and pointed out the whereabouts of his flock,—conspicuous enough, thanks to their gaudy attire.

"Barney's all right," said he; "and has a couple of splendid young horses coming on for Ballinasloe. Maybe you'd be wanting a pair by that time, Counsellor?"

"Not I! Where are you, though? I want you to give me the pleasure of your company at dinner on Tuesday. Is Killeen in town, or Daly?"

"No: but Father Desmond is; he's here above, stopping beside me."

Hogan wrote down both addresses in his pocket-book; and promising to call to see the young ladies in a day or two, followed his friend Saltasche, and they strolled on together watching the passers-by.

"I ought to have remained another week in Scotland," said Hogan, discontentedly. "What a day this would be by Dee side!"

"Ah!" said the other abstractedly, "or at Baia." Then recollecting himself, he started violently, and bit his lip.

"Baia! where's that?" said Hogan.

"Oh! name of a friend's place where I stay a good deal. By-the-by, I met Braddell, the member for Blankstown, you know: his wife was asking me could it be true Miss Bursford and you were engaged,—in fact, it seems to be the generally received opinion hereabouts."

Hogan looked at him with an angry frown, but did not reply. Just then they fell in with a large group standing all together by the water-side. The Raffertys now engaged Mr. Hogan's attention. Mrs. Rafferty almost immediately started the company into a walk, in the hope that the Member would distinguish one of her daughters by escorting her down the Pier as her cavalier. She was doomed to disappointment, however; Mr. Hogan singled out Miss Davoren, who had stopped as she passed to speak to them, for that honour. Her brother Dicky advanced beside Saltasche; and they speedily left the rest behind them, and started towards the end of the Pier.

Nellie was looking lovely: the sun lighted up her hair,

filling it with little golden shades, and the radiance and depth of the waters lying bathed in its warm embrace seemed mirrored in her blue eyes. Hogan, who had not seen her for some time, thought her more beautiful than ever.

"I have not seen you now since April,—since I was last here," he said. "What an age it has seemed to me!"

"Has it?" she replied. "And how have you amused yourself ever since in London?" A mocking glance accompanied the words.

"Amused myself? That is kind of you, Miss Nellie: and I am worked nearly to death. Ask Mr. Saltasche here, behind us. Let us climb up here: the bay must be looking pretty. Come." He led the way to the flight of steps at the end of the Pier; and they climbed up to the top and looked out to sea.

"Those boats look like seagulls, do they not? They must be becalmed," said Nellie.

"Come down here, to the water's edge; I have something to say to you," said Hogan, in a low voice. Then he held out his hand. She took it; and they descended together the shelving rampart wall down quite to the edge, where the sea grass, left bare by the tide, was shrivelling on the stones. The strong salt smell of the water and the seaweed came up; and the tiny murmur of the little pebbles as they swayed to the motion of the now turning tide.

"Nellie," said he, stooping down to her—she was standing farther down than he—"it is likely you will here some rumours of me from London, ere long; don't believe them, dear; promise you'll not heed them: won't you promise me?"

She turned round astonished, and looked up straight into his face. His eyes met hers for a second, then shifted uneasily; and his brows had an anxious, drawn expression.

"Rumours," she repeated vaguely. "What rumours? I sha'n't mind."

"As I told you before, Nellie, I'm not my own master. I hope to be soon; but things have gone very hard with

me of late, dear,—they have indeed. You will pay no
attention to anything? it's untrue."

"Nellie, I say, Nellie!" called Dicky, just as she was
framing a question. "Quick; till I show you Dermot
Blake. Come up! he's down there with Dorothy: we'd
better go to them."

"Allow me," said Hogan gravely, offering his hand and
stepping to one side to assist her. She took his hand to
step across to a rock. He pressed it, looking eagerly at
her; but her face showed nothing further than a sort of
anxious surprise.

"We have to dine with our cousin this afternoon, to
meet a Mr. Blake, her nephew, just home this morning
from India," Dicky explained. "See, Nell—that tall, sunburnt fellow down there."

Nellie and Dick left now, and followed Miss O'Hegarty;
who, leaning on the arm of the long-expected Dermot, was
parading the Pier. He was a very tall, broad-shouldered,
and athletic-looking man of thirty-four; greatly sunburnt,
as far as could be seen of his face, which was almost covered
by a huge tawny beard. He had bushy eyebrows, like his
aunt, but not her round, hard gray eyes. Dermot's were
dark gray-blue, with a merry quizzical expression in them.
Dorothy felt quite proud of him. One of the Bragintons
was on the Pier (from which it may be inferred that the
godly Lord Brayhead was not in the neighbourhood),
and Dorothy brought Dermot up to her with quite an
air, just as of the owner of an excellent *parti*, and who
is waiting for bidders. Miss O'Hegarty was to be a
personage of no small importance until her nephew was
disposed of.

"I really feel ashamed," she said, "to be seen with him;
he has such a colonial air,—just like a bushranger or gold
miner, you know. That complexion is really —— You
must do something for it, dear."

"There's the thanks she gives me! Why, aunt, I
stopped ten days in London on purpose to get myself fined
down before coming over—dressed myself at Poole's, too."

"Oh, pray *don't* take off the sunburn; I do admire it so.

You have no idea how becoming sunburn is," protested Miss Braginton.

Dermot grinned good-humouredly, twisting an end of his long moustache between his teeth.

"I'd have to get myself flayed to take it off. Here's a fellow coming up here just as brown as I am."

Dorothy bestowed a passing glance on Ned Shea as he passed by.

"My dear, that's some farmer—a hay-maker, or some working man. You don't see many gentlemen like that."

"I've been so long out of Ireland, I hardly recognise position by appearances that way, now. I declare in California there was an English earl twice as rough-looking as that man."

"The Pier is really crowded with very common people this summer. Every year it gets worse," said Miss Braginton. "Now, just look at these costumes—R. C.'s, my dear, of course."

"These costumes" were the Raffertys' and Malowney's, who looked like a walking flower-garden as they passed.

"R. C.'s! what's that for, eh?" asked Mr. Blake.

"Roman Catholic," explained Dorothy; "common people—trade, you know."

"Haw! Why, you know, ma'am, in Kerry the best families round are that persuasion. What dooced difference does it make?"

But Miss O'Hegarty never answered the question, for at that moment she spied the young Davorens approaching.

"Oh, here are Nellie and Dicky. Dermot, darling, these are Everilda's children. Don't you remember?—Everilda Davoren."

Dermot did not answer; he was too busy staring at the pretty slim girl in a pale-blue bonnet, with the lovely complexion and eyes, who was coming up, and blushing so prettily—and naturally too. Miss Braginton, who did not care to risk a possible comparison of her elderly charms with those of the new comer, dived back to her post of observation by the wall.

"We're cousins, you know—ain't we?" said Dermot, when the ceremony of introduction had been gone through. "Certainly we're cousins; I ought in simple duty to kiss you—yes, both of you; and faith, I'd do it too, only, you see, the very simplest acts are liable to misconstruction in this wicked world. Look here, ma'am; here's a seat for you till I take a stroll with my relations. I'll come back to you."

So talking, Mr. Blake planted Dorothy beside Miss Braginton, and marched off between Nellie and Dick.

"Bless us! what heaps of women. They ought to be packed off west, 'pon my word," continued the traveller. "Out in the west women are that scarce that if a man only sees a petticoat hanging on a bush he takes off his hat to it."

"Here comes my dear Miss Brangan," said Dick.

"Why does she bow so stiffly to you, pray?" asked Nellie.

"Well, a little lapse on my part. I was talking to the young woman the other day, and I unluckily mentioned a character famous in song,—'Charming Judy Branigan,' says I. My dear, she got in a fury all in one minute; and, said she, 'I'd have you know, Mr. Davoren, that my name's not Branigan, but Brangan.' I know why she was so huffy; her name *was* Branigan, but when the family got rich they changed it."

"Changed it? Why, pray?" asked Dermot, laughing.

"For gentility—to take the Irish out of it, of course. Here's a man coming up here; his name is Burke, and he has changed it back, as he says, to De Burgh; and there go the Byrnes, who spell themselves Burnes; and the Reillys, who call themselves Reallys. They're past counting. Dugan, whose father was Duggan; Roneys, who were Rooneys. Oh! look! look!—here come 'The World, the Flesh, and the Devil.'"

"What!" cried Dermot, staring at three over-dressed, elderly young women who were coming up.

"That's what they're called," explained Dicky; "and that swell yonder, he is a rich tallow-chandler, and he's called Count Chandelier."

"Why," said Dermot Blake, "you have as many nick-names here as we had at Yosemite or the North Fork. Come up on the top of the wall, and you will show me everybody; and perhaps, my dear cousin, you will allow me to smoke a cigar. ·You're coming up to dine with us in Royal Terrace, are you not?"

"Yes," replied Nellie, abstractedly.

She was looking down at Hogan and his friend Saltasche, who were standing amid a crowd of gentlemen talking and laughing together. What could be the rumour? What had he done? She thought he looked the handsomest and best-dressed man amongst them all. He had such a tone and bearing. Certainly London does improve people. The Raffertys were sitting on a bench near, and she could see that Mrs. Rafferty pointed out her friend, the Member for Peatstown, to every one who came up. They quite plumed themselves on his acquaintance. What in the world could the rumour be? Business? Maybe that Mr. Saltasche; but stay—was not Cousin Dorothy speaking of Diana Bursford? She was in London; could—no——"

Then a deep-chested laugh from Dermot Blake startled her. Dicky was pointing out some one below.

"So, eh, that's O'Rooney Hogan, M.P. Now, is it the man with the light zephyr coat? Hey, now! and that's the fellow they say my old flame, Di. Bursford, is to marry. How funny!" and Dermot stared at Hogan with his great eyes wide open. "Why, he's rather a good-looking fellow. See, Cousin Nellie,—what's your opinion? Oh! you know him, hey, do you?"

"Nellie, what's the matter with you? you're as white as a sheet," Dicky asked, abruptly.

"Ah, nothing!" she replied a little peevishly, for she felt confused by the sudden and inquisitive gaze Dermot Blake had turned upon her. "The sun is making me quite giddy. I have a bad headache."

"Have you, now?" asked Dermot, quite interested and anxious. "Come along down and take my arm; we'll go up to where Dorothy is."

They redescended the steps, and crossing to the outside

edge of the Pier, where there was the least dust, and where the *patchouli* and *frangipani* of the fine ladies did not offend them, they walked slowly on. Nellie passed the group where Hogan stood without raising her eyes. She could not, for Dermot Blake's were so closely bent on her. She was sick of the noise and glare and bustle, and longed to be away in some retired, shady nook, to think quietly over everything. She was trying to remember what Hogan had said at the head of the Pier—the exact words, his look and manner. It was no use. Dicky was chattering and laughing; and Dermot, who seemed capable of attending to both of them at the same time, appeared never to relax his watch. She was ready to cry with vexation; and when they at last reached Miss Dorothy, she insisted on sitting down beside her and Miss Braginton, and refused to walk again to the end to let Dicky show Dermot the beautiful yacht which had arrived last week from Cowes, and on board which the owner, a rich Manchester man, and all his family were living. They went off,—Dermot rather unwillingly, it seemed to her; and she, not being called on to take her part in Miss Braginton's discourse, sat and fretted and troubled to her heart's content. Dermot Blake—great, big, disagreeable, teasing creature—must have taken something into his head; and how in the world was she ever to sit opposite to him at dinner?

CHAPTER XXXV

" Wo so ein Köpfchen keinen Ausgang sieht
Stellt er sich gleich das Ende vor.
Es lebe, wer sich tapfer hält !
Du bist doch sonst so ziemlich eingeteufelt.
Nichts abgeschmackters find ich auf der Welt
Als ein Teufel, der verzweifelt."

"Ah—mine Gott! what shall pe done? He is gone with fifty dousand—perhaps a hundert—what shall I say?—all de money, Bruen!" shouted the senior partner. "Bruen, you fool! what is to be done?" And Mr. Stier dashed a slip of paper on the ground, and wringing his fat white hands, stamped up and down the hearthrug of the office in Cole Alley. Bruen, somewhat pale about his thin lips, sat stolidly in his chair.

"Well, he's gone this time in earnest; you have yourself to thank for it. I never was for allowing him to get the investing of the Leadmines capital—never! He got all the money he could lodged or invested in his name, or jointly with ours; forged our signatures. Easy affair that for him!" and Bruen shrugged his shoulders.

"He has daken every penny of eighty dousand pounds!" wailed Mr. Stier, utterly oblivious of his fine English pronunciation. "An dere is dat *Beacon:* I wish we were rid of dat *Beacon.* Ah!"

Just then the office door was thrown open, and Hogan, breathless, and with a face the colour of ashes, rushed in, and threw himself exhausted on a chair.

"What of this? Is he gone?" he gasped.

"Dere! read dat!" grunted the senior partner, jerking

him the telegram with scant courtesy of manner, and then
resuming his walk up and down the hearthrug.

Hogan drew a deep breath as' he read the pencilled
lines; and before he had finished the first half of the message, he uttered an inarticulate cry and fell off his chair in
a swoon.

The telegram was from Dublin, stating that Saltasche
was missing—that he had overdrawn his accounts at the
banks, and had taken securities, bonds, and cash, to the
amount of some thirty or forty thousand pounds. Moreover, that he had been gone two days before he was
missed.

"See, Stier: this won't do," said Bruen, advancing
hastily from his place. "Bernhardt and McKie are to be
here shortly, you know. Let's put him in the private
room."

A touch from Mr. Bruen's long finger, as he moved to
lift the shoulders of the unconscious Hogan, sent the bolt
of the outer door home. Stier and he then carried him
into an inner room, and laid him on the sofa. Then a jug
of water was fetched out of a cabinet, and poured over his
face.

"Pretty business for him this will be, too!" said the
senior partner, throwing up the window. As he turned
round he met his partner's eyes fixed on his with a peculiar
expression. "Eh, vat?" cried he.

Bruen frowned threateningly, and pursed up his mouth.

"Thinkest thou it is a sham—that they are con-
federates?" burst out Stier, speaking very rapidly, and
in German.

Mr. Bruen took the wrist of the unconscious Hogan in
his fingers, and felt his pulse carefully. Apparently the
result was not satisfactory; for he let it fall and shook his
head.

"We must pursue him at once. Send a messenger to
Scotland Yard, and—let me see': have we a photograph?'

"No. He may, though," returned Stier, nodding at the
prostrate figure. "But Saltasche will never be got—
never! Maybe is he in London dis minute."

Just then Hogan began to show signs of returning consciousness, and moved as if to raise himself. Bruen took
a flask of brandy out 'of a cabinet, and filling a glass,
handed it to him. He swallowed it at a draught, and rose
and stumbled to a chair before the open window. Bruen
followed him over; and placing himself with his back to
the light, keenly watching Hogan's bewildered face, said,—
     "Are you better? It was a strong shock that—hey?"
     Hogan did not seem to hear him. He was staring with
lack-lustre eyes out on the yard which lay before the
window. A hideous backyard, grimed with the smuts of
centuries, with blades of smoke-coloured grass struggling
for life among the cracked flags. A water-butt, dry months
ago, and whose staves were in a state of disruption, stood
in a corner beneath watershoots choked with birds' nests—
sooty sparrows' nests—straggling, shapeless tufts of straw
filched from the nearest mews or cabstand. A desolate,
overshadowed place, lying in gloom though the harvest sun
shone hot overhead. How well he remembered that out-
look for years to come! It seemed to have printed itself,
with every hideous detail, indelibly on his brain.
     "Take some more prandy?" said Stier, who had helped
himself to a dram.
     Hogan pressed his hands to his forehead, and started up.
"Yes—yes; I'm better. There will be an inquiry. My
God! I am utterly ruined. What is to be done? Let
us try and capture him. It was I who, at the last meeting
of the Leadmines, urged them to give him the funds for
investment; and there's the *Beacon*, and writing down the
Transcontinentals. Oh!" groaned he, letting himself fall
back in his chair.
     "Bah! what's the use of this?" broke in Bruen, con-
temptuously, walking away from the window. "There will
be an inquiry; and very likely the affair will be thrown
into Chancery, and a receiver appointed. The thing is—
set the detectives after him. Offer a reward to-night: five
hundred pounds. Are they doing anything in Dublin?
Better see if they will join us there. See here: I will go
to the police myself. Let me have his description. Height,

five-seven—hey?" And he began to jot down the items on a sheet of paper with a pencil. "Dark eyes and hair, aquiline nose, no whiskers or moustache. Have we no photograph?"

"I can get one," said Hogan, who remembered that the Bursfords had one in their album.

"Will you go to Dublin to-night, Mr. Hogan, and inquire into this affair?" asked Stier.

"Decidedly not!" returned Hogan, quickly. "I was his personal friend. I could not do it."

Hogan, indeed, thought there were few things in the world he would not do sooner than go over to Dublin on such an errand. Dublin would not see him until the Saltasche episode had been completely forgotten. How in the world could he face the Bishop? Barely eight months had been needed to realise all his sinister forebodings.

"Well, then, you will bring us the photograph, or send it without delay. And about the *Beacon.* Go on as usual; we shall send you the day's intelligence. By-the-bye, were your shares—the qualifying shares, you know, as Director of the Leadmines—made square?"

"Made square—fully paid up?" repeated Hogan. "Never: that is what troubles me. If I could only raise a thousand pounds, now, it would save me altogether."

"H'm!" sneered Bruen; "were I you, Mr. Hogan, I would raise it—and at once. Good afternoon. You will find me here to-night, if you need to settle anything further."

Hogan left Cole Alley in an unenviable frame of mind. He knew no one to whom he could apply for the money. He could give no security; and it must be forthcoming at once. Lord Brayhead was in Scotland; and even were he at hand, in London, there would be no use in applying to him. He was likely to be a heavy loser himself in the crash of the Leadmines; and, moreover, his Railway Bill having been shelved for another session—owing to no fault of Hogan's, though his lordship persisted in blaming him—he would be in little humour to accommodate the luckless advocate; and the idea of going to him and asking for the loan of money seemed to Hogan unbearable. He reached his lodgings in Half-Moon Street, and flung himself in his chair, utterly overcome. The heat of the room—though it was on the shady side of the street—was stifling; and it seemed to him that the open windows only let in dust and still hotter air from without; so he closed them and pulled down the blinds. Then he sat down in a cushioned chair by his writing-table, and unlocking a drawer, took out a vellum-bound book in which he kept an account of all his expenses; in this were sundry loose sheets of memorandums. With aching temples he read and wrote down calculations for nearly an hour. Nothing availed him; the blank fact remained, staring him in the face from column after column of black and red figures—bankruptcy, ruin, and disgrace.

Saltasche had carried off four thousand pounds of his. Nothing remained to him but a few weeks' pay from the *Beacon* and about two hundred pounds lying loose at his bankers'. He owed money, too; he had taken a suite of rooms in Half-Moon Street, and had furnished them pretty luxuriously. Nothing in Saltasche's queer *rococo* style,—polished bare floors and painted walls, and queer gimcrackery: Hogan had given an order to a first-class upholsterer, and had got what he liked—plenty of green velvet and gold, and looking-glass everywhere; Oxford Street *brimborions*, and prints which he knew must be good because he saw them almost in every house; the well-known Landseers and Holman Hunts, in fine, flaring frames; photographs there were also, in the inevitable Oxford borderings; and an enormous musical album, playing six tunes, and filled with bought portraits of dramatic and other celebrities. He had prided himself not a little on his "chambers" and their fittings, and had invited the Bursfords to lunch there one day, when all the arrangements had been completed, and the upholsterer's men had given the finishing touch. Diana, to tell the truth, had grimaced a little over the green velvet and gilt,—a combination which, doubtless on political rather than æsthetic grounds, is held by Dublin people to be excessively vulgar. She admired "The Combat," and "Dignity and Impudence," and "Christ the Light of the World," as if she beheld those rarities for the first time; went into raptures over the Bishop of Secunderabad, who was depicted sitting in profile, which did not suit him at all, with a tiny black skull-cap on his head, a pectoral cross, and his episcopal ring (a garnet as big as a teacup) finely displayed. Diana had become extremely High Church of late, went to confession, and dragged her mother, sorely against her will, to St. Alban's. She had frequently hinted her desire that Hogan should accompany her thither, and expressed herself utterly unable to understand why he declined; telling him the service was much more like that of his Church than theirs, and evidently expecting him to be overwhelmed by her condescension. She stuffed her prayer-book with markers and coloured ribbon, wore crosses perpetually, and talked of abstaining on Fridays.

Hogan threw down his pen after a while, exhausted. The feverish excitement caused by the dose of brandy had worn off, and the reaction left him almost helpless. Everything swam before his eyes in a mist, and his temples seemed ready to burst. He lay back in his chair for an hour or more, in a sort of stupor. The ticking of the French clock on the mantelpiece was the only sound he heard. He seemed to see Bruen's face; and his parting words, " I would raise it—and at once," rung through his head, and seemed as if they were set to the motion of the pendulum.

A knock at the door startled him. He opened it, and took a bundle of papers and a letter from the servant. The letter was from Diana Bursford; her large round writing, and blue and gold monogram, were well known to him. He laid it on the desk, and opening a press, drank a glass of wine before reading it. Then he returned to his desk and took up the letter. The post-mark was London: they ought to be at Dieppe. And he tore it hastily open.

" MY DEAR MR. HOGAN—We are back in Clarges Street. Pray come at once, and tell us what is this

2 F

dreadful news about Mr. Saltasche. Mamma is almost deranged. How fortunate that we are not involved in the awful catastrophe! Pray come at once.

"Ever, dear Mr. Hogan,

"Yours most sincerely,

"DIANA BURSFORD."

Hogan read it over slowly; then laid it down and seated himself in his chair with folded arms. "Not involved," he repeated to himself: "then their money is safe. Lucky for them!" Then he smiled to himself at the motive which had plainly prompted that piece of information. Saltasche had told him Diana had four thousand pounds. He repeated it over and over to himself. And now, how could he induce her to lend the fatal thousand pounds to him—lend it? There was one way he could get it—only one. He got up and walked about the room, with his hands pressed to his temples. Propose to Diana, and that within an hour's time, or else be convicted of fraud; or, if not actually disgraced, appear as the accessory of Saltasche. He might even have to resign his seat in Parliament. Then Nellie's face rose before him: he thought of the Sunday, three weeks ago, when they stood at the Pier's edge together, looking out at the silver stretch of water and the little yachts lying becalmed—their snowy sails hanging idle from the mast. He could almost see her sunlit hair and the wondering blue eyes that met his so shyly. And Diana? He glanced at his watch: nearly three o'clock. Then he bundled the papers and books all back into the desk, and locked it—his hand shaking nervously as he did so. He caught a glimpse of himself in a mirror as he passed, and started at the haggard face and tossed hair it showed. He went into his bedroom, and having washed, and brushed, and changed his coat and tie, he drank another glass of sherry, and started at a quick pace for Clarges Street.

Diana and her mother were in the drawing-room together; both pale and anxious-looking.

"Well, Mr. Hogan? Can this be true? Is Mr. Saltasche really gone? and are these dreadful rumours true?"

Hogan flung himself in a chair without answering. In a moment, as if he had paused to take breath, he replied,—
"Everything is true! He's nearly three days gone, and he has robbed every one. The detectives are after him. What have you heard?"

"Oh," began Diana, "the Greys are penniless. You know Mr. Grey had commuted. He entrusted the money to Mr. Saltasche—nearly four thousand pounds: it is all gone. The Helys have lost three thousand. Oh, I never could tell you all the people in Dublin he has ruined! And the funds of the Connemara Soup Society, and the Widows and Orphans of Scripture Readers Asylum."

"Oh dear!" cried Mrs. Bursford; "don't speak of it now, Diana. I can't endure to think of it. One whom I knew so long, and who was such a good friend to me. It is terrible!" And poor Mrs. Bursford began to cry.

"They have offered five hundred reward, you know," continued Hogan to Diana, in a low tone. "There's a description of him. By-the-by, I've been asked for a photograph: have you got one?"

"Oh, yes. Mamma, could you not give Mr. Hogan that last photograph of Mr. Saltasche? The police want to have one, he says."

"I'm astonished at you, Diana—I am, indeed!" cried the old lady. "I'll do nothing of the kind. Whatever the unfortunate man has done, he has spared us; and I shall not give it to them. I wonder at you, indeed, to think of such a thing!"

Thoroughly vexed, Mrs. Bursford left the room. Hogan rose and walked to the window. He rather admired the old lady for her outburst; and moreover, with the quick instinct peculiar to him, felt convinced by it, far more than by Diana's written assurance, that their money was intact. After a moment he came back and seated himself near Diana, in an arm-chair. He leaned one elbow on the chair, and supported his head in his hand without speaking. She was watching him anxiously.

"Is anything wrong, Mr. Hogan? Pray tell me: you look so haggard and worn!"

" I need be," he answered, slowly.   " I am on the brink
of destruction.   Nothing but a—a miracle can save me."

" Oh dear !   Now do tell me—do !   What is it ?   Has
he—has Mr. Saltasche——?"

" He has carried off the funds of the Leadmines Company.   He got them into his hands as treasurer, at my
recommendation as a director myself.   That's bad enough;
but I was not—not fully qualified to be a director at the
time.   Nine hundred and seventy pounds were due on my
shares—are due still ; and Saltasche has carried off every
penny I possessed.   Oh, Diana ! had I only one thousand,
I would be saved,—saved from utter ruin ! "   He laid his
head down on his hands, and groaned.

" Tell me clearly : is that the only thing that troubles
you ?" asked Diana, her keen blue eyes watching him
closely.   " One thousand pounds would leave you as you
were before this ?"

" Yes, absolutely.   That is the only pressure ; but I fear
it is a fatal one.   My God ! " he wailed, " I have no one
to turn to for help."

" You have ! " said Diana—a flush lighting up her face,
and a strange glitter in her eyes : " you have ! Let me,"
—and she laid her hand on his sleeve—" let me help you.
Take my money—all, every farthing.   I devote it to you
gladly."

It had come at last—the inevitable.   In a moment he
was on his knees before her, kissing her hands.

" Dearest, best girl !—truest, only friend !   Diana,
dearest, you must give me a title—an excuse : how otherwise could I ?   Say, dear, you will be mine—my wife."

The flush spread from Diana's cheeks over her brow ;
and there was an under-current of exultation in the tone
with which she replied, " Yes, then, since you will ;—but
here comes mamma."

CHAPTER XXXVI.

MISS DOROTHY O'HEGARTY was sitting with Nellie one fine September afternoon in the drawing-room at Green Lanes. The French window, which led into the garden, was open; and the relics of an afternoon tea were scattered about. Miss O'Hegarty was comfortably disposed in an easy-chair, tatting. Nellie, seated on a low chair beside her, her chin resting in the palm of one hand, was gazing dreamily down the garden, where Dermot Blake and Dicky were smoking in the espalier walk. Between them and her lay the flower-garden, all ablaze with scarlet and yellow; standard roses, now bearing their second crop, climbing tea-roses and jessamine, in full blossom, scented the air deliciously; the bees were at work still in the beds of mignonette, and brown and scarlet butterflies flitted to and fro. The peach-apples, dead ripe, showed their scarlet and yellow cheeks on the boughs; plums, covered with purple down, and apricots, sweltered on the red-brick walls. Everything was ripe: the flowers, for all their bloom, had the parched look that tells of coming decay; and every breath of air scattered rose-leaves and little jessamine stars on the turf.

Nellie was looking pale and languid; her lips trembled every now and again, and her eyebrows were drawn up fretfully. She sat quiet and silent, apparently listening to Dorothy's never-ending stream of talk; in reality her thoughts were far away.

"Two, six, pearl," began Dorothy, ticking off the number of stitches with a contented nod. Then, taking up evidently some previously discussed topic, "I do wonder how Diana can be such a fool!"

Up went Nellie's arms over her head, which she laid back on her joined hands ; and an expression of impatience, that was almost pain, contracted her brow. Not a word did she say.

"Idiot of a woman! She *has* three thousand pounds. People call it five, and no doubt this Mr. Hogan thinks it is that ; and it is that he's after, of course—the fellow. I have no doubt Emily Bursford is glad of anybody for her. She has had her share of trouble with her family. The sons were dreadful—dreadful scamps ; one of them married some creature, and is obliged to live out of society—in New Zealand somewhere. Oh, no!" Miss Dorothy continued, with a shake of her head that nearly displaced her spectacles, "I don't think the young man is getting at all such a catch as he imagines—at all. Then one died. People said he was the steady man of the family ; but anyhow, *he died.*" Dorothy said this in a dubious tone, as if the fact of dying was damaging *per se*, and must be held to be incriminating, as no proof to the contrary had been lodged. "Then there's Jervis to the good yet ; and a torture he is too."

Had Nellie been listening, she would have been surprised at this transition from the earlier views of the matter held by Dorothy. When the first news of Diana's engagement had reached the Fitzgerald Place *coterie*, surprise and indignation at the mésalliance had been the order of the day. But now the reaction—the inevitable reaction—had set in. Diana was going about Dublin with all the airs and graces of a *fiancée* desirous to make the most of her position, and showing thereby that she considered herself in no way to be making a bad match. This glaring defiance of law and order was not to be put up with ; so public opinion veered round to the gentleman's side. All the disadvantages of the Bursford family were held up in a strong light. Drelincourt's, Hutchinson's, and Jervis's misdeeds were raked up ; Monsignor Bursford, the pervert ; Diana's age : nothing was left undone ; and for a week or two it might be thought that the only adequate expression of her friends' sentiments would be a round-robin of condolence with O'Rooney Hogan, M.P.

"I wonder what her mother will do now? She'll have to give up her house. I suppose *they* will be living in London. Diana need not imagine he'll be taken up by people here. London will be the most convenient for him, and of course Diana will live there."

Nellie was biting her lips hard. Her elbows were taken down now, and her hands were clasped tight together in her lap.

"The way those Bursfords cleared off out of Dublin last spring," Dorothy went on like a musical-box wound up, "not a bit of me could guess why: Emily was that close over it. Blanche Braginton wasn't long finding it all out, though. I daresay Blanche wishes she were as comfortably settled with that old widower—the widow man, as Peter calls him——"

But Dorothy was speaking to the empty air now. Nellie had raised herself lightly from the low chair, and had glided through the open window. Dermot Blake, who seemed to have been watching her, raised his chin above the top of an intervening apple tree, and cast a glance of invitation towards her; but Nellie did not see, and passed, unheeding, round the corner of the house, and, lifting the latch of a green door, entered the poultry-yard.

The hens lay meditatively in holes which they had rooted under the sunniest wall, basking in the warmth, and scratching up clouds of dust. They barely unclosed one eye apiece to view the intruder. Their lord and master, perched on the side of a water-tub, pruned his feathers with dignified indifference. The pigeons, who were busy poaching in the food-pans, spread their wings and flew to the roof of the woodhouse, impatiently walking up and down the sloping tiles, and watching with their cunning yellow eyes for her disappearance. The terrier rushed at break-neck speed out of his barrel, where he had been sheltering from the sun; and, mounting on his short hind-legs, begged to be released.

Nellie saw nothing. She brushed past the water-tub, almost upsetting chanticleer, and into the woodhouse, latching the door after her. And there, amongst billets of wood, garden baskets, tools, and bunches of dried herbs and roots, she sat down on a block and began to sob. The storm had been gathering some time, and it had now burst. For a minute or two she was carried away by its vehemence.

Suddenly a laugh reached her ears from the garden. It was Dermot's laugh,—deep-chested and wholesome, like the bay of a great Newfoundland dog. She started up, remembering she would have to meet him again. She dried her eyes, and opened a little window hidden behind some bushes, to let in the air on her hot cheeks and brow. "Only a month ago!" she thought, as she called to mind the day at Kingstown—standing with him at the water's edge, the little weak ripples of the ebb-tide breaking among the seaweed at their feet. She almost saw him as he looked into her eyes when asking her for that strange promise. "Believe nothing: trust me, Nellie." She could hear the tones of his voice. She could see the bay lying calm and white under the August sun; and the salt acrid smell of the seaweed seemed to come back to her. And now! Could it be a dream? Diana Bursford was again in Dublin, and engaged to be his wife. "Wearing a ring, too," as Dermot Blake had said, in corroboration of Dorothy's intelligence; and Dermot had laughed as he had said it—indicating to Nellie, with a gesture of his brown hand, the engaged finger. He had been watching her closely, too, while Dorothy had been telling this great piece of news. What could he have meant by it? It was very impertinent of him, thought Nellie; and she pushed aside the currant bush that was growing before the window, and peeped out at Dermot striding up and down the walk. She looked from his huge shoulders and brown, manly face to Dicky, pale and careworn, and more haggard to-day than ever; and another shadow crossed her face. Dermot seemed in great spirits, laughing and stalking up and down the walk, on the right-hand side,

where the border of lemon-thyme was—just where Hogan
had walked with her that April day. Ah, how long ago!
How old it seemed now! She half closed her eyes,
dreamily. The soft moist fragrance of the April flowers,
violet and narcissus,—the little drops nestling in the cups
of the blossoms, and the low, earnest voice that stole away
her heart,—all came back to her. Then an angry feeling
rose in her. She put back the tears gathering in her eyes,
and bit her lip, summoning pride to her aid.

She closed the little window gently. Not so gently
that the sound did not reach the quick ear of Dermot
Blake, who had not hunted with the Red Indians without
learning some of their guile. He threw away his cigar,
and, crossing the flower-beds with great steps, entered the
poultry-yard as Nellie was coming out of the woodhouse.
Away flew the pigeons to the housetop; the hens, roused
from their siesta, clucked nervously; chanticleer flew from
the water-tub to the top of the barrel; and the terrier,
advancing as far as his chain would let him, snuffed and
fawned to the new-comer.

"Well, Mr. Blake?" said Nellie, shutting the woodhouse
door, and meeting the shrewd, kindly glance of his eyes
with one half-veiled and timorous, "How do you come
here?"

Dermot Blake mounted one foot on the edge of the tub,
and leaning his elbow on his knee, stroked his long beard
thoughtfully for a moment.

"Miss Nellie!" said he, then; "tell me—is it in there
that your hens lay their eggs, eh?"

"They do sometimes," she answered evasively, and
making a move to pass him; but he caught her by the
arm, and turned her round. "Look at me, Miss Nell;
you've been crying."

"Well, and—and—if I have, Mr. Blake?" flushing red,
and, with a poor attempt at dignity, trying to meet his
eyes, which, no longer laughing, but with something of
sternness and sadness in their depths, were bent upon her
face.

"If you have?" he repeated,—"if you have—wouldn't

you tell me why, Nell—eh? Nell, wouldn't you?" He still held her, waiting for an answer.

"No," she replied brusquely, and with a tremor of her lips that boded a fresh outburst. He let go her arm suddenly, and turned away. Nellie, with a feeling of relief, crossed the yard and opened the door. As she drew it to after her, she looked back shyly towards where he was standing. He was lighting a fresh cigar; Fly, the terrier, rolling in an ecstasy of pleading at his feet.

"Where on earth did you disappear to, child?" asked Miss O'Hegarty, when Nellie returned to her seat beside her. "I was wanting to ask you about Dicky. What is wrong with him—he looks so wretchedly?"

"He does, indeed," said Nellie. "I can't understand it."

"I think, really," said Dorothy, "he's given too much money to spend. That must be it. I declare one doesn't know what is coming over young people nowadays at all. There's Jasper Gore at Oxford; his aunt has been telling me he has gone through every farthing of his money. The luxury of his rooms—pictures, and china, and all the rest of it—was scandalous. His cousin did the same; and Dermot found him working on a railway in California. Not much pictures and china has he there. Everybody is gone mad, I declare. People old enough to know better doing the same thing. Look at Diana Bursford, now. There, I've dropped a stitch—must go back. See, Nellie dear. Nellie, you don't hear me: go and call Dermot—we must go. No, I won't go into the garden: it's too hot. Just gather me a flower or two, will you, and tell him to come?"

Seeing Nellie busy with her scissors among the flower-beds, Dermot advanced to help her.

"Are you cutting flowers for us?" asked he, reaching down a spray of roses high over her head. "What's the use, though, ma'am? Are we not going to Blakestown to-morrow?"

"Saturday, Dermot dear," cried Miss Dorothy from the window in answer. "I could not be ready any sooner."

"Grant me patience; I won't have a bird left. I'll go on by myself to-morrow, and you can come after."

But this Dorothy would not hear of. She had no notion of missing the *éclat* of the triumphant entry of this wandering heir into his seigniorial demesne; in fact, the reason of the delay was that she had ordered a special gown for the occasion. So she advanced her head as far as she could without getting out of her chair, and cried shrilly—

"Now, Dermot, how can you think of it? Blakestown won't be ready, it won't; and we must wait now till Saturday. Nellie, you'll be over the day after to-morrow, won't you?"

"Ha! Then I won't go to-morrow," said Dermot in a voice meant for Nellie's ear alone. "I mean to find out what those tears were for."

"Ah! because you are not going till Saturday."

"That's nice and complimentary, by Jove—isn't it? See now : tell me what sort of roses these are."

"Tea-roses."

"Take them, my dear : tea is good for the eyes," said he, with a meaning glance at hers.

"I wish you were in Blakestown, with all my heart."

"You can't mean it!" Then changing his bantering tone, "Nell! Nell! I say!"

"What do you say, Mr. Blake?"

"Give us that little rosebud. Just that one, now."

"No!"

"You won't! Give a fellow that little bit of forget-me-not. Nellie, I say, if you give *me* a bit of forget-me-not, I'll keep it." And Dermot accented the *me* emphatically, watching poor Nellie's face the while with mischievous eyes.

An indignant glance was all he got. She hastened back to Dorothy, tying the bouquet as she went with trembling hands.

Dorothy and her nephew walked down together to the station. "Poor old Di.!" said he, in answer to some remark of his aunt's; "she's a great deal too good for that fellow—a deal too good." He laughed as he spoke, though his tone was pitying.

"Humph!" grunted Miss O'Hegarty dubiously; "she hasn't so much——"

"Ah! no matter. This fellow and that Saltasche, the runaway stockjobber, always hunted in couples. And—ah—there was some talk going about him in London, then, a while back. May not be true at all," he added, hastily; "but Saltasche was an unfortunate connection. Yes, indeed, Di.'s too good for him—quite too good for him."

CHAPTER XXXVII

" Everyone that flatters thee
Is no friend in misery.
Words are easy like the wind ;
Faithful friends are hard to find.
Every man will be thy friend
Whilst thou hast wherewith to spend ;
But if store of crusts be scant
No man will supply thy want."

THE vacation was over, and the College boys were nearly all back at work. One day, shortly after the commencement of term, our old acquaintance Mr. Orpen and his friend Gagan were walking in the front gateway.

"Young Davoren's in a nice fix, is he not?" observed Mr. Orpen.

"This bill affair, do you mean? Yes, the little ass is in a fix. Mel. will kick up a shine, won't he? What's this the amount is now? Renewed twice,—and how much per cent?"

"Don't know nor care," answered Orpen, airily; "I fancy our brave Dicky will have to hook it. He's been going ahead nicely of late—got money to pay his tailor and bookseller, and then the fees. Moreover, Tad and he have been patronising their outfitters lately."

"And pawning the clothes—eh? Ha! ha! ha!" And Mr. Gagan laughed so violently that he found himself obliged to support his frame against a pillar. Orpen also indulged in a burst of hilarity, but in a quieter way.

"I shouldn't wonder," said he, scratching his chin thoughtfully, "if they'd both be off immediately—perhaps to-night."

"Laws, now!" said Gagan, "let's look for them after lecture, and find out what the beggars are up to."

"I shan't," said Orpen, flicking a crumb off his coat lapel with his handkerchief. "Young Davoren was with me this morning, trying to borrow a pound. What a notion I had of lending it to him!"

"Not by any manner of means," sneered Gagan, who had a fine opinion of his friend's prudence. "A precious flat Davoren must be, indeed."

"As for Tad," pursued Orpen, unheedingly, "he'll turn up all right; he's done it before, and his father bought him out."

"What, enlisted? are they going to enlist? Poor Dav.! what a greenie he always was!"

"Tad will enlist; the other fellar wants to go to sea,— thinks he'd like a voyage."

"I always knew what was before that fellow," continued Orpen: "all he wanted was rope, just rope enough—to hang himself. I've seen lots of fellars here, now, in my time, and I pretty well know their sort; but for a regular fool, I give it up to young Davoren—and Mahoney Quain, perhaps, too. Wanting to be equal with fellars that are twice as long on town, and know enough to buy and sell them. Pah! Why, the marker in Kelly's rooms here, in —— Street, used to get a half sov. at a time out of Davoren, just for telling him he made good strokes,—fact, I assure you: he thought he could play billiards."

Mr. Gagan expressed a fitting sense of contempt and disgust, and the gentlemen then went to lecture.

Meantime Dicky, unconscious of the elegy which his friends were composing over him, was sitting on a bench in a low public-house off Grafton Street, waiting for his friend Tad Griffiths. The bar of a dingy tavern, unillumined by gas, and looking out into a filthy, muddy lane, is not a cheerful place to be obliged to spend a couple of hours in. The heavy smell of stale tobacco and beer and damp sawdust was sickening; and Dicky felt his head almost reel between terror and anxiety and the effects of the vile atmosphere. He would have liked to have stood

at the door, but feared, lest he should be seen; and it was
necessary now that he should shun observation. So he
squeezed himself up into a corner where the projecting side
of a great cask almost hid him, and having borrowed a
newspaper, held it, under pretence of reading it, so as to
cover his face. Not a word could he see to read, although
he tried to. The lines all danced before his eyes, burning
like those of a person in fever. Every time the door
opened he shook and started, dreading to meet the eye of
some one in search of him: the tailor's clerk, to demand
payment for the goods he had ordered and pawned; the
bootmaker's son, who had threatened him already several
times; or, worst of all, a messenger to fetch him to explain
to his father the terrible affair of Melchisedech's bill,—
anything on earth would be better than that. Why had
he not asked Dermot Blake to help him out of his scrape,
when he was in Dublin six weeks ago; and why had he
misappropriated the other money? He might, had he not
listened to Orpen and Tad and Gagan, have saved his
money and paid off his share of the bill. Gagan had got
out of it long ago; so had Wylding. He and Tad were
the only two now. Then he thought of his mother,—the
poor bedridden woman, whose only joy it was to see him
and to hear him talk to her; for now she could scarcely
speak at all, having had a second stroke during the last
few months; and how he had neglected and forgotten her
of late; and what might not happen before he could return?
Dicky dropped the newspaper, and covered his face with
his hands.

"Are you sick?" said the frowzy barmaid, who was
knitting behind her counter; "have something?"

Seeing that he did not move, and noticing his paleness,
she filled out a glass of cherry-brandy and put it into his
hand. Scarcely had he touched it, when the door opened,
and in walked Tad Griffiths. He shook his head when he
saw the glass.

"Hollo, Dick! I told you not to do that," said he, reprovingly. "Did Orpen lend you the sovereign?" whispered he, sitting down beside him on the bench.

Dicky finished the cherry-brandy before he replied, with a shake of the head.

Tad looked grave. "Just like him," said he. · "In that case we must take a deck passage to Holyhead; all I have is a pound, and you have nothing at all. The boat starts at seven to-night, from the North Wall. Have you a great-coat?"

"No, I haven't. I've nothing but what I've got on. Oh, Tad!" cried Dicky, with a sudden burst of terror, "I'd like to go home first." And he looked eagerly into his companion's eyes for help or counsel.

"If you do, you'll need to start at once; it's after four. What do you want to go home for, you ass? You'll be home soon enough. Don't I tell you the governor bought me out of the Fusileers? He left me in a month—to cool me as he said. If you go home now, your governor will kill you over those bills and all the rest of it. Just let him find it out for himself; and then he'll be delighted to see you home by the time you get back from China or India, and all will be right as a trivet. Just give him time to forget everything, and then you'll come out all right and tight.

Dicky brightened on hearing this sanguine forecast, and consented to remain where they were until it was time to go to the boat. Tad sent out for sandwiches, and they had some more cherry-brandy. The barmaid entered into the conversation, which now assumed a cheerful, jocular cast; and at half-past six, flushed and excited, Dicky and his friend took their way on foot to the quay, to where the steamer was in readiness for the night trip to Holyhead. They took a deck passage over; which left them just money enough to get by rail to Chester, where the —th Foot was stationed,—in which regiment Tad intended to enlist. Fortune seemed to favour their schemes. They reached Holyhead next morning—cold, and miserably tired; and after a meagre breakfast started for Chester, whither Dicky accompanied his friend, and where they parted. Dicky went on to Liverpool, and had the good luck to find a ship just sailing for Gibraltar; on board which he engaged as cabin boy, having first sold his clothes to a Jew huckster. Twenty-four hours after leaving Dublin he was far out to sea.

At the same time, perhaps, that the two boys were making their entry into the historic city of Chester, Mr. Davoren was engaged in examining the contents of some blue envelopes which reached him by the midday post. Having perused them, he looked at his watch. Finding it to be just the time he might expect to meet his son coming out of college, he took an hour's leave, and mounting a car, was soon at the college gate. He watched the crowd of lads coming out ; and not seeing Dicky among them, asked the porter if he had seen him that day. The man replied that he had not; but catching sight of Orpen passing, he pointed him out, saying that gentleman might be able to inform him, as he was constantly in his company. Mr. Davoren accordingly accosted Orpen.

"Would you be good enough, sir, to tell me if you know where I can find Richard Davoren, my son ?"

Mr. Orpen raised his hat politely. "I have not seen him since yesterday morning when he called at my rooms— about a book of his, I think. About ten ; yes, ten o'clock."

"You have not seen him since ? or could you tell me if you know of any one who has ?"

"I have not, and I do not know any one who could tell you anything about him. I am very sorry indeed. Good day !"

Mr. Davoren then went to Dicky's tutor ; and from him he came away with a very angry face. He jumped on his car again, and returned to his office. There he found fresh trouble. A disreputable-looking man presented him with Mr. Melchisedech's document, and a request for thirty pounds to enable him, the drawer of the bill, to meet it. After a moment's thought Mr. Davoren wrote the name and address of his solicitor on an envelope, and desired the man to meet him there the following morning. Then, feeling unfit for any more work, he left his office and went home.

Nellie was sitting in her accustomed place in her mother's room; and seeing from her window her father, coming in at such an unusual hour, hastened down to know if anything was wrong.

"Wrong!" he shouted, angrily. "I should think there was, indeed! That young ruffian, your brother, has gone to the devil;" and he dashed down his stick and hat with violence on the floor.

"Oh! oh!" she cried, startled and alarmed, and perhaps almost more concerned for the paralytic patient above, whom a shock might kill, than for the cause of her father's violence and anger.

Mr. Davoren flung into the parlour, pushing the door after him with a crash that resounded through the house, and began to walk up and down, trampling the floor with his heavy boots in a perfect ecstasy of fury. Dicky had caused him a terrible annoyance and expense, and he was determined in no way to suppress his sensations. The disgrace, the vexation were overwhelming. He had no room for other considerations; and it was with a sort of anger that he encountered Nellie's hastily uttered reminder of the patient upstairs.

He ceased his march, and dropped into a chair.

"Every one but me, of course. God help me! What have I done that I should have such a curse in my children? How shall I bear it, after all I have done for him? No one did anything for me; and yet I gave *him* every advantage. I was willing to give him a profession. He got everything he wanted. Thousands and thousands would never have done what I did for him. And look at the way he treats me. I shall never forgive him—never!"

"Where is he? What has he done?" She gasped rather than spoke the words.

"Run in debt; borrowed right and left; made away with everything. Of course, he has run off now. No one knows where he is."

"Run off! Oh, my God! Run off!—it will kill mamma."

"Ay, indeed. God help me! nothing but disappointment and trouble everywhere before me. Last week I lost ten pounds, and now—look at this little monster. I had better go back to town, and inquire if he has let me in with any other shopkeepers. Heavens and earth! How shall I look any one in the face? Was there ever a being persecuted like me?"

So this distracted parent set off back to town; and Nellie, frightened to death and pale as a ghost, stole back upstairs to her post. She found her mother awake, her face turned towards the door, watching for her.

"Dicky,—tell him to come to me," said she, indistinctly, opening her eyes wide—blue, soft eyes, like her boy's. "Do you hear me?" she added, sharply; "send him."

Nellie breathed a prayer for aid, and put forth all her strength; then slowly, and trying hard to master her voice — breaking and trembling in spite of her, — replied,—

"Mamma, he is not in. I'll send him directly he comes."

"What? Where is he? I insist. He has not been here for days. This moment, Nellie: tell me where is Dicky?"

Her cheeks were flushed now, and her eyes seemed unnaturally large and bright. She tried to move, to raise herself. The thick tone had disappeared from her voice, and she spoke fast and nervously. Nellie's heart sank within her at this ominous sign.

"I assure you, mamma, you are doing yourself harm; indeed, I will bring him directly. I expect him now at once. Do lie down—let me settle the pillow. He will be in now directly."

"You are not speaking the truth. He must be ill. Nellie," said she, after a pause, looking with terrified eyes at Nellie's pale face, "is Dicky dead, that he has not come to me?"

"Oh, mamma; no, no. Why do you speak so? Why do you distress yourself? Believe me, he will be here directly—by dinner time; he will indeed."

Her mother spoke no more : she seemed worn out, and laid down her head, moaning faintly. The moment Nellie thought she could quit her safely, she slipped down stairs, and sent a servant for the doctor. How she wished Dorothy were near, or some one, to help her ! She feared that another stroke might supervene after the excitement her mother had gone through, and of which she feared a recurrence ; for she must know the truth some time, and if Dicky had really run away, it would certainly be the death of her mother. She sat down on a low stool before the fire, and in the darkness and solitude abandoned herself to bitter tears, and to thoughts that were angry as well as bitter. The heedless selfishness of Dicky, the callous indifference with which he had pursued his own ends, and the terrible result that might be entailed now ; the disgrace, the wretched fate in prospect for him, poor misguided child ;—all were passed in review. She had had her own troubles and heartaches, as we know, of late ; and this seemed to be the drop wanting to fill the cup to the brim. Until late in the evening she remained crouched before the fire. Her father did not return to dinner ; and it was the entry of the doctor that roused her at last.

He pronounced her mother to be in a highly dangerous state, and advised that some one be got to watch all night by her.

CHAPTER XXXVIII.

" What vertue is so fitting for a knight,
Or for a lady whom a knight should love,
As courtesie ; to bear themselves aright
To all of each degree as doth behove ?
For whether they be placed high above
Or low beneath, yet ought they well to know,
Their good ; that now them rightly may reprove
Of rudeness for not yielding what they owe ;
Great skill it is such duties timely to bestow."

Faërie Queene.

HOGAN had not followed his *fiancée* to Dublin. He preferred for many reasons to remain in London. For one,
he did not deem it prudent to turn his back on the
scandal, slight as it was, in which he had been involved
by the inquiry into the affairs of those companies whose
assets Mr. Saltasche had carried off. He had, thanks to
the timely aid afforded him by the Bursfords, weathered
the storm which had nearly engulfed him. As he acknowledged to himself at the time, he had escaped by a hair's-
breadth. There were ugly rumours about him in Dublin,
and we may be·sure in Peatstown too ; the Irish newspapers had fastened on them greedily. However, a *douceur*
to his supporter Mr. Killeen, of the *Peatstown Torch*, had,
he fancied, set that all right so far as his constituents were
concerned. There was ample time for everything to be
forgotten ere Dissolution should arrive. He did not want
to sever his connection· with the brokers in Cole Alley,
whose newspaper he still continued to edit, aided by Mr.
Chaffinch ; and he hoped to be able to raise money by
some lucky hit on 'Change, and to pay back the Burs-

ford's thousand pounds, and get out of his engagement to Diana.

The more he thought of it, the less he liked the prospect of this marriage. Although he had been overwhelmed with gratitude and relief at the time, as soon as the sensation of danger had been removed the impression began to wear off, and his gratitude gave way to an uneasy feeling of having purchased the accommodation at too high a price. He even began to tell himself that he had exaggerated the position, and that he had been taken at an unfair advantage. Nevertheless, he could see no way out of the difficulty. It seemed almost impossible to find anything like a paying speculation ; and Stier and Bruen appeared to think that his salary of five pounds a week ought to content him, and were disinclined to let him into any of the good things that might be going. The *Beacon*, too, was by no means the paying concern it had been. Stier and Bruen were very close-fisted in their dealings—unlike Saltasche ; and the financial articles were nothing like what they had been in his days.

He had not written to Nellie now for some time—only once, indeed, since their short conversation on the pier at Kingstown. A fortnight or so before Christmas he observed an intimation of her mother's death in an Irish paper, and wrote immediately a letter of condolence, as kindly and feelingly worded as he could make it. After an interval he received a short note of thanks, indited in a trembling, broken handwriting, and breathing of such sorrow and affliction that his heart—not too sympathetic, as we know—felt deeply touched. He wrote again to her, this time at length ; but as vaguely and guardedly as ever. He said nothing of his plans or prospects : the usual moan over his hard work, his loneliness, his dependence upon yet remote contingencies, and his hopes ; his mental sufferings that rumours so prejudicial to him, and so hurtful to the feelings of those who were interested in his welfare, should have gone forth. He trusted to time to set him right ; and so on.

There was something in it that jarred upon Nellie in

spite of herself; she compared the long involved sentences which said so much and meant so little with Dermot's straightforward way—the hints and half-sayings with his blunt outspokenness. She saw a good deal of Dermot just at this time. Then she remembered the unbecomingness of thinking of such things now; and she threw the letter —the only one of Hogan's she had ever treated so—into the fire before she had even finished reading it.

That very day Diana also received a letter from her intended, the tone of which displeased her mightily. There was some talk in it of an investment, by means of which he hoped to be able to repay certain and sundry obligations, contracted unwillingly though gratefully, etc. Diana drew down her eyebrows and her upper lip as she read. When she had finished, she handed the letter across the breakfast-table to her mother.

"What do you think of this? What ought you to do?" asked the elder lady, as she returned it.

"Go over at once, I think. I shall write to him to-morrow—not until to-morrow; or had you better do it, mamma?"

"Very well, Diana," assented Mrs. Bursford with a sigh; "perhaps I had. I can excuse your doing so, you know."

So the next day but one Mr. Hogan found a huge mono-grammed violet envelope on his table in Half-Moon Street. He opened it with some slight misgiving, and unfolded the following from his Diana's mother:—

"MY DEAR MR. HOGAN—

"As dear Diana is suffering from a slight headache, the task of acknowledging your letter of yesterday devolves upon me. Diana and I expect to be in London on Monday or Tuesday next. I hope we shall see you without delay in Clarges Street. We are somewhat astonished at some expressions in your letter which seem to indicate a possible misconception on your part of your and her joint position. However, we may leave all discussion on that

point, should there be (which I hope there will not) any
necessity for it, until we meet.

> " I remain, my dear Mr. Hogan,
>   " Yours most sincerely,
>   "EMILY BURSFORD."

Hogan laid down the letter with a deep sigh, and took
a few turns up and down the room. Then he seated himself at his desk, and wrote rapidly an affectionate inquiry
to Diana about her headache, demanding to be informed
on what evening or morning they might be expected at
Euston Square, that he might have the pleasure of being
of some service to them.

Diana, on perusing this missive, felt there was no occasion to hurry their departure from Dublin; and the event-
ful session of '73 had commenced before they were installed
once more in Clarges Street. Hogan was now almost
driven to bay. He was too pusillanimous to risk an open
rupture; and he cast about him in vain for some means of
paying back that hateful thousand pounds. He imagined,
foolish man, that if that could be accomplished he was
saved. The memorable struggle of the Government over
the ill-fated University Bill was carried on without any
assistance from him. He sat in moody silence on his
bench, as member after member entered his protest against
the measure. He might as well have been sitting in the
drawing-room in Clarges Street with his Circe. Then
came the resignation of the Ministry—the resignation
which they were obliged to withdraw, to the intense
delight of their supporters, and the fatuous self-glorifica-
tion of the Liberal Party in general. Hogan passed an
interval of terrible suspense until the answer of the
Opposition was made known. He began to realise what
his position would be if he failed to procure his re-election :
he would literally have to begin the world afresh, and that
with drawbacks so terrible that he doubted his power to
overcome them.

Diana also was very anxious. She felt it was high time
the affair was being settled one way or the other. She

knew that Hogan was penniless. He possessed, to be sure, some three or four thousand pounds' worth of stock, which at its present value was not good for as many shillings; but, as her intended said, there was no telling how or when it might go up in the market. Hogan had infected Diana with some of his habits—that of trusting in luck, for example, as we see. There had been no further attempt on his side to approach any pecuniary settlement of the debt between them. Diana and her mother were arranging the execution of a long-matured plan—namely, to remind a relative of theirs highly placed in the Government of a promise he had once made to Mrs. Bursford: that he would procure a Government appointment for her ne'er-do-well son Jervis. Diana contended that this promise could be transferred to Hogan; and if that gentleman would only come to an arrangement, this additional inducement could be made known to him.

Day after day he made his appearance in Clarges Street, and disappeared without making a sign. At last Diana, taking heart of grace, seized the opportunity of his mentioning casually the name of Lord Blanquière to relate—making the most of it, we may be assured—the tie between him and the Bursford family. Hogan seemed impressed, as she intended he should be; but as usual took his leave without saying anything in particular. As soon as he was gone, Mrs. Bursford, who had left the room purposely that he might declare himself without restraint, came in.

"Diana, it is time this was put an end to. To-morrow, when he comes here, I shall have a talk with him."

"I really think you must, mamma: we are now nearly six months engaged. I told him about Lord Blanquière; he seemed to take it in."

By "to-morrow" a great many things were settled that the Bursfords had not anticipated. The Ministry announced their intention of appealing to the country; and Hogan, M.P., was plain Mr. Hogan once more. Before eight o'clock in the morning he was in Clarges Street, and engaged in an impassioned discussion with the mother and daughter. Hogan was for starting at once for Peats-

town, so as to be in the field early: the Tories had been
at work this long time, he declared. Their registries were
in perfect order, and he feared a serious opposition. So
he was talking, nervous and flushed, when Mrs. Bursford
cut him short. Diana left the room, in obedience to a look
from her mother.

"Now, Mr. Hogan, may I ask you how long do you
intend my daughter's engagement to last?"

"Mrs. Bursford, my means at present, as you know,
do not permit me to marry. If I am re-elected——"

"Stop, Mr. Hogan. You will not be re-elected for Peatstown; you have not a chance of it. You have no means.
Now, Lord Blanquière, whom I saw yesterday evening, has
promised to use his influence to procure a Government post
for—ah—the person in whom I am interested——"

"Mrs. Bursford, I am willing to marry Diana now; but
you will hardly, I think, insist on her prospects and mine
being sacrificed to precipitation."

"You are willing to marry my daughter now?" said
the old lady. "Well and good, Mr. Hogan; and you
will allow, I think, that her prospects are as dear to me
as to you. However, now we shall go to business; and I
must tell you that you are losing time and money in
going over to Peatstown. I know Peatstown well, from
the Wyldoates' accounts. You are not advanced enough
in your ideas; and you have disappointed your friends
there. Now, if you will take my advice, you will ascertain your chances before you go even as far as Dublin."

Diana now came in, and joined her entreaties to the
arguments of her mother. Hogan consented to telegraph
to Dublin and to Peatstown, to Killeen, on whom he
fancied he could rely. If it then proved to be a fair
prospect of success, he could go. If not, there was nothing for it but to trust to Lord Blanquière's good offices.
So he took his leave of the ladies, and went down to the
Clubs, and to Westminster, to learn what was going on.
He felt stunned and apathetic now; and amongst the
angry, excited crowds who were discussing the news, he
seemed so calm and indifferent, that many eyed him

suspiciously, and asked each other could the member for Peatstown have got anything from the Government? There would be some crumbs of patronage to be divided. But what had Hogan done to deserve anything? So that hypothesis was abandoned.

Before returning to Clarges Street he turned into his own house, to see if any news had come from Dublin. There was a telegram from the Bishop, curt but significant. "Don't mind coming. D. Houlahan is gone down to Peatstown by the morning mail. I'll write to-day."

Dinny Houlahan—Dinny the Hare—gone down! That was a good joke indeed: and Hogan laid aside his hat and sat down in his easy chair. Dinny Houlahan was a barrister whose principles it were kindness to designate as uncertain. He had been in prison in '48. His enemies declared him to be an informer, and that the imprisonment was a mere blind—an expedient to "save the situation." However, he had suffered imprisonment in the cause; and, aided by an impartial jury, he had been instrumental in procuring the acquittal of a murderer of the agrarian type, as recently as the previous autumn. And this was the gentleman who, "with his blushing honours thick upon him," was to supplant Hogan. There was another telegram—one from Ned Shea: "You will have my support, and a hearty welcome; I cannot answer for anything more." This was enough. He rose from his chair, and took a couple of turns up and down the room. While so engaged, the servant came in with a note in her hand, It was from the Cole Alley Office, and was addressed "—Hogan, Esq."

"DEAR SIR—

"We regret to inform you that we have no further occasion for your services as managing editor of the *Beacon*. We have made arrangements to sell the paper to Schepeler, Ignatieff, and Co., of Fenchurch Street. We shall be most happy to recommend you to them, should you wish it. You will be pleased to hear that the detectives have at last got on the tract of Mr. Saltasche.

"Faithfully yours,
"STIER AND BRUEN."

Hogan stirred the fire, and burnt the three communications. He stood watching the shrivelled fragments as they floated up the chimney in the draught. A queer conceit entered his brain as he stood looking at them. The Bishop's telegram, which might be held to personify his Parliamentary career and its brief illusory existence, had scarcely kindled when it took wing, all ablaze, and disappeared into the region of smoke; Ned Shea's burnt out quite, and divided into crumbling atoms; while Stier and Bruen's thick double sheet lay for a while, and turned yellow and brown ere it kindled: even when the flame had exhausted itself, the writing seemed to glow, and the letters turned red again and twisted strangely. He remained a long time staring idly into the fire: and it was not until a single stroke of the clock warned him of the hour—half-past four—that he moved from his place on the rug.

Then to Clarges Street, where he found Diana in the most charming afternoon toilette waiting for him. She received the news of his determination to abandon the contest with the composure bred of foregone conviction. The afternoon passed rather pleasantly. Hogan did not mention the news about Saltasche; he hoped in his heart that the detectives might yet be baffled, for he by no means relished the idea of the inquiry that must ensue upon that gentleman's trial. Neither did he think it necessary to tell Diana or her mother that the editorship was gone from him; they were both left in the pleasant delusion that the pretendant had five pounds a week of his own. Before he left the house Diana had named the day—which the gentleman, with an eagerness that was very lover-like and was thoroughly sincere, begged might be fixed at as early a date as possible.

Mrs. Bursford declared emphatically that everything should be as yet conditional on Lord Blanquière's good offices. She was writing to his lordship by that post. The old lady was indeed at her davenport, scribbling away on her thickest-toned, most monogrammed paper. When Hogan took his leave, Diana followed him to the lobby.

"Lord Blanquière may not be able to do anything for us," she said, resting her hand on the balustrade, and looking at him scrutinisingly.

Hogan was equal to the occasion. He took her fingers in his.

"Dearest Diana," he said, "surely that need be no cause for further delay. I am no poorer than before." We must do him the justice to say, that in speaking thus he had an eye to the recommendation of Stier and Bruen, and a prospective if not an actual five pounds a week. "If Lord Blanquière can offer me a position, so much the better; if not——"

If not . . . there were two thousand pounds still of Diana's, and her mother's jointure of four hundred a year. Five hundred pounds would clear off his debts. And he could pull along, as he told himself, until something turned up.

If not . . . Diana filled up the hiatus by a glance expressive of unlimited capabilities of self-sacrifice and heroic undertakings.

"I suppose," she said, "now that you are not in Parliament, we shall live in Dublin. With mamma, you know, in Merrion Street?"

"No, no," he replied, sharply; "I must stay in London. Much better to have your mother remove from Dublin. She could live with us here infinitely more conveniently. How could I edit a newspaper from Dublin? You had better talk to her about that, Diana."

Then he went away; and Diana set to work to persuade her mother how much more suitable and convenient it would be to bring over her furniture to London, and establish herself with her son-in-law in some nice house in the Bayswater or Paddington district. How this proposal was received, we leave it to the reader to imagine.

CHAPTER XXXIX.

"L'homme n'est qu'un roseau le plus faible de l'univers ; mais c'est un roseau pensant. Il ne faut pas que l'univers entier s'arme pour l'écraser. Une vapeur, une goutte d'eau suffit pour le tuer. Mais quand l'univers l'écraserait, l'homme serait encore plus noble que ce qui le tue, parce qu'il sait qu'il meurt ; et l'avantage que l'univers a sur lui l'univers n'en sait rien. Ainsi toute notre dignité consiste dans la pensée."—*Pensées de Pascal.*

MONSIEUR AND MADAME DE PRÉDÉLIAC—for such was the *nom de guerre* adopted by Saltasche and Mrs. Poignarde —did not remain long in Baja. Almost directly after his arrival from London they took passages in a fishing-boat, and crossed to Algiers. Here a fortnight was sufficient to weary Mrs. Poignarde; and impelled by some sudden whim, they passed over to Marseilles. Everywhere the same lassitude and devouring *ennui* possessed her. She seemed as if consumed by some inward fire, urging her onwards eternally. Scarce a city in the south of Europe but saw them alight, and after a few days' feverish sojourn take wing again. North, south, east, or west, she cared not,—so that they were in motion. Wearying of the noise and bustle of Marseilles, they went on to Nice, and hired rooms at the chief hotel.

The morning after his arrival, Monsieur de Prédéliac sauntered into the smoking-room to have a look at the papers. Several gentlemen were lounging there; one pushed a pile of papers towards the new-comer. He, seeing them to be English, politely declined; and taking up a *Moniteur*, said in French,—

"Thank you ; I take the *Moniteur*."

"Did you see here," said one of the loungers, "there's a paragraph in the *Swiss Times*, saying the detectives are on the trail of that fellow Salt—something or other, who bolted with a pot of money last November?"

The *Moniteur* drooped ever so little, and Monsieur de Prédéliac's face wore an expression of interest too intense to be warranted by the accounts of the debates in the French Assembly, which were spread before him.

"Where's the *Swiss Times*? Oh! 'Traced to Naples. It is supposed sailed to Algiers or Ajaccio. Five hundred pounds reward!' They're very apt to catch him, don't you think, Ross?"

"Yes; especially as he is English. The accent is sure to betray him. So few can ever attain the pure tone."

"Very few. Ross, you are peculiarly blessed in that particular."

"Hee—ee! I've lived such years abroad, you know."

Presently Monsieur de Prédéliac laid down his *Moniteur*. The last speaker, impelled either by a desire to display his powers, or the almost equally irresistible temptation to practise his French, turned to him, and with an air of conscious power said,—

"*Monsieur, veuillez byong m' prêter voter journal?*"

"With pleasure," returned Monsieur de Prédéliac. "There is nothing in it. The debate is so poor: I blush for my countrymen. Ah! monsieur, we are fallen upon bad times. *La France* is truly in a pitiable state. Ah! Heaven!—pitiable!"

All this was uttered in the quickest, most idiomatic French, and accompanied by shrugs, grimaces, and gestures sufficient of themselves to bewilder anybody. The Englishman, who little expected such a volley in return for his adventurous random pebble, could only ejaculate,—

"Er — *vraiment*." His two friends pricked up their ears.

"Ah!" continued the mischievous Parisian. "In Paris, monsieur—in Paris the demoralisation is frightful to contemplate: no order, no security; business is at a standstill. With a Republic which to-morrow may be a Revolution,

and the day after a Commune, what security for anything?
Monsieur, there is not that!"

Here Monsieur de Prédéliac, forgetting that the gesture
was slightly incongruous with his aristocratic name, turned
the palm of his hand outwards, and with the nail of his
index finger slightly scraped the inside of one of his front
incisors.

"*Paz—za de zecurité, monsieur?*" he repeated.

"Er—*vraiment*," from the Englishman again; who, feeling his friends' eyes upon him, felt bound to do something.
A phrase occurred to him.

"Foo l'Empereur, maintenong——" But he could get
no further; his opponent cut in with a burst.

"Feu sa Majesté? Ah! monsieur, quelle perte terrible!
Lui et moi, nous étions comme des frères. Je lui dois tout
ce que j'ai, tout ce que je suis. Quand je dis ça comme
à vous, je suis toujours de Prédéliac." The aristocratic air
which accompanied this assertion was inimitable. "Mais
toute ma fortune, ma position, je les dois à lui—à mon
cher Louis. Car il était Louis pour moi. Quand nous
étions seuls, dans l'intimité, je le tutoyais. O! qu'il était
bon! Mais je suis égoïste dans mes regrets. La Patrie,
la France, demande mes pleurs."

"Er—*vraiment*" (this time rather frigidly); "vous devez
le regretter. Oh, oui—sans doute. Permettez: merci,"
—and the Englishman, feeling it high time to beat a
retreat, opened his *Moniteur* with as much dignity as he
could command.

"Voluble party that, hey, Ross?" observed one of the
bystanders, as Monsieur de Prédéliac left, having finished
his cigar.

"Er—yes; don't feel too sure about him. Those wandering Frenchies are seldom worth much. That fellow has a
sharp eye in his head—talks a deal too much. Hem—I
never like to let those sort of fellows go on too far, you
know; they're always delighted to get a chance. I'm
pretty well up to that sort of thing."

Monsieur de Prédéliac strolled out, in the hope of getting hold of a *Swiss Times* or *Galignani*. He was afraid to

be seen reading an English paper, lest suspicion should be aroused. And he knew well that a mere surmise, raised even in jest, would be greedily caught up by idlers such as he had just quitted,—delighted to have something sensational wherewith to kill time. He found what he wanted at last, and folding it up hurriedly, stuffed it into his pocket and returned to the hotel. Once safe in his own room, he hastened to read the paragraph, and had the pleasure of finding a tolerably accurate description of himself.

"Height, five-seven; stoutish figure." He grinned as he read this, and got up and walked to a great mirror opposite the window. "'Five-seven'—the rascals; I'm five-eight. 'No whiskers or moustache:' humph! 'Traced to Naples; it's conjectured is in Algiers.' No hurry, my lads; take it easy," he said, throwing down the paper and beginning to walk up and down the room. "I shall stay here unless something wonderful happens."

However, three days later found him at Monaco. Mrs. Poignarde got tired of Nice,—there were too many English. And it was windy; and she disliked the sea. And there were American women, who insisted, whether she liked it or not, on talking vile French to or at her. So they found themselves at Monaco, where the gaming tables at least promised some excitement.

They made their appearance at the roulette table the second night of their arrival. A Russian prince, the handsomest man in the Imperial Guards and one of the largest sheep-owners in the world, had had an unprecedented run of luck for two nights in succession. The excitement caused by this rare occurrence had spread everywhere, and the Conversation Salon was thronged with a curious host, gamblers eager to divine the "*système*," and gaping, listless sight-seers greedy of the sensation. The Russian sat unmoved—the cynosure of all eyes, silent and impassive, staking every time the maximum. He scarcely raised his eyes, even. The heat and glare were tremendous; but not one seemed conscious of it, so intense was the excitement. The croupier's hoarse voice was almost the only

2 H

one heard, except the sort of hoarse murmur that followed the transfer of the stakes; and English, German, French, and Italian tongues exchanged ejaculations.

Monsieur and Madame de Prédéliac managed to secure good places, almost opposite to the Russian. He was seated in a careless attitude; one hand thrown over the back of his chair, the white jewelled fingers of the other just resting on the rim of the table. His face was pale, but it was a natural paleness; the eyes, of violet blue, betrayed his race by their somewhat oblique setting; but the beautifully-formed mouth and perfect chin and nostrils amply compensated for a defect in itself so slight as almost to escape notice.

"*Rouge gagne. Couleur perd.*" The croupier's monotonous cry went on, his little black eyes glancing round the table with the quickness and brightness of a squirrel's. "*Faites votre jeu, messieurs, mesdames!*"

Mrs. Poignarde, watching the sweep of the index, felt that sudden greed that takes the least avaricious of us sometimes; and she looked up in Saltasche's face for permission. He nodded assent, with a pleased smile, and took a gold piece out of his pocket.

She took it from his hand, and leaning forward, placed it herself on the board. The other stakes were already laid. The croupier set the ball in motion; and after a moment or so she found herself the winner of twenty-five napoleons; the Russian had lost: his eyes lazily followed the *rouleau* to her hands from those of the croupier. She received them with a smile; and whispered something to Saltasche. He nodded assent, and she took five of the pieces out of the *rouleau*, and laid them on the table again. As she drew back to her place beside Saltasche, her eyes suddenly met those of the Prince, fixed in bold admiration upon her. A transient glitter shone in her eyes; and the heat of the place or the excitement tinged her cheeks with a faint flush. Saltasche did not see the eager gaze of the Prince; he was looking at Adelaide, and thinking of that day when she stood in the tent at the Rose Show, with the glow of the flowers reflected in her face. She was dressed in a black, close-fitting costume, unrelieved by any colour, and with soft ruffles of lace at her throat and wrists. A bonnet of black and white tulle, with a wreath of pale roses, lay on the thick braids which encircled her head; her right hand, gloveless, and sparkling with diamonds, rested on his sleeve. She stooped forward, watching the course of the ball whirling round the table: her lips were parted a little, showing the small white teeth; and the white eyelids drooped till their long lashes almost swept her cheek.

She lost this time her five gold pieces, which, with the Prince's fifty, were raked up by the croupier. The Russian saw nothing; his attention was riveted on her face.

The appetite newly awakened within her refused to be satisfied. Another glance to Saltasche, and she risked five more pieces. The Russian waited until her stake was placed; then, reaching over, laid a long *rouleau* beside it.

Again the ball swept round and round.

"*A vous, madame.*" And the croupier handed her five *rouleaus* of twenty-five each. She had won one hundred and twenty-five napoleons.

Astonished beyond measure, she forgot herself.

"Why, look!" she cried, in English, to Saltasche.

A hasty glance from him warned her. Greatly alarmed, he turned his eyes cautiously round the table. They had been heard, no doubt; but no one seemed to take any notice. One man, who had been standing near the Prince, and who belonged to his party, whispered something in his ear, and having received a whisper in return, left the room hurriedly. Saltasche followed him with his eyes; he felt some indefinable uneasiness. Could this have been a spy set to watch him? He waited for nearly half an hour, nervous and alarmed; then, unable to bear the suspense longer, he whispered to her to leave.

Once outside in the open air, he felt better. Another moment in the room, and he must have fainted.

"What is the matter, pray?" asked she, in a whisper; "what have I done? No one noticed that I said anything."

"Hush, hush!" said he; "come out here in this open place." They walked across a grass plot towards a broad terrace with benches set here and there, which the moonlight showed to be untenanted.

They sat down on one of them. Behind them was the light and noise of the Salle ; and the footsteps of the people going in and out could be heard distinctly. The groves of ilex and orange looked ghostly in the cold light of the moon, and the dry leaves rustled harshly in the wind.

"There was a man at the side, near me; he left when you said that in English. I fear they have traced me. That he is English I am convinced; and no doubt it is a detective. I wonder could they by any chance have got upon our track?"

"You ought to go at once; never mind me," replied Mrs. Poignarde, anxiously.

"Bah! How! If I am right, the gendarmes are on the alert, and every road will be watched. No, no; there is no chance if I am right."

"Why not get a horse now, at the hotel, ride off at a gallop and distance them? Disguise yourself. Once up the country——"

"Adelaide," whispered he in a strange tone, catching her by the wrist as he spoke, "look yonder by the orange trees—quickly—on a line with the end of this bench."

"A man's shadow," she faltered. "We are watched. Oh my God! we are lost!"

The shadow was that of one of the followers of the Russian, who had been sent by him to watch them home, in order to find out their address; and who, having watched for them outside, was lurking among the orange trees, waiting for them to move.

"Now to think of you, in case I try to escape. All I have to do is to give you the banker's receipt for the money I lodged in your name, in case this—this happened. How fortunate that we arranged that!"

"Will you not make an effort to escape?" she insisted, catching him by the arm. "Think of what you risk! Come, oh, come!"

"Ten years! I think," he said coolly, getting up quickly off his chair as he spoke.

She looked at him in bewilderment. His face was deadly pale, and his brows set in a painful frown; the lips, however, though smiling, were white; and he seemed to walk unsteadily.

"Adelaide," said he, whispering low as they walked along, "the game is up—no doubt of it. What else could that mean? I remember, too, that I noticed to-day we several times came on the same man in the wood; and as we were at dinner the waiter seemed to be a little strange in his manner: no doubt he has been bribed. It may be only fancy; but anyhow, I don't see much hope. I'll make an attempt to get off up country. If I could get to Turbia!"

By this time they had reached the *perron* of their hotel. They entered—casting, in spite of themselves, uneasy looks round. The porter in the hall, on seeing them come in, telegraphed a glance to a personage who was reading a paper in one of the embrasures. They saw the smile and nod with which the glance was received; and passed on, as fast as they could, up the grand staircase. She was so terrified that she could scarcely walk. It was the same man, who had made known to the porter his errand, and had been admitted into the hall in order to copy their names from the book.

The doors of their apartments locked, Adelaide flung herself on the sofa; but Saltasche set to work energetically, and having packed all the papers securely and confided them to her keeping, counted out some gold pieces and sewed them into the lining of his vest. This done, he unfolded a map and laid it on the table.

"I don't see what I can do, unless to get off into the mountains by way of Turbia, up the country—or maybe hold on along the coast to Ventimiglia, or some fishing village, and set out to sea. And that matter, anyhow, is a secondary consideration; how to elude the people who are watching the house is the question."

"You must wait until the moon has set," said she, walking over to the window and looking out. "I suppose between one and two it will be dark enough for you. Maybe sooner; see those clouds hanging over the sea."

Saltasche turned out the gas, and walking over to the window, took her hand and made her sit down beside him. The casement remained open, and the moonlight streamed in over her white, wan face; the dark circles round her eyes were livid, and her lips twitched and trembled. Outside the murmur of the ilex leaves came on the breeze, mingling with the noise of the waves breaking on the beach below; and now and again a bat flitted by, like a shadow, between them and the light. For a moment or two they were silent; looking out on the pine woods, the dark crests of which hid the distant sea. He was the first to speak.

"Adelaide, surely we have something to say to each other. If I—I am taken; have you thought of that?"

She shuddered convulsively, and withdrawing her hands from his, clasped them together.

"Adelaide, could you? Oh! no," he cried, the words breaking from him with a sort of sob. "Ten years—seven years: no, I could not ask it of you." His eyes sought hers with a hungry, searching look.

Still she remained silent, only clasping her hands tighter together.

"Adelaide! will you let me have that sweet hope to cheer me, to keep me alive in my prison? You will, will you not?" He fell on his knees before her.

She sprang away from him with a violent effort.

"Stop!" she cried, gasping with the effort. "No, no. I have deceived you long enough. We have been wrong —both of us wrong; but I most of all. Oh! shall I ever be forgiven? I never loved you—never! I deceived you from the first; and now this is the punishment of my crime: and all falls upon you."

He was standing now, looking at her and holding by the window-frame for support. Drops of sweat stood on his forehead, and he shivered as if in an ague.

"Forgive me! oh, forgive me," she moaned, kneeling to him; "and let me go free. Even had this not come upon us I must have left you—I must——"

"Enough!" said he. "Enough, my poor child: we have indeed need to forgive each other. There, there, sit down now, and only think what you are to do for yourself." He had mastered himself in one moment; to all outward appearance he was as calm as the day before. "The money is there; you will do as you choose with it. I shall not require any. For that matter, the affair may stand as we arranged it."

He walked up and down the room with long strides. Then he stopped suddenly beside the window-seat where she was lying rather than sitting, and looked at her compassionately.

"Tell me," said he: "that day at Inchicore, when you consented, did you deceive me knowingly then?"

"No, not then; but I wanted so to get away from Eric; and——"

"Ay; that's it;" he interrupted. "Fool—treble fool that I have been!" After a pause, "I am only losing valuable time. Adelaide, we must part. If I reach a place of safety I shall find a means to communicate with you. If not——"

"If not?" she repeated, her parched trembling lips scarcely able to frame the words.

"If not, you must judge how to act for yourself. Now, what I propose to do is this. See: these straps will lower me to the ground from the balcony. You will come when I am gone, and remove them, will you? That is my last request of you."

She only looked at him despairingly.

"Now," said he; and taking her by the hand again, he led her to a chair removed from the window. She gave him her hand, cold as ice, and obeyed him passively.

"Forgive me," said he; "we were both wrong, both: and goodbye."

She tried to rise, to speak; but voice and limbs failed her, and she sank in a swoon on the floor. He lifted and laid her on a sofa; then pressing a kiss on her lips, seized hastily the trunk straps which he had fastened together, and passed through the window on to the balcony.

The moon had set, and it was dark. Not a light could
be seen. The hotel windows were all closed for the night,
and the Conversation Salon was dark and silent. He passed
rapidly and gently past the windows and across the front
of the house ; and when he reached the corner where the
balcony ended, he stopped, and set to fasten the straps to
a rail. To cross and glide down was the work of a minute,
—the straps were long enough for him to reach the ground
without risking a fall,—and in a moment or two he had
reached the pine forest and was brushing at a rapid rate
through the undergrowth.—No easy task in the darkness.

All his efforts were bootless. Adelaide, whose over-
wrought frame had succumbed, remained unconscious until
daybreak. The strap was found hanging on the balcony
by the servants : the gendarmes were sent for, and insti-
tuted a search. In the midst of the commotion some English travellers, who had the evening before arrived from
Nice, called the landlord's attention to the *Galignani* paragraph, and the description of the absconding defaulter
Saltasche. The landlord, whom the mention of the five
hundred pounds' reward roused to an enthusiastic pitch of
zeal, telegraphed to Ventimiglia ; and just as the unfortunate Monsieur de Prédéliac, weary and footsore, walked
into the town, he was arrested and lodged in prison. It
did not take long to communicate with the detectives, who
had in fact succeeded in tracing him to Marseilles. They
hastened onwards, and in twelve hours' time Saltasche
was being conveyed in the mail train to Paris, *en route* for
Calais, Dover, and London ; guarded with the watchful
care that so valuable a prize demanded.

He was perfectly calm and unmoved, silent and moody,
for the greater part of the train journey. When once
they had reached Calais, he became quite cheery and talkative ; the detectives were by no means bad companions,
and showed themselves as indulgent as was compatible
with the exercise of their functions.

It was a fine clear evening when they reached Calais ;
and there was every prospect of a calm passage. They
went on board the mail boat early in the evening, in order

not to attract attention; and Saltasche was glad to lie down for a couple of hours. The detectives always remained at his side. After the boat started, one of them seated himself beside the berth where the prisoner was sleeping, or trying to sleep, and the other stretched himself on a sofa opposite.

Both had revolvers ready for use at a second's warning. They were puzzled greatly by the demeanour of their prisoner. He was neither sullen nor depressed; nor had he the feverish reckless exaltation which so often marks despair. He asked no favours, offered no bribes,—which especially astonished them, knowing as they did that he had enormous resources at his command.

Saltasche, meantime, lay on his back in the narrow miserable berth of the saloon cabin, listening in a sort of half-stupor to the hissing of the water rushing past at the other side of the planks. He was preoccupied now but by one thought — to get his guardians on deck before they arrived at Dover. He dreaded to show the least uneasiness—to give them the merest shade of suspicion. He knew the time they would arrive in Dover. No doubt the boat would be met there by Stier and Bruen, and others, greedy to feast their eyes on him. He smiled, thinking of the disappointment that awaited them.

The swing lamp was burning faintly. He could hear the heavy breathing of the sleeping man on the sofa; and turning his head cautiously and gently, saw that the detective beside his berth was watching him closely. Doubtless they meant to divide the watch until they reached Dover. He turned on his left side, with his back to the light, and took out his watch. With difficulty he managed to see the hands. Nearly two hours yet. He could wait for another hour, and see if they meant to relieve each other.

He closed his eyes, which were stiff and sore from the dust and want of sleep; but there arose a sort of phantasmagoria, and the scenes he had passed through in the last terrible days all returned. Adelaide's white face and wild imploring eyes, the moonlight shining on her long hair as she knelt in the window, rose before him. He was in the

wood again at Monaco—the brambles and the hard boughs
of the pine trees scratching his hands as he forced his way
through.   Then the train : the weary, endless journey, the
grating and jar, and the shrieks of the steam whistle ; the
trees flying past.   It was unbearable.   He turned around
impatiently, and this time without any effort at conceal-
ment looked again at his watch.

"I cannot sleep," he said to the watcher.   "Could we
go on deck for a turn ?"

The man hesitated.

"We're very tired ; and Johnston and I were thinking
of dividing this watch, you see."

"Bah !" said Saltasche.   "Call for some brandy, or say
a pint of champagne : that will do you more good than
sleep."

"You can have what you like, Mr. Saltasche ; nothing
for us, much obliged.   Shall I call for brandy !"

Brandy was brought in ; and Saltasche swallowed a
couple of glasses, to the evident content of his guards, who
declined to touch it.

"Now," said he, "let us go up.   I'm smothering here."

After some demur they agreed, and buttoning themselves well up in their overcoats, they passed up the companion ladder and on to the deck.

Saltasche drew a long breath as he stepped out of the
grease-laden, reeking atmosphere of the cabin.   The air
was fresh and chill ; and he pulled his great furred cloak
around him tightly.   It was a moonlit night, and the
crests of the waves shone and sparkled like snow-wreaths,
Between sky and water, low down, hung fleecy clouds ;
and at times a flying scud of vapour passed over the face
of the moon, and cast its shadow on the sea.   They passed
close by a great ship gliding southward—her masts and
rigging looking black and ghostlike.   The look-out man
in the bows of the steamer shouted some strange greeting
or warning.   No answer came back, save the deep bark of
a dog, frightened at the noise and lights.   They walked up
and down in silence for about a quarter of an hour.

"We can't see the shore," said one of the detectives at

last; "but we shall be in, I expect, in half an hour. There are fishing-boats away there, to the right."

"Ay," grumbled the other; "I shall not be sorry to get in. It is cold work, here."

"You will soon be at liberty, my friend," said Saltasche, blandly. "See: try a cigar, will you?"—and he took a case out of his pocket.

They stood for a moment while the lights were being struck. Saltasche noticed a pile of boxes, bales, and trunks, along the side. The taffrail was high, as the steamer was saloon-decked. A white deal packing-case projected slightly; from that it was an easy step to a black trunk on top; then one more, and he would be on the edge.

One of the men—he who was on the prisoner's right hand—turned a little aside as he struck a vesuvian on his boot-heel. Saltasche let slip his cloak, as if accidentally, off his shoulders. Both the officers stooped simultaneously to pick it up for him. Now was his chance. Three long rapid strides bring him to the pile by the side. One step on the white packing-case—his left foot reaches the black trunk. It shakes. No: he seizes the taffrail with his right hand.

The detectives, with a wild yell, follow him. One of them has him almost grasped by the foot. But Saltasche vaults over, with a vigorous spring. A splash, and he is in the water just abaft the paddle-wheel.

He did not sink. On the contrary, he was swimming. From the side they could see his face, calm and defiant, as the moonlight fell upon it, for a few minutes. The crests of the waves were not whiter. A life-preserver was flung out. It floated by within arm's reach of him. He seemed only to wait to have the boat lowered. Then, in sight of all, he threw up his arms over his head. There was a ground-swell now. A high wave raised and shook its white mane between them, and hid him for a moment. Was it the sound it made breaking against the bow? or was it a sea-bird's cry? Something between a laugh and a sob—and he was gone.

CHAPTER XL

"O ! ten times faster Venus' pigeons fly
To seal love's bonds new made, than they are wont
To keep obliged faith unforfeited."

Merchant of Venice.

Miss O'Hegarty and Dermot Blake were breakfasting together one frosty morning. It was chilly out of doors, as one might see from the fine red noses of the people who went by; but a blazing fire prevented the occupants of the room from feeling any discomfort. A huge pointer lay on the rug, thumping the floor with his thick tail as he gazed into his master's face, watching for the piece of dry toast or the drumstick which was certain to reward his patience. It was eleven o'clock; the breakfast was unusually late, for Dermot had only come up from Blakestown by the night mail, and had taken a good sleep to make up for his lost rest. Miss O'Hegarty, who had finished her breakfast some time, was reading the newspaper.

"Here it is at last!" she cried; "listen, Dermot. Now, I do declare!

"'At St. George's, Hanover Square. By the reverend,—um, um,—O'Rooney Hogan, Esq., barrister-at-law, to Diana, only daughter of the late Drelincourt Bursford, of Bursford Castle, County Armagh.'

"There now! She's done it at last, hasn't she? And he's not even an M.P."

"Not even as much as an M.P.," grinned Dermot, mightily tickled at the conceit. "Poor Diana! She's off at last."

"And that unfortunate mother of hers! Fancy,—she

has allowed herself to be bamboozled into bringing all her nice comfortable things, her furniture and everything, over to London; to live with them, by the way. Long that'll last, won't it?"

"Behave yourself, Spot, I say," said Dermot to the pointer, who had stuffed his moist nose almost into his master's hand. "Doesn't she agree with the son-in-law—hey, ma'am?"

"Not she: how would she? Low fellow!—a friend and companion of that Saltasche man, who drowned himself, you remember, when he was being brought home to be tried. A low fellow. Got into society here somehow, through Saltasche. Thank goodness, things are changed now. With a Conservative Government we may hope for a little decency."

"Yes, I recollect Saltasche," said Dermot, thoughtfully. "I saw him on the Pier that first Sunday I was there: the Sunday I met Nellie."

"Was it not an extraordinary thing that all the money should have been recovered, though? I declare I never heard of such a romance; and how it was, no one knows."

"What money?"

"Did you not hear, Dermot? Why, nearly sixty thousand pounds were placed by some person in the hands of the solicitors who were engaged by the company he had cheated. Nobody knows who it was. Poor Mr. Grey was telling me about it the other day. They say it was some lady: but one of the conditions under which the restitution was made was, that nothing should be said about the person who conducted the negotiations."

"Why, it's a perfect romance! Well, well, I hope that unfortunate Grey will get his money back."

"They have hopes of it. Poor things! it was an awful shock to them. They tell me that wretched Captain Poignarde, whose wife used to play so beautifully, is dead —died shortly after his arrival in India. She is teaching in London, and gets on remarkably well. I hope she'll get a pension."

"Who, ma'am? who are you talking of?"

"Augh! I am stupid. I forgot you did not know them. They had gone away, to be sure, before you came home. I had it on my mind to tell Nell about it."

"Dear me!" Dorothy began again after a pause, during which she had been engaged on her newspaper; "what a crowd of people were at the levee! Quite a different class, too, from last year's people. It used to be perfectly dreadful to see what the Castle was reduced to. It's really a comfort to one. Dermot, dear, you should have gone: really, now, you should."

"Lie down, Spot, you rascal. Is it the Castle you are talking about, ma'am? Not one bit of me. I'll never go near it."

"Well, now!" said Dorothy, looking up on hearing the clock strike, "Nellie ought to be here by this; she ought indeed. I told her to come over the first thing in the morning. Poor child! she's looking badly of late—very badly. It's wretched for her there by herself."

Dermot had finished his breakfast, and had turned round to the fire—the pointer's muzzle resting affectionately on his knee; and was looking thoughtfully into the red mass of coals.

"What's the date of that announcement of Di. Bursford's wedding?" asked he lazily, lifting the dog's ears between his fingers.

"Yesterday, I suppose: no, the day before," replied his aunt, looking at the date.

"I suppose it is in every paper in Dublin. Well! well! well!"

"Poor Emily Bursford! It is a trial for her. I quite foresee the end of that poor woman. This pair will have to emigrate as soon as that idgiot Diana has given him all her money; and then her mother will have to go into lodgings or a boarding-house. It all comes of bringing people out of their proper sphere in life. That Hogan man should have been left where he was."

"Well, I'll go and have a smoke in the greenhouse. When did you say Nellie was to be here?"

"If she's not here by twelve, I shan't expect her. I do wonder what is keeping the child. It is really——"

What it really was Dermot Blake never knew; he was off to the little greenhouse on the leads, to smoke.

Here he seated himself on a bench, and began to read the paper—blowing great wreaths of smoke from his cigar to the right and left of him. But Dermot did not read long; the paper was presently laid on a bench beside him, and he got up and began to walk up and down the tiled floor. His elbows brushed the fern-leaves, which hung down limp and rusty from the pots on the shelves at his side; and the pale white primulas trembled and let fall a blossom or two at the unwonted shock of his heavy tread. There was a mist, such as often comes with frost, outside; and the window-panes were thick with steam; but overhead he could see through an open pane that the day was clearing and there was a promise of sunshine. Until his cigar was finished, Dermot paced to and fro, meditating evidently, and frowning and biting his heavy moustache. At last, after a quarter of an hour spent thus, he passed through a door on the lobby into his own room; whence he emerged shortly, ready to go out. He went downstairs quietly, as if he desired to go out unobserved; but Spot, the parlour door being open, heard from the hearthrug the welcome sound of his master's walking-boots, and dashed out, leaping and yelling with excitement at the idea of a walk. Dermot nodded assent, as he selected a cane; and both set out.

When he got to the corner of the street he looked at his watch; he was late for the twelve o'clock train. He calculated that if Nellie came into town by it he ought to meet her on her way to Fitzgerald Place, within the next five minutes. So he and Spot strolled on together, keeping a sharp look-out for a slender figure in deep black. He met no one, however; and by the time he had crossed the bridge he had made up his mind that Nellie was not coming at all. It was too early to go to the club. He felt inclined to take a long walk: it seemed just the day for a smart tramp out into the country. And he thought he might as well walk out in the Green Lanes direction as in any other; so, whistling Spot to heel, he soon left the

thoroughfares behind, and was rapidly approaching the
country roads of Green Lanes. They looked muddy and
bleak, although the frost of the previous night had hardened
everything. Where the sun was shining the ground was
again loosened, and the traveller slipped from a footway
dry and hard, like iron, into soft, yielding slush.

Dermot soon found himself in the avenue in which the
Davorens' house was situated. And now, self-possessed
and decided as he usually was, he felt a little uncertain.
He had not been in the house since that day last September
when he had accompanied Dorothy to see the Davorens;
although he had frequently met Nellie in Fitzgerald Place.
He wondered what she would think of him. He could
easily say, however, that Dorothy had sent him; and he
cudgelled his brains for an excuse. By this time he had
reached the gates. The side-door was open, and he entered
the front. It looked desolate and gloomy enough : the
aloe tubs were damp-looking, and the green paint wanted
renewing; the front of the house was dark and sunless,
and the dead creepers and bare rose-trees hung down
neglected. Altogether it had a bleak, solitary look—widely
different from the aspect it had worn when he visited
it the previous summer. He looked up at the windows
as he approached the house, trying to discover a glimpse of
Nellie. But nothing could he see. The lattice panes were
untenanted and dark, in their framing of dead jessamine
and rose-branches.

A servant showed him into the parlour, saying she
believed Miss Davoren was there. The room was half
dark; and Dermot, coming in out of the strong sunlight,
for a moment was unable to see anything.

"How do you do, Mr. Blake!" said a quiet voice
beside him.

He started round. Nellie was sitting in a window
close to the door he had entered by ; and he had passed
without seeing her. She was sewing, and laid down her
work as she advanced to meet him.

It was the first time Dermot Blake had seen her since
her mother's death; and he was startled to find her so

changed. She looked pale and haggard; her eyes were
dull and lustreless; there were dark circles round them;
and the forehead wore a fretted, pained contraction.

"Nellie, poor child!" said he, "what trouble you've
been in?"

Dermot was no master of words; but the pressure of
his great hand and the kind sympathising look of his eyes
as he bent down close to her, carried with them whole
volumes of sincerity and unmistakable good-will.

She looked up gratefully, with tear-filled eyes, as she
held out her hand and murmured some inaudible words of
thanks.

Dermot sat down beside her, and leaning one elbow on
the back of his chair, pulled his whiskers with his fingers
thoughtfully. Nellie seemed struggling to keep back her
tears and to try and speak at the same time; and he did
not know what to say. Spot, who had of course rushed
into the parlour along with his master, having made the
circuit of the room in dog fashion, came up and laid his
head on his master's knee. Nellie at last managed to
speak.

"You came from Blakestown yesterday, did you, Mr.
Blake?"

"Yes," replied Dermot, quite cheerfully now that the
ice had been broken; "last night; fetched Spot up with
me: he's company, you know, when I go out to walk."

Then another pause ensued; and Dermot, desperate,
plunged headlong into the business of his visit.

"Nellie, why didn't you come over to us this morning?
You promised to come, you know."

"Oh, I couldn't do it—I couldn't indeed!"

"And why not, Nellie? Now, don't turn away that
way. Say why couldn't you come? What was it?"

But Dermot got no answer. He rose and walked down
to a far window looking out on the garden, wintry and
black, with only here and there an early crocus showing
its yellow head above the box edges. No sun shone into
it, and the hoar frost lay still on the beds. He looked
out for a moment only; then turned and walked back to

where she was sitting, and, standing drawn up to his full
height, fixed his great eyes upon her with a determined
look.

"Nellie," said he, standing and looking down at her ;
"I can guess why you didn't come."

A quick flush mounted over cheek and brow ; and her
eyes met his angrily for a moment—for a moment only,
then drooped in confusion. But if her eyes were timid,
not so her tongue.

"You have no right to talk to me so, Mr. Blake," she
began, in a would-be sturdy tone. "What do you mean?
It's most unkind of you ;" and then all the sturdiness vanished, and she began to cry outright.

"I don't mean it for unkindness, Nellie, and well you
know it ; tell the truth to me : it was because—because
of——"

Dermot did not finish the sentence. His eyes turned
meaningly to a paper lying on a table near him. And
then, taking both her hands in his, he sat down again beside
her nearer than before.

"Nellie, this is folly—wicked folly of you. No I you
needn't say one word ; I have known it all along. The
idea of you and that worthless scamp: it's atrocious !
Not a syllable will I hear from you. I have a right to
speak, and I will. He is a worthless scamp—a paltry
wretch ; and he sold himself to Saltasche, that schemer
who drowned himself the other day ; and he sold himself
again to other people ; and now he has sold himself to his
wife."

She had pulled away her hands and hidden her face in
them.

"Don't you know I'm speaking the truth, Nellie, dear?
Don't you know I feel for you—that I love you. Yes,
just that,—ever since the first day I saw you, I did.
Don't you hear me?"

Dermot tried to pull down her hands, to make her look
at him. Her hands fell suddenly ; and with a spring she
was away from the window to the hearthrug, looking at
him with eyes that sparkled with indignation.

"Yes, I do hear you; and I won't listen to you. You malign a man who never saw you, whom you don't know, on mere hearsay, and behind his back. It is unmanly—ungentlemanly."

"Stop," said he, quietly. "You don't know what you're saying. I can prove everything,—if proof be necessary," he added with a sneer. Then following her, he said, in a different tone,—

"I can't bear to think, Nellie, that you who have so many real trials, should add to your own burden. Dear child, forgive me if I have pained you. Put that fellow out of your head,—he never could have been in your heart, I'm sure, Nell,—and let us be friends."

He held out his hand. She raised her eyes timidly to his, and placed her hand in his broad palm.

"Now we understand each other. Come here and sit down a moment, and then go and get ready. I won't have you here by yourself any longer: it's not good for you. It's a horrible life. You'll kill yourself."

"Where am I to go?" she said, with a wistful look. "To Dorothy?"

"To Dorothy first, anyhow," replied Dermot, giving his moustache a twirl. "After that——After that, Blakestown, Nellie, and me."

"Nothing of the—— Oh! dear me! how dare you, Mr. Dermot Blake? Really——"

"Well, there?" and he released her. "I won't vex you; but, Nell, you will think of that. Say you will."

"Mr. Blake, what do you mean?" Nellie was stroking down her ruffled plumage at a safe distance, and looking at Dermot with eyes in which surprise at his audacity and vexation were blended together.

"Marry me. There now! You're the only girl I ever asked in my life, or cared to ask. I don't want to hurry you, dear. I'll wait as long as you like. Only give me some hope, Nellie."

Nellie was leaning against the window. She turned round and said gravely, "This is no time to talk of such things; we ought both to have remembered that——"

"Say you'll have me: I only want that. Of course we can put off everything till after Easter." Dermot's eyes were dancing with delight.

"After Easter, Mr. Blake! You must be mad!" Nellie looked at him with eyes of astonishment. "What on earth will Dorothy say?"

"Never mind. I don't; nor what any one else says, either. I may hope, then, may I, Nell? Say yes," whispered he imploringly, taking her hand in his: "yes, Dermot."

But Nellie would not answer at all; she drew her hand from his, gravely, and was turning as if to leave the room. But Dermot with two long steps was at the door before her and planted his broad back against it.

"Listen, Nellie," said he, holding up a warning finger; "mind what I say to you, I am in earnest: if you don't consent to marry me I'll start to-night to the other end of the world and never come back. And then," nodding his head, "you'll be sorry—and Dorothy——"

But Nellie had sunk into a chair and was crying. Dermot was beside her in a moment.

"Don't, my darling; there now, Nellie, I didn't mean a syllable of it. Oh! my poor child! what a brute I've been——"

"No, no!" she said through her tears.

"No—haven't I?" said he, suddenly. "I won't tease you, then; look up. Nell! look at me, I say." And Dermot succeeded in drawing down her hands. "I am really sorry, indeed I am. You'll forgive me?"

"Yes," she said.

"And we'll be friends, won't we?"

"Oh! yes, Dermot."

"Listen, though: sometime or another I may ask you again?"

"Oh! now don't"—and she began to cry again.

"Well, there now, I won't."

*　　　*　　　*　　　*　　　*

But he did, not very long after, and successfully.

CHAPTER XLI.

"DEAR MRS. BURSFORD—

"Your letter reached me in due time, and I must ask you to pardon my delay in replying to it.

"I find, upon inquiry, that the amount of patronage remaining at the disposal of the late Government is very limited indeed, and that there are an immense number of applicants for the few posts yet unfilled. Amongst them are so many persons who have substantial claims on the Ministry that I fear I would not be justified in holding out any hopes whatever of an appointment such as you mention. If there is any other way in which I can be of service to you, I beg, my dear Mrs. Bursford, that you will not fail to command me. With kindest regards to Miss Bursford,

"I am, yours most sincerely,
"BLANQUIÈRE."

Such was the letter which reached Mrs. Bursford one afternoon, nearly a week after she had written in accordance with Diana's behests to Lord Blanquière.

She took off her spectacles, and laid them on the mantelpiece on top of the letter. Then she sat down in her easy-chair to think over the affair. Would Hogan and Diana break off the match? In her heart Mrs. Bursford sincerely hoped so. She had objected to him from the first, and now she disliked him excessively. Still this last week she could have tolerated the match, so long as there was a prospect of a post of some sort being found for him. Now that was definitely settled. If they persisted in marrying, what on earth were they to live on ? To be sure there was his five pounds a week as editor of the *Beacon.* A most uncertain thing, no doubt. Diana would not be dissuaded by this check, she felt sure. No: that she would not! And the old lady nodded her head. Her only hope was that Hogan would cry off at the last moment. There would be the talk—the ill-natured comments—to be gone through over again. Well, they could live that down, as they had done before. Anything would be better than——

But here the door opened; and Diana, dressed for the afternoon in a charming costume of cashmere and silk—a Regent Street copy of Worth, with her blonde hair arranged in its most becoming manner—walked in. A glance at her mother told her that she had received some intelligence.

"There is Lord Blanquière's letter," said the elder lady, indicating its position by a glance.

Diana walked over quickly, and took it up. Her mother watched her face as she read. She noted the mortified, anxious look that spread over it—the raised, petulant eyebrows. Then, when she got to the end, the lips closed in moody determination ; and Mrs. Bursford knew by the expression of her daughter's face, as she laid down the missive, that she had chosen her part, and that dispute or expostulation was bootless.

"There is an end of that, then," she said shortly.

"I should say so, indeed," returned her mother. "Nothing for nothing nowadays. The Government has something else to do, indeed, I imagine, with its offices (you see what he says about persons who have no claims upon them), than give them to persons like this."

"I saw nothing of the kind, mamma," said Diana, flashing an angry look across the hearthrug. "You are a little late in the day with your observations. Pray, if you knew so much, why did you write to Lord Blanquière at all ? "

" Because I was a fool, I suppose. However, we are no worse off than before ; and it may be all for the best."

Then Mrs. Bursford put on her spectacles, and settled herself in her easy-chair comfortably, to conjure up pleasant visions over her netting of Hogan's withdrawal. She hoped that he would have more sense, as she put it, than her daughter. As for the thousand pounds, she was willing even to forego that. Mrs. Bursford's views were tolerably selfish. If her daughter married, it would be difficult for her to maintain the big house in Merrion Street by herself. Altogether, her comforts would be seriously interfered with. She liked society ; and as long as Diana was with her, had an excuse for frequenting those assemblages which she protested she attended only for her sake, but which in reality she enjoyed thoroughly. She must be relegated henceforth to the position of an old dowager whose occupation is gone. Moreover, Mrs. Bursford by no means subscribed to the fairy-tale dogma—"Married and lived happily ever after." She had a shrewd suspicion, confirmed by her own experience, that the prince and princess found the reverse side of the medal not quite so beautiful and sunshiny as it had been pictured to them ; and she foresaw a long and endless vista of trouble, torment, and wretchedness to come. Why Diana could not make up her mind to accept the inevitable puzzled her. She was now in her five-and-thirtieth year. Her temper was a trial, no doubt; but she had grown accustomed to that. Altogether, the old lady felt it a terrible grievance.

There was, to be sure, the probability that Hogan would back out. He might be very glad of the excuse afforded by Lord Blanquière's decision ; however, in a minute or two they would know that.

Diana, who had been sitting still, looking thoughtfully into the fire, rose now, and took down his lordship's letter again.

" You see what he says here, mamma. ' If there be any other way in which I can serve you.' That really looks as if he meant it. I am quite certain he could do something, and would, too, if we asked him."

Mrs. Bursford had not time to reply. The door was opened, and the servant announced Mr. Hogan.

He came in slowly, walking with a listless indolent step, which had lately become habitual to him; and having greeted both the ladies dropped languidly into a chair. The last three months had made a wonderful change in Hogan's appearance. Ten years could hardly have aged him more. All the fire and spirit of his face, the buoyancy of bearing, the bright confident tone that characterised him, were gone. He spoke with a depressed voice and indolently, as if this effort were beyond him, and his face bore marks of dissipation and late hours. In truth, of late he had not been keeping regular hours, to say the least of it. He had sought in vain to drown his remorse, and in wild, feverish excitement to get away from the memories that haunted him—the past that mocked him and the future that threatened. Nellie Davoren's face and wondering blue eyes swam before him in his dreams; and even in Clarges Street the scent of Diana's pots of violets carried him back to the garden at Green Lanes. He forgot the noise of the London Street, the sickly warmth of the heated room; Diana's voice fell unheeded on his ears. He was walking once more among the apple trees, in the fragrance of the new leaves and the moist sweet smell of the earth after the April shower : the old hopes, the foregone ambitions, rose before him and mocked him ; and he ground his teeth in vain anger at his own folly and his own treachery. There was no help for it now. He must go on ; he must drink the cup to the dregs. Sometimes, indeed, a wild vision of flight would pass before his brain ; but he lacked the courage and energy to realise its possibility, even— much less to carry it out. He abandoned himself to his fate. He let go all his aspirations, all his hopes of distinction, of success. Left to himself now, he must have come ere long to starvation ; his will and energies seemed paralysed, and he looked to Diana's cold, clear brain to help him, to maintain and stay him up.

After a while Mrs. Bursford, seeing that no mention was made by Diana of the communication from Lord Blanquière, withdrew, and left the pair to discuss their prospects together.

As soon as she was gone, Diana rose and handed the letter to Hogan. She said nothing, but stood while he read it, leaning one elbow on the chimney-piece, watching him anxiously.

"Just what I expected," was his comment when he had finished. "It was ill advised, I really think, to ask for anything from the Government. Something else, now—a secretaryship, or something of that sort—would be more practicable."

Diana drew a deep breath of relief. "You think, then, that we might apply to him in his private capacity?"

"I've no doubt he could do more that way. He is, as you say, under heavy obligations to your father."

"Oh dear, yes."

"Meantime, Diana, what do you think of this?"

"This" was a ring, which he took from a tiny morocco case—a circlet of dead gold, in which was set one large emerald surrounded by diamond sparks. The emerald had a flaw in it; but that was only perceptible to experts and to people who were told about it. The cost was forty-five pounds—that is, it would cost that sum when it should be paid for—which, it is hardly necessary to say, it was not.

Diana was enchanted. She admired emeralds above all precious stones in the world,—and the sweet little diamond sparks! How had he known so well, so exactly, what pleased her?

After a time Mrs. Bursford came in, and Diana acquainted her with her lover's decision. It was quite absurd to imagine that a Government appointment could be obtained in that way. She wondered how they could have been so silly as to imagine it possible. Dear Lord Blanquière would of course be only too happy to exert his influence privately. A secretaryship, now.

Hogan, standing with his back to the fire, watching, with a somewhat dreary smile, the emerald glistening on Diana's third finger, assented to all she said.

Mrs. Bursford smiled grimly. She too noticed the

2 K

engaged ring on her daughter's finger, but with very different feelings.

When Hogan was gone, Diana sat turning it round and round meditatively.

"I wonder what that cost?" said Mrs. Bursford, coldly.

"I am sure it was seventy or eighty pounds. Emeralds are very costly now—quite as much so as diamonds," said Diana.

"I hope not, indeed," was the sententious reply.

"It is lovely," went on Diana, holding up the ring close to her face, and turning it round with the thumb and forefinger of her right hand.

"I am glad you like it, my dear; that's all. You will have to pay for it, I have no doubt."

This went unnoticed by Diana. She was in a good humour now that no taunts could ruffle; and she merely smiled in reply to her mother's acrimonious saying.

"Then," continued Mrs. Bursford, "I suppose I may write to Lord Blanquière again at once. This day fortnight leaves quite little enough time on our hands."

That day fortnight Diana and Hogan were married.

Lord Blanquière wrote, after some months' delay, to say that an old friend of his, the governor of one of the South Sea Islands, who had been home on leave for a year, required a secretary, and that he would recommend Hogan to him in that capacity. The salary was small—three hundred a year; and he could offer no prospect of promotion. The secretary would have to reside permanently at Honolulu.

Miserable as this prospect was, Diana was glad to accept it. Her mother bid them adieu with more relief than sorrow. Her son-in-law had not turned out well. The Bragintons had terrible stories to tell of him. The idle time of an unemployed man is seldom too well spent; and for Hogan, who, since his marriage, had become perfectly reckless, a complete change of scene and occupation was necessary.

Mrs. Bursford returned to Dublin, to a solitary, lonely life. She brought Jervis home with her, thinking that the prodigal might repent and be a comfort to her old age; but she was soon obliged to send him back to Monaco, or whatever foreign haunt the gentleman most favoured. Dorothy O'Hegarty is very kind to her; and although the old woman is obliged to live in lodgings, she manages to assemble her friends round her again. For their delectation she makes the best of the accounts from Honolulu. She decries "mixed marriages" as bitterly as the Cardinal himself; and Dorothy, whose dear nephew Dermot is married to a Roman Catholic, is obliged to take up the cudgels in their defence, declaring, with perfect truth, that a happier couple than Mr. and Mrs. Dermot does not exist.

Dicky Davoren never came back. He left his ship at Rio Janeiro, where he obtained a situation in a merchant's office. Mrs. Dermot Blake hears good accounts of him from time to time. His friend Tad Griffiths was disappointed in his expectations. His father declined to buy him out a second time; and the young gentleman is now serving at the Cape of Good Hope. Mr. Orpen passed his examinations with credit, and took Orders the other day. Gagan is an M.D., and is studying for India. Miss O'Hegarty and Peter keep house together. The Dermot Blakes flatly refused to avail themselves of his invaluable services as major domo, and the old lady has made up her mind that if Peter left her she would miss him so much that it mightn't be good for her. She takes periodical flights to Blakestown, where Dermot and Nellie are delighted to have her. They seldom come up to town. Nellie's father is married again; and, except Dorothy, she has no ties in Dublin. Besides, Dermot hates town; and she is only happy where he is.

THE END.

Printed by R. & R. CLARK, *Edinburgh.*